SCRATCH DEEPER

SCRATCH DEEPER

Chris Simms

ÇRÈME de la CRIME

This first world edition published 2012
in Great Britain and 2013 in the USA by
Crème de la Crime, an imprint of
SEVERN HOUSE PUBLISHERS LTD of
19 Cedar Road, Sutton, Surrey, England, SM2 5DA.
Trade paperback edition first published
in Great Britain and the USA 2013 by
SEVERN HOUSE PUBLISHERS LTD.

British Library Cataloguing in Publication Data

Simms, Chris, 1969-
  Scratch deeper.
  1. Police–England–Manchester–Fiction. 2. Terrorism–
  Prevention–Fiction. 3. Detective and mystery stories.
  I. Title
  823.9'2-dc23

ISBN-13: 978-1-78029-035-5 (cased)
ISBN-13: 978-1-78029-535-0 (trade paper)

All Severn House titles are printed on acid-free paper.

Severn House Publishers support The Forest Stewardship Council [FSC],
the leading international forest certification organisation. All our titles that
are printed on Greenpeace-approved FSC-certified paper carry the FSC logo.

Typeset by Palimpsest Book Production Ltd.,
Falkirk, Stirlingshire, Scotland.
Printed and bound in Great Britain by
MPG Books Ltd., Bodmin, Cornwall.

'When everyone is dead, the Great Game is finished. Not before.'
Rudyard Kipling, 1865–1936

PROLOGUE

Reginald Appleton grunted from behind the gag, eyes bulging with terror. In his mind, the words he was roaring were clear. I heard you! Yes, I'll tell you! Please, please, don't hurt me any more.

The pressure on the back of his neck eased, allowing him to turn his head so his face wasn't pressed into the pillow. Nostrils flaring in and out, he filled his lungs, ears still ringing from the punches to his head.

'What is it?' the voice repeated.

The hatred contained in the question made Appleton feel ill. He nodded as vigorously as he could. There had been the faint trace of French in the man's voice. A local, then. Probably a Creole needing money.

Rough fingers pulled the thick band of rubber away from his lips and something was thrust towards his face. The device beeped and a red light came on. 'Say it.'

'Eleven, thirty-three, ninety-nine, zero, four,' he gasped. 'There are dollars—' The gag snapped back into place, rendering the end of the sentence incomprehensible.

He felt his lower arms being yanked as the person checked his wrists were still bound tight. A hand patted the stubby Henry Moore sculpture on the bedside table.

'Lie still. Don't move. If you move, I'll smash your skull in.'

Appleton jerked his head back and forth against the pillow to indicate that he understood. Footsteps quickly crossed the room and he was alone.

His heart was beating so strongly, it caused his shoulders to rock against the mattress. It's a burglary, he said to himself. Stay calm. He'll take the cash – how much is there? Ten, fifteen thousand dollars? He'll be happy with that. He'll go.

Something warm began to tickle behind his ear. Blood, he realized. My head must be bleeding. He felt it creeping under his chin and across his throat. Anais will be dismayed when she sees the sheets. Cleaning them is going to take hours.

Outside, the cicadas' grating buzz rose to a crescendo and abruptly stopped. Now came the soft, insistent sound of waves lapping the nearby beach. Something thudded in his study further down the bungalow's corridor. He recognized the sound – the door to the safe, swinging open and bumping against the wall. He'll be removing the cash. Probably my watch. Margaret's jewellery, too. The pearl necklace she always favoured when we dined out. It doesn't matter. They're only things.

The thin whine of a mosquito passed his ear and he knew how the man had got in. He lifted his head and was able to make out the neat hole cut in the screen that covered the window he'd left open. Arching his head brought into view the red button of the panic alarm mounted in the wall above his bed. He cursed himself; why on earth didn't you close the window? You grew complacent and now you're getting what you deserve.

The sound of the footsteps coming back caused the throbbing in his temples to quicken.

The shadowy form came into view. Appleton could see a small bag hanging from one hand. The person looked down at him and the old man closed his eyes so they were almost shut, like a child pretending to be asleep.

Then the figure walked over to the window. Appleton breathed out. He's going. Thank the Lord, he's going.

But the person placed the bag on the floor. The objects inside made a faint chink. He turned round and walked back to the bed. Now Appleton really did close his eyes. Please go. You've got what you want.

Hands gripped his shoulders. As he was turned on to his back, he felt the hairs of his chest pulling clear of the blood that must have pooled beneath him. His bound wrists dug painfully into the small of his back. Fringed by thick strands of long hair, the dark face looked down, all but a silhouette against the moon filling the window behind. The buzzing of the cicadas was starting up again.

'The password for your computer.'

Appleton's breath caught in his throat.

The thick band of rubber was peeled down. 'Password.'

Appleton felt tears sting his eyes. 'Lucinda64.'

As he gave his daughter's name and year of birth he sent up a silent prayer. Please let me see her face again.

The gag snapped back and the man vanished from view. Appleton stared at the ceiling. The tropical heat seemed to have vanished. He wanted the password. If this is a burglary, why would he want the password? He must be after something on the computer. Why not just take the hard drive? This doesn't make sense. I'm not important any more. I've retired.

He tilted his head back to stare at the red button. Could I turn myself over and get on to my knees? Raise myself up and press it with my forehead? *Smash your skull in*. That's what he said he'd do if I move.

He lay there until the cicadas fell silent again, allowing him to hear the plastic tap of his computer's keyboard. The printer started to whirr. This isn't a burglary. Jesus Christ, this isn't a burglary. I've got to do something.

He started rocking himself from side to side, trying to build up enough momentum to turn on to his front. No strength, he thought. Not since the hip replacement last year. He thought of his daughter and grandchildren back in Britain. James and Sophie running down the drive to meet him with their arms outstretched.

By bunching his hands into fists he was able to form a fulcrum at the base of his spine. He began to rock himself again and, with a push of his hands, finally flipped himself over. He was back in the patch of blood, now cool and sticky.

The keys continued to tap as he sucked air through his nostrils. Not enough oxygen was getting in. He felt dizzy and faint. Sweat was running down his temples. Or was it blood? You can't stop, he said to himself. Not now you've moved. Bit by bit, he brought his knees under his chest. Groaning with the effort, he managed to slowly raise his shoulders up. Down the corridor, the printer continued to click and whirr. The Henry Moore sculpture caught his eye and he had to look away. Nearly there, he thought, focusing on the red button and shuffling from one knee to the other. Almost close enough, almost close—

Something black moved in the periphery of his vision.

Appleton swivelled his eyes to the side.

The person stood watching. When he spoke, Appleton could tell he was smiling. 'I hope you've enjoyed your time on this island.' His voice dripped with contempt.

Appleton kept absolutely still, eyes full of fear.

The man shook his head as he reached for the stubby sculpture on the bedside table. His hand bounced as he measured the weight of it. 'Time to pay for what you did to my people.'

He raised the chunk of stone and Appleton's cheeks puffed out as he tried to scream. The base of the sculpture thudded into the back of his skull and the old man pitched forward. He saw Margaret, waiting for him in the bluebell woods where she so loved to walk. And then the lump of rock came down again, this time causing a fleshy crunch. Appleton slumped to his side and two thin lines of blood hissed into the air, pattering against the mahogany headboard. The sculpture was brought down again and again, shattering and then pulverizing facial bones beneath it.

Eventually, the man stopped. He gazed down at the corpse, his breath undisturbed by the effort. The dripping sculpture was dropped on to the blood-spattered bed and the cord tying Appleton's wrists was loosened enough for one hand to be pulled free. Carefully, the man lifted the slack arm up, straightened Appleton's forefinger out and carefully pressed it against the panic button.

As the shrill alarm drowned out the cicadas' song, he counted to ten then strode across the room, picked up the bag and climbed back through the hole in the mosquito screen.

ONE

Iona Khan got to the pedestrian crossing just as the little green man went out. Drat, she said to herself. Deansgate lay before her. One of Manchester's oldest roads, its lanes cut a wide swathe across the city.

Her thoughts went to the police station tucked halfway up the narrow side street on the opposite side of the road. I'm going to be late. Can't stand being late. Agitatedly flicking one forefinger and thumb, she reflected on why she was visiting the station. It was just over a month since she'd learned that her application for a place in Greater Manchester Police's Counter Terrorism Unit had been successful. Quite a result for someone who'd only joined the force four years ago.

And the timing couldn't have been better: the Labour Party's conference was due to start in two days' time and the Unit was flat out coordinating the security operation.

In terms of profile and importance, this was the Unit's big day. So when Iona was tasked with looking into a report of a foreign student using a false name, her initial reaction was one of disappointment. The assignment meant being marginalized from the Unit's number one priority. No place for her in the daily briefings, no part to play in making sure the conference went smoothly. A simple case of false identity. She'd made sure she didn't appear crestfallen as her boss had handed her the scant details. But, she'd been thinking all the while, couldn't something so inconsequential have waited until after the conference was over?

A car's engine being revved returned her to the present. In front of her, an elderly woman carrying a shopping bag was halfway across the road walking towards her, her head bowed as she took small, determined steps. Not for the first time, Iona thought the traffic lights simply didn't allow long enough for people to get across. The Porsche Cayenne's engine revved again, the vehicle's lines giving it a bullish appearance. Iona glanced at it. Come on, she said to herself. There's no need for that. The woman soldiered on, clearly perturbed by the fact that the safety of the kerb was still a dozen feet away. As cars in the far lanes began moving again, Iona realized the traffic lights must have started flashing orange.

The Porsche also started inching forward, its thick bumper now overhanging the white lines delineating the crossing point. Iona stepped out to give the elderly lady a hand and the vehicle's horn blared, making both of them jump. The driver poked his head out of the side window, a mobile phone pressed to his ear. 'Oi, the lights have fucking changed!' he shouted. 'Get out of the road!'

Iona pointed to the lady. 'I'm helping her!' She turned to the woman. 'Would you like a hand?'

Her eyes cut nervously to the vehicle menacing her. 'Thank you, yes.'

The driver of the Porsche now started trying to edge his vehicle round them. Iona watched in disbelief until its front corner had come to within inches of the lady's spindly legs. Right, that's it. She reached into the jacket of her brand-new trouser suit and produced her warrant card. 'You!' she barked, thrusting it towards the windscreen. 'Take your foot off the pedal. Now.'

His mouth dropped open. Yeah, Iona thought, you're not the first person to be surprised by someone like me having a police badge. The tone of the engine dropped, as did the driver's hand holding the mobile phone.

Iona stood her ground until the woman had made it safely to the pavement. 'OK, missy?' the driver called out amenably. 'OK for me to go?'

Missy? She regarded the man behind the wheel. 'Sir, pull over to the side of the road, please.'

He raked strands of oily-looking hair back over his head. 'Officer.' His voice was now infused with courtesy that rang fake. 'You were both causing an obstruction.'

'And you were talking on your phone at the wheel of your vehicle. Pull over so the cars behind you can get past.'

The condescending smile disappeared from his face. 'This is a fucking joke.'

Iona remained exactly where she was. 'Pull over, please.'

After noting down the man's details and informing him that he'd be receiving a notice of prosecution in the post, she watched the vehicle nudge its way into the slow-moving stream of traffic. A few seconds later, the lights changed again and she was able to hurry across Deansgate and up Bootle Street towards the Victorian police station where she'd started her career.

The edge of the side street had been dug up and then deserted by the workmen. As Iona skirted round the red and white plastic barriers she peered into the pit. Its sheer sides comprised of several layers. First, a couple of inches of tarmac sitting on an older layer of the same material. Then a gritty band of shale which, after about two feet, gave way to dark soil. In the dirty puddle at the bottom, half-submerged cables coiled like serpents in a swamp. Items of litter had blown in. A crisp packet. Several cigarette butts. A hamburger carton.

She continued on to the police station, made her way through the front doors of the building and glanced round the lobby. Behind the Perspex screen of the reception desk a civilian worker she didn't recognize was busily sorting through forms. On the wall above the woman a CCTV camera peered down.

Iona approached the desk and, aware no one else was in the waiting area to see her do it, went up on tiptoes. 'Excuse me,' she announced, warrant card at the ready. 'Detective Constable Khan to see Sergeant Ritter.'

TWO

The woman behind the reception desk regarded the badge next to Iona's photocard. 'Counter Terrorism Unit?' She sounded surprised as she picked up a phone.

Feeling self-conscious, Iona brushed back a strand of raven-black hair. I knew it, she thought. I should never have had it cut in a bob. Makes me look like a schoolboy. And a young one at that.

'Sergeant Ritter?' the woman asked. 'I have a Detective Constable Khan from the CTU here for you.' She nodded before addressing Iona. 'You can go through – head straight on and he'll meet you coming the other way.' The reinforced door at the far end of the counter clicked. Iona pushed it open and stepped through to the narrow corridor beyond.

She almost smiled. Since she'd worked here, the foyer might have been given a makeover so it resembled the lobby of a bank, but on this side things hadn't changed one bit. Memories came back of being fresh in police uniform, walking the beat round central Manchester, convinced – just like every other new recruit – that people were staring at her back with incredulous expressions.

A man was walking briskly towards her, late thirties, short hair in a side parting. 'Constable Khan? Sergeant Ritter.'

She held out a hand. 'Really sorry to be late, I got caught up with something on Deansgate.'

'Not a problem,' he replied as they shook. 'It's Bill, by the way.'

'Iona. This place hasn't changed.'

He moved aside to let a couple of uniforms squeeze past then started back up the corridor, glancing over his shoulder as he did so. 'You were based here?'

'Just a short stint,' she replied, following behind. 'My very first rotation on qualifying. Four years ago, now.'

'Oh. Well, I don't think the place has had much more than a lick of paint in all the time I've been here.'

'Which is?' Iona asked.

He blew air from the side of his mouth. 'Mid-nineties. Same time as the bomb – that was my welcome to the job.'

Iona's mind bounced back to June 1996. She'd only been eleven, but the events of that day were among her strongest childhood memories. Shopping with her mum in the maze of little streets that used to sit alongside the Arndale. Uniformed officers suddenly appearing, arms out, voices raised, alarm showing in their eyes.

It was the first time she'd properly appreciated what power the job conferred. The reassuring way a female officer had addressed her mum. Come on, let's get you both clear of this area. Iona had stared up at her, in awe of the officer's businesslike desire to protect. Right then she'd decided that's what she wanted to do in life.

They'd been herded up to the far end of Market Street. Bewildered and mildly scared, they were trapped in the crowd by the side of Debenhams when the thing had gone off. She still remembered the tremor beneath her feet, like an invisible tram was rumbling by. Then the billow of smoke rolling up from the direction of the Arndale, the echoing boom replaced by a chorus of shrill alarms, fine shards of glass tinkling down from the sky, shortly followed by scraps of paper. 'Still seems incredible no one died.'

'Doesn't it?' The man gestured to an open doorway. 'Right. What I've got for you – it's an odd one, really.'

She stepped through. There seemed to be even less space in the ground-floor rooms than she remembered.

'I'm over here.' The sergeant made his way to a desk in the corner. 'Don't suppose you've ever heard of a group called the Sub-Urban Explorers?'

Iona dragged a spare chair over from the next workstation, sat down and raised an eyebrow. 'No.'

'Didn't think you would have. Bunch of student types and general misfits from what I can make out. They grub around, finding ways into the various passages which run under Manchester.'

Iona had heard rumours of the many secret tunnels which were believed to lie beneath the city's streets. Her mind went back to the hole in the road outside the station. The pool of water at the bottom. You never really consider what's under your feet, she thought, as Ritter opened a file. 'This lot like to creep along them, taking photos and posting reports. It's all on their website.'

Iona sat forward to examine the printout. A standard forum-style page, with a list of titles and dates.

Medlock Culvert, June.

Bunker storm drain, June.

The Works drain, August.

Lumb Clough Brook, sewer overflow, August.

Cathedral steps, September.

'Each to their own,' she murmured.

'True,' Ritter responded. 'If you overlook the fact half these places are out-of-bounds to the public, private property and general deathtraps.'

'And crawling with rats, I should think,' Iona added.

Ritter shuddered. 'Which is why I'm only too happy to be passing this on to you.'

'Yeah, thanks for that.' Iona gave a quick grin. 'So, where does this false identity come into it?'

Ritter flicked over a couple of sheets. 'OK. This is from someone referring to himself as an intermediary for the Sub-Urban Explorers, or SUEs. The actual members of the group are wary about meeting – in case we try to arrest them.'

'They don't think we've got better things to do?'

'This lot? They're nothing if not paranoid. You can guess the type – we're agents of a fascist state, they're fighting for freedom.'

Iona nodded wearily. 'We're out to get them and harvest their DNA. Feed their data into our evil state computers . . .'

'You've got it,' Ritter smirked. 'Until someone mugs them and runs off with their laptop, then they're suddenly very keen to get in touch.'

They shared a smile.

'According to this intermediary, the group were approached a while back by a newcomer who wanted to become a member. He was a . . . lightly tanned gentleman.'

Iona caught the hitch in the comment and glanced up. 'It's OK, you don't have to be all politically correct with me. Lightly tanned, meaning what?'

Ritter eased back in his seat as he consulted his notes. 'He described the person as Middle Eastern.'

'So Arabic?'

'I suppose so.'

Iona nodded. 'Go on.'

'This gentleman seemed particularly interested in any tunnels that might be in the vicinity of the G-Mex, or what's known nowadays as the Manchester Centre.'

An alarm bell began to ring in Iona's mind: that little detail hadn't been mentioned by her boss when he'd handed the job to her. The Manchester Centre was the enormous convention building in the middle of the city where the Labour Party conference was about to begin. Voice now serious, she asked, 'This newcomer – is he still with the group?'

'No. They wanted to concentrate on a new tunnel system they'd found beneath the university. The guy stopped showing up and emails to his address now come back as undeliverable.' He closed the file and slid it towards her. 'Over to you.'

She placed it on her lap and brushed her fingers lightly back and forth across the cover. 'How do they know his ID was fake?'

'He told them he was called Muttiah, over from Sri Lanka on a student visa studying maths. Then, a week ago, one of the members of the group who goes by the name of Hidden Shadow –'

Iona frowned. 'Hidden Shadow?'

'His user name on the forum. They all use silly tags. Oldskool, Buddah, Skiprat. I said they're a bit sad. Hidden—'

'Sorry to butt in; is the name Muttiah one of these tags as well?'

Ritter shook his head. 'I asked that. The guy said he wasn't bothered with a tag – Muttiah was fine.'

'OK.'

'So, Hidden Shadow was outside Central Library and saw the man calling himself Muttiah. He raises a hand in greeting and gets blanked for his trouble. This Muttiah was now wearing smart clothes and he was with another person of similar appearance. Hidden Shadow lives up to his name and follows the two of them to the Local Studies section. He keeps behind a bookcase and listens in. Neither of them are speaking English, but the older one's asking the younger one loads of questions. Except he keeps addressing him as Vasen – or something sounding very similar.'

Iona hooked a stray strand of hair behind her ear. 'Interesting. Maybe a surname?'

The sergeant shrugged. 'Possibly. The reason I reported it to you guys is because, after about fifteen minutes, they return the book to the shelves and leave. Hidden Shadow scoots over – if that's what shadows do –'

'Maybe glides?'

Ritter smiled. 'Glides. Yeah, that's better. He glides over to see what they were studying. The book is an architectural account of the convention centre, right up to the plans for an annex, built on the side of the main building a few years ago.'

This investigation, Iona thought, isn't looking so trivial, after all. She kept the emotion out of her voice. 'Anything else?'

'I contacted the university. No Sri Lankan student called Muttiah is currently enrolled on a mathematics course.'

'How about Vasen?'

'Nope. It was at that point I thought it best to call you lot in.'

'Right.' Iona lifted the file. 'Looks like I'd better speak to this group. Have you contact details for this intermediary?'

'It's all very cloak-and-dagger. There's a mobile number and an email address on the sheet at the back.'

'Did you actually meet him?'

'Only talked on the phone.'

'Well, no time like the present.' She turned to the back of the file and took her mobile out. 'He's got a funny name as his email address. Doc-P.' She put her phone on loudspeaker and keyed in the mobile number.

'Who is this?'

Iona could immediately tell he was local; probably from the southern part of the city. She allowed some of the same accent to seep into her voice. 'Hello, this is Detective Khan. Who am I speaking to, please?'

'Police?'

'Yes, I work with the Counter Terrorism Unit. You spoke to a colleague about an individual who joined the Sub-Urban Explorers. My colleague passed that information to me.'

'Counter what?'

'Terrorism Unit.'

'Oh.'

Iona caught the hesitancy in the man's voice. He was now obviously feeling intimidated. 'Don't worry,' she said reassuringly. 'I'm only involved because this person appears to have been using a false identity. Something we're currently obliged to check out in cases of foreign nationals.'

'Oh.'

'Can we meet . . . sorry, I feel funny calling you Doc-P. Got a first name?'

'Yeah, Toby.'

'Can we meet, Toby? I'd like to get some more details from the people you . . . represent.'

'They need an assurance, first. That nothing they tell you will be used against them.'

'See what I mean?' Ritter whispered.

She rolled her eyes at the sergeant. 'You have my word. My questions will only relate to the individual who was using the name Muttiah. What you guys get up to in your own time is of absolutely no concern to me.'

'And it will be just you?'

'Yes, if that's what you want.'

'It is.'

'Then it will be.'

There was a pause. 'OK. We can meet in town this evening.'

Iona thought about her plans to have tea over at her mum and dad's. A Khan tradition on a Friday evening. Oh, well, not this week. 'Great. Will the Sub-Urban Explorers be there?'

'Not at the initial place we meet.'

She rubbed a finger across her forehead, keeping the exasperation from her voice. 'But we'll go on to meet them?'

'Only if you're alone.'

Like I couldn't have support just round the corner, Iona thought. 'OK. Where and when?'

'You know the Cornerhouse?'

She pictured the Art House cinema on the junction of Whitworth Street and Oxford Road. 'I do.'

'I'll be in the bar there. Eight tonight?'

I can make it for tea at the folks' after all, she thought. 'Fine.' She flashed a mischievous grin at Ritter. 'Oh, Toby. This being a blind date, how will I know who you are?'

'Oh, yeah. Well . . . I'm six feet tall, twenty-two and I've got blond hair in short dreadlocks. I'll be wearing a maroon top with Howie's written across the chest. You?'

'I'm five foot three, mid-twenties . . . and I'm not describing my chest to you.'

Silence.

'Relax, Toby, I'm joking.'

'Oh, right.' He sounded both bemused and intrigued. 'What's your name again?'

'Detective Constable Khan.'

'Khan? So you're . . .' He let the question hang.

'Half Scottish, half Pakistani. I'll be wearing a charcoal trouser suit. See you at eight.' She pressed red and stood.

Ritter was chuckling. 'Which side of the family is from Pakistan?' he asked.

'My dad's. He came here in the seventies to do a PhD in Persian Studies.'

'Here in Manchester?'

'No, up in Glasgow. That's where he met my mum.'

'Ah.' He held up a finger. 'Hence the name Iona.'

'You've got it.' She smiled.

'And is she an academic, too?'

'Mum? No, far from it. She was working as a typist in the history department's office. They moved down here when dad was offered a place lecturing at the University of Manchester. I was six.'

'I thought I couldn't hear any Scottish accent.'

Iona wrinkled her nose. 'No. But you should see my headbutt.' She switched her voice to thick Glaswegian. 'It's beazer.'

Ritter's laughter filled the room as Iona lifted her turquoise eyes to the ceiling. 'Are the incident rooms still upstairs?'

'Yeah, mainly on the floor above. Need me to show you up?'

'No, don't worry. I thought I'd say hello to an old colleague. Another sergeant, as it happens. Jim Stephens?'

'Jim? Yeah, he's up in room eight. Drug-dealing case, I believe.'

'Great, cheers.' Iona started heading for the door, file held up. 'I'll let you know how this goes.'

THREE

U p on the second floor, Iona opened the swing doors and scanned the corridor ahead. Room eight was at the other end and, as she neared it, she could hear Jim's voice inside. Right, she thought, slowing her step. How to play this?

Hesitantly, she peeped through the half-open door. Jim was standing at the far end of the room facing a large map of the city centre. She took in the immaculate creases in the shirt and trousers of his police uniform. Nothing changes, she thought, eyes lingering on his shoulders then dropping to the tight curve of his buttocks. She'd had three other boyfriends in her life and none of them had been quite like Jim.

Memories of life before they'd broken up caused a pang of sadness to stir. Lazy Sunday evenings on the sofa at his place, the hiss of the iron as he went over both of their uniforms interspersing his impersonations of whoever happened to be on the telly. She smiled at how rubbish his attempts at accents always were – not that it stopped him from trying. It was one of the qualities she loved in him most; not taking himself too seriously.

Jim was removing what appeared to be stills from CCTV footage. The images formed a thick border around the map. Two people, one in civilian clothes and one in uniform, were seated at the large table in the middle of the room, tidying piles of paper into folders. A brew table with a kettle on was just inside the door, several empty cups next to the tea and coffee. Iona sensed an investigation coming to an unsuccessful close. When Jim spoke, she could immediately tell the enthusiasm in his voice was forced.

'Hey-ho, we'll get another chance to nail this bunch. I'll put a bet on that – I have a theory about these things.'

Iona found herself studying his profile. A young Paul Newman, that's how her mum fondly described him. The guy was horribly good-looking, she had to admit. Light brown hair that had been allowed to grow slightly tousled. It was still, essentially, a soldier's cut, but it was only when he turned his head that the movie-star comparison really floundered.

The scars were a lot more noticeable on the right-hand side of his face: particularly the one at the corner of his eye. Despite the army surgeon's best efforts, the skin there was pinched, giving her ex a slightly haunted look in moments when he let his jovial exterior slip. Then there were the burn marks showing just above his collar. Ridges and lesions that, she knew, half-covered his chest. She'd run her fingers over them so often.

Yet again she found herself wondering just what had happened during his time as a squaddie out in Iraq. He'd come close to telling her a couple of times when he'd been especially drunk. Whatever it was, the incident had left him with a deep sense of shame and remorse. He didn't know it, but the emotions would often surface when he slept, causing him to turn his head from side to side, the muscles of his jaw bulging out. It always amazed her that someone with such issues in his personal life held it together so well at work.

'My money,' Jim continued briskly, as he tapped his finger on a photo that had been blown up larger than the others, 'is on this character being back on our radar first.' Arms now crossed, Jim stared at the close-up of the man's face. Iona could make out a shaved head and leering mouth. 'Law of Jug Ears, that's my theory.' He tried to put on a Mancunian accent but only succeeded in sounding like someone with a blocked-up nose. 'The dumber the criminal, the worse their ears stick out.'

His two colleagues started laughing.

'What's wrong with that? Seriously, someone should do a study on it,' Jim protested.

Iona listened to the laughter die down. I know, she wanted to chip in, he always goes on about the jug ears thing. Instead, she rattled a teaspoon in one of the empty mugs.

All three heads immediately turned.

'What the bloody hell are you doing gate-crashing my debriefing?' Jim asked, blue eyes sparkling.

'Cuppa tea?' she asked in a squawky voice. 'Who wants a nice cuppa tea?'

He glanced at his watch. 'Let's break there. Julie, Matt – this is Iona and she can't make a decent brew to save her life.'

The pair regarded her uncertainly.

'Seriously,' Iona said. 'Does anyone want a drink?'

With polite shakes of their heads, the two got to their feet and headed for the door, Matt muttering about having to get to the bank, Julie saying she needed to check emails.

Once they were gone, Iona looked at Jim with the beginnings of a smile. 'Hello, there.'

He kept to his side of the room and nodded. 'Hi.'

Still sore, she thought, now wondering whether she should have popped in at all. It was Jim who'd told her that the Counter Terrorism Unit was increasing its numbers. They'd ended up both applying for a place, but only Iona had got in. She put her file down and flicked the kettle on. 'Keeping busy, then?'

He turned to the montage of images and let out an exasperated sigh. 'Just crashed and burned on a technicality. The CPS' fault, not ours – thank God.'

Iona was spooning coffee into a pair of clean mugs. She was about to add a sugar to Jim's when he said, 'Just milk, cheers.'

She glanced across with surprise. 'Since when?'

He patted his stomach. 'Got to watch the gut.'

'You're joking?'

He shook his head.

Oh, please, Iona thought. No way you're getting fat. I know where this is coming from: not getting into the CTU. Now you're afraid life is passing you by. 'I think you can allow yourself a bit of sugar for a while yet. There aren't many guys in their mid-thirties in as good shape as you.' She splashed milk into the cups and carried them over, a glance going to the wall. 'Drugs thing, was it?'

Jim took the drink she was holding out and also turned to the images. 'Almost a month's worth of surveillance work. Not sure how many hours we spent fiddling about with footage from council CCTV. You know when you've just had enough of something?' He cast a despondent look around the room.

She waited for him to ask how her new job was going but his eyes were on the collection once more. 'So what else is new?'

'Mmm?' He looked at her. 'Same old, same old. Helping out with a misper as soon as we clear this room. Young lass went missing two days ago.'

Iona nodded knowingly. 'Boyfriend or partner?'

'Single, according to her parents.'

'Does it seem like they're right?'

'Apparently; from what a couple of her close friends have stated.'

'No recent partners she . . .'

'What?' Jim jumped in. 'Dumped?'

Their eyes touched for a moment before Iona looked away. You know the reason why we broke up, she thought. And until you cut out the drinking and share with someone whatever's eating you, none of your relationships are going to survive.

The silence began to grow heavy. Looking slightly embarrassed, Jim tasted his coffee and grimaced. He walked over to the brew table and added a spoonful of sugar. Iona studied his back as he resolutely stirred his drink. His movements were stiff. Tense. I shouldn't have come up here, she thought. It's too soon. 'Well, suppose I'd better be making a move. They'll be expecting me back.'

She crossed over to the doorway and paused to take a couple of sips, not wanting it to appear too obvious she was abandoning her drink. She felt his hand on her arm.

'Hey,' he said softly. 'Why don't you pop over to mine this evening? I'll cook – we haven't caught up with each other in weeks.'

Damn, she thought. I was afraid this would happen. 'You know . . .' Her voice had lifted slightly and she wondered why she was sounding apologetic. 'I'm due round at mum and dad's. Friday night, remember?'

'Yeah, but after that?'

She made a face. 'To be honest, Jim, I'm really knackered. I've been running around loads since . . . you know, switching to this new role.'

She could see the hurt on his face and guilt surged through her. How, she asked herself, do you always make me feel in the wrong?

His eyes had dropped. 'Yeah, I noticed the new outfit.'

She brushed uncertainly at her lapel. 'Do I look all right?'

He pushed his lower lip up. 'Yeah.'

Cheers, Iona thought. That was really convincing.

'You didn't say what brought you here.' He glanced at the folder she'd left on the table beside them.

She lifted one shoulder momentarily, careful to underplay things. 'Some bloke using a fake ID. I'm surprised it even ended up with the CTU. I don't know – the inspector I've been paired with is off sick. Probably couldn't think of anything else to give me.'

'You mean they've got you flying solo with it?' He was trying to sound encouraging.

'First one.'

He considered her answer, the haunted look creeping across his face. 'What sort of a fake ID – passport or something?'

'No, not even that. He was using one name with a group of associates then was overheard being addressed differently by someone else.'

'What?' Jim sounded incredulous. 'The mighty CTU are handling that? Hardly a threat to national security, is it?' The laugh that escaped him carried within it a note of scorn.

The sound cut right through her. Thanks a bunch, Iona thought. I've only tried to be nice here. 'It could be when the person is of Middle Eastern appearance, studying at the uni on a temporary student visa and showing an unhealthy interest in the venue for the Labour Party conference.'

The sarcastic grin fell from Jim's lips and he blinked. 'Middle Eastern appearance?'

Great, Iona thought. Now I've really rubbed his nose in it. 'Well . . . he was dark-haired and tanned.'

He crossed his arms. 'Ah – there you have it.'

'What do you mean?'

'Come on, Iona.'

Frowning, she sought out his eyes. 'What?'

'Surely you can see . . . you know . . . why they chucked it your way.'

She stepped back, hoping this wasn't heading in the direction she thought it was. 'Sorry?'

He hesitated a moment. 'You want me to spell it out?'

She felt anger rising up. 'Yes, I think you should.'

'Forget it. Ignore me.'

'No, come on, Jim. Spell it out, please.'

He took a deep breath as if to say, here we go. 'The nature of CTU stuff – it usually involves ethnics. They needed a few non-white applicants onboard to deflect the usual bullshit accusations.'

Ethnics? Iona stared at him in disbelief. 'I never thought I'd hear you say something like that.'

'Like what?'

'That the only reason I got in was because I'm half-Pakistani.'

He lifted a hand. 'Not the only reason, obviously. But you know what I mean . . .'

She put her cup down on the table too quickly. Coffee sloshed over the side. 'No, I don't know what you mean.'

He spread both palms. 'Surely you agree it was a factor?'

It had occurred to her once or twice. But she wasn't about to admit it. All she could do was shake her head as she snatched up her file.

As she stepped through the door, he spoke from behind her. 'Iona, that came out all wrong. Please, don't just storm off.'

Now in the corridor, she turned round, wondering where the Jim she'd fallen in love with had gone. 'You need to be careful. You are turning into one bitter and twisted man.'

FOUR

Iona pulled up behind her parents' gleaming Audi A5. Definitely getting trendier in their old age, she thought, reflecting on their gradual transition from bulky, but practical, Volvos when she and her sister were growing up to the sleeker, racier model now on the drive.

Her gaze travelled to the decrepit old caravan parked behind it. Faint traces of moss had begun to establish themselves in the joints connecting the body panels. Now I just have to persuade them to get rid of that old heap and start going on cruises or something.

Memories of travelling from one midge-infested Scottish caravan site to another returned as she locked her Nissan Micra and walked up to the front door. Seconds after the bell chimed she could see a tall figure through the stained-glass window set into the centre of the door. Dad, she thought affectionately, as his stooped form got closer. The door swung open to reveal Wasim wearing slippers, jeans and the usual old cardigan.

'Iona,' he smiled, bending to give her a hug. 'Look at you in your smart work clothes.'

She searched out his deep brown eyes, so kind and considerate.

'Are they OK? Not too . . . sober? I don't want to appear like an accountant. But not some kind of media type either.'

'No, no,' he replied reassuringly as her mother, Moira, appeared at the kitchen end of the corridor. Wasim glanced back at her. 'Iona looks great, don't you think?'

Moira's blue eyes twinkled with pride as she rested one forefinger against her lips. 'Mmmm . . . something missing. I know!' Her Scots accent contrasted sharply with Wasim's sonorous tones. 'A bit of colour for your lapel; your deputy head girl's badge from school!'

Iona glanced fearfully from one parent to the other. 'I look like a school kid. I do, don't I?'

'Nonsense,' Wasim said, suppressing a smile. 'Don't listen to your mother.'

Moira let out a throaty laugh, one arm now outstretched. 'I'm messing with you. You look the business, my love. It's just still bloody weird you being out of that police uniform.'

Shoulders relaxing slightly, Iona approached her mother and embraced her.

'Just finishing this email,' Wasim said, retreating back into his study.

The two women stepped into the kitchen and Iona looked at the old circular oak table. It had only been laid for three. Moira caught where her daughter was looking and said, 'Fenella is stuck at the hospital. There are loads ahead of her still waiting for their scans.'

'Shame,' Iona replied, thinking of her older sister who was expecting twins. 'I was really looking forward to seeing the photo.'

'She'll be here later – it won't take all evening.'

Iona flicked a hand towards the door. 'I can't stay long, Mum. Work stuff. Sorry.'

Moira looked momentarily disappointed. 'Not to worry, we've got you for a short while.' She lowered her voice so it didn't carry beyond the kitchen. 'How's it going with Jim? Is he still taking it badly?'

Iona pursed her lips. It didn't help, she thought, that Jim and her mum had got along so brilliantly. 'We argued, Mum.'

A pained look appeared on Moira's face. 'What about?' she whispered.

Iona hesitated before replying. If there was one way to wipe out any warm feelings her mum still had for Jim, it would be to tell her what he'd said earlier on. She recalled incidents outside the playground at her primary school in Glasgow. There were no other Asian kids in her class. The parents of any child who used the word Paki soon regretted their kid's language when Moira stormed up to them, demanding to know where their kid had learned the word. 'It's not . . . I'd rather not talk about it.'

The silence that followed was punctuated by a steady dripping sound coming from the direction of the sink. Iona glanced at the dodgy tap. The wrench and spanner that had been lying on the window sill when she'd last visited were still there. 'Not fixed yet?'

Moira gave an exasperated wave. 'Oh, your father had another go. But you know how he is with stuff like that.' She was about to say something more, but stopped herself.

Yeah, I know, Iona thought. Jim would have mended it in less than a minute. Just like he re-attached the loose curtain rail in the telly room, repaired the lawnmower when it started misfiring, sorted your boiler when it kept cutting out . . .

'Sorry, hen,' Moira said. 'I didn't mean to, you know.' They heard the door to Wasim's study open and Moira whispered quickly, 'Maybe talk about it later?'

Iona nodded. Almost everything she'd ever done had been a source of pride for her parents – until she'd joined the police. Wasim tried not to show it, but her choice of career obviously troubled him. The fact she'd also started seeing a colleague who'd previously served in the army bothered him even more.

Moira had picked up an open bottle of red. 'A wee splash?'

'Just a dash,' Iona replied, taking her usual place as Wasim wandered in with a newspaper and almost-empty glass of wine.

'Iona has some work things to do later, Was,' Moira announced, half-filling a glass.

'Really?' he asked, extending his own in Moira's direction.

'Afraid so,' Iona said.

'So come on, then,' her mum asked, topping up her and Wasim's drinks. 'How's it all going? You don't know how many people are still commenting on the newspaper article about you.'

Iona cringed as she thought about the recent piece in the *Manchester Evening Chronicle*. Someone – and she had yet to find out who – had tipped off the news desk that Iona, one of only three female officers with Asian blood in the entire Greater Manchester Police, had just started working for the CTU. 'Maybe they wouldn't be commenting on it if you weren't wandering the streets of Altrincham shoving it in everyone's faces,' she countered.

Grinning, Wasim sat down as Moira raised her fingertips to the base of her throat. '*Moi?* Would I do such a thing?'

'Yes,' Iona smiled, catching sight of the paper her dad was unfolding. '*The Times*? Dad, I thought you refused to have anything to do with Murdoch's evil empire.'

Saying nothing, Wasim shook the sheets straight. The front page headline caught Iona's eye. New information coming to light over the extent of the United State's extraordinary rendition program.

'The paper boy missed us again and it was the only thing they had left when I went to the shop,' Moira said. 'Anyway, what have they got you working on now? It must be manic with that conference about to start.'

She looked up at her mum, embarrassed to admit she hadn't been given a part to play in the operation. Her finger searched out the groove in the edge of the table that she had carved with a craft knife almost two decades before. How many hours, it occurred to her, did I sit here doing my homework?

'According to this,' her father announced before she could reply, 'the event might be blessed with a visit from Blair himself, along with a few other New Labour cronies – I mean architects.'

'Blair? Surprised the party can afford him,' Iona smirked. 'What does he charge for an appearance, nowadays?'

'Don't get me bloody started,' Wasim muttered. 'And that bloody ridiculous perma-tan he now sports? It certainly isn't from time he's spent out and about as the Middle East peace envoy.'

Moira was straightening up from before the oven door. 'Come on, you still haven't said what you're up to,' she said, placing a metal baking tray on the table. Inside it was a layer of roasted vegetables.

'That really smells delicious,' Iona said, avoiding the question by leaning forward to see the food. 'What is it?'

'From my new cookbook,' Wasim announced proudly. 'Baked artichokes, broad beans and parsley.'

'He's going all Mediterranean on us,' Moira said, putting on a posh voice, as she placed a bowl of chopped-up pitta breads beside it. 'Ever since the doctor said his curries are pushing his cholesterol up. Now, for the third bloody time, what are you up to at work?

Are you in the security area? Will we see you on the telly, hovering about in the background, looking all official?'

Iona tried to sound nonchalant as she watched Wasim spoon food on to their plates. 'I doubt it. I'm looking into a case of false-identity use. Someone claiming to be a Sri Lankan student who was showing a keen interest in the tunnels beneath the city.'

'Oh,' Moira said, 'that is spooky.'

Wasim passed her a plate. 'Dig in. This fellow was showing a considerable interest to whom?'

Iona savoured the aromas drifting up. 'A group who like to sneak about exploring them.'

'I recall Granada did a documentary about the tunnels years ago. Do you remember it, Moira?'

'Vaguely,' she said, surveying the plate he'd just handed her. 'There's an entire network of them, isn't there?'

'Mostly uncharted,' Wasim concurred. 'Old mine-workings, passageways, corridors. Even catacombs; it was fascinating.'

Moira clicked her fingers. 'What was that special word? For underground streams and rivers – the ones they built over.'

'Culverts,' Wasim answered. 'A few of those, too.'

'Well,' Iona said, 'this person was very interested to learn about any in the vicinity of the convention centre.'

'Couldn't you have said something?' Moira asked disapprovingly.

Iona turned to her, feeling defensive. 'Mum – just because I'm not working on the actual security operation for the convention centre . . .' She could hear the tetchiness in her reply and softened her tone. 'It doesn't mean this incident isn't potentially important.'

Moira's eyebrows were raised. 'I wasn't meaning that, hen. I meant getting you to investigate anything to do with tunnels. Hardly a strong point, is it? Given your thing with small spaces.'

'Oh that,' Iona breathed as she sat back. 'Well, I doubt I'll end up having to actually go down any.'

'Touch wood,' Moira responded, pressing her fingertips against the table.

FIVE

Iona climbed the stairs of the Cornerhouse to the first-floor bar. It had been done out in a rustic style, all chunky wood and natural stone. She scanned the tables of drinkers: most seemed of a similarish age to her. There were lots of trendy glasses and shaved heads, but no blonde dreadlocks to be seen.

Stepping round a few people at the top of the stairs, she approached the bar and started trying to catch the eye of the bloke behind it. He wandered over with a sceptical look on his face.

Do not ask me for proof of age, she thought. I'll curl up and die if you do. 'Hi, there,' she said brightly. 'A slim-line tonic, please.'

His face relaxed as he nodded. You were, Iona thought. How embarrassing.

He prepared the drink and placed it on the slate counter. 'That's three pounds fifty.'

Iona almost coughed. Three quid fifty? For a tiny bottle of tonic? Worrying how that would look on her expenses form, she fished a fiver out of her pocket. 'I'll need a receipt, thanks.'

There was a stool free at the end of the bar, so she moved it to the corner and climbed on. Her toes barely reached its foot rail. As she waited for Toby to appear, she ran her eyes over the tables of people once again. None seemed to be the least bit perturbed about spending God-knew-how-much on bottles of wine and fancy little plates of nibbles. She wondered what they all did for a living: whatever it was, it obviously paid far better than the police.

Her gaze caught on a guy with neatly combed hair and a North Face gilet looking about for his friends. A young woman with bright scarlet hair burst out laughing at a nearby table. 'No way, that is outrageous!' she exclaimed. 'What are you like!'

Iona sipped her drink and saw the guy in the North Face gilet was now standing near a rack of leaflets detailing forthcoming films. No drink. He was pretending to study a flyer. Their eyes met for an instant. It's you, Iona realized. You're Toby. Either that, or you're about to come over and try to chat me up. She studied her glass, wondering how long it would be before he made his approach.

A minute later, the man came across. 'Is your name Khan?'

She looked at him, feigning confusion. 'Yes.'

'I'm Toby.' He dropped his voice. 'You know. Doc-P?'

'Really? You had me looking for someone with blonde dread-locks.' She raised her glass. 'Well done.'

The young man smiled. 'Yeah, well, I wanted to make sure you were on your own.'

Iona made sure her amusement didn't show. 'I hope you can see I am.'

'Yup.' He glanced at her drink. 'They're waiting for us at a place not far from here.'

'OK. Hang on.' Iona drained the tonic in one, catching his look of surprise as she placed the empty glass back down. 'Cost three quid fifty, that did.'

Toby led the way down the stairs, out the door and on to Oxford Street, where he started heading towards the library. Following behind, Iona thought about the security surrounding the site of the Labour Party conference just a short walk away. A ring of steel, as her colleagues in the CTU referred to it. The phrase had also found its way into the papers.

She'd taken a detour on the way home from work a couple of times to surreptitiously survey the oval-shaped anti-ram bollards linked by thick metal bars that closed off the roads. The double fence that formed the perimeter of the secure zone had now been in place for over a week. Access was only possible through the temporary buildings that had been erected at designated points and only to members of the public carrying special passes. Once the event started, the same conditions would apply to police officers. From reports she'd scanned in the office, she also knew mobile CCTV units and dozens of extra officers were set to be stationed around the perimeter – the rooftops of several tall buildings in the vicinity had also been requisitioned as sniper points.

They reached the mouth of a side road and Toby altered direction to a set of steps vanishing beneath ground level. As Iona registered the name on the awning above the entrance, she felt her heart sink. The Temple of Convenience, once a public toilet, now a subterranean bar – and a very small one at that.

Come on, she told herself. It's only a few steps down: nothing you can't handle. It might be cramped down there, but it's not a problem.

'You all right?' Toby had descended three steps and was looking back at her with a quizzical expression.

Iona nodded. 'Absolutely. Lead the way.'

She followed him to the bottom of the stairs and into a poorly lit and narrow space with a tiny counter at the far end. Small square tables lined each side of the room. Lou Reed was playing on a vintage Wurlitzer jukebox and the place was half-full of drinkers.

Toby had approached a corner table where two men also of about twenty were eagerly finishing off a packet of crisps that had been opened out on the table. They had a slightly geeky air about them. Like the sort, Iona thought, you see in Forbidden Planet, sitting around painting their latest *Lord of the Rings* figurines.

'This is her,' Toby announced, sitting down and looking up at Iona.

Seeing both had almost finished their bottles of Budvar, Iona circled a finger. 'Can I get you another?'

The one with the cropped hair fended her offer away with a raised hand.

OK, Iona said to herself. So you're in charge. She took the fourth seat at the table and, trying not to dwell on how low the ceiling was, took out a notebook and pen. 'My name's Iona Khan.'

Both nodded, saying nothing.

'What should I call you two?'

'I'm Hidden Shadow,' the one in a checked shirt answered.

The one with the cropped hair just glared at her, seemingly reluctant to say anything.

Iona nodded. 'I really appreciate you agreeing to see me. As I've said to Toby, what you tell me will not have any repercussions for yourselves.'

'There was a lot of debate about whether to report this or not,' the one with cropped hair announced moodily. 'What we do, it's not the sort of thing you lot exactly approve of. Or the council, or site security.'

'I can imagine,' Iona responded, beginning to wonder what else they might be into. G20 protests? Breaking through to the runway at Manchester airport to stage sit-ins? Harassing scientists linked to animal experiments? Activist types rarely confined their activities to just one issue. 'What you do doesn't bother me. In fact, I'm very interested by it – from a personal point of view. I didn't know there were that many tunnels beneath the city.'

'Miles of them.' This from Hidden Shadow as he swept hair back over the collar of his checked shirt.

Iona wondered if she could get through the entire interview without having to use the name Hidden Shadow. 'Forgive my ignorance, but why are there so many? Do most cities have them?'

Hidden Shadow's nostrils widened as he drew in air. 'Not as many as Manchester,' he announced on the outward breath. 'Thing to remember about Manchester is the whole place sits on a bed of sandstone. Dead easy to dig into. That and the way the city evolved so quickly, layers built on layers in such a rush; no one stopping to record what they were covering over.'

He's right, Iona realized, memories of a history lesson activated by his comment. Manchester hadn't been planned. Like an unexpected baby, the teacher had described it. Dragged kicking and screaming into the world. From minor rural town to the world's first industrial powerhouse in a few short decades. She remembered reading about the breathtaking speed of its expansion – how the population mushroomed in the early 1800s to quadruple its original size in just fifty years. The frenzied building of mills, warehouses, factories, railways and canals. An industrial vortex, sucking in people from all around, workers crammed into terraced houses, one outside lavatory for hundreds. The smell of poverty amid the swirl of chimney smoke.

'And you explore them, when? At weekends? I presume at night.'

'Mostly,' he replied. 'But not exclusively. Sometimes an opening's exposed on a building site and our window of opportunity is only small. I've slipped past security and gone down during my lunch hour. Knackered my suit and everything.'

'Where do you work?' Iona immediately saw the question was the wrong one. 'Sorry. What do you do in these tunnels?'

'Just document them,' Cropped-hair replied while looking off to the side. 'Leave nothing behind but footprints: that's our motto.'

Iona dipped her head in understanding. It was the sort of philosophy the world could do with more of.

'We take photos, video footage,' he continued, still not making eye contact. 'Try and see where they lead . . .'

'And where do they lead?' Iona asked, her own eyes wide to create an air of innocent curiosity.

'Depends which tunnel,' he muttered.

'Some stretch for hundreds of metres,' Hidden Shadow cut in. 'Especially the ones below the cathedral. One time, we followed—'

Cropped-hair clicked his tongue. 'Stick to what we agreed.'

His partner closed his mouth and crossed his arms.

Iona twiddled her pen. Hidden Shadow seems very eager to impress, she thought, targeting him with her next question. 'Can I ask why you go down them?'

The three men exchanged glances before he spoke again. 'You heard of the mountaineer, George Mallory?'

'Don't think so,' Iona responded.

'He died while trying to make the first ascent of Everest. Before he set off, a journalist asked him why he wanted to climb it. His reply?'

Iona shook her head.

'"Because it's there".' He sat back.

'Plus,' Cropped-hair added, 'it's our heritage; the city's. The council's attitude is totally out of order. Not only do they deny access, they deny many of the tunnels even exist. Including ones we've been down. There are records of some of them – why they were built. But they're kept under lock and key. Bastards. They didn't dig them, they don't own them.'

Actually, Iona thought, if they're on city council land, they do. 'Probably just Health and Safety concerns,' she said. 'Usual sort of rubbish.'

Hidden Shadow shook his head. 'Fuck that. They're just pen-pushing, faceless officials. Servants of the state.'

Here we go, thought Iona. Have a rage against the machine. Still, at least they weren't causing trouble during their explorations. Spraying graffiti or stuff like that. She glanced about, remembered her surroundings and tried not to think about when she could head up the stairs and back out into the open. There was the interview to get through first. 'Listen, you sure you don't want a drink? I wouldn't mind one.'

The same shifty looks bounced round the group again. Like, she thought, to say yes would be to somehow incriminate themselves. She pointed to the empty packet of crisps. 'I wouldn't worry. If I want your DNA, I'll just take that. You were both licking your fingers then dabbing the last little bits out.'

Their eyes widened in alarm.

'I'm joking.' Iona sighed, getting to her feet. 'Three Budvars, yeah?'

They all nodded.

As Iona returned, one hand grasping the necks of three bottles, a gin and tonic in her other, she could see the three of them in whispered conversation. 'Here you go,' she said, plonking the drinks down. 'So, this newcomer to the group. Can you take me through it?'

'Right,' Cropped-hair said. 'We're really careful about taking on new members. Unless it's someone we already know, initial contact usually comes through the forum. I keep a Gmail address up there and he started PMing me about two months ago.'

Private message, Iona thought, scribbling away.

'Stuff about wanting to join, how into what we were doing he was. I ignored him, waited for him to actually read the process of getting in.'

'Which is?' Iona asked, glancing up.

'Posting a few explorations of your own.'

'People can do that – put details of their own trips straight on to your site?'

''Course. Anyone can join the forum. Loads do just to read and comment on what we do. Doesn't mean you're an actual member of the Sub-Urban Explorers. Post reports of your own trips – preferably ones not been done before – and we'll consider letting you in.'

'OK – so this newcomer. He had an email address for you to reply to?' Iona's pen was ready.

'Did,' Cropped-hair stated. 'It's no longer active.'

Doesn't matter, Iona thought. I'm sure our tech guys can still trace it. 'What was it, anyway?'

'A darkmail address. You won't get anywhere with it.'

A good part of her CTU training had covered the use of the Internet for covert communication. Still, she thought, no harm making out I don't know what on earth they're on about. 'Darkmail?'

'You do much on the Net?' This from Toby, now sitting forward.

'Of course. Google, mainly. BBC News. Facebook and Twitter, when I get a chance. Plus,' she gave a wink, 'Streetmap is good for when we need to raid an address. Have a good look from all angles online first, far more subtle.'

Toby sighed like that was so yesterday. 'You and half the burglars in this city. OK, when you do one of your Google searches, think of it like dragging a net across the surface of a very deep lake. What you catch is the stuff designed to float – to get caught. There's so much more deep down that doesn't come up. That's the darknet, including email addresses that will lead you absolutely nowhere.'

Iona raised her eyebrows, feigning surprise. 'Do you have it anyway? I know my boss will only ask.'

With a sigh, Cropped-hair took out an iPhone and brushed his way through a few screens. 'Ready?'

Iona nodded and copied down what seemed to be just a random sequence of numbers and letters. She searched in vain for anything that might even indicate which country the address belonged to. Nothing.

'Good luck with it,' Cropped-hair said, putting the device away.

'Cheers,' Iona replied. 'So, what can you tell me about this guy?'

SIX

Iona took another sip of her gin and tonic. The alcohol was definitely hitting home, countering the feelings of discomfort caused by the confines of the bar.

'What can we tell you about this guy?' Hidden Shadow repeated, as he thought for a moment. 'Well, he then posts a couple of trips he's done on his own. Nothing impressive – just a couple of the better-known sewerage tunnels, like the Amory Street storm drain.'

'Yeah,' Cropped-hair interjected. 'Like that's a big deal. Not.'

They're loosening up, too, Iona thought. Amazing what a bit of booze can do. 'Why didn't that impress you?' she asked.

Hidden Shadow looked at her like she was an alien. 'Been done to death. That's why. Anyone can get in.' He put on an American accent. 'It ain't no thing.'

'Too right,' Toby agreed forcefully.

Iona glanced at him. You're chucking your opinions in now, too. That's good. 'So he's not doing so well at making an impression.'

'Until,' Cropped-hair said, 'he had a go at the Cornbrook. On his own. Now that is a serious mooch.'

'Epic,' Hidden Shadow concurred.

'What is it?' Iona asked.

'A drain,' Cropped-hair replied. 'Runs for over five clicks, from Cornbrook—'

'The Metro stop going out to Salford Quays?' Iona asked.

'Yeah, near there. Runs below the city to come out near Ardwick.'

Iona tried to gauge distances in her head. Easily over five kilometres, like they said.

'It is,' Cropped-hair elaborated, 'a shit-fest of massive proportions. Probably the toughest drain in Manchester.'

'Parts where you're knee-deep in fester,' Hidden Shadow added. 'Methane releases, the lot. All manner of debris to wade through.'

'And the tunnel is never more than four feet high,' Cropped-hair said. 'So you're bent double the entire way.'

The impact of their words – and the images they created – was causing Iona's pulse to speed up. 'If I were into betting, I could be tempted into believing you've also been down it.' She smiled.

'Down it?' Hidden Shadow grinned. 'We were the first to complete it. That thing is our bitch.' He held up a hand and Cropped-hair gave him a high-five. Lowering his arm, he looked at Iona. 'This is all off the record, right? Anything we've done?'

She nodded. 'Within reason, of course. But if you mean exploring tunnels, it honestly does not concern me.'

He leaned to the side and whispered something to Cropped-hair. The other man looked dubious and murmured a reply. Hidden Shadow whispered something else. 'Come on,' he said more loudly. 'It's cool.'

Cropped-hair gave a reluctant nod.

Hidden Shadow turned to Iona. 'You want to see the inside of a storm drain?'

'Now?' She looked around. 'I don't think . . . I mean, my shoes – I'm hardly – '

He grinned. 'We don't mean actually going down one.'

Cropped-hair sniggered as he produced his iPhone. 'Watch this.' He selected a file, started the footage playing and handed her the device. 'There's sound, if you can hear it above the noise in here.'

The title, Bunker Storm Drain, faded from the screen and a drumbeat started up. The view was outside, looking across a concrete channel about ten feet wide. Stinging nettles and brambles drooped over each side. The picture zoomed in on a semi-circular opening at ground level. A hand appeared in front of the camera, thumb raised.

The image cut and was replaced by the outline of a figure directing a powerful lamp up the low tunnel. He was wearing waders and had a bandana over his face. Iona could tell it was Hidden Shadow. The camera swung round to show a thick layer of litter on the floor.

It homed in on a lump of matted fur – a cat maybe, or the remains of a fox. Whatever it was, it must have stank. Iona was wondering where the second light source was coming from when Cropped-hair said, 'Many cameras have built-in spotlights. Burns battery power, but can be useful.'

As Hidden Shadow started making his way forward the song's tempo increased, synthesizer notes now layered over the frantic drum rhythms. The footage cut to another section of tunnel. A tripod had been set up with the lamp now mounted on it. Hidden Shadow was thigh-deep in sludgy water, pointing out the complicated-looking brickwork forming the rim of a circular opening in the wall. The liquid seeping over its edge was lumpy and orange. More was oozing between the bricks in the smaller tunnel's roof.

'What's known as a shrinker,' Hidden Shadow said, peering at the screen from across the table.

Iona glanced up.

'Wide opening, gets narrow the further in you crawl. Bummers to back your way out of.'

Just the thought of it sent a shudder down her legs. An ankle knocked against the table leg, making their drinks wobble.

Another cut, now the view was off some kind of ledge, looking down on to a smooth, glassy surface. The tunnel seemed to have got bigger. A hand reached out and let go of an empty sweet wrapper. As soon as it touched the surface, it shot off to the side. Iona realized it was water – and it was moving fast. The camera tracked it for a few metres before it was swallowed by the blackness beyond.

'That's the main tunnel, the bit before was just an overflow,' Hidden Shadow explained.

'How deep is it?' Iona asked.

'Hard to say,' Cropped-hair responded. 'Three, four feet? More than enough to sweep you off your feet.'

'What if one of you slipped and fell in? Where would you end up?'

'Just don't slip,' Hidden Shadow laughed.

The footage cut again, Hidden Shadow on the ledge, peering upwards, bathed in a shaft of daylight. It looked for a moment like he was in the beam of space ship and Iona could imagine him rising into the air. The camera drew closer and tilted up. A shaft, one side of it lined by a row of rusty rungs. Sheets of cobwebs stretched across it, dead leaves and twigs causing them to droop. The top of the shaft was capped by some kind of perforated cover through which the sunlight was shining. Hidden Shadow made a spider with one hand and crawled it through the air towards the camera's lens.

The next scene was him approaching a circle of bright light – the mouth of the tunnel. The song came to a stop as he turned and saluted. The picture faded out.

Iona stared at the screen for a moment longer before handing the iPhone back. 'You're mad.'

They were clearly delighted by her comment.

'So, back to Cornbrook,' Hidden Shadow said. 'Which, by the way, makes the Bunker look like a Sunday stroll. In fact, we nearly gave up after four-and-a-half clicks. Backs were killing us. Only reason we carried on was we couldn't shift any liddage to get the fuck out –'

Iona shot him a questioning look. 'Liddage?'

'Man-hole covers.'

'You mean,' she said, voice slightly hoarse, 'you could have been trapped down there?'

'No way we wanted to turn back,' Cropped-hair continued. 'Plus, our GPS told us, if we did surface, it would be in some rather on-top locations. Busy areas with traffic and cameras, you know? So we pressed on to the finish, finally popped a manhole only to find a dome cam directly above us.'

'Yeah,' Hidden Shadow laughed. 'Not wanting to outstay our welcome, so to speak, we got moving. Had to schlep right across town to our dry gear, sun coming up, head-to-toe in the most acrid gunk imaginable.'

They looked proudly at each other.

Iona dropped her gaze to her notes. What a pair of weirdos.

'When he tried it, our man clocked up a fail a few hundred metres in,' Hidden Shadow said. 'Started pouring down and the poop-flow got too strong for him.'

'Oh, my God,' Iona said. 'There's a danger of these things flooding while you're down there?'

'Well,' Cropped-hair said, looking amused, 'they are storm drains.'

'Obviously,' Hidden Shadow added, 'you pick a dry spell to do them. Which he didn't. Then, a few weeks after that, he posted something that really got our attention. He made it up on to the town hall roof. Took some amazing photos across the city, many from the top of the clock tower.'

'I thought you were only into below-ground stuff?'

'Primarily, yes. But we'll go up cranes or on to a roof if the opportunity presents itself.'

Iona pictured the neo-Gothic architecture of the civic building. The clock tower was frighteningly tall. 'He's got a head for heights, then.'

Hidden Shadow sat forward. 'Also an ability with locks.' The other two nodded. 'That's not an easy building to access. Majorly difficult, in fact.'

'Doing it was deserving of respect,' Cropped-hair stated.

'So we contacted him,' Hidden Shadow continued. 'We met in the student union on Oxford Street. He was really keen to visit the tunnels under the cathedral at first. But they've been well gone through.'

'They have?' Iona asked, giving them her wide-eyed look again. 'Are there many?'

'Under the cathedral?' Hidden Shadow looked bored. 'It's riddled with them. They spread out in all directions. Get to most via the crypt or the passage below the main tower. It's hardly a secret. Next, he wants a look round the Victoria Arches.'

Confused, Iona looked at him.

'Dug out originally to store goods being transported up and down the River Irwell. No one's quite sure when. Then they were used as air-raid shelters during World War II. Right in front of the cathedral, they are. You can see them looking back across the river from Bridge Street.'

Iona clicked her fingers, picturing the steep walls dropping down to the dirty water. 'They look like giant bricked-up windows? Set a few metres above water level?'

'That's them. Over three-and-a-half-thousand people used to shelter in there during the Blitz.'

'Really?' Iona said. 'That's a lot of bodies.'

'Each archway leads into a cavernous great hall, all interconnected by narrow corridors.'

'You've been in them, too?'

'Plenty of times.'

'How do you get in?'

He looked at her. 'Trade secret. There used to be wooden stairs going down to them from Bridge Street, but they were torn down when the council decided to brick the entrances up. There are other

ways in, though – including where the wardens' posts used to be.
You just need to know where to look.'

Cropped-hair raised a finger. 'All this stuff? You're not teasing
anything out of us you can't read about on our website. Hope you
realize that.'

Iona looked at him. Damn, that was starting to go really well. 'I
wasn't trying to. So, what's down there now?'

'Not a lot. Part of a tramway gantry. Bits of old pipes, broken
bricks – the usual stuff. There's meant to be a way through to the
cathedral tunnels but we've never had any luck finding it. We might
have done if Hidden Shadow here isn't always so keen to get out.'
He smirked at his mate.

'Sometimes, you hear things,' Hidden Shadow said uncomfortably.
'Moaning sounds. The back part of the arches must be almost
touching the cathedral crypt, we reckon.'

A little smile had appeared on Toby's lips. 'Like there's a ghost
trapped down there.'

Hidden Shadow was staring at his feet. 'Take the piss. You
wouldn't think it was so funny if you actually heard it. Not down
there in the pitch black, just the sound of dripping water all around.'

'OK,' she said, 'leaving the haunted stuff to one side. This person's
interested in the areas below the cathedral . . .'

Across the table, Cropped-hair held up his finger again. 'At first
he was. Then he starts trying to pump us for information about the
Deansgate tunnel – which, of course, he gets no joy with.'

Iona paused again in her note-taking. 'You've lost me again.
Deansgate tunnel?'

'It's a bit of a legend.'

Iona thought about Deansgate's wide lanes. How the little old
lady had been stranded at the mid-point with the four-wheel
drive edging towards her. 'And what? It goes from one side to
the other?'

'Not across it,' Hidden Shadow said. 'Under it.'

Iona blinked. 'Sorry?'

'And it's big enough to drive a coach and horses through.'

Iona sat back. 'You're saying there's a tunnel beneath one of the
city's major roads and no one can actually find a way into it?'

Hidden Shadow rocked his bottle from side to side. 'We didn't
say no one can get into it. I made it into a short section once – but
it had been bricked up after about forty metres. The council are

bound to be aware of it – but life's far easier if they just deny it exists.'

'But surely something like that couldn't be covered up? Pardon the pun.'

From the sudden way they all shifted in their seats, Iona sensed she'd touched a collective nerve.

Hidden Shadow swigged the last of his beer down before speaking. 'You're trying to tell me, the authorities don't try and keep stuff secret from the public? We're in the age of WikiLeaks, dude. Calling people like us conspiracy theorists won't wash any more.'

Fair point, Iona said to herself. She was aware of a few cover-ups herself. Like a couple of years ago when the big screens that had been erected in Piccadilly Gardens to show the UEFA cup final had suddenly gone off. It wasn't, she knew, because of any technical fault as official announcements had claimed. It was because senior brass had taken the decision to cut the power when crowds swelled to dangerous levels. They just hadn't anticipated the thousands of infuriated Glaswegians who then rioted through the centre of the city.

'So which bit of Deansgate is it meant to be beneath?' she asked.

'Which bit?' A wry smile was on Cropped-hair's face. 'It doesn't run under just part of it – the thing goes its entire length.'

Iona wasn't sure if she'd heard correctly. 'From one end to the other?'

'Correct.'

She did a mental scan of the city. Deansgate started adjacent to the cathedral and then ran in a straight line all the way to Deansgate train station. In between those two points lay such city landmarks as The John Rylands Library, Kendals department store and the Great Northern Railway Terminal; now a leisure complex housing a cinema, gym and several bars. She realized the convention centre was located not far to the side of Deansgate, at the train station end of it. The alarm bell that had rung in her mind when talking with Sergeant Ritter started up again, more loudly this time. 'Talk me through when you saw this person again.'

Hidden Shadow let out a burp. 'OK, so you know he walked right past me outside Central Library?'

Iona gave a nod.

'I wasn't sure if it was him, at first. The way he was dressed was so different. Then again, he may not have recognized me with a tie on and my hair all neat—'

'Can you give me a physical description?' Iona cut in.

Hidden Shadow looked momentarily irritated at being interrupted. 'He's quite tall – kind of gangly. Yeah?' He looked at his companion for confirmation.

Cropped-hair nodded. 'About six feet, maybe just over. Probably ten stone, maximum. Thin shoulders, long neck. Quite a sharp face, high cheekbones, jaw – you know – angular.'

Toby tapped his throat. 'Big Adam's apple.'

'Yeah, big Adam's apple,' the other two chorused.

'Hair?' Iona asked.

'Black and thick,' Hidden Shadow replied. 'Swept over in a side parting. Imagine a fast bowler in the Sri Lankan cricket team – that would be pretty much him.'

Iona noted everything down. 'You said he was dressed differently. What was he wearing? A suit?'

'No – chino-style trousers,' Hidden Shadow replied. 'And a shirt. Sensible clothes, certainly not the jeans and hoodies he usually wore. So I follow him in and up to the second floor – where they have a good look at those architectural plans.'

'They being the one calling himself Muttiah and his companion?' Iona realized her businesslike tone was now destroying the interview's laid-back approach she'd so carefully cultivated. 'Can you describe the other one?'

Hidden Shadow thought for a moment. 'Shorter, for a start. And he was wearing a baseball cap. He took it off inside the library and I could see he was a bit older. Meaner-looking, too.'

'Why do you say that?'

'Don't know,' he shrugged. 'Just the expression on his face – he looked angry. Similar features, just older and angrier.'

New voices caused the volume of noise in the bar to suddenly increase. Iona glanced to her side: a group of people were filing in, creating a wall of bodies between her and the bottom of the stairs. A sense of being trapped suddenly flooded her and she felt the muscles in her legs tense. Looking down, she fought back the urge to jump from her seat and barge her way out. 'How old, would you say?'

'About thirty, at the most. Hair was short – looked like it would have been curly if it was longer.'

'And about how tall?'

'Oh, five-and-a-half feet, maybe less.' He focused on Iona. 'Not that much taller than you. And he looked in good shape. Wiry sort of build to him, like a rock climber. When they got to the stairs in the library, he was up them like a shot. Two at a time, proper I-mean-business style. That's when I first realized he's not calling the other one Muttiah. He looked back at the first landing and goes, "Vasen!" Then he beckoned, like he was saying to hurry up.'

Sounds like this other guy was in charge, Iona thought. Maybe a more senior person in whatever organisation they're part of – if any. 'And they're not speaking English?'

'No – not sure what it was. But once they're at the book shelves, it's Vasen this and Vasen that.'

'Would you recognize the language if you heard it again?' Iona wondered how easy it would be to get hold of a Sri Lankan audio tape. Probably simplest to go on YouTube and have a search there.

'I'm not sure.'

'But – previously – Muttiah claimed to be from Sri Lanka.'

'That's what he said.'

'Which would make him more South Asian than Middle Eastern.'

'I suppose. But, no offence, if the person's wearing Western clothes, how can you easily tell? I mean, his skin was quite dark, hair black, eyes brown. I don't mean to sound racist, but you get my point?'

Iona nodded, aware her heart was beating more quickly than normal. The new arrivals were speaking too loudly, filling the place with a barrage of sound. 'The companion,' she said more loudly. 'You said facially, they were similar.'

'Yeah – I'd say related. Like an older brother or something. I actually thought he could have been there for the Muttiah bloke's graduation ceremony – it would have explained the smart clothes.'

Iona tried to cut out the surrounding noise and think. The foyer of the library had to have CCTV. 'And you first saw them outside the library?'

'Yeah. The front steps. I was coming down, they were going in.'

'Can you remember when exactly this was?'

'End of my lunch break. Last Wednesday.'

'Which is when, sometime around two o'clock?'

'Yup – five to.'

That's my first task for tomorrow morning right there, Iona thought. Try and get a CCTV image of them. Until then, they remain faceless. She checked herself from thinking too far ahead:

it might not be so easy to arrange another meeting with these guys. Just because it's bloody noisy and cramped down here, she thought, is not an excuse to rush things. You know Wallace will be looking for any gaps in the interview. 'Anything more you can tell me about Muttiah? Did he ever mention where he lived, what he did when he wasn't with you, places he liked to eat at? That kind of stuff.'

Cropped-hair shook his head. 'Looking back, it was always strictly tunnels with him. No idle chit-chat, just questions about if we'd seen this place, do we know a way into that.'

'He never hung around after a trip? Came down here for a drink?'

'We offered, but he said he didn't touch alcohol. And he couldn't stand loud places. We didn't pressure him.'

'You never asked him about Sri Lanka? What it was like over there?'

'I did once,' Hidden Shadow replied. 'You know, about the Tamil Tigers and the civil war. He definitely wasn't keen to talk about it. I thought maybe he'd lost his family. Something horrific like that.'

'OK.' Iona put her pen down and surveyed the group with what she hoped was a calm, controlled expression. She realized the wall behind them was glistening; condensation, from all the people squashed in. Her chest felt tight. 'If you remember anything else – and I mean anything – here's my number.' She placed three of her freshly printed cards on the table. First I've handed out, she thought. Apart from the ones to mum and dad. 'Call me anytime.'

As the leader lifted one off the table, Iona stole a glance at the exit sign. 'Thanks for taking the trouble to see me. You did the right thing here.'

Cropped-hair sat back and crossed his arms. 'You think it could be something? A bomb plot?'

Iona put her notebook away, now just wanting to get out. 'Any report like this has to be followed up.'

Hidden Shadow made a hissing sound through his teeth. 'That's not what he asked.'

She glanced at him. 'I can't say at this stage. I'll need to contact the university for details about foreign students. But, initially, yes; it does give me cause for concern.'

The admission seemed to go down well, like they could be involved in something serious. Talking fodder for their next trip.

'Obviously,' she added, 'our arrangement to keep this between ourselves works two ways. Quid pro quo, as Doctor Lecter said to Clarice Starling.'

Cropped-hair's face lit up. 'Like it,' he smiled. 'Yeah. Of course.'

His eyes went to Hidden Shadow and, from the glance they shared, Iona wasn't sure if they'd be keeping their side of the bargain. She got to her feet and looked at Toby. 'If anything else comes up on my side, more questions or the need for photo identification, do I go through you?'

He turned to Cropped-hair, who nodded.

'Yup,' Toby replied.

'OK. Thanks again.' She reached into her pocket, took out a tenner and put it on the table. 'And have another drink on me.'

The three of them looked delighted as she burrowed her way across the packed bar and jogged thankfully up the steps. Back out in the open air, she placed a hand on the railings, breathing deeply as she looked up at the night sky. Seems like I've been down there for hours, she thought, a light breeze making her damp shirt feel suddenly cold.

As her heartbeat returned to normal, her mind turned to how she could access the footage from any cameras overlooking the library's entrance. Her mobile beeped and she realized there would have been no signal in the subterranean bar. Looking at the screen, she saw the message was from Jim. Hang on, she thought. Jim. He's just been through the exact process with the drug-dealing case. His parting comment rang in her head and another thought occurred: I'm not sure if I can face speaking to him. Not tonight, anyway.

She put her phone away and glanced at her watch. Eight forty-three. In about thirty-six hours, she realized, these streets will be crawling with delegates for the Labour Party conference.

SEVEN

The phone line clicked as Iona was placed on hold. She looked up from her desk. As usual, the office was very quiet. Many members of the Unit would be over at Gold Command, the operations centre set up especially for the Labour Party conference in the sports hall of the Police Training College at Sedgeley Park.

Others would be at the Silver and Bronze posts located closer to the convention centre itself. That left a few civilian support workers and her.

Her eyes settled on the screensaver that someone in the IT department had loaded on to everyone's monitor. Operation Protector, the block lettering boldly announced. The digital numbers below it read, fourteen hours, forty-three minutes. It was a countdown to midnight: when the security operation went live.

She examined the empty desk opposite hers. Detective Inspector Dave Ellis. The person meant to be her work partner, showing her the ropes, making her feel part of the team. Presently laid up at home with a slipped disc.

On getting in that morning, she'd tried to summon the will to call Jim and ask how he'd got hold of all the CCTV images relating to the case he was wrapping up. I've helped in so many cases where evidence from council CCTV featured, she chastised herself, and not once did it occur to me where all the images were actually recorded.

After a minute's agonizing, she'd decided to prioritize contacting the University of Manchester to ask how she could obtain a list of all foreign nationals currently in the city on student visas.

The task, as the staff member in the admissions office had told her, was made considerably easier by the fact the present institution was the result of a merger, some seven years before, between The Victoria University of Manchester and the Manchester Institute of Science and Technology. The new establishment had close to forty thousand students, and not only were the seven thousand or so overseas ones on student visas listed by the admissions office, they were also categorized by nationality, sex and ethnic origin.

Iona had asked the staff member to bring up all those from Sri Lanka. As expected, Muttiah and Vasen were not among the nine names revealed. Examining the ethnic categories on the university's online form, Iona asked the person to separate off all males who'd ticked 'Asian', 'African' or 'Any other black background' as their ethnic group and email the names over.

This had resulted in a list of just under two thousand, alphabetically listed, surnames. She scanned carefully through the lot. No Christian or surnames of Muttiah, as Iona expected. Worse, no Vasens either. In fact, none of the names beginning with V even came close to the name which Hidden Shadow thought he'd heard being used.

She'd tapped her pen against her lower teeth. It was no surprise the mystery person had lied about being Sri Lankan. But if he wasn't actually over on a student visa either, the search for him would make finding a needle in a haystack seem simple.

She'd sunk lower in her seat, suddenly sensing that the grim reality of most police work was about to apply to this case: a slow, methodical sift of information. And, with the conference about to start, it was something she didn't have time to do.

Studying the names again, she recalled that Hidden Shadow had mentioned something. What was it? She closed her eyes. It had been towards the end of the interview, when she was dying to get out of that bar. Something to do with the pair being in smart clothes outside the library. Like they were dressed for a graduation ceremony, that was it!

She called the person in the university's admissions office back. 'Do you keep a list of recent graduates? Or, better, the foreign nationals who've completed the course they were granted a student visa to undertake?'

'We do.'

'Great. Can I have all male names then for last year, please? Same ethnic search parameters as before. Oh, and any chance the alphabetical order can be by the Christian name this time, not surname?'

'I think I can do that.'

Ten minutes later, she had a new list, numbering one thousand three hundred and fourteen. She scanned for those that began with M. No Muttiah. She continued to those that began with V. There were eight.

Vasava.

Vasilios.

Vassen.

Vedanga.

Victor.

Vimal.

Viraj.

Vougay.

Her eyes went back to the third. Vassen. Surname of Bhujun, from Mauritius. Of course, the university staff member had explained, there were also foreign nationals studying at Salford University and Manchester Metropolitan University, not to mention the various other Further Education institutions dotted about the city.

But Iona had a good feeling about Vassen Bhujun and, judging from what the police officer in Mauritius had just reported, her hunch had saved countless valuable hours of searching.

At that moment there was another click as the police officer came back on the line. 'Sorry for keeping you.'

'That's OK. What time is it in Mauritius, by the way?' Iona asked, transferring the phone to her other hand and reaching for a notepad.

'Twenty past two in the afternoon,' the woman replied, a mix of what seemed to be Caribbean and French in her accent. 'Four hours ahead of you.'

'Oh. Afternoon then. And you're an inspector?'

'That's correct,' the voice said.

She glanced at Dave Ellis' empty chair. 'We have the same rank over here.'

'I know. The police force here is modelled on yours. We were a British colony until 1968.'

'I didn't realize.' Feeling a little sheepish, she checked around – but there was no one to have overheard her minor gaffe. 'Sorry, I didn't catch your name.'

'Sheila Moruba,' the inspector replied. 'So, checking with immigration, we have no record of Vassen Bhujun re-entering the country.'

'But, according to the university he was enrolled at over here, his course has already finished.'

'We might be a small country, Detective Khan. Less than one-and-a-half million. But our immigration systems are as modern as yours.'

'Sorry – I wasn't implying they weren't.'

There was a slight pause. 'Well, Vassen Bhujun has not passed through Customs and Immigration since leaving for Britain over a year ago.'

Which means if he is still here, Iona thought, it's illegally. 'OK, thanks very much.'

'You also asked if he is known to us.'

'Yes,' Iona replied. 'I appreciate you can't just send me his criminal record – if he even has one. But, you know, it tends to be the same names that crop up again and again. At least it is here in Manchester.'

'I can tell you – in confidence – he has no record. But his name recently came up as a possible associate of a man we've issued an arrest warrant for.'

'Who's the man?'

'A relative of his, Ranjit Bhujun – the prime suspect in an ongoing murder investigation.'

'Really?' Iona's mind went back to what Hidden Shadow had said. The man with Vassen had looked like an older brother or uncle. 'What kind of a relative?'

'Cousin.'

Iona felt a little jolt of adrenaline. 'But Vassen wasn't involved?'

'No. Vassen was in Britain when the murder was committed – his address was searched in case Ranjit was hiding there. The rooms were empty.'

'When did this murder take place, then?'

'Around six months ago. It was unusual in the sense that the victim was British.'

Iona imagined a tourist mugging gone wrong. Some poor soul straying into the wrong part of town. 'A holidaymaker?'

'No. The person owned a property here. On a very exclusive part of the island. He was killed in his bed.'

'So it was a burglary?'

'The file is with the Major Crimes Investigation Team. If you put in a formal request, I imagine they'd share it with you.'

'OK, I'll arrange for that as soon as possible. But can you give me any details in the meantime? I'm really up against it here.'

'Yes – I remember the incident well. You may, too. The case made the news for two reasons. Firstly, it was a very brutal and senseless murder. The thief had already emptied the contents of the safe when the owner of the property managed to free a hand and hit the button for the panic alarm above his bed.'

'Free a hand? He'd been tied up?'

'Yes. The assailant had got in through an open window of the villa. Cut through the mosquito screen, bound and gagged the victim, then forced him to divulge the combination for the safe. When it was being emptied, the victim set off the alarm. The thief returned to the bedroom and bludgeoned him to death. As I said, brutal and senseless.'

'So a burglary gone wrong.'

'I believe that was the final conclusion.'

'You mentioned a second reason why it stood out.'

'Yes – the victim. He was quite a prominent figure here on the island. At least in official circles.'

'Who was he?'

'Reginald Appleton.'

Iona screwed her eyes shut. The name sounded vaguely familiar. 'Appleton . . . what did he do in Mauritius?'

'He had a retirement property here, a very large one. In Britain, he was a Lord – a very senior part of your legal system.'

Iona opened her eyes. 'The Law Lord? You're talking about the judge: that Appleton? I do remember, it made the news here . . .'

'The whole thing is very embarrassing. Especially as the prime suspect has not been caught.'

'Ranjit Bhujun is still at large?'

'Yes – though not thought to be in Mauritius any longer.'

So your borders aren't quite as watertight as you were making out, Iona thought. Which is understandable, considering you're an island, like us. She considered the fact Vassen had been seen with another man of a similar appearance. Am I dealing with some kind of terrorist cell? I need that CCTV footage, she realized. And I need more information on Appleton as well. 'OK, thanks Sheila. I'll get a proper request for the file on the murder. Speak to you soon.'

While replacing the receiver with one hand, she was typing into the search box of Google with the other. Appleton, Law Lord.

EIGHT

Ten minutes later, Iona had contacted the UK Border Agency. As she waited for the person to get back to her, she turned to the Wikipedia entry she'd printed off for Reginald Appleton. Four pages of dense text. Iona skimmed over the opening pages.

Born in 1937, in Kent, educated privately and then at Queen's College, Oxford, where he won the Vinerian Scholarship. Called to the Bar in 1965, made a QC just eleven years later in 1976 and then a judge in 1980.

All par for the course so far, Iona thought, reflecting for a moment on her own – failed – application to Oxford. Still, she gave a quick smile, if I had got in I'd have probably ended as a merchant banker or something similar. Living in London, working in the Square Mile, hours from my family. No, three years reading maths at Newcastle University and then into the police is suiting me just fine.

But this guy, she thought; he'd been born into the establishment and was obviously destined to become part of the establishment. Made a Judge of the High Court of Justice, Chancery Division in 1984 followed by a Lord Justice of Appeal from 1991 to 1996. Then, at fifty-nine years old, he was appointed Lord of Appeal in Ordinary and created a life peer by the title Baron Appleton. Retired as a Law Lord in 2009, just prior to the title changing to Justice of the Supreme Court.

At which point, Iona thought, he invested in a property on Mauritius. No doubt the plan had been to see out his twilight years in a tropical climate, cocktails on the verandah, fresh seafood and stunning sunsets. Except the poor man had been battered to death in his bed.

The next section detailed the man's life outside his role as a Law Lord. Had received a blue from Oxford for rowing. Married in 1962. His wife, Margaret, had died of cancer in 2003. He was a jazz aficionado and had published what was widely regarded as one of the finest biographies of the pianist, Oscar Peterson. In 1995, his eldest daughter, Lucinda, had married the son of Tristram Dell – a senior civil servant who – until his retirement – had worked in the Foreign Office. The man had also graduated from Oxford in the early fifties.

Iona's eyes stopped moving. Did the two men know each other before their respective children got married? Were they more than just contemporaries?

She moved to the next section, titled Selected List of Cases Decided. A series of bullet points detailed various actions. One plc company versus another, a shipping corporation versus a chartered bank, a private name versus an insurance company. Then, in the early years of the new millennium, a series of decisions where the defendant was listed as either the Secretary of State for the Home Department or the Secretary of State for Foreign and Commonwealth Affairs. She searched for any more details on what the cases had been about. Just dates and a few letters that obviously denoted some kind of reference code.

The final subheading read, Opinions in Terrorism Cases. Iona's eyes narrowed. Of course, she thought; the man was a Law Lord in the years following on directly from 9/11. The start of the Bush and Blair administrations' so-called War on Terror. She sat forward, eyes now fixed on the text. Appleton had been involved in a variety of judgements. Again, the cases were listed, but with no accompanying detail.

The concluding few lines stated that, in the long tradition of English judges deferring to the executive in matters of national security, Appleton had been no exception. Which meant, Iona thought, going along with the government.

She highlighted one of the decisions where the defendant was listed as Secretary of State for the Home Department and fed it back into Google. An obscure legal website came up. The judgement related to the detention without charge of several foreign prisoners that were being held in Belmarsh prison under the Anti-terrorism, Crime and Security Act 2001.

Iona brushed hair back from her face. This was all getting very murky. The nature of Appleton's job had made him a symbol of the British establishment. Then he was involved in cases like that. A terrorist's dream target, surely. She glanced uneasily towards the corridor leading past the stairs up to her boss' office. If this cousin – the prime suspect in the Appleton murder is over here – and the Labour Party conference is about to kick off, we could have a problem. Her dad's words came back to her; the observation Blair and his old cronies were due to be sweeping into town. This, she thought, is something Wallace needs to know about.

The phone to her side went off. 'Constable – I mean, Detective Constable Khan speaking.'

'Forgot your rank there? It's Dominic Edwards.'

The Border Agency official I spoke to earlier, Iona thought. 'That and being in a new office. Keep setting off to my old one in the mornings.'

He chuckled. 'I've had a search on the system.'

She tilted her head so she could wedge the phone against her shoulder. The strand of hair she'd tucked back over her other ear fell forward again and she blew at it from the corner of her mouth. 'Did you have more luck than me?' she asked, pulling off the cap of a biro.

'Afraid not. You're right – Vassen Bhujun was granted a student visa to undertake a one-year course at the University of Manchester. That visa expired in June, but there is no record of him leaving the country.'

'So you have his file?'

'Yes – right here.'

'Is there a photo with it?'

He gave a little cough. 'I believe there was a human error – that's polite-speak for someone dropping a bollock. No photo with the paperwork.'

Iona sighed. 'OK. So he shouldn't still be here. How many other people in the country on student visas promptly vanish when it expires?'

'You want the official number or the real one?'

'Real one, please.'

'We don't know.'

She frowned. 'Roughly, then. Thousands?'

'Higher.'

'Ten thousand?'

'Keep going.'

'Twenty thousand?'

'Keep going.'

'Bloody hell. So, what happens in those scenarios?'

'You want the official version or the real one?'

She sensed a quagmire of unknown depth. 'Let's have the official version this time.'

'We send out enforcement officers to check their last known address, flag their names with various government agencies, pro-actively pursue any leads we might unearth. In reality, if they change name, they aren't going to be troubled by us. Especially if they start working cash-in-hand.'

'Thought you might say something like that,' Iona muttered gloomily.

'Sorry.'

'Hey – not your fault.'

'Anyway, that's the good news. You want the bad?'

She took hold of the receiver and tilted her head to look up at the ceiling. 'The bad?'

'He's a possible terrorist suspect, is he not?'

'Absolutely.'

'His paperwork lists the subject he was here to study.'

Iona closed her eyes. Damn, I should have asked that of the university. 'What was it?'

'Chemical engineering.'

'Well,' Iona said, getting to her feet, 'that's just pants. Thanks, Dominic. Time I spoke to my boss about this.'

NINE

'This is looking a bit tasty,' Superintendent Paul Wallace said, rubbing his hands together. 'Especially the Appleton murder.'

Iona took in the nasal-twang in the man's voice. Wallace was a born and bred Mancunian who'd grown up on the east side of the city where some of its poorest neighbourhoods were found. She had heard somewhere that he was ex-army, but she wasn't sure of any details. What she did know was that he'd been in the CTU from its inception. A beak-like nose, slightly hooded eyes and a fuzz of brown hair made him look faintly like something out of the muppets.

He glanced at his monitor once again. 'According to this old article from *The Daily Telegraph*, the attack was so ferocious they had to ID him off fingerprints. If dental records were a no-no, there couldn't have been much left of his face.'

Iona grimaced, partly at the suspicion that her boss was slightly thrilled by the grisly detail. It had occurred to Iona on more than one occasion that Wallace would have excelled as a criminal. But then again, she concluded, many of her fellow colleagues in the CTU looked like they might too. It was probably what made them so good at their jobs. 'That level of violence,' she said. 'Doesn't that normally suggest the attacker knew the victim?'

Wallace sniffed. 'You're right. Overkill, I think they call it over in the Major Incident Team.'

'I vaguely remember it being on the news,' Iona replied. 'Headlines asking if there was a dark side to paradise, that type of stuff. Won't MI6 have taken an interest in something like this? A figure of the establishment, involved in some high-level stuff . . .'

'Probably. I'll ask the question.'

One of Iona's hands was hanging down at the side of her chair. She crossed her fingers. 'Do you want me to follow up on this student character?'

'Shit-bag,' Wallace muttered, eyes now on the university printout with Vassen Bhujun's name highlighted. 'Coming here and taking advantage of our educational system.' He glanced at Iona. 'You went to uni, didn't you?'

'Yeah, Newcastle.'

Wallace curled a lip. 'Is it true the Geordies count themselves more Scot than English?'

She thought the question an odd one, especially considering the amount of contempt he'd heaped on the word Scot. Doesn't he realize, she wondered, that I'm half Scottish? 'I don't know, really. It was mainly other students I mixed with.'

'Right,' he replied uninterestedly. 'I heard they are. We could always rebuild Hadrian's Wall for them, couldn't we? Make it so the thing goes round the south of the city this time; that would put them firmly on the kilt-wearers' side.'

She gave a half-hearted smile. He's definitely forgotten I was born in Glasgow.

'Fuck's sake, lighten-up, Iona,' he chided her with a grin. 'I'm only arsing around. Bit of joking – it's what the CTU runs on.' He looked down at the thin file Sergeant Ritter had passed on to her. Then he traced a finger across the notes Iona had typed up after her meeting with the Sub-Urban Explorers. 'So your proposed next actions are to obtain visual identifications of our mystery Mauritians and to see what kind of an impression the one called Vassen Bhujun had on his tutor at the university?'

'Yes, sir. And request the file on the murder Vassen's cousin is the PS for.'

The silence stretched out and she found herself trying to beam thoughts through the top of her boss' bowed head. Say yes. Say yes. Say yes.

He looked up. 'Can I be straight with you?'

The question caught her by surprise. 'Yes.'

He lifted the corner of Ritter's file. 'This thing that came out of Bootle Street. I put it your way because – with DI Ellis off sick – it seemed a nice one to ease you in with. You know a lot of our work here is intelligence gathering – this would allow you to do exactly that, with no major consequences if you didn't make much headway.'

Iona kept her eyes on him, not trusting herself to speak. So I did get the case because it appeared unimportant. Thanks a bunch.

He sat back and lifted his eyebrows. 'That got your goat, has it?'

Iona gave a quick smile. 'We're being straight here?'

He nodded.

'Then, yes. It has.'

He looked amused. 'You're new to this unit, Iona. Fresh into the job. It wouldn't be in anyone's interest to let you run before you can walk.' There was a ping of an email arriving. His eyes cut to the screen and he cursed. 'Despite the amount of credible threats I've got piling up here.'

Iona felt herself flush. Could the man be any more patronizing?

'Tell you what, give us a bit of time to think about it,' he announced, sliding her report and Ritter's file to one side and clicking his mouse. 'If that's all right with you.'

Iona gave a curt nod and made for the door.

'Excuse me?'

She looked back with a frown. 'I didn't say anything.'

'Really?' he said, eyes on his monitor. 'Thought I heard a "Yes, sir" there.'

Iona took a breath in. 'Yes, sir.'

But Wallace now appeared oblivious to her presence.

Back at her desk, Iona's gaze caught on the small square of newspaper that someone had neatly Sellotaped to the top of her monitor several days before. It was the headline from the piece on her the *Manchester Evening Chronicle* had published. No reporter had ever spoken to Iona directly, and the paper had been kind enough not to feature a recent photo of her, but that hadn't stopped them unearthing plenty of information on her past. First was the fact she'd won a scholarship to Manchester High School for Girls through her prowess at hockey. Obviously inherited – the article had alleged – from her university lecturer father, Wasim Khan, who had represented Pakistan at hockey in the 1976 and 1980 Olympic Games. While at the school, Iona had risen to the position of deputy head girl and had also excelled at chess.

The paper had even got hold of a grainy copy of her school hockey team's photo. Iona was middle of the front row, several inches shorter than most of her team mates. The fact she was the side's top scorer, the caption stated, led to her nickname, *The Baby-Faced Assassin*.

It was these words that had formed the headline. Now they were firmly attached above her computer screen. *The Baby-Faced Assassin*. At first, she'd just laughed it off and left it there. But the week before, someone had asked her something and, rather than use her name, had used the word *Baby*.

She hadn't been sure what to do. The prospect of having *The Baby-Faced Assassin* as a work nickname didn't seem too bad. But what if everyone started shortening it to *Baby*? That made her uncomfortable. Surely it would label her as ineffectual, even ridiculous? Should she just quietly remove the clipping? But if she did, would her new colleagues class her as precious and lacking a sense of humour?

Realizing she was dwelling on the dilemma yet again, she pushed the thoughts away and looked round the near-deserted office. So what am I meant to do now?

Wallace's words came back to her. *Give us a bit of time to think about it*. She tapped her fingers on the armrests of her chair in frustration. He'll never know, she said to herself, that I continued with my lines of enquiry. After all, half of them are ongoing; I can always claim the people concerned rang me back. She allowed herself a small smile as she reached for the phone.

The same person in the admissions office at The University of Manchester answered. Iona' first question was to enquire if the university would have in their system any photograph of Vassen Bhujun.

'There should be one for his NUS card,' the person responded. 'Though I imagine those of the last year's graduates may well have been archived. I'm not sure.'

'Would you mind finding that out and getting back to me?'

'OK.'

'Any idea of how long that might take? I'm sorry to press you.'

'I'll get on to it right away.'

'Thanks. The other thing I need to know is who Vassen Bhujun's tutor was in the chemical engineering department.'

Within a minute, Iona had the man's name and contact details. Ian Coe. A down-to-earth-sounding name for a professor, Iona thought as she keyed in his phone number and listened to it ring.

'Ian here.' The young-sounding voice had a pleasant timbre to it. She guessed he was somewhere in his thirties.

'Hello, this is Detective Constable Khan speaking, Greater Manchester Police.'

A slight delay. 'I . . . sorry, the police?'

Iona gave a slow nod. 'Yes, that's right. I'm calling about an ex-tutee of yours. I'd appreciate the chance to speak to you about him.'

'Oh . . . right, sorry. You threw me there.' He gave a quick chuckle. 'What's his name?'

'Vassen Bhujun. He graduated last year. An overseas student – from Mauritius.'

'Bhujun, Bhujun – it's not ringing any bells, I'm afraid. If you give me a chance to dig out last year's list . . .'

'Professor Coe, how about you do that while I drive over? I can be with you in no time.'

'In no time,' he mused. 'I take it this is urgent?'

'Very.'

'Well, I'm here in my office for the next hour or so, if that's any—'

'I'll be there in fifteen minutes.'

'Right . . . jolly good . . . you know where to find me?'

Iona looked down at her pad. 'Office twelve, third floor, Faculty of Chemical Engineering, Lower Albion Street.'

'That's it. I'll have his notes ready, Detective Constable . . .'

'Khan. See you shortly.' She hung up, wondering what else needed covering off. Loads. For a start was confirmation the person the Sub-Urban Explorer saw outside the library was actually Vassen Bhujun, chemical engineering graduate from The University of Manchester. The person's mugshot for the NUS card – when it came – was only one half of what was needed, Iona realized. CCTV footage of the person who blanked Hidden Shadow was the other. Jim was the guy with the knowledge about that.

She thought about the verbal sludge he'd left on her answerphone the previous evening. He'd sounded really pissed. Biting at her lower lip, she pondered whether to ring him. Oh, crap, she decided: his parting comment to me in the incident room at Bootle Street was personal; my need to speak to him is professional. That takes priority. She reached for her mobile, brought up his number and pressed the green button.

'Iona?' His voice sounded cautious, even a little contrite.

'Morning. How's the head?'

'All right, why?'

'I could hardly understand a word of that message you left me last night.'

Silence.

'You don't remember, do you?' Iona asked.

'No . . . I mean, yes. I kind of do.' He cleared his throat. 'When did I . . .?

'Before nine in the evening, Jim. You were really pissed. And really ranting.'

'Sorry, got carried away . . . a few with the boys after work.' His voice dropped. 'Actually . . . I do remember some of it. And I mean what I said, Iona.'

She sighed. Did he mean the stuff about me being Wallace's puppet? Or the self-pitying declaration of love? She wasn't sure which was worse. 'You know those stills you had pinned to the wall? The ones taken outside the library?' At the other end of the line she heard someone in the background start to speak.

'Well, well.' His voice was now all cheerful. Iona instantly knew he had adopted his usual persona for the benefit of whoever was in the vicinity. 'Not arsed making contact for weeks, now I can't get her off my back.'

Very funny, Iona thought. 'Did they come from council-run CCTV?'

'That's right.'

'How did you get hold of the footage? Is there a department or something like that I can call?'

'You can call? Why?'

'This case I'm working on. My guy was spotted right outside the library.'

'Have you got an exact time and date?'

She thought about the notes she'd taken in The Temple of Convenience. 'Yes.'

'Was it in the past four weeks?'

'Yes.'

'Then you're in luck. Everything's deleted after one month. But if it's in the last four weeks and you know exactly when, it's a piece of piss. Do you want me to have a word? I have the number for my guy in the control room right here.'

'You do?' Iona hesitated, uneasy about accepting his offer of help. 'I'm not sure when I'll be able to visit. Where is it, the town hall or something?'

'You know the massive NCP car park attached to the back of the Arndale?'

'Yes.'

'In there.'

'The car park?'

'You've never been there?'

Iona pictured the grim, windowless, structure. Naked concrete, strip lights and exhaust fumes. 'The Arndale's NCP? Why on earth is the control room there?'

'The entire city's CCTV system is run by the NCP. They did a deal with the council – you give us all the city centre car parks to run, we'll install you a state-of-the-art CCTV system and control room. They were linking up cameras for all their car parking sites anyway, so it was no great hassle to cover the streets, too.'

'Suppose it makes sense. So where exactly is it?'

'Well, it's a bit strange.' Jim had lowered his voice to sound mysterious. 'A bit weird.' He stretched out the final word, voice dying slowly away.

She refused to smile; why did he always have to clown around? 'And why's that?' she asked in a businesslike way.

'Basically, it's in between levels. Kind of floor three and a half.'

'Jim,' she said, unable to keep the beginnings of a smile from her face. 'I think you've been reading too many Harry Potter books.'

Her ex laughed. 'It's true! The car park lift only has uneven floor numbers. One, three, five and so on. So you go up to three, get out, walk up the ramp to the level above and there it is.'

'Floor four, then.'

'All right, misery-chops,' he said light-heartedly. 'Floor four if you want to ruin it all and be boring.'

'Got a phone number for it?' she asked. 'Or do I just attach a message to my owl?'

She could tell from his voice that he was grinning. 'I'll text you his name and number.'

'Cheers.'

'And Iona – what I said to you in the incident room yesterday? That was out of order.'

She waited for an actual apology.

'Iona? Did you hear? I'm a dickhead. I wasn't thinking when I blurted it out.'

Wasn't thinking? That's not saying sorry. Not even close.

'Iona – we really need to talk. There are things . . . things you need to know.'

She dreaded the thought of him begging for another chance. Saying no left her feeling so bloody awful. 'Listen,' she said quickly. 'I've got to go, OK? I'll give you a buzz.'

Before he could say anything more, she cut the call.

TEN

Iona's footsteps echoed on the stone floor as she strode along the third-floor corridor of the Faculty of Chemical Engineering. From somewhere deep in the building there came the dull thrum of vibrating machinery. Outside the row of windows to her left towered a huge cylindrical vat with lettering on the side: BOC Liquid Nitrogen. The place was more like an industrial plant.

The door to Professor Coe's office was the last one on the right. The wooden box attached to the wall next to it had a few corners of envelopes and sheets of paper poking through its slot. She knocked twice and her hand was still in the air when he called out from inside.

'Come on in!'

The door opened on a modest office with white walls and a wooden floor. A leafy plant on the cabinet in one corner softened things a bit. She spotted an expensive-looking mountain bike leaning against the wall next to it. Suspension on the rear and front forks, just like Jim's. She felt a little stab in her chest. Ian Coe was half out of his seat, a hand held towards the empty chair on the other side of his desk.

He was, as she had suspected, about thirty-five. Pale brown hair, cut short. Oval lenses to his rimless glasses. Kind, intelligent eyes. 'Hello, there, Detective – please, take a seat.'

'Hello,' she replied, taking out her identification.

He waved it away. 'I vaguely remember the piece in *The Chronicle*. Your father lectures here too?'

Iona felt herself blush. That stupid, damned article. 'He does, yes.' They shook hands across the piles of paper covering his desk. 'You seem to have as much form-filling as we do,' she observed as they both took their seats.

He glanced down with a look of irritation. 'These? Requisition forms for missing equipment are what these are. We've just had the departmental audit signed off. Better late than never. Anyway, I'd offer you a drink, but it means a walk down to a rather soulless canteen.'

Iona was taking her notebook out. 'That's fine. As you guessed on the phone, I'm a bit short on time.'

'Yes.' He turned to a printout draped across the keyboard of his computer. 'My tutorial notes for Vassen Bhujun.'

Iona looked hopeful. 'Don't suppose you have his photo?'

An uncomfortable expression flashed across the professor's face. 'No. Is he . . . Is this about making an identification?'

Iona caught what he was getting at and shook her head. 'There is no body. We just need to trace him.'

'Is he not back home in Mauritius?'

'No.' Iona clicked her pen. 'How did he strike you as a student?'

Ian lifted a shoulder. 'What am I expected to say? I can tell you he was very conscientious. Attendance record was one hundred per cent. No issues with handing work in late. Always turned up for his tutorials on time.'

'And what about as a person?'

The professor sat back. 'Perfectly normal. I mean . . .' A hand was briefly raised. 'Detective, I'll be honest. He was one of hundreds of students. I'm not here to provide pastoral care. He had no issues keeping up with course work. In fact, I see here, he graduated with a first.'

'How much would his course have cost?'

'Overseas student? MSc in Chemical Engineering? He wouldn't have got much change from twenty thousand pounds. Students like him are a valued source of revenue for the university.'

'Almost twenty thousand?'

'Yes – I can't say offhand exactly what he was charged. But the standard rate is around that.'

'And his course lasted a year?'

The professor nodded. 'The money came from some kind of benevolent fund, by the looks of it. The RA Foundation.'

Iona jotted it down. 'Did he specialize in a particular area of chemical engineering?'

'You mean his thesis? Yes – he was analysing ways of using liquid chromatography to purify proteins and other polymers.'

Iona raised her eyebrows in question.

He crossed his legs. 'Liquid chromatography is a separation technique – a form of purification – used in all manner of manu-facturing processes.' He checked his notes. 'Bhujun was interested in producing a low-cost substitute for cocoa butter. He aimed to blend it with sugar – I gather that's the main cash crop of Mauritius. Chocolate bars: he was hoping to make cheap chocolate bars.'

Iona scribbled away. 'We're talking in confidence here, Professor.' She looked up and waited for his nod. 'Can this liquid chromatography be used in illegal ways? Say, for instance, in the manufacture of explosives?'

The professor's gaze lost its focus as the question sank in. 'Explosives?' He took off his glasses. 'I . . . I really wouldn't know.' His eyes narrowed. 'That article in the newspaper. You'd joined the Counter Terrorism Unit, hadn't you?'

'That's correct.'

He looked out the window and she knew he'd put it together. The Labour Party conference. 'Do you mean weapon grade explosives?'

'I'm asking you.'

'I'd need to contact a colleague. It's not my area of expertise.'

'How quickly could you do that?'

He slid his glasses back on. 'Couple of hours? If not before.'

Iona put her pen away. 'Thanks for your time, Professor. Here's my card. If you can call me as soon as you've had a quiet word with that colleague.'

'Of course, of course,' he murmured, taking the card with a troubled look in his eyes.

ELEVEN

She was back in the office within an hour of setting off to see the professor, a bag with a sandwich and drink dangling from one hand. As she approached her desk, she scanned it for any yellow Post-it notes: Wallace's preferred method of leaving messages. No sign of one. A civilian worker she got on well with was waiting by the printer in the centre of the room.

She gave him a nod and sidled over, feeling like a schoolgirl sneaking back into class. 'Hi, Euan, has Wallace been after me?'

The man looked across to the doors. 'Don't think so,' he replied in a hushed tone. 'Nothing stuck to your screen?'

Iona shook her head.

'Looks like you've got away with it, then.' He gave her a wink.

She held up a hand with two fingers crossed and moved back to her desk. No Post-it note, but there was an email from the university admissions department waiting in her inbox. When she saw the subject line, she dumped the food bag on the floor, sat down and opened the attachment without bothering to read the accompanying message.

An inner box materialized, the screen blinked and she found herself staring at the face of a young man. Her immediate reaction was that the Sub-Urban Explorers were right: he looked like a lanky bowler for a cricket team. A thick fringe of black hair was swept to the side, its lower edge almost connecting with the eyebrows.

The face was thin, a mixture of adolescence not-quite-shaken-off and something else. Iona pondered what. Not eating enough, she concluded, taking in the spindly neck with its Adam's apple sticking out like a bolus of trapped food. She focused on his eyes. Dark and somehow forlorn.

'That him?'

The voice was so close to her ear, Iona flinched. A glance to her side revealed Paul Wallace leaning in towards her screen. She caught a whiff of his stale breath. 'Yes, the university just sent it.'

Wallace didn't move. He was invading her personal space but she couldn't wheel her chair away because his forearm was now resting across the back of it. Warm air washed across her cheek as he breathed out. 'Shifty-looking cun—' He caught the end of the word. 'Character.'

Her seat rocked as he pushed himself upright. She watched him reach towards the adjacent desk and drag over the empty chair from in front of it.

'Been looking into this Mauritius connection,' he announced, plonking himself down and resting some sheets of paper across his crotch. 'Oh, I've put in the request with the Mauritian police. The Appleton file is being sent direct to you.'

'You're letting me run with this?'

He tilted his head. 'Yeah, why not?'

Her fist clenched with triumph. 'Thanks, sir.'

Wallace's forefinger came up. 'Reporting direct to me, all right? Depending on what you find, we bring in support. Which – you realize – will be of a rank that's senior to you.'

Iona didn't care; if the threat was a genuine one, it would be her name on the report that had raised the alarm. She'd have a score on the board. 'Absolutely, sir, I understand.'

'Good. Now,' he lifted the printed sheets, 'the ethnic make-up of Mauritius. Did you realize there's a sizeable Muslim population on the island?'

Iona swivelled her chair to face him. 'No, I didn't.'

He tapped the upper-most sheet. 'Hindu, fifty-two per cent. Christian, thirty-five per cent. Muslims? Sixteen per cent.' He gave her a meaningful look. 'Out of a population of about one point two million, that's a couple of hundred thousand of them.'

Not liking how Wallace had phrased the comment, Iona reached for her pad. Wallace stopped her with a shake of the sheets. 'You can have these. Looking more closely at the numbers, approximately ninety-five per cent are Sunni. Need I say who's behind most of the mayhem out in Iraq and the Middle East? Port Louis, the Mauritian capital, has the highest concentration. That's where there are loads of mosques.' He lowered the sheets and, as he glanced at Vassen's photo on her screen, she caught the look of distaste in his eyes. 'I think it merits further investigation.'

Iona turned briefly to the young man's photo. 'I'd say he's of Indian descent, sir. The name sounds South Asian to me, too.'

'Your point being?'

'That would make it more likely he's Hindu. What are the stats on that part of the population?'

Wallace didn't look down fast enough to hide the irritation on his face. 'Hindu? Let's see . . . says here, like the Muslims, brought in as indentured labour by the British in the 1800s.' He looked up. 'That means slaves?'

'Bound to a specific employer, I think.'

'Right. Thousands were shipped over to work the sugar planta-tions, core of the island's economy—'

'That's what Bhujun's tutor –' She stopped speaking. Shit! A glance at Wallace. His eyes were fixed on her. 'When I spoke to him just earlier . . .' She waved in the direction of her phone. 'He said Bhujun's thesis was about making cheap chocolate; the sugar for it being locally produced.'

Wallace eyed her for a moment longer. 'Well, this is your shout, DC Khan. We need to know exactly what our boy here – and his little sidekick from outside the library – are all about.' He dropped the printouts on her desk as he stood. 'Don't need any more help, do you?'

Iona looked up at him hopefully. 'What are you offering?'

'Fuck all,' he laughed then pointed at the screensaver on an adjacent desk. 'Not with Operation Protector going live in less than twelve hours' time.'

TWELVE

Iona immediately reached for the sheets of paper Wallace had left. As she looked them over, she couldn't help frowning. A yellow pen had been used to highlight every mention of the word Muslim, Islam or mosque. Where the figure stated the size of the Muslim population, exclamation marks had been added. Nothing else on the printout seemed to have interested the man.

A sense of uneasiness was nagging at her as she looked around the room full of empty desks, picturing the person who normally sat at each one. I'm one of three female officers, and the only one – male or female – who isn't white. Maybe Jim did have a point when he said . . . no, she told herself. Don't start thinking like him.

She'd finished off her tuna and sweetcorn sandwich and was screwing up the wrapper when the phone on her desk started to ring. Focusing on a waste-paper basket three desks away, she lobbed the ball of paper into the air. It hit the bottom of the bin without touching the sides.

'Get in!' Euan called over from his corner desk.

She flashed him a smile as she picked up the receiver. 'Iona Khan speaking.'

'Detective Constable Khan?'

Male voice with a vaguely continental accent. She guessed belonging to someone well into their forties. 'That's correct.'

'This is Superintendent Veerapen, Major Crimes Investigation Unit, Mauritius Police Force.'

She sat up. 'Hello . . . Sorry, I wasn't expecting your call.' She frowned. 'And I didn't quite catch your name.'

'Superintendent Harish Veerapen. Harish is fine.'

Similar accent, Iona thought, to the female inspector's. Just a touch more French. 'Thanks for getting in touch, Harish.'

'That is my pleasure. I have sent the Appleton file to your email

address, as requested. But I find it always helps to discuss a case
rather than rely on the notes alone.'

'Absolutely,' Iona replied, clicking on her inbox. No sign of the
file as yet. She reached for her pen. 'So you were directly involved
with the case?'

'Senior investigating officer.'

'And what were your impressions about the murder?'

'Monstrous. And a tragic waste of a life. I think my colleague
mentioned the thief had already gained access to the safe.'

'Yes, she mentioned Appleton was killed when he raised the
alarm.'

'That's right – the maid was woken by it. She saw the suspect
running from the scene.'

Iona put an elbow on the table and rested her forehead on the
tips of her fingers. Something seemed odd here. 'Why kill him?'

'Pardon?'

'I'm just wondering, why kill him?'

'Who knows what goes on in this type of person's mind?'

'True. But that would have taken up valuable time, surely? Why
not just run when the alarm went off?'

'Rage. Anger at Appleton raising the alarm and forcing him to
flee the scene sooner than he wanted to. Many items of great value
had been overlooked.'

'What were those?'

'The murder weapon, for one.'

'Really?'

'A stone sculpture – an early one by a British artist. Henry Moore?'

The name was faintly familiar. 'Expensive, I take it?'

'Well, we've had to take special precautions in storing it as evidence.
It is currently in a vault here at our headquarters in Port Louis.'

'And this was used to bludgeon Appleton with?'

'Yes – there are plenty of crime-scene photos with the file. They
are not pleasant.'

Fingerprint ID of the body, Iona thought. Yuk. 'So whoever
murdered him was then seen leaving by the maid . . .'

'Yes. She turned on the lights in her rooms at the side of the villa
and observed a single male, who was carrying a bag, running across
the lawn. The first officers arrived at the scene within ten minutes.'

Iona still couldn't shake the feeling something was out of place.
'How do you know it was Appleton who raised the alarm?'

'I beg your pardon?' The man was starting to sound exasperated.

Iona didn't know where the hell she was going with her questions. 'Could the alarm have been triggered by something else? The safe being opened?'

'Ah, I see. No, it was Appleton,' he stated emphatically.

'Because . . .?'

'He was found slumped at the top of his bed and it was his bloody fingerprint on the panic button above it.'

Iona lifted her chin. 'I see. Sorry for going on . . . I was just trying to get it all straight in my head.'

'If it is of reassurance, British Embassy staff were closely involved in the investigation. And someone flew over from your security services – MI6.'

'Did they?' Iona murmured, thinking that Wallace's request to see the Appleton file would surely have triggered a flag with the security services down in London. *Funny how a superintendent halfway round the world can get back to me faster than them.* 'So he checked the crime scene over, too?'

'Yes – but alone. He played his cards very close to his breast.'

'Chest,' Iona remarked.

'Chest, yes. Close to his chest. But he quickly agreed – a burglary that escalated into something far more tragic.'

'Your colleague mentioned to me that you have a prime suspect.'

'Ranjit Bhujun.'

'Why him?'

'Forensic evidence left on the Henry Moore sculpture and the doorframe leading into Mr Appleton's bedroom.'

'Fingerprints?'

'Yes.'

'He didn't bother wearing gloves?'

'No. When we searched the accommodation of Mr Bhujun, it was clear it had been vacated several days before. There has been no sign of him since, despite one of the largest searches we have ever conducted. We believe it unlikely he is still here on Mauritius.'

Iona saw a box materializing in the bottom right-hand corner of her screen. 'Your email just came through.'

'Good. The photo of Ranjit is several years old, I'd better warn you. You should also be aware Ranjit had several debts, including rent owing on the place where he was staying. The man was in desperate need of cash. May I ask why you are interested in Vassen Bhujun, the cousin of Ranjit?'

Careful now, Iona thought. I don't know what I might be straying into here. 'His visa permitting him to study here as a student expired. But we have reason to believe he is still in the country.'

'And that is what concerns Greater Manchester Police's Counter Terrorism Unit?' The sarcasm in his voice was plain to hear.

'Harish, I'm sorry to sound cagey. But you know how it is – this investigation is ongoing.'

'As is ours. I sent you the file on Appleton. Now you are acting like the representative from MI6.'

Iona sighed. 'OK. He's been making enquiries in Manchester about . . .' She searched for a suitable term. 'The city's infrastructure. I don't know if you're aware, but Manchester is about to play host to the Labour Party's annual conference. The place will be awash with Members of Parliament in one day's time.'

'I see. Thank you for being candid with me.'

'No problem. But my enquiries? Can I ask that you play them close to your chest?'

'Of course. If I can be of any further assistance, please call.'

'Thank you.' After hanging up, Iona opened the superintendent's email. It included several attachments. Spotting a JPEG labelled Ranjit Bhujun, she clicked on it.

A police identification photograph took over the centre of her screen. Thick strands of black hair, not far off dreadlocks. Gaunt face and high cheekbones. She brought Vassen's photo back up and aligned the images side by side on her screen. The two were obviously related, but where Vassen possessed a youthful, innocent glow, Ranjit did not.

He stared out, sullen and hostile. Iona realized the man might have been born on a tropical paradise halfway around the world, but his face showed the same sour defiance she saw on the faces of the lowlifes it was her duty to deal with every day in Manchester. She was still staring into Ranjit's eyes when her phone gave a beep.

THIRTEEN

S he checked the screen: a text from Jim. The details for his contact in the CCTV control room – a man called Colin Wray. Good timing, she thought, reaching for the phone on her desk and keying in the number.

After explaining the urgency of what she needed, Wray said that a quarter-past-one slot had come free, if she could make it over in time for that.

'I'll be there,' Iona replied, checking the clock on the corner of her screen. Twenty-five minutes' time. She turned her attention to the photo of Ranjit Bhujun once again. He looked dodgy, that was for sure. But was he more than just a burglar who had turned violent?

After minimizing the image of him and Vassen, she scrutinized the other attachments. A folder marked crime-scene photographs. Clicking on it opened up a bank of thumbnails across her screen. Her eyes skirted those of a figure in a bed drenched with blood.

The third row of images switched to another room: Appleton's study, she guessed, clicking on one. As usual with crime-scene photographs, the combination of arc-light glare and camera flash had robbed the room of all warmth and homeliness. She spotted the wall-safe, its door hanging open, documents and paperwork spilling on to the floor. A lamp lay on its side, the green glass of its shade broken.

The next image was of Appleton's desk – a large, wooden one with a computer and keyboard on one side. Letters and printouts covered the centre part of the work area, and the upper drawer was half open. A large, framed photograph stood next to the printer. Iona could make out a female form in white at the centre of the assembled people. That's a wedding dress, she thought, recalling something in Appleton's Wikipedia entry about a daughter. Lucy or similar. Bushes covered in exotic-looking blooms flanked the gathering, and encroaching at the top of the image were a few wispy palm fronds. A wedding on Mauritius by the looks of it, Iona concluded, closing down the screen and clicking on the crime-scene report.

The Mauritius police emblem topped the form, followed by fields detailing the senior investigating officer's name, date, location and time of incident.

She read through the details of Appleton's property – purchased in 2008. Iona's eyes came to a halt. That was the year before he retired as a Law Lord. Obviously had lined up the island as a potential retirement spot on a previous visit. Maybe the daughter's wedding.

The section giving background details of the victim provided more of an explanation: Appleton had visited Mauritius in 2003 while sitting in session as a Law Lord.

'Sitting in session,' Iona murmured, a frown on her face. 'And what, exactly, is that?' Whatever it was, he'd returned to do it again in 2007. Wondering how anything got done before the Internet, she brought up Google and keyed in, Law Lord, sitting in session, Mauritius.

A site titled, The Judicial Committee of the Privy Council topped the results. Aware she was due over in the CCTV control room, Iona read the introductory screen as fast as she could.

The final court of appeal for several Commonwealth countries as well as the United Kingdom's overseas territories, Crown dependencies and military sovereign base areas.

Five senior judges normally sit to hear Commonwealth appeals. Asked, over the years, for final rulings in a wide variety of laws, including pre-revolutionary French law from Quebec, medieval Norman law from the Channel Islands and Muslim, Buddhist and Hindu law from India.

Iona sat back. So, Appleton had visited Mauritius twice in his capacity as a Law Lord to settle cases that, for whatever reason, the court system on Mauritius felt unable to resolve. The buck had stopped with Appleton – and with his decision the last hopes of many people who felt wronged had been ended.

She thought about the man's violent death once again. Burglary gone wrong or something more? And, if so, how did it all link to a chemical engineering student with an interest in Manchester's tunnel system?

There was a contacts link at the base of the screen. Iona hurriedly keyed in the phone number and explained to the person who answered that she needed details of the cases heard by Reginald Appleton on the two occasions he'd sat in session on Mauritius.

'You'll need Ayo for information on that,' the man replied. 'You do realize it's a Saturday, though?'

Iona wrinkled her nose in anticipation of bad news. 'She's not in at weekends then?'

'I can put you through to her office. You may be in luck. We're approaching the Michaelmas term so there's a lot to sort out.'

The phone hadn't completed its second ring before it was answered by a cheerful-sounding female with a strong London accent. 'Ayodele Onako speaking.'

Iona introduced herself and began to outline what she needed.

'It was so, so awful,' the woman blurted, 'hearing that news about Reginald.'

Iona could detect genuine grief in the other woman's softly spoken words. 'Sorry, Ayodele—'

'Ayo, please.'

'Sorry, Ayo. The man who put me through, he didn't actually tell me what your role is there.'

'Me?' Her voice had lifted once again. 'Oh, I just try to keep everything running smoothly. Organizing Law Lords – or Justices as they're now known – isn't everyone's cup of tea. But I love it.' She let out a throaty chuckle.

Iona guessed the answer glossed over a mountain of work. 'Would you be able to get the case details?'

'I was out there in 2007.'

'Pardon?' Iona replied, glancing at the time. Almost one. I need to get going for my slot at the CCTV control room.

'When the Law Lords went out there in 2007, I accompanied them – to run the field office. They put us up in a very nice hotel, I can tell you.' That deep chuckle once again.

'Really? So how does it work, this sitting in session business?'

'It's always at the invitation of the particular country's government. Generally, they wait until the number of appeals merit flying the Law Lords out there.'

'How many cases would that be?'

'Maybe eight? Each one usually takes half a day to a day; visits are always for one week.'

'Can you remember any details from the 2007 cases?'

She drew out her words. 'Well, let me think . . . to be honest, I rarely sit in court any more – my days of being a clerk are long over.'

'Were the cases criminal ones?'

'Criminal and civil. Both. There was one to do with the need to have a licence for tourist-related businesses, if I remember correctly. Another was an appeal against the Mauritius tax authority.'

'Were the people who were making the appeals—'

'The appellants.'

'Were the appellants individuals?'

'Individuals and groups. The tax authority one – that involved a whole load of businesses. Over a hundred, I think. Oh, yes, there was a criminal case that involved a sole appellant. He'd been charged with a drugs offence – cultivating cannabis, I think. His appeal was against receiving a penal sentence. I think he lost.'

Iona imagined Ranjit's face. 'I don't suppose you remember his name?'

'Detective, my memory isn't that good!'

Iona nodded in understanding, eyes going to the screen clock once more. 'Ayo, I've got an appointment I really must get to.' She paused. 'This is really cheeky, but is there any way you could check for me if a particular individual featured in any of the rulings where the appellant lost? From 2003 or 2007.'

'I could try. How soon would you need to know?'

Iona screwed her eyes shut. 'Today?' she asked hopefully.

A hoot of delight came down the line. 'How did you know I love a challenge?'

'I don't. But I would really appreciate your help, Ayo. It . . . it's very important.'

The lady's voice dropped again. 'Iona, are you asking me to do this because you think there's a link to Reginald's murder?'

'In confidence: yes.'

'The police assured us it was a burglary. A small-time criminal – someone with previous convictions.'

'It probably was,' Iona replied, getting to her feet. 'But I need to check it out for myself.'

'Well, Iona, now I know this is about getting justice for Reginald, you can count on me. And if I can't find time this afternoon, I will make it my bedtime reading for tonight. Tell me, what is the name of this person?'

'Ranjit Bhujun.'

FOURTEEN

I ona looked up at the soulless structure of the Arndale's NCP. Like something out of Stalinist Russia, she thought, squeezing round a small gap to the side of one ticket barrier.

A yellow line on the floor showed the way towards a stairwell. To her right a ramp led down from the floor above, an impressive spectrum of car paint smeared on the wall of the sharp bend.

Something must have been wrong with the spring in the hinge of the swing door to the stairwell because it flew open on her shove to crack loudly against the wall. The noise reverberated off the bare walls. 'Oops,' Iona whispered.

Tarnished silver lift doors were directly ahead, pay machines to her side. A metal yellow box was secured to the ceiling above, and behind the glass at the front end, the eye of a lens was visible.

Iona pressed for the lift and the doors opened immediately. No smell of urine, she thought with mild surprise, peeping in. Jim had been right: there weren't any even floor numbers. She pressed three, ignoring the tremor of nerves as the doors slid shut, trapping her within the lift's cramped confines.

When she stepped out on to level three, she saw a concrete ramp to her left, the obligatory scrapes of paint adorning that wall, too. Not liking the idea of meeting a vehicle coming down, she hurried up the incline, listening all the while for the sound of an approaching engine.

The far side of the floor above was dominated by a long row of obscured-glass windows. Beyond their tinted panes, Iona could just make out an expanse of glowing lights. The way they subtly shifted and altered made the place look more like a cocktail lounge or upmarket bar. She half-expected to hear the dull thud of a bass line as she neared the double doors at the centre. An intercom unit was mounted at the top of a waist-high metal pole. 'Detective Constable Iona Khan, CTU. I have a one-fifteen appointment.'

The door clicked. 'Please enter.'

She stepped into a reception area with a sofa, potted plant and camera in the ceiling. Before she could sit down a side door opened and a middle-aged man wearing black trousers and a charcoal-grey top with the NCP logo on its chest stepped out. 'Colin Wray; I'm the team leader on duty today.'

'Hello, there. Iona Khan.'

After shaking hands, Wray swiped an ID card and showed Iona through to a narrow passageway lined with staff lockers. He swiped again at the far end and Iona followed him into the darkened room beyond.

'Sorry about the low ceiling,' Colin said. 'That's what comes of building a control room within the confines of a car park.'

'No problem.' She added her signature to the signing-in book and was led by Colin round a partition wall. Two rows of desks stretched the length of the main room, operators with headsets manning the front one. Iona saw they were all wearing the same grey NCP top, sitting in grey chairs on a grey carpet. The quiet way they all were murmuring made them seem like worshippers; disciples at prayer.

All were facing a bank of six enormous floor-to-ceiling screens. They comprised of many smaller images, each one a different view from around the city. Every few seconds, each image would shift to another. A real-time recording of a day in the life of Manchester, Iona thought. Segmented and scrutinized for the sake of public safety. 'That's really quite something.'

'Isn't it?' Colin replied, circling to the centre desk in the deserted second row. 'This is me. Supervisor's spot.'

Iona noticed the small bubble of black glass in the ceiling just behind his desk. But who, she wondered, is watching you? A familiar two-tone beep caused her head to turn. She examined the front row. 'Is someone here patched into the police network?'

Colin looked slightly defensive as he touched a radio unit on the corner of his desk. 'We all are.'

Iona made an effort not to look taken aback. 'Really?'

The team leader nodded. 'We have been for a year or two now. Once we'd established a sufficient level of trust with the powers-that-be on your side of things.'

'So are you employees of the NCP or the police?'

'The NCP, but everyone has been vetted by Greater Manchester Police to act as a civilian worker.' He pointed to a pair of walky-talkies next to the police radio unit. 'We're also linked to Storenet and Nitenet – the communications system run by the many shops and drinking establishments our good city boasts.'

Iona glanced at the banks of screens and thought, these guys have a better idea of what's happening on the streets than we do.

The operator directly in front of them started to speak in softly modulated tones. 'What's the problem, sir? Your credit card's not working? Don't worry, that machine you're at can be a bit temperamental. Yes, I can see you. Yes, right now. From the little camera in the ceiling to your left. That's it; you're looking straight at it. OK, sir. If you could try cleaning the magnetic strip of your card. Wiping it on your sleeve should be fine. Good. Now try swiping it in the machine again. Success? That's fine, sir. My pleasure. Drive safely now.'

Iona was impressed; she could name quite a few officers who could have done with going on the customer relations course this lot had obviously been through. She looked at the three screens on Colin's desk. 'How does this all work?'

The team leader gestured to a chair and she sat down. 'OK. These two monitors give me the view from specific cameras – so, currently, I'm tapped into one at the end of Market Street and one mounted on the roof of the Great Northern Warehouse.'

Iona looked down on people making their way along the streets.

'The third monitor is just a normal computer screen for logging incidents,' Colin continued, reaching for a joystick mounted at the centre of his desk. 'This lets me turn, tilt and zoom.'

Iona raised her eyebrows. 'And how powerful are these things?'

'Oh, very. Watch.' The view from the top of the Great Northern tilted up until they were looking across Manchester's rooftops. Then suddenly, they were surging over them, homing in on the curving structure in the distance. It soon filled the screen, individual panels on its smooth surface clearly visible. 'The Imperial War Museum over at Salford Quays.'

Iona leaned back. 'What's that? Two, three miles away?'

'Something like that. Or we can go in close.' Colin zoomed back and then tilted the view down on to the junction of Deansgate and Quay Streets. Iona remembered helping the old lady across it the previous day. The team leader focused in on a car turning left and hit a button. The image froze. Using the arrow buttons on his keyboard, he then positioned the cross hairs over the front of the vehicle and expanded it out. The vehicle's registration filled the screen. He then tracked up and to the right and zoomed in again. The date printed on the car's tax disc was clearly visible. 'And that's from not far under two hundred metres. This is the best system in the country – as good as the one covering the Square Mile in London.' He pointed to the giant screen at the end of the row. 'That Barco will be allocated solely for the conference's secure zone.'

'The Ring of Steel,' Iona murmured.

Colin smiled. 'Indeed. Generally, we have a few guests up here during the conference – people from MI5, Special Branch, a few from your unit.' He tapped a button and the frozen image of the car was replaced by a view of traffic as it continued to negotiate the busy junction. 'Where did the incident you're interested in take place?'

'Outside Central Library.'

'The main entrance? By the tram stop in Saint Peter's Square?'

'Yes.'

'I think that's covered by at least two cameras. Date and time?'

Iona took out her notebook. 'About one fifty-five in the afternoon, on the seventeenth.'

The team leader turned to his computer monitor, brought up a form and entered the details in. 'No problem. Let's make it ten minutes either side of that time to be safe. I'll get Jamie to action it.' He raised his chin and spoke over the top of the row of monitors. 'Is Jamie about?'

One of the operatives glanced back. 'Lunch break.'

Colin grunted. 'He's our main guy for Alpha One coverage. I'll get him on it when he reappears. He can then transfer the relevant footage to a disc and have it delivered to you later today.'

'That's it?' Iona asked, taken aback by how quick the service was.

'That's it.'

'And can I play this footage? Freeze it, zoom in, that sort of stuff?'

'Of course. It comes loaded with a media player to enable that. Just put it into the CD slot of your computer – it's very easy to use.'

Iona smiled. 'Well, Colin – I have to say how impressive this is.'

'We aim to please.'

'I don't know what this all cost the NCP, but I think the council got a very good deal.'

Colin winked. 'You should see the weekly revenues from the city centre car parks.'

FIFTEEN

Right, Iona thought, stepping back out of the CCTV control room lobby. Time I had a look round the convention centre itself. As she set off back down the ramp, her mobile began to ring. Jim's name flashed up on the screen. Feeling guilty, she let it ring out. By the time she'd reached the floor below a message alert had pinged. She accessed it as she trotted down the rest of the stairs.

'Iona, it's me. Did you get my text OK? I assume you did. Listen, I know you're pissed off. I don't blame you, having to deal with an idiot like me. Can we talk? I . . . I really need to talk to you. It's hard to say what I need to over the phone. If we could meet up? It's important. Call me, OK?'

So, she thought, you know I'm pissed off. Congratulations. Try actually apologizing for the crap you came out with in that incident room and I might ring you back.

At the bottom, she turned right and opened the exit door to the side of the pay machine. A long corridor led into the Arndale. She weighed it up; a stroll through the busy surroundings of a shopping centre or back through the grim interior of a car park. Neither option particularly appealed, but at least cutting through the Arndale got her out closer to where the Labour Party conference was being held.

When she emerged on to the pedestrianized Market Street, it was with a renewed interest in the black poles topped by half-spheres of darkened glass. The cameras, she realized, were everywhere. By the time she'd turned the corner on to Cross Street she'd counted five, and on reaching the town hall her total was up to twelve. Another four were dotted about Albert Square. They're probably, she thought, up in that dim room watching me now.

She continued past the library and on to Mount Street where a couple of police vans were parked on the wide pavement outside the grandiose Midland Hotel. Her way forward was now blocked by a line of the anti-ram bollards linked by stout metal arms. The pavement on the other side led to the front of the convention centre with its enormous clock sheltered by the overhang of its curved roof. The seven-foot-high security fence barred her way.

'No access, I'm afraid,' a uniformed officer said, stepping towards her. 'Where are you after getting to, love?'

Iona clocked another two officers to the side of the vans, these ones clutching semi-automatic weapons. She fished out her badge, hoping no colleague was about to appear and ask what she was doing down here. 'I'm with the CTU.'

The officer scrutinized it a little too carefully. 'So you are. You need to come through?'

'Please.'

She was waved towards the security-check building that had been erected at the side of the Midland Hotel. Another officer checked her badge.

'You realize that as from midnight tonight, you need a valid pass to get beyond this point?' he asked.

'Yeah,' Iona responded, painfully aware that only CTU officers assigned to Operation Protector had been issued them. 'I do.'

He led her past the metal detecting machines to the doors at the other end.

'Thanks,' Iona said, walking down the ramp and making her way across a plaza being scrubbed clean by half-a-dozen council workers. The spotless paving stretched across to some wide steps that swept up to the convention centre's main entrance. A couple of commercial vans were parked at the bottom and four private security staff were grouped at the top.

As Iona climbed up she took a good look around. Beyond the security fence on her left was the Bridgewater Hall, home to the famous Hallé orchestra. Running past it on one side was the Rochdale canal, which then snaked out to the bleak industrial landscape of Trafford Park.

Looming high into the sky directly behind the convention centre was the monolithic outline of the Beetham Tower, Manchester's highest building. As her eyes travelled up it, she remembered the time Jim had taken her on the big wheel by Selfridges – the tower had dwarfed even that. Her gaze settled momentarily on the building's mid-point: what was known locally as the Sky Bar, a trendy cocktail lounge that separated the Hilton's hotel rooms below it from the private apartments above. She tilted her head to look at the very top where, she knew, the sniper team coordinating all the other rooftop rifle positions would be stationed.

Away to her right was the rear of the five-star Radisson Edwardian

Hotel, and hidden behind that, the Great Northern Warehouse which overlooked Deansgate. The road – and any tunnel beneath it – passed within a hundred metres of the convention centre. Close enough to represent a threat? She approached the group of security staff. 'Excuse me.'

They all looked round.

'Is there a supervisor I could speak to? My name's Detective Khan, Counter Terrorism Unit.'

'Two seconds, boss.' The man who'd replied then spoke into a microphone pinned to the top of his padded jacket. 'Is Simon about? Got an officer from the CTU here needs to see him.' He nodded and looked back at Iona. 'Three minutes?'

'Thanks.' Iona turned round and leaned her elbows on the railings. A man was wheeling a trolley laden with white plinths up the sloping walkway, followed by another with a trolley full of palm plants and bouquets of exotic flowers. The wheels of their trolleys clunked every time they crossed the joints in the paving. A tall, elegantly dressed lady holding a clipboard gave them directions as they reached the main doors into the convention centre.

From a flight of steps at the side of the building there appeared three men, one smart, two in jeans and trainers. They reached the railings beside Iona and, surveying the plaza below, started discussing camera angles. Iona realized she'd seen the distinguished-looking one on the television. The presenter of some kind of late-night current affairs programme.

'Officer?'

She turned to see a balding black man with a neat moustache approaching. Must be six foot six tall, she thought. In his left hand was a walkie-talkie.

'Simon Armitage, security supervisor.'

Holding out her warrant card, Iona stepped towards him. 'Detective Khan, CTU.' Once they'd shaken hands, she glanced about. 'You guys must be busy.'

Armitage rolled his eyes. 'Full on, it's been. And the thing hasn't even started yet. Three days of madness when it does.'

'I bet. Is it OK to pinch a few minutes of your time?'

He glanced at his wrist watch, seemingly oblivious to the vast clock face directly above him. 'Yeah – will ten minutes do? I've got a progress meeting at quarter to three.'

'Should be fine, thanks,' Iona replied, looking briefly towards the TV presenter. I don't want him overhearing anything juicy, she thought. 'Have you been involved with these things before?'

'Yes – the Conservatives last year, then Labour's before that.'

'Seems funny how they politely take it in turns.'

Armitage looked baffled. 'What, like they should be fighting over the venue?'

Iona nodded. 'That's how they normally act, don't they? Arguing and squabbling like school kids.'

The security supervisor looked amused. 'I hadn't thought of it like that. I suppose so.'

Iona took a few steps away from the TV people and turned in the direction of the Midland Hotel, on the far side of the plaza. She studied the Victorian splendour of its ornate balconies and intricately patterned brickwork, wondering how best to voice her concerns. 'This might seem funny me asking you about security arrangements, but I only recently joined the CTU.'

'Fine with me,' he replied. 'Are you over at Gold Command for the duration? Working under ACC Lawson?'

'No.' She hoped she hadn't sounded as awkward as she felt.

'Whereabouts then?'

She looked up at him. 'Actually, I'm not involved directly with the security operation. I'm working on a related case. But my boss reports into Lawson.'

He looked confused. 'OK. It's just I've got to know a few of your colleagues in the CTU over the years. Who's your boss?'

'Superintendent Paul Wallace.'

'Wallace?' Something like a shadow passed across Armitage's face. 'How do you find working with him?'

The question had been posed flat, all the casual curiosity in the man's voice gone. Iona tried to make eye contact, but the man was making a point of studying his walkie-talkie. 'He's very good at what he does. Why? Do you know him?'

Armitage sniffed. 'Not really. We've crossed paths. I doubt he'd know who I am, though.'

She felt there was plenty missing from the man's reply and was wondering whether to ask anything more when Armitage gestured to the plaza.

'What do you need to know?'

'Well, apart from the convention centre itself, what else does the secure zone encompass?'

Armitage nodded at the rear of the Midland. 'That place, obviously. It's where the majority of politicians are booked in.'

'Seems logical,' Iona commented. 'You couldn't get much closer to where the action is.'

'Nice and easy to wobble back after a hard day of discussing politics.' He raised an imaginary glass to his lips.

She tilted her head. 'You get that going on?'

Armitage gave a knowing nod. 'Plenty.' His eyes cut to the hotel. 'Back when they were built, the two buildings were joined by a walkway covered by a glass canopy. Passengers arriving at the rail terminal could then proceed directly to their hotel rooms. No nasty Manchester rain to soak the wife's ostrich-feather hat.'

'Of course.' Iona glanced behind her at the convention centre. 'I forgot it was originally a rail terminal.'

'Central Station. The Midland Hotel and the Great Northern Warehouse were all part of the same development. Passengers to one place, freight to another.'

'Nice little set-up,' Iona mused. 'But the secure zone doesn't stretch round the Great Northern, too?'

'No. It includes the Radisson Edwardian but that's it.' He gestured to the other hotel on the far side of the plaza. 'Also fully booked by politicians, assistants, researchers, delegates, lobbyists and God-knows-who.'

'How many people actually attend it then?'

Armitage puffed his cheeks out. 'In total, over ten thousand. Right now, you'll be lucky to find an empty hotel room anywhere in central Manchester.'

Iona pictured the hordes of people who would be descending on the centre the very next day. Was some kind of terrorist cell hoping to also sneak in? 'And access is only through the security point like the one I came through?'

'Correct – and only with a valid pass, no matter who you are.'

'How does a member of the public get hold of a pass?'

'Join the Labour Party and then pay the application fee for the conference. You get a photocard pass after submitting your passport and driving licence details. Plus you need a reference – someone to vouch for you.'

'Do you guys take care of all that?'

'No – they use an organizer who specializes in secure events.

The actual checks on each delegate are carried out in conjunction with Greater Manchester Police. You didn't know?'

Iona hadn't been told about it. But then again, she thought, that's no surprise. 'And that process applies to . . .?'

'Everyone. Party members, parliamentary staff, corporate and charity reps, exhibitors and technicians, media personnel, the lot.'

She nodded at the workers now walking back to the floristry van. 'Including them?'

Armitage studied the men for a moment. 'They look like people employed by the conference centre direct. In which case, they will have been booked in advance and had temporary passes issued by the centre specifically for the work they're carrying out.'

'And how many outside contractors will be accessing the secure zone between now and the conference finishing?'

Armitage shook his head. 'Including caterers, cleaners, waiters, bar staff, all that stuff?'

Iona nodded.

'Not sure. Hundreds? I know the list has been looked at by your people. Shall we go inside? I can dig a copy out if you want.'

Iona looked around, unsure if focusing on contractors should be a priority. It didn't seem likely Vassen Bhujun would be using his real name, anyway.

'Are you responding to specific intelligence?' Armitage asked, breaking her train of thought.

She pondered the question. What am I responding to? A potential terrorist plot by an unknown group over from Mauritius, one of them with an interest in Manchester's mysterious tunnels. It all seemed a bit shaky. 'Tell you what, can you just walk me round a bit more? It'll give me a chance to . . . assess things.'

Armitage shrugged. 'OK. You mean inside the centre?'

'No. Outside, if that's all right.'

'Follow me.' Armitage led her along the walkway hugging the perimeter of the building.

Iona noted several poles topped by clusters of cameras. Others were secured to the upper parts of the centre's outer walls. 'You have your own CCTV control room inside?'

'We do. It was all upgraded a year ago. Top-notch equipment.' He trotted down some stone steps which led to a fenced-off section of wheelie bins. Even they had a camera trained on them. Beyond, a brick arch led into an underground car park. 'The trains used to enter the terminal from that direction,' Armitage stated, pointing to the rear of the half-empty car park and then sweeping his arm over his head. 'Travelling over giant arches that are all gone now, obviously. Freight would be shunted off to the Great Northern which had upper and lower platforms, much like Grand Central in New York. From there, the goods could be carried on to their destinations by three different methods.'

Iona heard the clink of bottles coming from the underground car park. A van with a wine merchant's logo had been backed towards a double doorway leading into the basement of the centre. A man was stacking boxes of Moët on to a porter's trolley being held by a colleague. A third person emerged from the centre itself, pushing an empty cart before him. 'How do you get access to down here – other than by surrounding roads?'

Armitage considered the question. 'You can't. There are two ways in from Windmill and Watson Streets. Obviously this area is a potential security risk because of the volume of cars that will be parked here. Every delegate has to give the registration of their vehicle when applying for a pass – whether they're arriving in that vehicle or not. The access points I mentioned are permanently manned and only vehicles with registrations showing on the log are allowed through. A unit of sniffer dogs will be on-site too, by this evening. They'll be led round for regular checks.'

How the hell, she wondered, could you attack this place? With each political convention held here, the security systems would have been refined and then refined again. She walked up a couple of the steps to bring her on more of a level with Armitage. 'Can I ask what you did before this job, Simon?'

'British Army for sixteen years. Why?'

Army, Iona thought, shrugging a shoulder. Like Wallace, like Jim, like so many people in the police or security industry. 'What did you do?'

'Helped implement security systems for overseas operating bases.'

Iona looked at the wall beside her. 'And as it goes, this place is pretty much watertight?'

Armitage narrowed his eyes. 'Nothing's ever one hundred per cent. But put it this way, when I was working abroad – Northern Ireland, Iraq, Afghanistan – I put security systems in place that gave a fraction of the protection we have here. Minefields and machine gun towers excluded, of course.' He flashed Iona a smile.

'Right.' She tried to smile back. Was there a threat? Or, she thought, am I at risk of looking an idiot here?

Armitage glanced at his watch. 'Hate to say this, but I've got my quarter-to-three meeting.'

'Of course, sorry.' She turned round and they started climbing the steps side by side. The sound of more bottles being unloaded brought back a remark Armitage had just made. 'You mentioned freight was moved on from the Great Northern Warehouse by three different methods. Road and rail were two?'

'Yup.'

'So what was the third?' Her phone started to ring and she held up a finger, glancing at the screen. Unknown number. 'Sorry,' she said to Armitage before taking the call. 'Detective Khan speaking.'

'Hello, it's Ian Coe here. You visited me at the university earlier—'

'Professor,' Iona cut in. The man sounded tense, almost panicky. 'Did you speak to that colleague?'

'Not yet. He'll be available soon. It's something else, something I should have twigged when you were here. The internal audit I mentioned, it was there, literally under my nose. I can't believe I didn't—'

'Not so fast.' Iona replied, trying to keep up with the rush of words. 'Internal audit?'

'The paperwork all over my desk. The requisition forms for missing equipment?'

'Yes, I remember.'

'One item that vanished . . . it was worth over five thousand pounds. Vassen Bhujun's thesis was on using liquid chromatography to purify proteins. He used that exact piece of equipment – more than any other student.'

'What was it?'

'A GF Healthcare Frac-900. I have the form for it here in my hand. Bhujun often worked unsupervised in the laboratory where it was kept—'

'What is a Frac-900?'

'A fraction collector. For high performance liquid chromatography. Enough to manufacture large amounts of purified product. Laboratory-size amounts.'

Oh my God, Iona thought. Is he building a bomb? 'I'll be in touch.' She ended the call, the thought crashing around like a pinball in her skull.

'That sounded urgent,' Armitage stated.

'Yes,' she murmured. 'It was.' She started hurrying up the steps, scrolling through her address book for Wallace's number.

'The third method,' Armitage announced behind her. 'For transporting freight from the Great Northern Warehouse . . .'

'Mmm?' Iona replied, barely listening to the man's words. Bhujun had the knowledge and the means for producing large amounts of material.

'It was by canal.'

'What was?'

'The third method they used.'

'Canal?' Iona paused on the top step and looked down. There's no canal leading from the Great Northern, she thought, lowering her phone. It's all roads and pavements. 'Was that filled in at some stage?'

'You know the canal that runs along the side of the Bridgewater Hall?'

Iona nodded. 'The Rochdale. It leads out to Trafford Park.'

'Way back when, there was a little spur that came off it. It passed right under our feet, below the Great Northern and connected with a river across town. The Irwell, I think –'

Iona felt her heart drop. 'There's an underground canal that passes beneath the convention centre?'

'Was,' Armitage replied. 'It was drained of water and closed decades back. Never made any money for the company that dug it.'

Iona pointed both forefingers down at her feet. 'Here? Directly below us? There's a tunnel?'

'That's right. But it's been sealed off for years.'

Iona raised her mobile once more. That's how they'll do it. That's how they'll carry out their attack.

SIXTEEN

Iona paced up and down the pavement outside the coffee shop. When she'd rung Wallace, her revelation about the tunnel had seemed to leave the man momentarily lost for words.

'Who told you about it again?' he'd finally asked.

'A security supervisor at the convention centre. He knew all about the history of the place – what it was originally—'

'You've been looking round the convention centre itself?' He'd sounded mildly taken aback.

'Yes . . .' Iona had realized the visit wasn't strictly related to the search for Vassen Bhujun and his mysterious accomplice. Surely, she asked herself, Wallace isn't about to start getting funny about that? 'Sir – the tunnel runs right under where I'm standing.'

'OK – stay put,' he'd replied after another second's silence. 'There's a silver command post near to you – I think they have responsibility for perimeter security. I'll call you back.'

Unable to just stand around waiting, Iona crossed the spotless flagstones of the plaza, trying to visualize the forgotten tunnel beneath her feet. An underground canal. If it was big enough to carry barges, how much material could have been piled there by a would-be bomber? Enough to blow the place sky-high. Her mobile had gone off again as she was approaching the security-check building.

'They're sending someone for you,' Wallace had announced. 'A constable called Davis.'

'Constable?' Iona asked, shocked at the lack of response. She'd been expecting a lot more people than just a junior rank in a uniform. Maybe he was only escorting her back to the command post where she'd brief the rest of the team. She swallowed; perhaps even ACC Lawson would be there.

'Yes, a constable. He shouldn't be long. Instructions are for you to wait outside the Starbucks to the side of the library. The one on the corner of Peter Street.'

Iona knew it – the place was on the next street from the convention centre. She was there in under a minute. Now, over five minutes later, the constable had still failed to arrive. Where was he? She glanced impatiently at the screen of her mobile once again, wondering whether to call Wallace back. This was bloody ridiculous.

'Detective Constable Khan?'

She turned to see a uniform barely out of his teens walking casually towards her.

'That's a funny five minutes,' Iona snapped, closing the space between them, wondering how long it would take them to get back to the command post.

The younger man's smile fell, along with his outstretched hand. 'I came as fast as I could.'

Not fast enough, Iona thought. 'Has anyone actually filled you in on what's going on?'

The officer had recovered a bit of his poise. 'Yes,' he replied, reaching into his pocket and removing a small plastic bag. Inside it were two keys. 'I've come equipped.'

Equipped? Iona wanted to throw her arms out in frustration. Was this for real? Her eyes settled on the bag for an instant. 'What are those?'

'We'll need them to get down to the tunnel.'

'Down to . . .' Iona's words dried up. 'To what?'

'The tunnel.'

'Sorry?' She wasn't sure if there was a trace of amusement in the man's eyes.

'The tunnel that runs under the convention centre? Access to it is via a flight of stairs in the Great Northern Warehouse.'

'A flight of stairs? You know about the tunnel?'

'Of course. It's already been inspected and the entrance secured.'

'It has?'

He nodded. 'Two weeks ago. If not longer.'

Iona ignored a stray strand of hair, beginning to sense she'd just made a complete fool of herself. 'I didn't realize.'

'No? No one mentioned it to you?'

No, they didn't, she thought as Wallace's face flashed up in her mind. Sheepishly, she extended a hand. 'Sorry . . . I didn't ask your name.'

A brief smile as they shook. 'Constable Mark Davis.' He produced a card and held it out. 'Here's my number – in case you ever need anything else.'

She took it, now feeling awkward and embarrassed. 'Mark, sorry for being short with you – I had no idea we were aware of this place. Who inspected it?'

'The same people who do it every year before the conference – a few from the CTU and a couple of people from Special Branch. Plus a sniffer dog. But it's no trouble to double-check it if you want.'

Iona was now wondering if Wallace had been aware of the tunnel, too. 'Well, I don't know . . . I mean, if it's been inspected and sealed already . . .'

The constable waved the bag with the keys inside. 'It's no trouble.'

Opposite them was the Radisson Edwardian. Just beyond it, a security barrier blocked off the top of Peter Street. Davis was now halfway across the empty road heading towards the old warehouse a little further along it.

As Iona began to follow, she went over her phone call with

Wallace in her mind. He'd seemed genuinely shocked. But was it shock over the fact I was ringing him with knowledge about a tunnel? Surely he must have known about it if it was inspected every year. She stepped off the pavement, suspicion that her boss had let her embarrass herself swiftly growing.

By the time she caught up with the constable, he was rounding the rim of a shallow tier of seats leading down to a lawned area. In front of them loomed the sombre structure of the gigantic warehouse. As they reached the entrance, glass doors slid open to reveal its renovated interior. Immediately on their left were the blacked-out windows of a failed bar. Iona could make out the empty tables and chairs inside. 'Where is this entrance?' she asked, footsteps clicking on the shiny tiled floor.

'Just up here. I rang ahead – should be someone to meet us.' He led her round the base of an escalator which rose up to the shops, cinema and leisure centre on the floor above. Beyond the escalator was a bare corridor lined with a row of unoccupied shop units. It turned left to reveal a room with plain glass windows. 'Here we go.'

Iona could see a man with a neatly trimmed beard waiting inside. The centre of the room was taken up by a table with a white architect's model of the building they were now in.

Davis opened the door. 'Brian Elliott? Constable Davis of the CTU. Was it you I spoke to?'

'Indeed it was.'

The room had the dusty aroma of disuse. As the man approached them, Iona took in his brown corduroys and navy jumper with a name badge. She realized he was looking at her. 'Sorry – Detective Constable Khan, also of the CTU.' The walls of the room were covered in framed photos of the warehouse from the time it was used to store freight.

'Not the busiest of jobs, as you can see.' Elliot pointed at the model in the room's centre. 'It hasn't attracted quite the interest the developers hoped it would. The cinema complex does quite well, but that's about it.'

Iona frowned, still unsure of what was going on. She circled a finger. 'Where are we?'

'The visitor centre,' he replied. 'Or what was meant to be the visitor centre. It's too rarely used to warrant the name.'

'So,' Constable Davis announced. 'We need to check the tunnel.'

'No problem.' Elliot turned to a monitor set in the wall and reached for the joystick mounted on the stand below it. The black and white view on the screen swivelled round to reveal what appeared to be the inside of a large, deserted warehouse. Bare brick walls and then a few steps leading down from a raised area at the side. 'The only thing I ever see moving down there are rats. Obviously, you are in possession of all our keys at present, but I'll gladly show you about. It'll give me something to do.'

A feeling of nausea rose suddenly from the pit of Iona's stomach. Oh, no, she thought, they're talking about actually going down there.

Davis took out the bag containing the keys. 'Lead the way then, Brian.'

Her sense of dread mounting, Iona watched as Brian removed three torches from the bottom drawer of a desk. He held two out. 'Only the loading bay is lit. Once you enter the tunnel itself, it's pitch black.'

Iona cleared her throat. 'Um . . . you mean we're going into the tunnel? Right now?'

Davis glanced at her with a look of surprise. 'That's the idea.'

'Right.' Iona nodded, aware he was scrutinizing her. I don't believe this, a voice inside her head wailed. I do not believe this. 'How . . . how far is it to get down there?'

Elliot didn't need to think. 'Just shy of sixty metres.' He glanced down at their feet and gestured at Iona's shiny shoes. 'You don't mind if they get a bit dirty, do you?'

Aware her indecision had been clocked by Davis, Iona fought to regain her composure. She firmly believed the constable would be reporting everything about this visit back. 'How dirty are we talking?' she replied, trying to smile. 'These are Jimmy Choos, I hope you realize?'

'Jimmy whats?' Elliot asked.

'I'm joking.' Iona winked at Davis. 'Marks and Spencer's finest, more like.'

The constable grinned. 'There'll be a few puddles and a lot of the floor is just bare earth. But you'll be all right.'

At the rear of the room was a grey metal door. A line of anti-tamper tape bearing the GMP logo stretched across it and on to the frame. Handing his torch to Iona, Davis stepped forward, scraped back the corner with a fingernail and peeled the entire length away. The thin material instantly buckled with countless little creases. He scrunched it into a ball before removing the heavy padlock halfway up. Next, he selected the other key and turned it in the lock below the door's handle.

Behind the two men, Iona glanced nervously about. Was it her fear or did it seem reckless to start wandering around what could be the site of an intended terrorist attack? 'Are you certain this is the only way to access this tunnel?'

Elliot nodded. 'Absolutely.'

'What about each end of it? Surely it comes out somewhere?'

'Both entrances were filled with tonnes of rubble and concrete then bricked up years ago. I suppose you could dig your way through – if you had enough men and heavy equipment.'

Iona weighed up the response. OK, she thought. Looks like we're going down there. She took a deep breath.

'Last thing,' Brian said, glancing back. 'You might want to button your jacket up. It's pretty chilly down there.'

SEVENTEEN

On the other side of the door was a narrow passage with a concrete floor and walls. Elliot set off along it, talking over his shoulder. 'Is this a routine check?'

'Yes,' Iona replied before Constable Davis could speak.

At the end of the passage a steep flight of steps came into view. Grasping the handrail, Elliot began to descend, followed by Constable Davis. Iona trailed behind.

After two flights the steps were replaced by metal ones and, peering over the handrail, Iona guessed they were a third of the way down the shaft. White tiles now lined the walls, the grout between them furred by some kind of prickly growth. Like going into the basement of an abandoned mental asylum, Iona thought, as sweat began to prickle her armpits.

After another two flights the walls were just bare brick. In places a deposit resembling limescale had oozed from the surfaces to form tiny, frozen waterfalls of grey. The clang of their feet on the dimpled steps was the only sound and Iona tried to think of a deserted beach, sun hovering over a distant horizon. 'This was once a canal then?' Her voice echoed slightly.

'That's right,' Elliot called back. 'The Manchester and Salford Junction Canal. It was built as a way of circumventing the congested city streets and high levies being charged by the Bridgewater Canal Company.'

He cleared the final steps and moved to the side of a thin corridor. 'I actually work as a Blue Badge guide in the evenings. You can have the whole history, if you want.'

'Why not?' Davis replied. 'I've been wondering about this place.'

Iona was trying not to think about how far below ground they were. Her feet didn't want to leave the last step. To the side of it, a green bait box had been placed at the base of the tunnel wall. 'Are there loads of rats down here?'

Elliot tilted his head. 'They'll have scarpered long before we reached the last flight. I wouldn't worry.' He placed his torch under one arm and rubbed his hands together. 'So, the canal – which opened for business in 1839 – linked the Rochdale Canal, by the side of the Bridgewater Hall, to the River Irwell across town. Total length is about five hundred yards.' He turned round and strode off down the corridor, followed by Davis.

Iona took a last glance up towards the surface and then set off after the two men. They emerged into a cavernous hall with smaller, arched openings at each end. A cloying smell of damp earth permeated the air.

The sense of space caused Iona's feelings of anxiety to subside a little and she felt her breathing ease. This isn't so bad, she said to herself. As long as we don't have to squeeze into anywhere narrow, I can do this.

In the middle of the curving brick roof above her was the ubiquitous half-sphere of darkened glass. The CCTV camera, she realized. The images we could see on the monitor in the visitor centre. Next to it was a smoke alarm. Between the naked light bulbs dotting the ceiling hung spindly stalactites. Some, Iona guessed, were several feet long. A drip detached itself from one and hit the glistening earth below with a little plip.

Elliot approached some railings and pointed down. When he spoke, Iona could see his breath in the chill air. 'The canal was widened here to create a loading bay for the narrow boats. A lot of the coal from the mines in Bolton and Bury was carried into the city from this point.'

'Why did it close?' asked Davis.

'Never made any money. Just before it opened, the Bridgewater Canal Company slashed its levies for using the Castlefield locks. Then the railways, when they started to spread, offered a far faster means of transport.'

Iona visualized the frantic levels of activity that established Manchester as England's industrial powerhouse. The fortunes made and lost in that brief window of time.

'It was decided to turn it into an air-raid shelter in World War Two,' Elliot continued. 'The water was drained and a new lining of bricks put in, along with four generators to draw down fresh air, chemical toilets and rows of three-tier bunks.'

Davis looked around. 'For how many people?'

'The Air Raids Committee report put capacity at five thousand people. But I've seen documents in the archives stating thirty-six thousand bunk beds were brought down here. Who knows the actual amounts.'

Constable Davis glanced at Iona. 'That's about half the crowd who turn up to see United at Old Trafford. A lot of people.'

'But I bet they weren't down here eating prawn sandwiches,' she shot back.

Chuckling, Elliot made his way down the steps and on to the old canal bed. 'OK – I assume you want to check underneath the convention centre?'

'Please,' Davis answered.

As they followed Elliot towards the mouth of the left-hand tunnel Iona examined the black opening with apprehension. 'How . . . how cramped will it be in the tunnel?'

'Pleasantly spacious, as a matter of fact,' Elliot answered. 'The narrow boats it was built to accommodate were quite wide.'

'Like ant hills,' Davis remarked, pointing to the little mounds of powdery earth dotting the floor.

'Aren't they?' Elliot responded. 'It's trickle-down from the ceiling.'

A sudden image of the bricks collapsing under endless tonnes of mud and stone flashed up in Iona's mind. Don't be stupid, she told herself, pushing the thought aside.

Elliot stopped short of the entrance and turned his torch on. At the side of the archway faint letters below an arrow said, To Bay Three. 'From here on we provide our own light.'

The trio of spots cast by their torches bobbed and danced as they picked their way slowly along the dark tunnel. Every now and again Elliot would direct the beam of his torch ahead to provide a dizzying glimpse of the low roof stretching away. Iona could feel her heartbeat had picked up. Dozens of stalactites hung down, like streamers from a party held a lifetime ago.

Occasionally, she directed her torch off to the side and examined the waist-high towpath running alongside them. Scattered along it were fragments of broken brick, the odd length of cable or gnarled and rusted bits of metal. She passed some stacked pieces of wood, the uppermost ones rotted to a thick layer of splinters. Everything was encased in a grainy layer of brick dust and the sound of dripping water was all around.

'Brian?' Constable Davis whispered theatrically.

'Yes?'

'Has anyone ever died down here?'

'As a matter of fact, they have.'

They walked on in silence for a few more seconds, Iona clearly able to hear the thud of her heart.

'Brian?' Davis again.

'Yes?'

'What happened?'

The other man gave a low laugh. 'A boatman called Samuel Bennett drowned. He was returning to his vessel from the pub and fell in. His body floated out of the tunnel a few days later.'

'Will you two stop it?' Iona hissed. There was a splashing noise and she looked down. A shallow expanse of watery brown sludge was at her feet. As she stepped carefully over the remainder of the puddle both men suppressed their giggles.

They reached a partition wall that stretched across the tunnel. An open doorway at one side led into the next bay. Elliot shone his torch to the right. A row of brick cubicles lined a side recess. 'Some of the air-raid toilets. The third one along still has one in it.' The beam picked out what looked like a large metal top-hat turned upside down. Rust had half eaten the rim away and what remained of the wooden door was spread across the floor.

Several bays later, they emerged into a wider area with a flight of stairs stretching up.

'What was an entrance,' Elliot said. 'These steps once led all the way up to the street.'

'Hang on,' Iona cut in. 'You said there were no other ways to get down here.'

'There aren't,' Elliot replied, torchlight etching deep shadows across his face. 'They dug it as an extra air-raid shelter entrance but it's been bricked in and concreted over.'

'Where did it come out?' Iona pointed her torch beam up the steep steps. Darkness defeated the thin shaft of light after about ten metres.

'Grape Street.'

He led the way up to the first landing where an archway had been built into the right-hand wall. 'Through here, mind the step.'

They entered another passageway that, judging from the echoes, opened into something far bigger. She played her torch beam about and realized the space they were now entering made the loading bay seem poky.

'Where are we?' Davis asked at her side.

'Directly below Central Station, the last main passenger railway terminus to be built in Manchester,' Elliot announced with a flourish.

And now the convention centre, Iona thought, climbing down a knee-high ledge on to bare earth. She aimed her torch up. The beam was just able to illuminate colossal spans of brick. The ceiling they supported was slightly shiny and black. 'Is that the actual underside of the convention centre's floor?'

'Correct.'

Iona pictured the mass of people scurrying about on it, all completely oblivious to what was below their very feet.

'That main arch,' Elliot remarked, jumping down beside her and shining his torch to their left, 'is the second largest unsupported span in Britain. Exceeded only by one down in London's Saint Pancras station. Shall we check around?'

'If you don't mind,' Iona replied, feeling like she was in a cathedral during a power cut.

'What actually are we looking for?' asked Davis.

Good question, Iona thought. A pile of recently dug earth? Bricks removed from a wall? A stack of strange-looking sacks with a timer on the top? 'I don't know. Just anything to indicate people have been down here.'

They skirted round the base of the wall, looking for any signs of recent disturbance. Nothing. An opening on the far side gave access to a smaller, lower room.

'And in here?' Elliot asked.

'We've come this far,' Iona replied, beginning to sense the search was pointless.

As they looked for anything suspicious, Iona became aware of the intense silence. It seemed she could actually feel it, pressing in from every direction. The desire to be out of the place was starting to grow. She gave a cough. 'Well, seems secure enough to me. Sorry if I used up your time for nothing.'

Elliot's torch swung round and his face showed faintly in its reflected glow. 'Happy to head back?'

'I am. Constable Davis?'

The spot of his torch drew closer. 'Fine with me.'

As the electric light from the loading bay grew stronger, Iona felt relief starting to wash over her. By the time they stepped out of the tunnel itself, she could have pumped an arm up and down. She looked fondly at the bright bulbs above. 'I feel like an explorer making it back to civilization.'

'I know how you feel.' Elliot smiled.

Up in the visitor centre, Davis relocked the door and removed a roll of anti-tamper tape from his pocket.

Iona watched as he started to carefully stretch a length of it across the door and its frame. Did Wallace, she asked herself, set me up for this? Thinking about it, he didn't actually express any surprise at the tunnel's existence – he just asked me how I knew about it. But why would he let me make a fool of myself?

She thought about the report from the Sub-Urban Explorers: Vassen's interest in the tunnel system was real. Surely he and his mystery friend were planning something. She saw Elliot was arranging papers on the desk. 'Do you know of many other tunnels beneath the city?'

'Oh, yes,' he replied, 'it's riddled with them.'

'Like?'

'The Duke's tunnel.'

'What's that?'

Elliot sat on the edge of his desk. 'It branched off from the River Medlock and ran under the city centre before ending at what's now the approach to Piccadilly Station. It was used to transport coal from the Duke of Bridgewater's mines at Worsely.'

Nowhere near here, Iona thought. 'Is it still there?'

'It had silted up by the early eighteen hundreds, after the level of the Medlock rose a few feet. Bricked up not long after.'

'Any others?'

'Victoria arches?'

'Yup – I've heard about them. Any others? Ones near here?' Iona asked.

Elliot thought a moment. 'Not that I know of. I've heard mention of them stretching out from beneath the cathedral. And there's a proper honeycomb under the campus of what was UMIST.'

What the Sub-Urban Explorers were trying to access, Iona thought. 'What about,' she asked, 'one running beneath the length of Deansgate?'

'Oh, that.' Elliot shot a glance at Davis. 'I don't believe it. Surely a tunnel of that scale would be charted somewhere.'

'But you've heard it mentioned?'

His eyes flicked to Davis another time. 'Yes.'

She turned to the constable. 'Have you heard anything about it?'

He shrugged. 'There are copies of some old maps – I saw them at our command post.'

Iona turned to him. 'Whose are they?'

'Council ones, I think.'

'And?' From the corner of her eye, she saw Elliot had leaned forward.

'All I can say is, anything deemed a potential risk has already been examined. Just like the one below us.' He turned away to double-check the padlock and Iona gave a sigh, wondering exactly what the maps showed.

EIGHTEEN

Iona walked nervously along the corridor leading to the CTU's main office in Orion House. After parting company with Constable Davis, she'd watched as he hurried off in the direction of Deansgate. Wherever the silver command post was that he'd come from, he'd be back at it well before she got to her desk.

The question in her mind was, how fast would the news of her error spread? Would raising an alert about a tunnel already checked and secured be a source of amusement for her new colleagues? Or were people too busy to pause and give her a hard time?

Two detectives stepped out into the corridor and started walking towards her. Anxiously, she kept her eyes on their faces and was able to see their expressions change as they realized who was approaching. One smirked as they passed her by.

Was that me? Was he grinning because of me? She paused with her hand on the office door. Well, I'm about to find out. She pushed it open to see that the office was a little busier than normal. A few uniforms on one side, a sprinkling of detectives at their desks. Several heads turned in her direction but no one seemed that interested in her presence.

Maybe I was worrying for nothing, she thought, as she made her way across to her workstation, searching for any yellow Post-it notes as she got closer. There was something in front of her keyboard. It was cylindrical and grey. No, not cylindrical. A cylinder cut in half. Cardboard tubes – the ones from the middle of toilet rolls. Three had been Sellotaped together. There was writing on the side: The Manchester and Salford Junction Canal. At the entrance to the miniature tunnel stood a little figure fashioned from Blu-tack. She looked about. Faces grinned back at her and people started to clap.

'Nice work, Baby!' someone called.

Laughter broke out.

'She'll boldly go where no man has gone before!'

'Is it a badger? Is it a fox? No, it's a human mole!'

Knowing she was bright red, Iona tried to smile. 'Very funny, you lot. Ingenious.'

The laughter wasn't dying down.

Gingerly, she picked up the toilet rolls and dropped them in her bin. 'Were these things clean or do I need to wash my hands?'

An inspector – some huge guy with a squashed nose and cropped hair – paused as he passed her desk. 'It's your shoes you need to clean. Been exploring, have you?'

Iona looked down at her mud-spattered shoes and held up a hand in acknowledgement. Even Euan, the civilian support worker she got on with, was trying to suppress his giggles. She sank into her chair and went to stick the little Blu-tack figure on top of her monitor. Someone had trimmed the newspaper clipping down so it now read, Baby.

The laughter began to fade and she noticed a plastic case on the corner of her desk.

FAO: Detective Constable Khan, CTU. From: Manchester Operations Centre.

The CCTV footage, she thought, as her phone started to ring. 'DC Khan speaking.'

'Detective?' It was Wallace, phoning down from the floor above. 'Pop up to see me, would you?'

He was slouching in his chair, one hand draped on the edge of his desk, eyebrows half-raised.

'Sir,' Iona said, stepping inside.

He lifted a finger and pointed to the empty seat opposite him.

She crossed the room as quickly as she could and sat down, glad to tuck her dirty shoes out of sight.

'Tunnel was clear, then?' Wallace asked.

She nodded. 'Yes, it was, sir.'

'Good.' He tapped his fingers. 'I'm glad they only sent a constable along with the keys. We've all got enough on our plates as it is.'

'Sir, I'm sorry. If I'd known its existence was logged, I wouldn't have . . . wouldn't have . . .'

'Jumped the gun so badly?'

She caught his eye. OK, she thought. So I jumped the gun. But did you let me? 'It just seemed that no one knew about it –'

Wallace sat up. 'No. You assumed no one knew. Which is the type of thing that happens when you stray into an operation you have no part in. Why were you down at the conference centre site, anyway?'

She gave a flustered shrug. 'When I came out of the CCTV control room, it seemed to be an appropriate step – to, you know, check what I thought was a site at imminent risk of attack.'

'Really? At risk from a student that – and here's the assume word again – you thought was making a bomb?'

'Yes, sir.'

'With a piece of equipment you assumed could be used to manufacture explosive material?'

'Yes.'

'Have you much knowledge of explosives, Detective?'

'Well, I did the course as part of my training. On how to recognize the different types.'

'And what part would high pressure liquid chromatography play in making a bomb?'

She realized the university professor hadn't actually confirmed the Frac-900 could be used to manufacture explosives. Damn. 'I . . . I don't know.'

'Well, Detective. Most explosives I've dealt with – and I have a decade in the British Army behind me – are compounds. Different things, bonded together. Carbon monoxide, carbon dioxide, nitrogen. You remember seeing that grainy white powder on your course?'

Iona wanted to bow her head. 'Yes, sir.'

'What was it called?'

'PETN.'

'Correct. Pentaerythritol tetranitrate. An organic compound. What is liquid chromatography used for?'

'Purifying proteins.'

'Separating things out.' Wallace tapped his fingertips together. 'Not combining them. Stay back after class, Detective. It's extra chemistry lessons for you.'

She glanced up but he wasn't smiling.

'It is,' he said, 'a classic case of two and two making five. You hear about a tunnel and believe only you in the CTU know about it. You hear about a piece of missing laboratory equipment and, just because the person you're searching for had access to that piece of equipment, you leap to the conclusion he stole it. Then you make the further assumption the equipment is being used to manufacture explosives. Let that be a lesson, Detective. Don't let your suspicions cloud your judgement.'

She felt like a schoolgirl. 'Sir.'

'Now, apart from charging round the convention centre – oh, and popping over to visit Vassen's tutor in the chemical engineering department . . .'

She blinked with surprise. He'd clocked it. When I mentioned talking to Professor Coe earlier on, he knew I was glossing over things.

He waved a hand as if to say he couldn't be bothered dealing with her minor act of deceit. 'Where are you with the Mauritius link?'

'I have the footage from outside the library now on disc. It's waiting for me at my desk. I need to try and ascertain if the associate of Vassen is, indeed, the suspect in Appleton's murder.'

'Looked into the existence of any community from Mauritius in the north-west?'

'No, sir. I haven't had time.'

'Well, you're in luck, because I have. A simple search on Google has brought up a couple of interesting things. I bet you didn't know there's a football team made up of Mauritians currently living over here?'

Iona shook her head.

'There is. The Mauricien Exiles. They play in the first division of the Bury Sunday League,' he put a finger on a sheet of paper, 'alongside other well-known teams such as Radcliffe Town, Bridge Tavern and Whitefield Wands. I also contacted The Border Agency on your behalf.' He turned the uppermost sheet over. 'They've provided me with some names of Mauritian passport holders living in the area. Over forty, as a matter of fact. Addresses included.'

'Right,' Iona said, leaning forward to take the sheets he was now holding out. 'I don't suppose any have the surname Bhujun?'

He snorted. 'We should be so lucky. However, many of these people seem to be located in and around Bury. Never know, our guys may be lodging with one; the community doesn't appear to be very big.

'There's a separate thing you need to know about.' He looked straight at her. 'We've received reports that a Muslim cleric with extreme views is now at a particular mosque in Bury. The Jamia Masjd on Oram Street. It's not the first time this particular mosque has been associated with extremists. This particular cleric? The last time he popped up was in Wootton Basset, shouting abuse at the coffins of our boys being flown back from Iraq and Afghanistan. Calling them murderers of innocent Muslims.

'What I'm wondering is this: could there be a connection? Might our characters from Mauritius be visiting this mosque? Because if they are, it will save us – sorry, you – one heck of a lot of hunting around.'

Iona was struggling to cope with the sudden change of tack. She cleared her throat. 'I'm not quite sure what you're asking me to do, sir. Set up camera surveillance on this mosque?'

Wallace laughed. 'In the area where it's located? They'd sniff us out in no time. Besides, there are no resources for that, Detective. Not at present.'

She remained silent, watching as her senior officer studied the ceiling above her.

'The reports about the presence of this particular cleric are – as yet – unconfirmed. We could do with knowing if he's really there. Better than that, we could do with knowing if he's planning any kind of demo at the conference centre. It would be just his style.'

'Sorry, sir. If cameras are out, are you asking me to visit this mosque in an undercover role?'

Wallace's gaze dropped to her face for a moment before he broke eye contact to check something on his screen. 'Would you be comfortable doing that?'

Iona swallowed. The shift in focus – from trying to trace Vassen to investigating a mosque in Bury was so sudden. Wallace was talking about a covert visit. 'I'm. . . . I'm not sure, sir.'

'Thing is with this tunnel, Detective. It's a minor blip – something the team will rib you about for a while. It would be forgotten a lot faster if we could get you doing something of real significance.'

Her mind seemed to be stalling as the implication of his comment sank in; the search for Vassen and his accomplice wasn't really important. It had been trivial, inconsequential; a task for the baby of the team. But now he was offering her something worthwhile. A way to redeem herself in everyone's eyes. 'But – for a start, I'm not a Muslim. I've never even visited a mosque.'

He hunched a shoulder. 'You wouldn't be expected to deliver a sermon, Detective. We know this mosque allows women in through a separate entrance to the men. You could probably see if this particular cleric is there. Maybe get wind of what he's up to. Have a think, OK? In my view, it would be a very productive use of your time. Especially if this pair from Mauritius are also linked to it. That would be something worth our attention.'

She couldn't get over how everything had been flipped on its head. 'And the tunnels, sir? That's no longer a priority?'

'Detective, if you're dealing with vermin, would you prefer to trap them once they're running around in your kitchen, shitting in your cupboards and spoiling your food – or would you prefer to find their nest and deal with them there?' He bared his teeth in the semblance of a smile. 'It's the same with these types. Better to track down where they're operating from – in Bury or elsewhere.'

Iona nodded uncertainly. 'What should I do with the CCTV footage? Is it worth trying to confirm whether the person outside the library is the one suspected of killing Appleton?'

Wallace thought for a moment. 'Yes, it is. At the least, it will give us an up-to-date image of him. You'll find that useful if you decide about looking into the Bury thing in more detail.'

You mean sneaking into a mosque, Iona thought. One with apparent links to extremists. Her legs felt a little shaky as she stood. 'I'll get on to it, sir.'

His attention had switched to the documents on his desk. 'Don't take too long letting me know what you decide,' he muttered.

'Sir.' She paused in the act of turning, wondering whether to ask the question still rattling around in her head. Was Wallace aware of the tunnel? Because if he was, he purposefully let me make a fool of myself. She had to know. 'Sir, the underground canal. Did you have prior knowledge of it before I called it in?'

He sighed, head staying down. 'The canal? Detective, there are many, many concerns relating to the security of the convention centre.'

She nodded, aware she was now hovering in front of his desk.

He glanced up, but only as far as her stomach. 'That is all, Detective.'

'Sir.' She retreated towards the door, wondering whether he'd just deliberately avoided her question.

NINETEEN

Back in the main office, Iona was relieved to see the most of the day shift's desks were now deserted. She glanced at her watch. No wonder, it was getting on for half-six.

She headed over to her workstation and sat down. The message light on her desk phone was blinking so she lifted the receiver and pressed the button. Professor Coe's voice on the line.

'Yes, hello . . . Detective Khan. It's Professor Coe from the university. Apologies for the delay in getting back to you. The colleague I mentioned has been extremely busy.'

Iona leaned back in her chair. I know what's coming, she thought.

'He's not aware of any method of explosives manufacture where the Frac-900 could be of any use. I won't bore you with the details, but the process involves combining, not isolating, elements. I hope that's of some use and . . . I wish you success, with your investigation.'

Yeah, thanks, Iona thought, replacing the receiver. If only you'd got back to me a bit quicker. Letting out a sigh, she looked at the little Blu-tack figure on her monitor: its legs had buckled and the thing had keeled over on its side. Know how you feel, she thought, reaching for the CD case the CCTV control room had sent over.

As the disc began to whirr in her computer, she studied the handwritten note that had been placed inside the case.

As requested – footage from outside Central Library, 17 September, 1.45–2.05 p.m. Not included: footage from the tram platform.

She frowned. Tram platform? Why mention that? A window opened up on her screen; the image was from on high, looking across the front of the library towards the Midland Hotel. Figures were frozen in the field of view. A suited man on his mobile phone. A couple of young lads in jeans and hooded tops. Two females in white headdresses, bags over their shoulders. A courier, pushing his bike.

Superimposed in the top corner was SP1; in the other was a time stamp. Iona pressed play and watched. The people immediately resumed their business – the young lads heading in the direction of the burger place just up from the Temple of Convenience. The two females in white headdresses walked up the library steps, the courier wheeled his bike forwards, passing from view directly below the camera. More office workers entered the picture. The businessman finished his call and disappeared in the direction of the town hall.

After five minutes of footage, she saw the Sub-Urban Explorer calling himself Hidden Shadow emerge from beneath the library's portico. At the same time two men entered the edge of the screen from the direction of the Midland Hotel.

Iona hit pause. One was Vassen, no doubt about it. Lanky and with a mop of black hair that he was running a hand through, working his fingers back and forth as he did so.

The other one was shorter, thick shoulders hunched up. But he was wearing a baseball cap. Damn it, she thought, did Hidden Shadow mention any baseball cap in that underground bar? She let the footage resume and watched as the pair climbed the steps and proceeded past the Sub-Urban Explorer. The face of the shorter one was obscured the whole time. Hidden Shadow, one hand half-raised, looked over his shoulder and, after a moment's hesitation, turned on his heel and followed them in.

Iona fast-forwarded through the remaining footage until the view changed. This camera angle was lower and appeared to be from the direction of Oxford Street, looking past the cenotaph and across the tram tracks towards the library's entrance. Even worse, she groaned to herself. The view would be from behind the two Mauritians. After a few minutes Hidden Shadow appeared, but the distance was so great he was all but unrecognizable. Vassen and his companion entered from the left with only the backs of their heads showing. 'Typical,' Iona muttered, watching the scene play out.

She sat back and let out a sigh of frustration. Had Hidden Shadow mentioned a baseball cap? She reached for her notes from their meeting. Yes, he had. Who, she asked herself, wears a shirt, chinos and a baseball cap? Only someone deliberately trying to keep his face hidden, she concluded. Or someone not particularly up on Western fashions. She traced a finger down her notes. Result! Whoever the mystery companion was, Hidden Shadow said he'd taken his cap off on entering the library. She smiled; there was the solution. She just needed to take Ranjit's mugshot from the police file and show it to Hidden Shadow. He can confirm if they really are one and the same person.

Opening her top drawer, she brought out her copy of Ritter's file and turned to Toby's mobile number. It rang through to answerphone.

'You want Toby?' The Mexican accent was totally overdone. 'He no here. Leave him a message. Maybe he call you back.'

'Hello, Toby, this is Detective Constable Khan here. This message is extremely urgent so please call me the moment you get it. I need to speak to your friend, Hidden Shadow.' She left her number then went straight to text and left him the same request. Saturday night, she said to herself. Almost seven o'clock. I hope he's not ferreting about in some sewage drain for the evening.

She reached for her mouse and rewound to the first camera's footage. Hidden Shadow appeared from under the portico, Vassen and his friend stepped into view. The lower half of the friend's face was visible for a fleeting second. She dragged the bar at the base of the screen back a fraction, froze the image and tried to expand the menu box to show more than just Play, Pause and Stop. It wouldn't display anything else. Where's the zoom? A right click of the mouse opened a box with the option of saving, moving or closing. How, she wondered, do you operate this? The bloke in the control room definitely said you could enlarge stuff. 'Why won't you work?' she growled under her breath, moving the cursor back to their faces and clicking repeatedly.

'Iona, you OK?'

Euan was standing by her desk, a concerned look on his face. 'I've had better days,' she announced quietly.

He frowned. 'I'm really sorry about earlier. You know – when everyone was having a giggle about—'

'Forget it. Euan, do you know how to work these media-player things?'

He examined her screen for a moment and then waved his hands theatrically. 'Don't ask me about stuff like that! I can't even figure out how my niece's Leapster works.'

She smiled up at him before turning back to the monitor. 'You should be able to manipulate the image – crop it, blow it up, things like that.'

'No, sorry, love. It's double-dutch to me. Listen.' He lowered his voice. 'If I'd known how cruel they were going to be with you, I would never have just stood by.'

She looked around, realizing they were now the only two people in her half of the office. 'Cruel? Did you think it was cruel?'

'I'd say so,' he replied uneasily. 'It was obvious you weren't happy.'

She pursed her lips. 'Just embarrassed, really. But thanks.' She leaned closer to her screen, hoping he'd say goodnight so she could focus on getting the media player to work.

'They probably felt they had free reign – because of Wallace.'

She looked back at him. 'Sorry?'

Euan nodded down at her bin. 'That joke with the toilet rolls.'

Iona checked around to make sure no one was in ear-shot. 'That was Wallace?'

'He didn't actually make it; but it was his idea.'

Iona felt like her chair was sinking down. 'How do you mean it was his idea?'

'When he came in and had a word with a few of them – saying about how you thought you'd uncovered a bomb plot. The tunnel that had already been inspected?'

Iona nodded. Word had come from Wallace, then. Not the uniform sent from the silver command post. I don't believe it. 'He knew about the tunnel?'

Euan's hand fluttered. 'He said to write the name of it on the side of the tubes. So . . . yeah, he seemed to know.'

She shook her head. If he knew the tunnel's name, he must have been aware of the situation all along. Which means he deliberately used it as a way of humiliating me. Why? She felt tears stinging her lower eyelids. Why would he do that? Suddenly, she felt very vulnerable. 'Thanks, Euan.' She reached up and squeezed his hand. 'Thanks for letting me know.'

He hung on to her fingers. 'My pleasure, darling.' He glanced across the empty desks. 'Don't show them any weakness. This lot – half of them think they're bloody Rambo. And don't stay too late, will you?'

'No.' She smiled as he made his way towards the doors. The implications of what he'd revealed were billowing out in her head. What was going on? The sense that Wallace had some kind of agenda was now unshakeable. Why would he encourage me to look into the Vassen thing and then use it to ridicule me? Was it a way of putting me in my place because he thought I'd overstepped the mark? And the mosque in Bury. What was all that about?

She tried to focus on the image of Vassen and his companion on her screen. But the rows of empty desks at the edges of her vision seemed to be crowding in. She glanced to her side. There were a few officers on the far side of the room. Two were leaning back in the seats and quietly chatting. One caught her eye and then looked away. The office had taken on an oppressive air and she knew that her ability to concentrate had been shattered. Home, she decided. I'll take the disc home and try to go over the footage there.

TWENTY

Clusters of people were out on the streets of Whalley Range. Couples going for meals. Groups heading for the pubs and bars in Chorlton. People walking with a purpose, the prospect of a night out injecting their legs with energy.

Iona parked her Nissan Micra outside the large semi-detached house where she rented a room. The place looked dark and deserted. She turned the key in the front door and, as soon as it opened, the harsh beeps of the burglar alarm greeted her. So everyone's out, she said to herself as she keyed in the code. And why wouldn't they be? Most normal people my age are.

She flicked on the hallway lights and wandered down to the kitchen. Jo, junior member of a firm of architects in town, had left a scrawled note on the kitchen table.

We're in The Lion. Maybe going on to the Warehouse Project later. Catch us up?

Iona pictured the pub overlooking Chorlton Green. It would be packed, probably with quite a few twenty-something unattached men. How many weeks is it since I've had a good snog, let alone anything else? She thought sadly of her time with Jim. That's where I'd normally be now, she reflected. At his place sitting on the sofa, music on, dissecting their respective days over a bottle of wine . . .

She opened the fridge, selected a can of diet coke then made her way slowly up the stairs to her first-floor room. The top step gave its customary creak, the noise made larger by the surrounding silence.

After unlocking her door, she threw her jacket and bag on the bed and turned on the laptop on the desk in the corner. As it clicked and whirred, she scanned her shelf of CDs. Nothing took her fancy. She searched again more slowly. Too jolly, too mellow, too heavy, too upbeat, too loud. Giving up, she pressed the button for the radio. A frantic dance track blared out and she turned the machine off.

She took the CD out from her carry case. The laptop loaded it up without problem and she gazed at the window filling the screen. Right, she said to herself. You've got a play button. She clicked on it and the silent footage started up once more.

Hidden Shadow appeared from under the portico; Vassen and his friend stepped into view. She paused, un-paused, paused, un-paused until the moment Vassen's companion lifted his chin. The lower part of his nose, mouth and jaw were in view. But without zooming in a lot closer, the image was useless.

She checked her mobile for any new messages. The last text was from Jim. Nothing from Toby. She called him again and got the same stupid Mexican message.

'Hello, Toby. DC Khan speaking. It's now . . . twenty past nine, Saturday night. When you get this message, please call me. It's not a problem how late. Thanks.'

She put the phone down and reached for the computer's mouse. Methodically, she worked her way through the tool bar at the top of the screen. Not a single way of playing about with the image came up. Her eyes went to her mobile once again. There was one person, she thought, who would definitely know how this damn thing works. The same person who's always been there, giving me advice, telling me how to play it with all the office politics that goes on. Jim. He'll know.

'Fucking move. Go. Go. Go!'
   'Where?'
   'There!'
   'There?'
   'Yes.'
   'You sure?'
   'That or die.'
   'Holy shit, OK.' He swallowed. 'Here I go.'
The sound of breathing became snatched and erratic as quick footsteps crunched on the gritty surface. He was halfway across the empty road when tracer rounds began to whip overhead. Milliseconds later the crackle of automatic fire filled the air.
   'Don't stop, stay low.'
   'Holy shit! Holy shit!'
   'The humvee. Get behind that fucked-up humvee! OK. Now switch to the rocket launcher. Do it, before they try sneaking round the side.'
   Sharp clangs as bullets ricocheted off the burnt-out vehicle's armour.
   'Where's the fucking air support?'
   'You don't get it. Not at this stage.'
   'Shit! Where are they firing from? That building with the smashed-in roof?'
   'No, the palm trees. They're prepping an RPG, you need to let rip with that rocket, right now.'
   'What am I aiming at?'
   'The middle tree will do.'
   The thin barrel on the screen changed to something far thicker.
   'Soon as you fire, switch back to the M16.' The man on the end of the sofa looked back down at the little mound of powder on the coffee table and continued separating some of it to the side. 'You can pick the fuckers off when they break cover. There'll be four of them.'

A third man, this one sitting in an armchair in the corner of the room aimed the remote at the sound system and upped the volume even higher.

'Time to die, you rag-head fuckers.' The view on the TV screen lifted, rising above the humvee's bonnet to reveal a little cluster of palm trees about twenty-five metres away. On the side of the half-collapsed building next to them was a poster, faded Arabic letters just visible. In the distance, a ripple of dusty-looking hills met with the sun-bleached sky.

The rocket launcher recoiled and a faint arc of smoke vanished in the direction of the trees. A bright ball of orange, followed by bits of trunk flying out. The palm fronds were still shaking violently as the rocket launcher was replaced by M16.

Four figures – their heads and faces obscured by red-checked material – broke to the left.

'Light them up,' the man at the end of the sofa stated quietly.

The one sitting at the centre of the sofa was hunched forward, body tense, controller held towards the TV. 'Fuck you, fuck you, fuck you!' he yelled, spent cartridges flying from the weapon as its muzzle flashed.

The one in the armchair started laughing manically. 'Oh, yeah, stroke my bell-end, you pussy-fucks.'

Little puffs of red vapour appeared behind three of the sprinting men and they spun and collapsed. The last one turned and tried to raise a pipe-like weapon on to his shoulder. M16 clattered again and he flew backward.

A message filled the screen. Area cleared.

'Yes!' the man with the controller was panting as he lowered it to his lap and sat back. 'Never made it this far before!'

The man next to him had got down on one knee. A straw hovered over the powder as he drew in air through his nose. The thin white line on the coffee table started to evaporate.

The one holding the controller watched him then turned to the third man in the armchair. 'What's his name again?'

'Gary,' he replied, nodding to the music as he finished off his can of Stella.

'Fuck all else to do inside but play them games,' Gary said, looking up.

The one with the controller studied him admiringly. 'What were you inside for, again?'

Gary got to his feet and rotated heavily muscled shoulders. 'This and that. A raid on a Paki shop that went wrong.' He paced over to the flat's front window and looked down on the street below. 'Good to be out, it is.'

'Lee,' the one in the armchair said, thrusting a can towards the sofa. 'You need to fucking catch-up, mate.'

Lee placed the controller to his side, opened the can and gulped deeply.

As he did so, Gary caught the man in the armchair's eye and prompted him with a little nod.

Martin raised himself up. 'So, what's the plan?'

Lee lowered his can. 'Next map? I've not done the airfield.'

Gary's eyes went to slits as he glanced at the screen. 'Fuck that. Spent fucking months stuck in a cell doing that.' He turned to the window, drinking in the massed lights of Bury. 'You like wasting rag-heads, Lee?'

'Fuck, yeah.'

'Should have seen some of the ones you get inside. Weasely little shits. Half of them shouldn't have even been over here in the first place.'

Martin cracked open another can of Stella. 'Three meals a day. Probably couldn't believe their luck.'

Gary flexed his head from side to side. 'Used to see them scurrying off for their prayers. Arses in the air, muttering in foreign.'

Lee's face was sour. 'They should put them on a plane home. Why are they even in this country?'

Gary gave Martin another look.

Tapping the side of his can, Martin said, 'Lee, they still let you keep that works van at weekends?'

Lee nodded.

Gary perched on the edge of the sofa, one knee jigging up and down. 'What do you keep here, mate? In case someone tries to break in?'

Lee stared at him for a moment then nodded in the direction of the cupboard in the corner. 'Baseball bat.'

'That it? Got a toolbox with your job?'

'Yeah.' The reply took a moment to come out. 'At nights I keep it in that same cupboard.'

Gary was on his feet. 'Sound.' He crossed the room, pulled open the cupboard doors and crouched down. An aluminium baseball bat was placed on the dirty carpet. 'Nice.' The toolbox came out next. The catches clicked and the lid was lifted back.

As Gary rummaged about, Martin was mouthing along to the music, his eyes slightly glazed.

Gary stood, a long screwdriver hanging from one hand, a claw hammer from the other. He was grinning. 'Lee. You a talker or a doer?'

TWENTY-ONE

As Iona approached Jim's front door, she tried to smooth her nerves. It was, she realized as she pressed the bell, the first time she'd visited since breaking things off with him. She stepped back, clasping her carry case in front of her.

The door was opened a little too quickly and he regarded her with an anxious look.

You look as uncomfortable as me about this, she thought.

'Hi,' he said tentatively, stepping back. 'Come in.'

'Thanks.' As she squeezed through the gap between him and his mountain bike propped in the corridor, she caught a sweet and fruity aroma. Alcohol, she thought.

'I'm in the telly room,' he announced, now awkwardly squeezing round her.

She caught his eyes and saw they had a dull shine. How much, she wondered, has he had? And will it have been beer or spirits? He always gets morose if it's spirits.

The telly room was as neat as ever. Her glance touched on the framed photo of the two of them high above Manchester, pressed against each other in the pod of the big wheel. She felt a needle of dismay that he still had it on his shelf. On the coffee table was an open bottle of wine and two glasses, one half full. She waited for an offer of a seat.

'Would you like a drink?' he asked, heading towards his usual armchair. When he saw she was waiting just inside the door, he looked momentarily disappointed. 'Sofa's free. Do you want tea? Coffee? I opened a bottle of wine . . .'

'Umm, I'm OK for the moment, thanks.'

'OK.' He sat down in the armchair as she took the mid-point of the sofa.

'So, what's the score?' he asked, reaching for his glass. 'The footage from the control room won't play?'

'It'll play,' she replied, opening her case and sliding the laptop out. 'But I can't figure out how you zoom in and all that stuff.'

He frowned. 'Weird.'

As the device booted-up, she tried to fill the silence between them. 'He said it was straightforward, but . . . I don't know . . . it's probably something really simple. I can't see how it can be too complicated; these things usually aren't, are they?' Realizing she was babbling, she took the CD out of its case and slotted it into the laptop. Another couple of seconds and the window of the media player appeared in the middle of the screen. 'I can see the play, pause and stop buttons . . .'

'Let's take a look.' He plonked himself down beside her. As he hunched forward their thighs came into contact. 'Right, I see.' He placed a finger on the track pad and moved the cursor to the top right-hand corner of the media player's window. There was a tiny double-line symbol next to the cross for closing it down. 'Somehow, your toolbar has been minimized.' He clicked on it and a range of new buttons slid down. 'There you go. Zoom in and out, play speeds – half, quarter, eighth and sixteenth. Adjustments for brightness and contrast. No idea what the last ones on the right are for.'

Iona felt like a complete idiot. One click. A two-second job. 'Thanks.' She started to consider how quickly she could wrap things up and get back home.

'Who's the target, then?'

'Oh. Here.' By leaning forward, she inadvertently brought more of their legs against each other. Nightmare, she said to herself, allowing the footage to progress up to when Vassen and his companion came into view. 'That's them? See there? The one with the baseball cap just looked up slightly.'

Jim moved the footage back to the point where the pair entered the picture. He then resumed the footage at eighth speed. They watched as Vassen ruffled his hair in slow motion. 'Needs to use Head and Shoulders,' Jim murmured. 'Dandruff problem like that.' The companion started to lift his chin and Jim's finger hovered over the pause button. 'Here's a neat little trick.' When the lower half of his face was exposed he pressed the button then dragged out a dotted line around the person's head. 'Always makes me feel like Deckard, when I do this.'

'Deckard?'

'You know, when he says to give him hard copy.'

Mystified, Iona gave a little shake of her head.

Jim wrinkled his nose. 'My all-time favourite film?'

'Oh, right.' She shot a glance at his collector's edition of *Blade Runner*, sitting in its special metal presentation box on a shelf below the telly. 'How could I forget.'

Jim moved the cursor to another icon in the media player's toolbar and expanded out the field until the person's face dominated the frame.

'Nice work,' Iona said appreciatively.

'He's a blue,' Jim said, taking a sip of wine.

'Mmm?' Iona was reaching for her case.

'Manchester City badge on his cap. Those things are two-a-penny round town. Get them in any souvenir shop.'

She extracted the mugshot of Ranjit Bhujun she'd printed off earlier and held it next to the laptop's screen. Resting her chin on her other hand, she studied the image for a moment. 'No way to tell it's definitely him, is there?'

'Not really. Worth getting a copy, though.' Jim selected another icon from the toolbar. A smaller box appeared asking where he wanted to save the image. 'Got a memory stick? The printer's in the front room.'

'Somewhere in here.' She rummaged around and handed it to him. 'The view from the other camera is even worse – it's situated a lot further away and almost behind them.'

He stuck the memory stick in the USB port and, as the image was transferred, reached across Iona's legs for the CD case. 'Not included – footage from the tram platform,' he said, reading the label.

'I wasn't sure about that,' Iona replied, knees pressed firmly together. She glanced at the bottle of white. There were droplets clinging to the glass. Cold Muscadet, she thought. What we always treated ourselves to on a Friday evening.

'The council also has cameras on every tram platform,' Jim explained. 'You've got the stop directly in front of the library. Saint Peter's Square. The control room operative, was it Jamie Compton?'

Iona shrugged. 'It just got delivered across by someone.'

'Well, whoever it was, he means there's a chance your guys will be caught on that one – cameras are directed at the platform but some pick up people passing in the vicinity. How long were they in the library for?'

She took her notebook out. 'Not sure. The witness waited until they left – it couldn't have been long because he was at the end of his lunch hour.'

Jim tapped the rim of his glass. 'Sure you don't want any?'

She shook her head.

'OK.' He poured himself another glass. 'You need to think wider here. They didn't just appear at the edge of Saint Peter's Square. They approached it from somewhere. Similarly, when they left the library, it was to go somewhere. Maybe home.' He gave her a meaningful look.

'Of course,' Iona whispered, feeling a tingle of excitement. The bottle of wine was like a magnet to her eyes. 'Actually, mind if I do have a drink?'

'Go for it.' He passed her the bottle. 'So, you need to check the cameras ten, fifteen minutes on. The tram platform ones tend to be positioned at a lower level, too. Might get a look under the rim of that baseball cap. Of course, if they actually caught a tram, you're really laughing.'

'Onboard cameras, you mean?' Iona asked, taking a sip of her drink. That tasted good.

'Those are the responsibility of the Greater Manchester transport system or whatever it's called. Might be good for a face-shot. What I'm thinking is this: assume they did catch a tram. You then study platform footage along the line to see the stop they get off at. Then you're getting close to where they're operating from.'

Iona nodded eagerly. 'That would be brilliant.'

Jim removed the memory stick. 'I'll get you hard copy,' he said with an American drawl in his voice.

'And can you print me another copy of Ranjit's mugshot? It's on the memory stick under his name.'

Once he was out of the room, Iona stood. The investigation was moving forward. Not sure if it was the wine causing fresh energy to rush through her, she circled the coffee table, pausing in the doorway leading to the kitchen. Her eyes were moving about and she realized she was examining the room, searching for signs of anyone other than Jim. No low-fat versions of mayonnaise or salad dressing next to the bottles of sauces near the cooker. The recycling crate near the bin was almost overflowing with crumpled cans of Stella.

'Here you go.'

She whirled round, mortified at being caught snooping. 'Great! Thanks.'

He placed the printouts next to the mugshot and sat back in the armchair. 'I don't think it helps much.'

'No,' she murmured, looking down at the images as she retook her seat. 'I can't get hold of the one person who could say for certain.'

'How's work in general?' he asked casually. 'Is it still just you on this?'

She nodded. 'Dave Ellis, the detective I've been paired with, is off for the foreseeable future. I feel a bit, I don't know, detached from the rest of the office. Still settling in, I suppose.'

'But you're getting on all right with the rest of the team?'

She tilted her glass, eyes on the shifting liquid inside. The newspaper clipping of Baby. The toilet rolls. Wallace and his mind games.

'Iona?'

Her vision had started to waver and she knew that, if she looked up, he'd immediately know something was wrong. 'Yeah.'

'You sure? You don't sound very convinced.'

She kept her head bowed. Oh, no, she thought. Don't start crying. Not now.

'Iona?'

It was no use. She lifted her chin and looked at him with eyes that were brimming with tears. 'Jim? I don't know what's going on.'

TWENTY-TWO

He started to get out of the armchair but she held up a hand to indicate that he shouldn't come any closer. 'I'm OK.' After a couple of deep breaths, she felt more in control of her emotions. She found a pack of tissues in her handbag and dabbed at her eyes. 'It's probably just me.'

Jim was on the edge of his seat, wine glass cradled in his hands. 'What's happened?'

She reached for her own glass and took a large sip. 'I made a bad decision today. Not a disastrous one – but not a good one either. Now I'm copping a load of flack . . . which is fair enough. That's how it works in any station, I know that. But this . . . it just doesn't feel right.'

He sat back, a wary look now on his face. 'Tell me.'

She tried to explain the day's sequence of events, and at the mention of Wallace, his lips tightened. By the time she'd described how it had been her boss' idea to set up the toilet-roll arrangement, his face was white.

'What?' she asked, perplexed by his reaction. 'Do you think he's being out of order?'

When Jim spoke, his voice was different. Low and almost menacing. 'Anything else been happening to make you feel uncomfortable?'

She searched his face before replying. 'Yes. That article the *Manchester Evening Chronicle* ran? Remember it?'

He nodded. 'Probably some bright spark's idea in the press office.'

'Probably. No one has ever owned up to it. The headline was, "The Baby-Faced Assassin". My nickname in the hockey team at school. That got stuck to my monitor, which seemed—'

'Who stuck it there?'

'I don't know.'

'No one held their hand up?'

'No.'

He ran a finger round the rim of his glass. 'Go on.'

The sense that his questions were leading to something had started to unsettle her. 'Today it got trimmed down to just Baby. That's what they've started calling me.'

He looked up, eyes glittering with anger. 'Who?'

'Pretty much everyone, now. Certainly all the more senior detectives. I'm not sure how to react. I mean, it feels demeaning. Or am I overreacting? I don't want to get labelled a humourless cow—'

'Take it down.'

'Sorry?'

'Take it down, Iona. You don't want that on your monitor. Do other detectives call each other things like that?'

She considered the question. 'No. It's all Browny or Smithy or Greggsy. Like they're in a football team.'

'Exactly. I know you want to fit in, but you need to take it down. Someone addresses you as Baby, ignore them. Don't even look at them until its Detective or Iona or Khany, if they want. They'll soon learn. What else?'

She wondered about mentioning how Wallace was trying to steer the focus of the investigation towards the mosque in Bury. But to do so would give credence to Jim's comment in the incident room at Booth Street – the one about how her race had helped her get into the CTU. 'Not really.'

Jim seemed to be weighing something up. He shifted forward in his seat, refilled his glass then looked at her almost as an afterthought. 'Top up?'

'A splash, thanks.'

He poured more in, replaced the bottle and stared at the floor.

'Jim? What's on your mind?'

His shoulders rose as he took a long breath in. 'It's how he operates.'

She didn't want him to be talking about her boss; it opened up so many horrible possibilities. 'Who?'

He drained a good third of his drink. 'Wallace.'

She felt like the sofa had started to buckle around her. 'How do you mean?'

'I doubt he was behind that story getting into the *Chronicle*. But I'll put money on him being the person who stuck the clipping to your monitor.'

'Why?'

'I said, it's how he operates.'

'But how do you know? You've never worked with him, have you?' As he lifted his glass again, she saw that his hand was shaking slightly. 'Have you?'

'Not in the police.'

'Then . . .' Suddenly, it clicked. The army! He was talking about the army – something he was never willing to do. Wallace had said he'd also served in it when he was berating me about explosives. 'Where did you work with him?' she asked cautiously.

He finished his drink, tipped more in and set the bottle down. 'Iraq.'

'While you were a squaddie?'

He lowered his head. 'He was my CO. We were both in the Kings Regiment – it's where you go if you sign up in Manchester. We were posted to the same base out there. Not really a base, even. A fortified compound in a town north of Basra.'

Oh my God, she thought. The thing that happened – he said once it was to do with Iraq. Is he opening the lid on that box? 'Did you have some kind of run-in with him out there?'

Jim said nothing for a few seconds. 'I was trying to warn you, Iona. That message on your answerphone I left – about how he'll use you.'

The drunken rant, she thought. Or was it? The look on the face of Simon Armitage – the security guy at the convention centre – came back to her. When she said she worked under Wallace. The measured way he asked her how she found him. 'Warn me about what?'

His eyes crept up to meet her face. 'I didn't have any major issues with the man because of two reasons. One was my colour.'

Iona felt the sofa tilt again. 'He's racist, you're saying.'

Jim's smile was grim. 'Out there, anyone who wasn't white got treated differently by him. With soldiers, it was subtle. Who got the shit jobs, who got the cushy ones. Iraqis? They . . . to him they weren't even people. Just a threat – not to be trusted. Iona, he's a nasty piece of work. I'm sorry if the way I went about trying to tell you—'

'He wants me to check out a mosque. One over in Bury. It's been linked with certain extremists.'

'Extremists?' A note of alarm had entered Jim's voice. 'What do you mean, check it out?'

'Visit it. That was the implication. Jim, I've never set foot in a mosque in my life. You know how mum and dad raised me and Fenella.'

'He wants to send you into a mosque dressed up like a Muslim woman?'

'I'd have to be to get in. Long sleeves, ankles covered. Something covering my head, at least.'

'What about back-up?'

'He didn't mention any. Everyone's so busy with the conference about to start. None of this was a formal request – it was more about me dropping in at a prayer session and looking around.'

Jim was gripping his glass so tightly, she was afraid it might shatter. The last of his wine was gulped down. 'There is no way – no bloody way – an officer with no training and no detailed briefing would be sent into a situation like that. He's testing you, Iona. Seeing how far you're prepared to go.'

'I don't get you.'

'You're new to his team, right? He's seeing if he can trust you. The fact – and I am so sorry to say this Iona, I really am – the fact you're part Pakistani will be a problem for him. He'll have doubts about where your loyalties lie, I know it. So he's seeing what you'll do to keep him sweet, to be part of his team . . .'

His words trailed away and Iona got the impression he was no longer talking about her situation; he was remembering something that had involved him.

He shook his head. 'Bastard. The guy is a complete bastard.' He jumped up. 'More wine? I'll get a bottle.' He crossed into the kitchen without waiting for a reply.

Iona kept very still. This was making her want to be sick. Fighting to control the waves of queasiness, a thought hit home: while they were discussing Wallace, there was still a chance of getting to the truth about the incident in Iraq.

He walked back in, unscrewing the cap. Another glass for him, a top-up for her. 'Jim,' she said softly, no intention of touching her drink. 'You didn't have any major issues with Wallace for two reasons.' He seemed lost in thought. 'Jim? Did you hear—'

'I did, yes.'

'What was the other reason?'

When he looked up at her, she almost had to break eye contact. There was such intense emotion on his face. Anger. Shame. Despair. This is it, she realized. This is the thing that torments him when he's asleep. 'Jim?'

His eyes were moist. He blinked. 'I . . . I . . . it doesn't matter.' He drank again.

She wanted to reach out and take his hand. 'Jim, we're both mixed up with this man. I need to know what it is, what you're not saying.'

He dragged air in through his nose and she could see the muscles in his jaw working. When he spoke, he sounded hoarse. 'I did as he asked.' A tiny groan came from his throat. Physical pain. 'I did as he asked.'

'What did you do?' she whispered.

He gritted his teeth, head going slowly from side to side. Trying to deny the memories.

'Jim? Tell me. Please.'

Suddenly he was out of his chair and running for the kitchen. He reached the sink as a column of liquid shot from his mouth. By the time she got to his side, wine was gurgling noisily down the plughole. She rubbed a hand up and down his back as he continued to throw it up. 'That's good, Jim. Get it out.' She realized he was sobbing between retches. A long drool of spit hung from the end of his lips. He let his forehead lean against the edge of the sink for a second and then he started to slide towards the tiled floor, knees drawing up under him.

She crouched at his side and ran a hand through his hair. An arm wrapped round her waist as he tipped forward, causing her to lose her balance. She ended up on the floor with him, his head in her lap. Eventually his breathing calmed. As she stroked the side of his head, she was able to feel his pulse through a vein in his temple.

His eyes were closed as he mumbled, 'He was so young.'

'Who was?' she breathed, wishing she could turn off the harsh strip light glaring down on them. 'Who was so young?'

'The kid we killed.'

Cigarette smoke swirled round the interior of the van. Gary spoke up from its rear. 'The places they eat. Trays of lentil slop, dog meat on skewers, all that shite. That's where to find them.'

Lee glanced in the rear-view mirror. 'There are a couple on Woodhill Road. They stay open late.'

Martin was drumming his fingers on the dash board. 'You all hear that?' he drawled. 'We're a-havin us a Paki hunt!'

The van headed through a few sets of lights before turning on to a road lined with shops. A couple of jewellers, shutters drawn down. A sari-makers, rolls of brightly coloured material in the window. On the pavement outside a grocery store a man with a long beard and a little lace cap was reaching up with a hooked stick to lower the awning.

As the van cruised past, Martin wound down the front passenger window. The sudden rush of air ripped into the haze of cigarette smoke as he slapped the side of the vehicle with his palm. 'We're coming for you, mullah-motherfucker!'

Gary's hand shot forward and he slapped the side of Martin's head. 'Shut it!'

Martin brought his arm back inside. 'He's a fucking—'

'Keep quiet. What if he rings the pigs? White van just went past my shop, some gobby dickhead shouting abuse . . .'

'Sorry,' Martin replied.

Gary was now sitting forward, forearms resting on the back of the front seats. The road curved gently to the left. Up ahead were the bright signs of a couple of food places.

'There's two,' said Lee, now sounding nervous.

A couple of men emerged from one. The taller one was thin with a mop of dark hair. His companion was much shorter, hair shaved close. Hanging from his right hand was a white bag.

'Slow,' Gary hissed.

Lee touched the brakes and dropped down a gear. Gary quickly checked the road behind. No traffic. All eyes were on the pair as they ambled along, deep in conversation. They reached the top of an alley and set off down it.

'Where'll that lead?' Gary's voice quivered with excitement.

'Just a cut-through, probably. To the next road,' Martin whispered.

'Pull over,' Gary commanded.

The van came to a stop and Gary reached down to the floor. He handed the screwdriver to Martin and the hammer to Lee. 'Let's go take these fuckers out, yeah?'

Martin deep-breathed as he reached for his door handle. 'Yeah.'

'I'll stay in the van,' Lee suddenly announced, putting the hammer in his lap.

Martin looked over his shoulder. 'Fuck off.'

'No, serious. We can get away quicker if I do.'

Martin swivelled the other way to look at Gary.

'Fuck him,' Gary said. 'Could tell he was a shitter.' He spoke into Lee's ear. 'You drive round to the next road. Wait for us at the other end of the alley. What will you do?'

Lee kept looking straight ahead. 'Drive round. Wait for you.'

'Good lad. And remember, these are your tools. So make sure you're there.'

The rear doors opened and Gary jumped out. Slamming them shut behind him, he set off across the pavement, baseball bat held close to his side. Martin followed him through the pool of orange light cast by the street lamp above the end of the alley. Then they were into the shadows beyond.

The two men were about twenty metres in front, heads bowed as they talked. Six-foot-high concrete panels ran along either side of the alley, giving it a canyon-like feel. Names, comments and pictures covered the stone-grey surfaces.

At the halfway point, the alley jinked to the left, another street lamp lighting the way. Gary and Martin were now ten metres behind the pair. Some small noise caused the two men to look back: they saw a pair of white men charging at them, one with a baseball bat raised to shoulder level. The bag hit the ground, rice spilling from the top. The taller of the two was slower to get moving and, as he struggled to keep up with his shorter companion, he began to stumble.

The baseball bat connected with the back of one thigh, driving the knee coming forward into the rear of the other. He sprawled forward. 'Ranjit!' he yelled. 'Ranj—'

The baseball bat came down again, this time across his back, cutting the word off.

Gary watched the shorter man sprinting away before looking down. 'Your rat mate's left you.'

The man on the ground was getting to his knees, one forearm raised. 'Ranjit!'

Martin stepped forward and swung a foot. The kick caught the man in the throat. He fell back against the concrete panels and started to make a croaking noise. 'Speakey English, you fuck.'

He coughed a couple of times then reached out and tried to stroke at Martin's shoes. 'Please,' he rasped.

Martin kicked the man's hand away. 'Get the fuck off me.'

'Fucking embarrassing.' Gary lifted the bat again, his eyes fixed on the whorl in the thick black hair at the top of the man's head.

A shadow – moving low and fast – entered the periphery of Gary's vision. He felt a heavy impact and the next thing he knew, he was lying on his back, the street lamp shining down at him. The concrete fence shook and he saw Martin bouncing off it and falling over, screwdriver clattering to the ground. Gary realized he was winded: all he could do was silently open and close his mouth.

Martin had got on to all fours when the silhouette reappeared, this time rising high into the air. It landed with both feet on the base of Martin's spine. He went flat and still. The dark figure started to look round and Gary turned on his side and tried to curl into a ball. He felt a knee jam into his back and a hand slid under his chin. Leathery fingers started to force his chin up, exposing his throat. The blade of a knife glinted and still he couldn't get in any air to scream.

'Ranjit!' The other one's voice. 'Ranjit!' Rapid words were spoken. Gary couldn't understand what was being said but he recognized the pleading note in the flow of the younger man's words.

For a moment the only sound was rapid breathing coming from just above him. Then the grip on Gary's chin eased as the man's weight shifted. An instant later it felt like one buttock, then the other, was punched. Finally his lungs were able to inflate and he started to bellow as red-hot pain lanced out from where he'd been stabbed.

TWENTY-THREE

Iona clicked her front door shut behind her. She could hear morning TV in the kitchen as she started for the stairs up to her room.

'Iona? Is that you?'

Curse it, she thought. I just wanted to grab a quick shower and get back to the office. She paused, one hand on the banister. 'Yeah, hi, Jo. Good night, last night?'

Her housemate appeared in the kitchen doorway. She was wearing tartan pyjamas and suede slippers with fluffy tops. 'Yes.' Her eyes travelled up and down Iona. 'You weren't in the office all night, were you?'

Iona glanced down at her crumpled work suit. 'Oh, no. I . . . just finished late.'

Jo cocked her head to the side, an impish look in her eyes. 'So, where've you been?'

Iona hooked a strand of hair over her ear. 'Just sorting some stuff.'

'Just sorting some stuff?' Jo let out a deep and dirty laugh. 'Yeah, it looks like you've been sorted. Anyone I know?'

'Jo!' Iona couldn't keep from smiling. 'You are such a potty-mouth.'

'Come on, you can tell Aunty Jo.' She beckoned. 'I'll make tea.'

Iona gestured to the stairs. 'I've really got to be back in work.'

She raised her lower lip. 'Seriously? It's Sunday morning – not even ten o'clock.' She clicked a finger and pointed behind her. 'The Labour Party conference, yeah? They've got camera crews down there right now.'

Iona could hear the enthusiastic tones of the TV presenter. The one with the thinning hair and floppy hands whose show was a Sunday morning fixture on the BBC.

'At least give me a clue,' Jo said. 'Work colleague? Blind date? Someone you just collared outside the kebab shop?'

'I was at Jim's.'

'No!' She widened her eyes and clamped a hand over her mouth. 'No! Is that good? I thought he was history.'

Iona's hand wiggled at her side. 'I don't know.'

'You don't know? You can't just start doing him again – well, you can. But . . . I can't believe it. Jim? He's a bit gorgeous, I have to admit—'

'Jo, I slept on the sofa. We had a lot of stuff that needed to be discussed.'

Her friend's face was now serious. 'OK, but do you reckon . . . you know . . . are you getting back with him?'

Iona shrugged as she started up to her room. 'One step at a time.'

Once in her room, she turned her little telly on. They were filming, she realized, by the entry point she'd used to get into the secure zone. The camera was looking over the perimeter fence to the front of the Midland Hotel. It lingered on the Labour banner draped above the front entrance before panning down to street level.

The road was heaving with people. Among them she could see numerous protestors and activists trying to hand leaflets to delegates as they made their way into the mouth of a fenced-off corridor leading to the security-check building.

She saw people in wheelchairs chanting their cause, an elderly man holding up a placard that read, Nukiller Power – a crime against God. Next to him a group of children wearing T-shirts which bore the words, Kids Count. Two elderly women were struggling to lift a banner emblazoned with Christians against the Cuts.

Patches of yellow were sprinkled about: police officers in high-visibility jackets. She studied her fellow officers, men and women quietly keeping an eye on things.

You're all targets, Iona thought, eyes fixed to the screen. All of you are targets.

Her phone beeped as she was putting on her dressing gown, ready to nip down the corridor to the shower. An 0207 number; someone calling from London. 'Hello, Consta— Detective Constable Khan speaking.'

'Good morning, Detective. It's Ayo here. I hope this isn't too early?'

'Not at all, Ayo,' she replied, remembering that the other woman had promised to go over all the cases Reginald Appleton had been involved in during the two times he'd sat in session on Mauritius.

'I've been through all the files. I would have called late last night, but it was the witching hour by the time I'd finished.'

'You've been such a help, Ayo, really I—'

'I wouldn't thank me too much, Iona. The man's name didn't feature.'

Iona felt her shoulders droop. 'Really?'

'I'm afraid not. No person with the surname Bhujun. I also took the precaution to check the name against Reginald's UK rulings as a Law Lord. No joy there, either.'

'You were able to check them all, including the ones linked to terror suspects?'

'Yes. The name didn't feature.'

Iona tilted her head back and blew out air in exasperation. 'Not to worry. It's massively appreciated anyway.'

'My pleasure. Do let me know if I can help any other way.'

'Will do, thanks Ayo.' After hanging up, she dropped the phone on her bed. Damn, damn, damn. Still, she thought, turning to the door, Jim would be in the CCTV control room by now, reviewing the footage outside the library to see where Vassen and his friend were headed. At least that line of enquiry was still very much alive.

Navin Ramgoolan sat in his kitchen, stacks of leaflets arranged on the table before him.

He thought about his young nephew, Vassen Bhujun. An enquiring mind. A young man blessed with intelligence. Intelligence that had been recognized – first with a grant for school and university on Mauritius and then with a scholarship to undertake his Masters degree in England. He could have had such a bright future. But not now. Now the cousin, Ranjit, had arrived, things could only end badly.

There was something dark about Ranjit. Something dark and disturbing.

Navin looked at his leaflets. The events of almost fifty years before had been a catastrophe for them all. A disaster on which humiliation and then injustice had been heaped. I, Navin thought, appreciate that humiliation as much as anyone. Twelve years I've lived here in Britain, battling for our rights to be recognized. But never have I broken the law. Never have I turned to crime. Why must I resort to something like this?

He heard two sets of footsteps coming down the stairs. It was them. Their shadowy forms got closer and Navin cleared his throat in readiness to speak. 'Vassen. It is . . .' His words died. 'What has happened to you?'

His nephew moved awkwardly into the well-lit room. He was limping slightly and his lips were swollen. An angry graze stood out on his chin. 'I was attacked, Uncle.'

Putting his glasses on, Navin got out of his chair and approached the younger man for a closer look. 'Who attacked you?' He shot a suspicious glance at Ranjit, who was skulking in the doorway.

'Two men. Locals, I think. They meant to really hurt me, Uncle. If Ranjit hadn't been there to fight them off I think I would now be in hospital. Maybe worse.'

Navin had placed his fingertips under Vassen's chin, gently lifting his nephew's head back for a better look. 'Who were these men?'

'I don't know,' Vassen answered, twisting his head away from his uncle's probing fingers. 'Thugs. That's all.'

'Where else are you hurt?'

'My back. They hit me across it with a bat.'

'Why did they attack you?'

'Why?' Vassen replied. 'Who knows? Because our skin is a different colour to theirs. Because they had a bad day and needed to take it out on someone.'

Navin cast a begrudging look in Ranjit's direction. 'And you? Are you injured?'

'No.'

'Well, come in. Don't stand there. Sit down. Have some breakfast.' He removed a loaf of bread from a cupboard. 'Thank you for helping Vassen.'

Ranjit acknowledged the comment with a nod. 'It was nothing.' He sat down and gestured at the leaflets. 'You are still going to do it?'

Navin peered over the top of his spectacles at the stacks of leaflets. 'Of course. It will be the best chance I ever get to bring attention to our cause.'

'Even though it will bring such trouble down on you?'

The old man picked up his security pass from the corner of the table. 'What will be, will be.' Sadness subdued his voice. 'My membership of the party has not helped get justice for our people. They care about us no more than any of the other political parties. All of them are the same.'

Ranjit looked hungrily at the pass as the old man ran its red lanyard through his fingers. Age had made the skin on his hands slack and wrinkled. 'And is it tomorrow you'll go?'

Navin looked up. 'Tomorrow? Yes.' He sounded almost regretful. 'When Blair and Brown are on stage. I will do it then, when the television coverage is best.' He looked at the clock on the wall. 'I must go,' he announced, taking his brown overcoat off the peg by the back door and placing a flat cap on his head before letting himself out.

TWENTY-FOUR

Jim had never seen so many people in the CCTV control room. Every desk before the two Barco screens dedicated to the convention centre and surrounding streets was occupied by an operator, their faces bathed by the giant screens' glow.

In the shadows behind them stood men in suits – many with southern accents. Most had their arms crossed and a constant murmur flowed among them. Occasionally, someone would move off to the side to take a call on their mobile phone.

The views on the bank of screens showed the ex-railway terminal from every angle. Other cameras were on the entry points, the operators constantly working the joysticks to scan the queues of people waiting to get in.

A tall man with streaks of grey hair reached out and placed a hand on the shoulder of the operator sitting before him. 'Can you go in on that camera? Twenty-two?'

The operator nodded and he tapped a few keys. The view from camera twenty-two appeared on his desk monitor. 'Zoom in on centre screen?' he asked.

'No.' The man pointed to the left-hand edge. A small group were gathered near a lamp post. 'That lot.' Above their heads a banner read, Extraordinary Rendition – We Demand the Truth. Their mouths were opening and closing in unison, some kind of chant. 'Facial captures for each one.'

The operator went in closer, froze the image and then expanded a square-shaped field with a perforated line over each person's face.

Another click on the keyboard brought up a command panel. The operator worked his cursor across the facial boxes, clicking on each one before selecting copy.

Jim turned back to his own screen. The supervisor had looked suitably pissed-off when Jim had asked to see eleven-day-old footage from outside the library.

'This can't wait for a less busy time?' he'd asked.

'Colin,' Jim replied, keeping his voice low. 'If it could, believe me, I would not be here. I'm not asking for an operator to burn me any footage. Just dump me on a corner desk. I can do the searching myself.'

The supervisor had led him to the far end and sat him down at a spare workstation. 'Twenty minutes. Then the full day shift arrives and I'll need this and every other seat in here.'

'No problem; cheers, Colin.'

It had taken almost ten minutes to access the footage from outside the library at two o'clock on the seventeenth. Selecting camera forty-eight, the one positioned beyond the cenotaph, Jim skipped forward ten minutes. At eleven minutes past, Vassen and his companion left the library, trotting down the steps in the direction of the camera before heading to the right. The companion walked purposefully along, baseball cap on, head down.

Cursing, Jim watched until they disappeared from view. He tapped his fingers; the angle they were walking at meant they would have passed the tram platforms. 'Come on,' he whispered, going to the main menu. He selected the tram platform cameras and scrolled down to St Peter's Square. Two options: inbound trams approaching from the direction of Salford on the city's outskirts. Or outbound, going the other way. Jim clicked on outbound. The view was from the end of the platform towards where the trams approached from Mosley Street.

The footage resumed, but after watching for three minutes, Vassen and his friend hadn't appeared. Aware time was ticking on, Jim went back to the menu. Last chance was if they passed the camera on the opposite platform. If they didn't, he'd have to start trawling footage from the nearby streets, and that could take hours. He selected inbound. This view was from the other end of the tram stop, looking along the platform and towards where trams trundled in from Salford.

After a few seconds, Vassen and his mate appeared. Jim felt his fingers clench on the joystick mounted in the centre of the desk. The two men quickly proceeded to directly below the camera where just the tops of their heads were visible. They stopped. 'Come on, do something, will you?' Jim said under his breath. 'Step round the woman with blonde hair. Look up. Check the sky. Just do something.' They remained still and Jim felt his eyes widen. Are they waiting for a tram? Oh, sweet Jesus, they're waiting for a bloody tram! He sat forward. This could lead back to wherever they were based.

The pair remained on the spot until a tram appeared, moving along the tracks which ran along side of the Midland Hotel. It came to a stop and he watched them both get on board. As soon as the tram began to pull away, he leaned across to the next desk. 'Excuse me. You know the trams; how do you go about getting the timings for between stations? I need to track one on its way from Saint Peter's Square.'

The operator removed a folder from his top drawer. 'Timetable in there, mate. Just work on it taking two minutes between each stop and you can't go wrong.'

'Thanks.'

Jim checked his watch; it was now less than ten minutes before the day shift arrived. He ran a finger along the timetable. St Peter's Square to Mosley Street. How likely was it they'd only catch a tram to a stop a couple of hundred metres away? Not very, he decided, moving on to Market Street. Again, hardly worth the journey. Next stop was Shudehill, a fairly decent walk from the library.

He scrolled through the tram platform menu, selected Shudehill and entered a time of two fifteen. The platform view came up as the tram pulled to a halt. Five people got on, two got off. A pair of teenage girls.

He checked his watch. Seven minutes until the day shift. The next stop was Victoria station, connecting point for trains going off in all sorts of directions. He typed in two seventeen and pressed play. The tram was already in and he could see the platform was busy with waiting passengers. Jim cut to quarter speed as the tram's doors opened. People started spilling out of each carriage, five, ten, twenty, thirty of them. He froze the image and started zooming in. No baseball cap. He let the footage continue, watching until the tram moved forward once again. Making certain they hadn't disembarked there had cost another minute.

Next stop: Woodlands Road, a residential area on the city's

outskirts. He added two more minutes to the timer. The tram pulled in: no baseball cap or tall lad alighted. Three minutes until the day shift was meant to start.

Crumpsall, Bowker Vale and Heaton Park revealed nothing. By the time the tram got to Prestwich, Jim could hear new voices coming into the room. Eyes glued resolutely to the screen, he became aware of a person by his side. Jim spoke from the corner of his mouth. 'Just a second, OK? Then you can have your seat.'

Nothing at Prestwich. Same for Besses o' th' Barn. Now Colin's voice, coming from the row in front. 'Jim? You're holding up my day shift.'

He glanced up. 'I've just got three more stops until the end of the line. Please, mate.'

Colin looked like steam was about to erupt from both ears. 'One more minute, OK?'

Jim scrolled to Whitefield and moved the timer on two minutes. Six people got off, none any good. Second to last stop was Radcliffe. Over a dozen alighted and Jim was frantically scanning them when Colin appeared next to him and leaned down to whisper, 'Jim, don't make me look a complete arsehole in my own office. Not today of all days. I gave you until eight o'clock. It's now almost five past.'

'I know, I know.' Jim clicked on the final stop, added two minutes to the timer and pressed play. 'I'm moving, OK? Let me get my things together and I'm off.' He handed the train timetable back to the neighbouring worker and lifted his jacket from the back of the chair. 'Thanks, Colin. Really sorry I ran over a bit on the old time.'

The supervisor started trying to usher Jim away from the desk. 'You know this is the big one. Any other time and it wouldn't have been a problem.'

'Appreciated.' He made a show of patting his pockets, trying to spin things out for a second or two longer. 'Nearly forgot my phone, there.' He turned round to retrieve it. On screen, the tram had stopped and a mass of passengers were moving along the platform.

As Jim leaned closer to the screen, Colin spoke behind him. 'Come on now, Jim. I've been reasonable.'

'This is it, mate. Just a second more . . .' Middle-aged women with shopping bags, a young couple – the woman pushing the buggy as the man struggled to light a cigarette. Behind them, a gaggle of young lads, some with their hoods up.

'Jim –'

He glimpsed a taller male with a floppy black fringe. Vassen! The flow of people shifted and Jim saw the baseball cap for a split second. No clear view of the face, but it was him. It was the two of them. Holding up a hand in thanks, Jim started towards the exit, phone pressed against his ear. 'Iona, I've got them! They caught a tram to Bury. Did you get that? They got off at Bury.'

TWENTY-FIVE

'**B**ury?' Iona said. 'You're sure?' She looked up at the ceiling – could Wallace have been on to something after all? The mosque with that cleric was in Bury. She realized the screensaver on her office computer had changed: now the conference had started, the ticking clock had been replaced by five words. OPERATION PROTECTOR IS NOW LIVE. The words drifted slowly up to bounce off the top of the screen and begin a lazy descent. If they're going to launch an attack, she thought, it could be at any moment.

'Iona?'

'Sorry, what?'

'I said the NCP's network doesn't extend that far out of Manchester. But there'll be street cameras run by the town council in Bury. Private ones, too. Petrol station forecourts, entrances to office buildings, that kind of stuff. Once Colin has bedded down the day shift, I'll go back in and try to find out more.'

Thoughts were bombarding Iona as Jim spoke. Bury. Might the Mauritians be linked to the same mosque?

She reached across her desk and lifted the items Wallace had helpfully left there at some point. Below the file on the cleric was the list of Mauritian nationals and their addresses. All were dotted about the Bury area. No time to start checking them, she thought, not working on my own.

She glanced at the TV mounted on the opposite wall. It was tuned into BBC News 24 – coverage was now from inside the main hall of the conference. In the foreground were rows of exhibition stands. She saw signs for trade unions alongside those for Amnesty International, Liberty and Save the Children. People were crammed in among them, most moving slowly to the main seating area beyond. All of them were at risk.

'Iona, are you still there?'

She turned from the images. 'Sorry, yes. What did you say?'

'I asked what you'll do next. Has Wallace showed his face yet?'

'No.' She pictured him up in his office on the floor above. She could still hardly believe what Jim had told her the previous night – the gleeful brutality of it. How it had then been covered up. The story had ensured that the snatches of sleep she'd got were brief and troubled. 'He's probably upstairs.'

'So what now?'

She slid one of Wallace's printouts closer. The one with details of the football team. 'Two seconds, I'm just typing something in.' She keyed the name Mauricien Exiles into Google and pressed enter. A homepage came up, a montage of players in a pale blue and claret strip. Tabs at the edge of the screen read, About Us, Join our Team, Fixtures, Results, League, Gallery. No Bhujun among the names of the squad.

'What are you up to?' Jim asked.

'Browsing a site. Hang on.'

She clicked on Gallery. More shots of football matches. The Mauritian team looked young and slimly built – unlike many of the teams of players they were up against. No sign of Vassen or his mate. A line at the base of the screen read, Last updated March 2010. The photos were well out of date.

She clicked on fixtures and the current season came up. At least they've maintained this bit, she thought, searching out the day's date from the table filling the screen. A home match versus AFC Elton. She looked at the time; kick-off was in fifty minutes. 'I'm driving up to Bury.'

'Why? What will you do there?'

'I don't know.' She thought about the mosque again. 'There's a football team made up of Mauritian ex-pats. They're playing a match later this morning. I can check them and their supporters out. You can be digging up what you can in the meantime.'

'I don't like the idea of you driving up there on your own.'

'Jim, I'll be fine. They play in a public park, it's not a risk.' She was back on Google typing in the postcode for the Jamia Masjd mosque. There it was, two minutes' walk from the town centre.

'That's all you'll do? Visit the park and then go back to the office?'

'Unless you work out where they went in Bury.'

'If I do that, I'll be driving straight up to you.'

'Jim, this isn't your shout. I don't want you to get in trouble.'

'It's my day off. Nothing to stop me deciding if I fancy wandering round Bury on a grey Sunday.'

She smiled, glad to know he was there for her. 'Call me with anything useful, yeah?'

'You've got it. And Iona, have you got rid—'

'I'm doing it right now,' she replied. 'Speak to you later.' She cut the call before reaching up and tearing the word Baby from her monitor. Then she squashed the Blu-tack figure into a lump and lobbed it into her bin. A detective a couple of desks away was silently watching. She locked eyes with him. 'Problem?'

He shook his head as he turned back to what he was doing. 'None at all.'

The drive to Bury took much less time than Iona thought. Coming off the M66 motorway at the second junction, she followed the Rochdale Road right into the town centre, passing the tram terminal on her right. Rows of bus stops were before the low building and she couldn't help looking for her two suspects among the people sheltering from the chill breeze in the Perspex shelters.

The road curved round to the far side of the town centre where larger, more modern buildings began to spring up. Bunting had been strung along the fence of a car showroom. The brightly coloured triangles swayed back and forth, the only things moving on the forecourt. Her eyes cut to the other side of the road and she spotted the brand-new police headquarters set back in the middle of what appeared to be former industrial wasteland.

As she waited for the set of lights in front of her to change, she reflected on the town. Like many others to the north of Manchester, Bury's population had been altered by large numbers of immigrants arriving from Asia.

Problems sometimes flared up – not as serious as the race riots that had ravaged many nearby towns in Yorkshire – but tensions still existed between the more established communities and the newly formed ones.

The lights glowed green and she filtered to the left, searching for signs to the recreation ground the Mauricien Exiles called home. A few minutes later, she was parking her car on a side road. The unkempt expanse of grass before her was dotted with dry leaves, blown from the cluster of trees at the far side of the park. What remained of their foliage was brown and Iona shivered involuntarily: winter would be here soon.

A couple of people were attaching nets to rusty goalposts while, out on the pitch, players warmed up. The Mauritians, in their claret and blue strip, were bunched together in their half, several footballs ping-ponging about between them. A smattering of people wrapped in coats and hats were lined up along each side. Wives, girlfriends and other people somehow connected to the team, she concluded. By the look of it, the visiting supporters had taken the left-hand touchline.

Iona went over what little training she'd completed for undertaking covert operations. Number one priority was to ensure the target remained unaware they were even being watched. And the best way to achieve that – apart from not drawing attention to yourself – was to let as few people as possible know that a surveillance operation was underway.

According to the training officer, you never knew which side a person was on. And that included officers from the local police force. She checked the photos she'd stored on her phone once again. The Bhujuns' mugshots were on it, allowing her to check likenesses while pretending to be sending a text or making a call.

That's a point, she thought, turning the handset over in her palm. Toby – the contact for the Sub-Urban Explorers – hasn't rung me back. She brought his number up again and called it. After two rings the line clicked and a recorded message said the number was temporarily unavailable. Iona frowned; has he just turned his mobile off on me? She tried again and got the same message before it even began to ring. He must have seen my number on his screen. Is he deliberately avoiding my calls? Quickly she typed him a text: Urgent message from DC Khan – call me.

A whistle sounded and she saw the match was now underway. After climbing out of her warm car, she zipped up her padded jacket and made her way round to the visiting team's touchline, reasoning that anyone connected to the Exiles would assume she was with them.

Eyes on the match, she studied the Mauritian players. Some seemed like they could be from India or Sri Lanka, some appeared to be part African-Caribbean. None were Vassen; that much was obvious. He would have stood out like that tall player England sometimes used. Crazy-legs Crane, Jim called him. There were, however, several shorter members of the team. Late twenties, early thirties, shaved heads and stubble.

She found herself studying one player who seemed to be especially competitive – using his shoulder to barge opposition players, tearing around after the ball with an intense look, swearing when anything went wrong. He was about five foot four, at the most.

Lifting her phone, she studied the image of Ranjit for a second. The player out on the pitch looked very similar. About the right age, too.

She listened to the voices, hoping to hear the name Ranjit called out. Eventually, he scored, punching the air with delight as he ran back for the restart. A thought occurred to Iona. She took out her notepad and pen then walked round the pitch. As she passed the Mauricien Exiles' substitutes, she felt their eyes on her.

'Good morning,' one said, flashing her a wide grin. 'If only our supporters were as beautiful as you.'

The player next to him cuffed him across the back of the head and they began to laugh. Blushing slightly, she approached an elderly man wearing a flat cap who seemed to be shouting the most instructions. 'Excuse me.'

He glanced down at her distractedly. 'Yes?'

She looked at the side of his face. He had a kindly air, even with his attention on the match. Like a cuddly uncle. 'I write the blog for AFC Elton. What was the name of your player who just scored?'

'Oh, that's Guillaume,' the old man answered, looking at the play. 'Widdy! Push up more, don't stand so deep!'

Damn, thought Iona, not Ranjit. She started writing the name down, no idea if she was spelling it correctly.

'That's not right,' he said, peering down at her pad. 'The team sheet is there. In my file sitting on the kit bag.'

'Ah, right, thanks.' She turned to the canvas holdall. A red file was laid across it. She crouched down and opened it. The sheet of paper in the uppermost sleeve contained a list of names. She glanced at the letterhead which read, Mauricien Exiles, Manager – Navin Ramgoolan. Coach – Pravind Dulloo.

Tracing a finger down the list of players, it took her three seconds to see no Bhujun or Ranjit featured. Flipping the file closed, she thanked the old man and returned to her spot. When the half-time whistle sounded, she used the opportunity to walk back to where her car was parked.

What next? She asked herself, sitting back in the driver's seat. But she knew the answer already. She took the *A to Z* out of her glove compartment and sought out the little symbol for a place of worship. The Jamia Masjd mosque. Barely the distance of a fingernail away.

She drove back to the set of lights by the garage and took the third exit down Bolton Street, knowing it would lead to the road which ran right past the mosque. Just a look, she said to herself. Nothing more than that.

Jim slid a chair alongside the operator. When he'd walked back into the main part of the room, he thought Colin was about to start physically shoving him towards the doors. It had taken a lot of quiet persuasion – bordering on pleading – before the supervisor had finally relented.

'Only when there's nothing else coming in, understood? If we need him for anything – even a little old lady needing help with the ticket machine in a car park – he drops your stuff to do it.'

'Absolutely,' Jim had replied. 'That's fine.'

Colin had shown him to one of the operators monitoring the outlying areas of the city. 'Howard? Can you take Sergeant Stephens here through some footage. He'll give you the day and times. This is low priority, OK? I want you to break off if needed for anything else.'

Jim sat forward in the chair. 'Right, Howard, thanks for doing this. First, can we go to the platform cameras at the tram terminal in Bury? I need to see who gets on the ones going into Manchester on the seventeenth. Can we start with the very first tram of the day?'

TWENTY-SIX

J amia Masjd mosque was on a narrow street – mainly residential properties with a few small shops. Most, including a halal butcher's, were closed for the day. She saw a convenience store had its lights on, as did a tiny newsagent's.

The mosque formed one half of a large semi-detached house that stood out from the smaller, terraced houses on each side. The front of the white building had obviously been modified – a very sturdy-looking double door was flanked either side by narrow windows, each rising to a point. The clouded glass filling the frames was engraved with Arabic calligraphy. Every window was protected by a metal grill. Positioned directly above the doors was a sign, the top of which consisted of tiny Arabic letters. The bottom read, Jamia Masjd. Iona parked further down the road from it and pretended to take a call on her mobile, eyes on the rear-view mirror.

It was hard to tell if the place was locked or not; no one seemed to be going in or out. After a few minutes, two people appeared from the rear of the building. Females, Iona realized, both wearing headscarves and loose clothing that went down to their ankles and wrists. A separate entrance for women, Iona thought, remembering Wallace's words about how the mosque permitted their presence. Talking very quietly, they walked past her car and round the corner. Iona was debating whether to take a look round the back of the building when three Asian youths, seventeen at most, emerged from the convenience store.

Leaning against the railings outside the entrance, they began to open cans of soft drinks while continuing their conversation. All were wearing jeans, trainers and casual tops. One had a zigzag pattern etched into his short black hair. Their speech was fast, accompanied by jabbing hand movements and bursts of laughter. They were barely ten feet in front of her vehicle and, Iona realized, now aware of her presence.

Time, she thought, to go. She brought her imaginary call to a close and began to pull out. They all stopped talking as she passed, one ducking low for a better look at her.

At the end of the road, she turned right and, checking to see no vehicle had trailed her from the direction of the mosque, followed the road back to the big roundabout. She took the exit leading to the police station, following the approach road to a sign that read: Police Vehicles Only.

At the rear entrance a civilian worker buzzed her through then directed her to an office further into the building, saying that's where the duty sergeant could be found.

As Iona walked along the corridor, she conjectured on how much it would be safe for her to divulge. The fact she was CTU was bound to raise the officer's eyebrows and – she had to assume – quickly become a source of conversation in the empty corridors of the newly built station.

The duty sergeant was a large man in his late thirties, with blotchy red cheeks and a sparse covering of grey hair clinging to the sides of his head. 'Morning,' she announced, pausing in the doorway with her warrant card ready. 'Front desk said you'd be here.'

He looked up, apparently surprised at the presence of someone else.

'DC Iona Khan.' She approached the table he was working at, a hand outstretched.

'Morning,' he said, shaking it after another moment's hesitation. 'Sergeant Ray Healey. Sorry – I'm used to having this place all to myself on a Sunday morning. Everyone tends to be in the canteen if we're quiet.'

'Best place to be on a Sunday morning.'

'It is. So, how can I help?'

'I'm trying to trace the whereabouts of a young male, early twenties, seen disembarking from the tram and heading into Bury at about half past two on the seventeenth.'

He sat back. 'You're a few days behind him, then.'

'Yes.'

'Is he on the system? Last known address in this area?'

'No.' She perched on the edge of the adjacent table and placed her hands in her lap. 'I'm not even sure of his name.'

'Not even . . .' He paused. 'Where did you say you're from again?'

'The Counter Terrorism Unit.'

The eyebrows went up, just as expected. 'Oh, right. Is this serious?'

She nodded and he pulled himself upright. 'Got a description for this person then?'

'Well, kind of.' She began to swing a foot back and forth then brought it to a stop, worried it was making her appear evasive. 'He's on the footage from the platform CCTV. I was wondering, how good are the cameras round the town centre? I was hoping to pick him up after he left the terminal.'

The sergeant rubbed at a corner of one eye. 'Not bad. Especially near the bus station and main precinct. A lot of pubs in that area. Gets patchy beyond there, though.'

'Does Bury Council own them?'

He nodded. 'They do. But they're very good at sharing.'

She pondered how to tackle the issue of Vassen and his companion's nationality without giving the sergeant more detail. 'What are the chances of me being able to get hold of anyone on a Sunday?'

'At the council?' He looked amused by the suggestion. 'I have a number, if you hang on.'

As he started leafing through a file on an adjacent desk. Iona looked down at the pieces of paper covering the table he'd been sitting at. Log printouts – a list of all the incidents that had been reported in during the last twelve hours. 'A lively Saturday night, then?'

He glanced over his shoulder. 'Average. I was picking out any priority crimes for the review in an hour's time.'

'What counts as priority for you in Bury at the moment?'

'Same as all over, though we're having a crackdown on burglary. Missing our target on that, we are. And racially motivated incidents, which we had yesterday evening. Some idiots in a van on the Woodhill Road shouting abuse.' He picked up the file and brought it back to the table. 'Any racial stuff we respond to immediately with a patrol car. Before the car got there, another report came in of an altercation close by involving two white males and two Asian males. So now I have to decide whether to count them as one incident.'

Iona cocked her head. 'Was anyone arrested?'

'No, they'd all cleared off pretty sharpish. White males were observed leaving the scene in a van.'

'What about the two Asians?'

'They didn't hang around either. Uniforms are still out there taking statements.'

'Off who?'

'The local resident who rang it in. Here's the number for the council, if you want it.'

Iona thought for a moment. 'Does the Woodland Road area have much of an Asian community?'

'It does. Pretty much the centre of it, as a matter of fact.' He lowered the file. 'This young male you're after. What would his ethnic background be?'

Iona pushed herself off the edge of the table and stood. 'That we're not sure about at the moment.' Feeling him scrutinize her, she hoped her tone had sounded convincing. 'I wouldn't mind having a quick word with that resident myself, though.'

'Be my guest,' he responded, handing her the log sheet. 'That's got the contact details for the officers who've been dispatched to the scene. You've also got the details for the shop owner who was threatened by the occupant of the van and the witness to the altercation – an old boy whose flat overlooks one end of the alleyway where the incident took place. Want me to have the radio room let the attending officers know you're on your way?'

'Thanks.' Iona took the sheet. 'And Sergeant Healey? We'll need to keep back the fact I'm CTU. Last thing I need is that blaring out of their handsets while they're interviewing a witness.'

'Understood. What should I say?'

'How about I'm from Community Relations? Working out of the city centre.'

'Sounds plausible. Community Relations it is.'

'In fact,' Iona added, 'if any of your colleagues ask, it would be helpful if you could say that's where I'm from.'

TWENTY-SEVEN

Iona turned into the narrow roads that bordered on Woodhill Road. Hudcar was the first street in and, sixty metres along, was a pavement sign indicating no bikes. It was positioned at the mouth of an alley cutting back towards the main road with its cluster of takeaways, grocery stores and late-night shops.

She pulled in and looked across the road. Directly opposite was a three-storey concrete-clad building with row after row of identical windows. Seventies-style architecture; probably regarded as modern-looking when built. Now bland and functional, at best.

The patrol car had managed to find a parking space on the building's forecourt. Jogging across the road, Iona assessed the sight-lines to the alley. They were good, with a streetlight helpfully positioned right where the cut-through joined the pavement of Hudcar Street. The witness would have had a decent view across.

She buzzed flat eight, home to a Mr Cooper.

'Who is it, please?' a brusque voice asked a few seconds later.

'Iona Khan – I'm from Community Relations? I believe you're talking to a couple of officers about last night's incident?'

'I am.'

Iona stared at the perforated grill. It didn't emit a buzz. 'May I come in then?'

'The more, the merrier. Please push the door.'

She gave it a shove and stepped into the lobby area. A notice board with details for Dial-a-Ride, posters for coffee mornings and advertisements for ballroom dancing classes. A sign pointing up the stairs directed her to flats seven to twenty-four. Cooper's was on the first floor and, on stepping into the short corridor, she saw a tall, elderly man standing half out of a doorway. He was holding himself very upright as he raised a hand. 'This way, Officer.'

As she got nearer, she took in the fact he was wearing a shirt and tie under his oatmeal cardigan. Grey flannel trousers with creases as neat as the ones Jim liked to press into his uniform. I bet you're ex-Forces, Iona thought, holding a hand out. 'Mr Cooper?'

He finished whatever he was saying to the people in his flat and looked her up and down with bright, intelligent eyes. 'Identification?'

Iona flinched with surprise then started reaching for her warrant card.

'I'll let you off this time.' He moved aside, face stern, though one eyebrow was wavering.

Is he joking with me? Iona wondered, lowering her hand. She gave him a tight smile as she stepped through the door.

'They let them in small nowadays – the police.'

She shot him a sideways glance but could see no mocking expression on his face.

'I remember when,' he continued, 'you had to be a strapping six-footer, at the least. Mind you, I don't think female officers were even allowed in then. Not to walk the beat, anyway.'

She turned to properly face him in the short corridor. There was definitely a mischievous gleam in his eye and she decided to risk a riposte. 'Well, things change, sir. We even have radios nowadays – not tin whistles.'

His face broke into a grin and the stiffness went from his shoulders. 'Ha! Very good, very good. A sense of humour – that will get you far in life. Now, a cup of tea?'

Relieved that she'd judged him correctly, Iona returned the smile. 'I'm fine, thank you.'

'OK. Your colleagues are in the front room, straight ahead.'

On entering, she saw two male officers squashed up on a small sofa, both balancing cups and saucers on their knees. One gave her a pained expression, as if to say, I know, I know, just tolerate him and we can be out of here soon.

'Please,' Cooper said, appearing next to her. 'You have the seat.'

She realized that, apart from the sofa, the modest room only had one armchair. 'I don't mind standing. I've been in my car most of the day.'

'Absolutely not.' Between the wall and a line of shelves stretching from floor to ceiling was a narrow gap. From it, he removed a wooden fold-up chair and opened it out. 'I keep this for when my daughter and her husband visit with my grandson.' He paused a beat. 'You might notice it's a little dusty.'

It was obvious there was no way he'd allow her the deckchair. She sat down and looked around. The comment about dust had obviously been made in jest; the entire place couldn't have been more clean and tidy. Military background, no doubt about it, she decided.

'We were running over what Mr Cooper saw last night,' the officer on the left announced. He placed his cup and saucer on the small table before him. 'It was just after eleven thirty, wasn't it, sir?'

Oh, no, Iona thought, hearing that the officer was using that special voice people reserve for addressing infants or the elderly.

'That's correct,' Cooper said, placing his hands on his knees and looking more serious. 'Shouting at first. One voice. Male. The same word. Rancid. I put my book to one side, turned my reading lamp off and looked out.'

Iona glanced at the book on the window sill beside her. *Point of Departure* by Robin Cook.

'The shout came again,' Cooper continued. 'My, I thought, the vocabulary is finally moving on from sick, which is the word I seem to hear most often. This is sick, that is sick—'

'And two Asian males appeared first,' the other officer cut in.

Cooper nodded, turning to Iona. 'Forgive me for speaking plainly, but they were of a similar colour to you. Indian, I'd say?' He arched an eyebrow as the two uniforms regarded her with uncomfortable expressions.

Casually, she hunched a shoulder. 'I'm half-Pakistani, as a matter of fact. For my forms, would Asian be best? That includes India, Pakistan, Sri Lanka, Bangladesh. Accurate enough?'

'Absolutely.'

'And what about physical descriptions? Did you get that far?'

The uniform on the left began to read. 'One was six foot or just over. Adult, early twenties, dark hair to his collar, thin build. The other was shorter, shaved head. Possibly older, athletic build.'

Interesting, Iona thought. The description fits my guys. She trod her hopes back down. 'How short, would you say?'

Cooper lifted his chin slightly. 'Five-three? And he was helping the taller one, who was limping and had a hand to his face – like he'd taken a knock. My view was obscured as they first came out – by the van the other two eventually got in to.'

Iona's eyes bounced between the pair of officers on the sofa. 'The others being the two white males?'

'Yes,' Cooper replied. 'A few minutes later, they also emerged.'

'And they got into this van?'

Cooper nodded.

'Was there anything written on it?'

The left-hand uniform gave a cough. 'A. J. Nell or Neil, Plumbing.'

'There was a telephone number, I'm sure. But I couldn't make it out,' Cooper added.

Iona shook her head. 'This is incredibly useful, don't worry.'

'The Asians proceeded right,' the uniform announced, reading from his notes. 'Continuing along the pavement towards the junction with Coniston Road, at which point they passed from Mr Cooper's sight. Then, about three minutes later, two white males, also in their twenties, made their way from the alley.'

'Those two had come off worse.' Cooper wagged a finger. 'Even though one had a baseball bat. He was using it as a kind of walking stick. The driver of the van – young man, too – had to open the back doors up. Between him and the other one – who was bleeding from the head – they got him into the vehicle. He was swearing all the time, the injured one. Stabbed, he kept saying. He stabbed me.'

The older uniform looked at Iona. 'We'll do a check on local A&E departments.'

She nodded. 'And run a check on all local plumbers, I suppose.'

'Of course.'

Iona addressed Mr Cooper. 'Sir, if we were to obtain photographic records of any of these people, do you think you could say if they were the ones you saw?'

'Who? The white males in the van?'

'Yes. And also the ones of Asian appearance.'

'I'd certainly give it a go. That street light brings out the shadows on a person's face, but I'd try.'

'Great.' Iona looked out the window. The alleyway was directly opposite, no tree branches or hedge to obscure the view. And the old boy obviously still had his marbles. She checked along the window sill but couldn't see any glasses.

'Thanks for your help, Mr Cooper,' the older of the uniforms said. 'If anything else comes up, I hope you don't mind if we call on you again.'

'Not at all,' he said, getting back to his feet.

Iona stood and held out a hand. 'Thank you, sir.'

There was a crafty look in his eye as he inclined his head. 'My pleasure . . . is it Detective Constable?'

'Yes,' she replied, slightly uneasy at his interest.

'Detective Constable Khan of Community Relations?'

'Yes.'

He gave a knowing nod as the uniforms gathered their things.

Once out of the flat, the two uniforms set off along the corridor. 'Glad to get out of there,' the younger one muttered. 'Did you see all the military books on his shelves? Thought he was going to start up about the war at any moment.'

Ignoring the comment, Iona addressed the older officer. 'Have you canvassed the surrounding properties?'

'Yes. Nothing doing.'

'Including the houses on the other side of the road, near the alley?'

He looked at her. 'Yes, Detective Constable, we did.'

'Sorry.' She gave a quick smile. 'I didn't mean to tell you how to do your job. So you'll also follow up on the plumber and check the local hospitals?'

'Where did you say you were from again?' He now sounded mildly annoyed. 'A Manchester office?'

'That's right.'

'And will you be taking responsibility for making enquiries in the Asian community round here for the other two?'

'If your boss is happy for me to do so.' Iona let them pull ahead. 'Just need to check something else with Mr Cooper. I'll catch you up back at the station.'

Cooper didn't seem surprised to see her when he opened the door.

'Mr Cooper, something just occurred to me—'

'Would you like to come in?'

'No need,' she said, double-checking the two uniforms had set off down the stairs. 'The word you heard being shouted. You thought it was rancid. Any chance it could have been a name?'

'A name? Rancid? You mean a nickname?'

'No, a name that sounded similar to rancid.'

'Well, now you say, it was more like a cry for help. A very scared cry at that.'

Shouting to his mate, Iona thought. She lowered her voice. 'Could the word you heard being called have been Ranjit?'

'Ranjit?'

She nodded and, after a moment's thought, Cooper did too. 'And you're really in, what was it you said, Community Relations?'

She tried to look surprised. 'Yes. Why?'

He bent down to bring his face closer. 'My guess is you're too sharp for Community Relations – whatever that's supposed to be.'

She gestured to the side. 'Thanks for your help. I'd better be going.'

He was still smiling as he stepped back and closed the door.

TWENTY-EIGHT

Iona crossed the road to where her car was parked. She looked at the mouth of the alley and the stretch of hedge bordering the road. Then she examined the pavement for any drops of blood or anything left behind. All the while she was able to feel Cooper's gaze upon her. Finally, she glanced back to the block of flats. He nodded at her from behind his window, unconcerned that she knew he was watching.

She nodded in return then approached the alley itself. It ran straight for about fifteen metres then jinked to the right. She walked slowly up it, eyes sweeping from left to right. Sweet wrappers, crumpled cans and broken glass seemed to be the most common elements of the litter lining its edges.

At the bend was another street lamp, the base of the pole a tangled mass of graffiti. She crouched down; a few pear-shaped droplets of something dark had hit the fence panels to the left of it. Blood. From their shape, she guessed they had flown out from a point that was about waist height. There were more spots on the ground. Some act of violence had definitely taken place here.

Looking further along the alley, she saw that it stretched for another twenty-five or so metres before joining with the next road. Woodhill, she thought. On the ground ten metres in front of her was a plain white plastic bag. It had something in it. Looking in from above, she could see a takeaway menu and two cartons inside. The lid of one had been dislodged. It was full of rice.

If it had contained a half-finished tray of chips or the remains of a kebab, she could understand. But someone had dropped an entire meal, untouched. Why?

She continued on to the main road, stepped out on to the pavement and looked either way. Houses to the left, a couple of takeaway places about fifty metres to the right. Much further along, she could see more shops, one with an awning and crates of produce out the front. The grocer's, she wondered, where the original call about a van had come from? The sign outside the takeaway place nearest to her read Al Kebabish. Back at the abandoned bag of food, she reached in and slid out the takeaway menu that had been placed alongside the order. Al Kebabish.

The man behind the counter was humming to himself as he stacked small bottles in an upright fridge. Beneath the glass counter was an impressive selection of food. Iona recognized samosas, bhajis and pakoras alongside skewers of lamb, coated in a sauce and ready to be cooked over a bed of charcoal in the corner. Filling the far wall was an enormous takeaway menu. 'Hello, there,' she said, smile at the ready.

He glanced over his shoulder. 'Hello. What can I get you?'

Heavy accent, she thought. 'Are you the owner here?'

He turned round, a suspicious look on his face. 'Why?'

'Don't worry, I'm not from environmental health or anything like that.'

'So where are you from?'

'I work in Community Relations, alongside the police.' She removed her warrant card and held it up for a moment. 'There was a report last night of a white van in this area. Its occupants were threatening people. The owner of the grocer's further along? He called us to report they'd shouted racist abuse at him. Were you working here last night?'

'I didn't hear anything.'

'OK. Did any of your customers mention a van to you? We're very keen to trace the vehicle.'

He looked sceptical. 'A bit of offensive language? Wouldn't it be better if you stopped the BNP coming here and handing out their leaflets?'

She rolled her eyes. 'I only wish we could, believe me.' She checked the doorway behind her. 'We think it was more serious than just offensive language. They might have assaulted a couple of males round the corner from here. There was some kind of disturbance.'

'Really?' Now he looked interested.

'Within minutes of the call from the grocery store. How busy were you last night?'

'Usual – mostly deliveries until ten, then a few passers-by later on.'

'Did you have anyone in here ordering food at, say, twenty past eleven?'

His eyes settled on the window behind her as he thought. 'Maybe.'

'Sir, if there was, there's a very good chance they saw this van. They may have even been approached. The victims of the assault have yet to report it, so we're just going off a call from a member of the public at this time.' She could tell he was deciding whether to say anything more. 'Sir? This is in the interests of your community. If people get away with whatever happened last night, they'll come back bolder next time.'

His fingers scratched at his sleeve and he avoided her eyes. You know something, she thought. You know who you were serving at around that time. Now you're wondering if they were the ones who were attacked.

'If they call in again, I'll get them to ring you.'

Them, Iona thought. You are talking about my guys, I'm sure. 'Sir, that's really appreciated. But what if they don't come back? They could possess vital information.'

'Listen, one of them's been popping in a bit recently. I'll mention it to him. But if he hasn't contacted you, I'm not putting your lot on to him, OK?'

Aware that exerting too much pressure would only create suspicion, Iona nodded gratefully. 'That's fine, thank you. He just needs to ring Bury Police Station. The incident has been logged.' She turned to go then looked back. 'Oh. The witness who reported the possible assault. He said one of the Asians was tall. Thin build, floppy fringe?' She let the question hang, eyes not leaving his face.

The take away owner gave a reluctant nod. 'That's him.'

Iona retraced her steps, her mind buzzing. It was Vassen and his mate, surely. Tall, thin, floppy fringe. A name called out that sounded very similar to rancid. She looked at the houses in the vicinity. They must be living within walking distance of here. Her heart thudded faster at the thought.

She came to a halt by the takeaway bag, trying to decide whether to retrieve some evidence bags from her car when her phone started to ring. 'Jim,' she said, seeing his name on the screen. 'How's it going your end?'

'Good. Where are you?'

'I called in at the cop shop in Bury. Something very interesting was on the log of overnights.'

'What?'

Unable to tell if anyone beyond the fences either side of her could hear what she was saying, Iona continued towards her car. 'I'll fill you in later. A racially aggravated incident.'

'Right . . .' Jim sounded slightly confused. 'You want my news?'

'Of course.'

'I've got them coming into town on the day in question – they boarded the nine forty from Bury and disembarked at Victoria Station twenty-four minutes later.'

'Jim, that's brilliant. I don't suppose the footage . . .'

'No clear shots, I'm afraid. Our man with the baseball cap is beginning to remind me of that one from the Pet Shop Boys. Could never see his bloody face either.'

'Pet Shop Boys?'

'The pop group? Oh, forget it. You're too young. Anyway, they leave via the exit on to Long Millgate, where the station's CCTV coverage ends. Few things, though.'

Iona was now at her car. No sign of Cooper in his window. She unlocked the vehicle, got in and shut the door. 'Go on.'

'First, the short one's carrying a rucksack on the way into town. Full of stuff, by the look of it. Second, Long Millgate – do you know where it leads?'

'Nope.'

'Deansgate. Runs right past the cathedral.'

Iona sat back. 'Vassen's interest in the fabled Deansgate tunnel. It fits.'

'There's more.'

'There is?'

'Oh, yes. The footage you obtained where they reappear outside the library just before two in the afternoon. That's four hours later. When they do, it's minus the rucksack. So that's been left somewhere. And Vassen, when he's walking along ruffling his hair? I don't reckon that's dandruff he's shaking out. I reckon it's dust.'

Iona swallowed. 'A tunnel. They've been down a tunnel.'

TWENTY-NINE

After hanging up, Iona looked across the road. She could see Cooper back in his spot, nose buried in a book.

He opened his front door with the same knowing smile. 'Detective Constable Iona Khan.'

'Hi, there. May I come in?'

'Please.'

She walked into his front room and waited for him to indicate that she could sit. 'Thank you,' she said when he pointed to the sofa.

'Would you like a drink, coffee or tea?'

She placed her carry case beside her. 'No, I'm fine, thanks.'

'So,' he stated, taking the armchair by the window. 'How did searching the alley go? I don't think those two uniformed officers more than glanced down it.'

'There had definitely been some kind of disturbance.'

'You seem to be doing an awful lot under your remit of Community Relations.' The same mischievous look was back in his eyes.

She looked away and found herself gazing at the packed bookshelves. Biographies of great leaders, politicians, studies of famous battles, a whole section on the Second World War. 'Mr Cooper, were you in the army?'

'I was.'

'For how long?'

'Longer, I suspect, than you've been alive.'

She looked back at him, searching once more for any indication he was belittling her.

'Not that I'd ever ask a lady her age,' he hastily added. 'I served for thirty-three years.'

'Thirty-three? That's . . . quite a stint. In one,' she searched for the correct term, 'bit?'

'No, several bits,' he smiled. 'I started in the regular army – as a squaddie. Then moved to the Paras then moved again.'

'You've seen a lot of the world, I bet.'

'Oh, here and there.'

She had the impression that was an enormous understatement. 'Which parts did you enjoy most?'

'Detective, one jungle is much like another. One mountain as cold as the next. Deserts are deserts, wherever you are. Sadly, I wasn't there for sightseeing trips. Often, I hardly moved out of the coffin-sized hole I'd dug.'

She glanced at the bookshelves again. Jim had often mentioned the extreme feats of endurance members of the SAS put themselves through: lying for days in one spot while gathering intelligence on a target, all bodily waste going into plastic bags. She couldn't see any books on the elite unit. 'That was after you moved on from the Paras?'

'It was. Now, I think you know the area of the army I was in. What I'm wondering is, what part of the police are you in?'

She kept eye contact. 'Counter Terrorism Unit.'

His nod was slow and measured. 'A lot of resources have been ploughed into that. A sought-after unit to be in, I imagine.'

She reached for her carry-case. 'Mr Cooper –'

'Bob.'

'Bob, I have a couple of images here. Do you think they might be the people you saw coming out of that alley?'

'I'll do my best.'

She removed the mugshots of Vassen and his companion.

'Something told me you weren't really looking for the white guys,' he said, taking the printouts and studying each one. He tapped on Vassen's face. 'Him. Not sure about the other. He was on the far side of the taller one, who obscured my view.'

She took a deep breath. 'How sure are you?'

'Sure as I can be.'

It was them, she thought. It had to be. She directed a quick look out at the mouth of the alley. They had been right there, only hours ago. 'Mr Coo— Sorry, Bob. There's a takeaway place on the next street. I think the man you identified visits it quite regularly.'

Bob's eyes lit up as he handed the printouts back. 'You need an observer? I have some experience in that particular field.'

Iona smiled, removing one of her cards as she did so. 'Then I'm sure you know the drill. If you see either of them, here's my mobile number.'

He took the card and slid it into the pages of his Robin Cook memoirs. 'My new bookmark.'

'Obviously, this is all in the strictest—'

'How aware are the officers who were here before?'

'Sorry?'

'In case they come back. I need to know what they know about you.'

'They have been told I'm from Community Relations, that's all.'

'Fine,' he replied.

She gathered her things and stood. 'Don't worry about seeing me out. And thank you, Bob. Call me, whatever time it is.'

'Understood.'

From the way he was sitting there, Iona suspected he'd already started his vigil. 'Of course, I don't expect you to pee in a carrier bag.'

'No?' He clicked his fingers in mock-frustration.

*   *   *

The drive back to Bury's police station took her past the town's library and then a large church. As its bell tolled out, Iona slowed to allow some members of the departing congregation to cross the road. The sign before it said, St Mary's Roman Catholic Church. Sunday Mass was at eleven thirty. On the front step was a figure putting on a flat cap.

She was looking away when the flat cap registered in her mind. Her eyes returned to the church entrance. The man was chatting warmly to the priest. The old guy from the side of the football pitch, she realized, watching as he reached out to clasp the vicar's hand. She moved forward once more, passing some kind of council offices, all the lights off. As she turned the corner, her mobile started to ring and she checked the screen. Wallace. Just seeing his name filled her with revulsion. 'Hello, sir,' she said, pulling over.

'Where are you, Detective?'

'Up in Bury, sir.'

'You are?' He sounded surprised. 'Doing what?'

'Looking into the Mauritian community, as you asked. I've been observing a football match involving that team whose details you gave me.'

'Anything interesting?'

'No sign of our pair from outside the library.'

'How about the mosque? I need intelligence on that place. Have you given it more thought?'

'Been there, sir. Only for a quick drive past. It seemed pretty quiet.'

If he was pleased, it didn't show in his voice. 'And now you are . . .?'

'Heading back to Bury Police Station to liaise with officers there. Another thing; there was a racially aggravated incident last night I'd like to look into.'

'When will you be back?'

'Mid afternoon, hopefully?'

'Update me when you get in, Detective.'

'Sir.' She dropped the phone and wiped her fingers on the side of the seat.

Back at the station, she found the duty sergeant just coming out of his review meeting, a sheaf of papers in his hand. Motioning to her, he led the way back to the room he'd been in earlier. 'Any luck?'

'Some,' Iona replied, stepping inside. 'Can you arrange for a scene-of-crime unit to drive out to the alley? There's an abandoned takeaway and some blood spatter about halfway along it. It wasn't right for a Community Relations officer to start collecting evidence.'

'Didn't my officers check that area?'

'Didn't seem so,' Iona mumbled, aware she'd just shown them up. 'Weren't they due to follow up on the white van?'

He twisted round and retrieved a piece of paper from the table behind him. 'A. J. Neill, plumber. There was a website with contact details.'

'Have they tried ringing?'

'No – I said to leave it with me for the moment. Sent them to deal with a couple of burglaries out in Freetown.'

'Thanks, Sergeant. Mind if I make the call?'

'That's what I thought you'd want to do.'

THIRTY

Iona listened to the person's mobile phone ring. If you owned a plumbing business, she reasoned, you'd have your phone switched on at weekends, surely? Burst pipes, broken washing machines, that kind of thing. Just when she thought it was about to go to answerphone, the call was picked up.

'Adrian here.'

The man sounded a lot older than Bob Cooper had made out. 'A. J. Neill, plumbers?'

'That's me. What's the problem?'

'I'm with the Greater Manchester Police.'

'Police? This isn't a call about plumbing?'

'No. I'm calling about an incident last night. In Bury.'

'I'm not sure I follow you – I'm up in Cumbria. Is this to do with my house? Have I been burgled?'

It's not him, Iona thought. He wasn't driving the van. 'There's no need for concern, sir. Do you own a work van?'

'Yes.'

'Is it with you at the moment?'

'No, Lee has it. Don't say he's crashed it, is that it? He's written the thing off?'

'No, there's no cause for concern, sir. There was a road traffic accident last night at a junction in Bury. Your van wasn't involved, but CCTV from the scene picked up the vehicle going past. We believe the driver may have witnessed the collision.'

'Lee?'

'Is that an employee of yours? Does he have the keys for it?'

'Yeah, Lee Madsen. If I'm away, I leave it with him in case of any call outs. You want his number?'

'Yes, please.'

'So . . . there's no problem? I mean, no one's died?'

'No, everyone's fine. We're trying to find out who was at fault, that's all.'

'Well, that's a relief. OK, I have his number here. Shall I read it out?'

'Thanks. And if you have an address for him, that would be great, too.'

A check on the PNC showed Iona that Lee Madsen, twenty-two years old, had three previous convictions. One for shoplifting and two for burglary. Served eight weeks in a young offenders' institute back in 2006. Kept himself clean, since then. He'll also have, Iona reflected, experience dealing with the police.

Minutes later, she was standing in front of a semi-detached house, regarding the two buzzers outside the front door. She was familiar with the arrangement. The front door would lead into a communal hall. There'd be two doors beyond – one giving access to the flat on the ground floor, one giving access to the flat on the first floor. The fact Madsen's buzzer was for the first floor was good, she decided. Assuming she could get him downstairs to answer her call, there would be no need to enter a property on her own that could well contain three violent males.

She took another look at the van parked on the other side of the road. It appeared like it was fresh from a car wash and she wondered if the inside had been cleaned just as meticulously.

She lifted the flap to the letterbox and peeped through. Stairs in front, no sound of a TV or radio drifting down. She pressed the button and listened as an angry buzz rang out.

Straightening back up, she waited. No response. She pressed again, following it with a quick succession of bangs with the heel of her hand. The skin was still tingling when she heard footsteps coming down the stairs.

'Who is it?' a voice asked from the other side of the door.

'Police. Open up, please.'

It opened a fraction and a young man with messy hair looked out to see a warrant card inches from his face.

'Open it properly, would you?'

Eyes that were still puffy from sleep momentarily tried to focus. He then checked over her shoulder and looked back at her with a frown. 'What's this about?'

'You know what it's about, Lee. Open the door.'

He delayed for a split second longer, then swung it back. Iona put her warrant card away, taking in his bare feet, tracksuit bottoms and baggy T-shirt as she did so. He was about six feet tall. The fact he was also two steps above her gave him a massive height advantage. Worse than that, his crotch was not far from the level of her face. 'Who's upstairs, Lee?'

'You what?'

'Who else is in your flat?'

He shook his head. 'No one. Why?'

'You lying to me, Lee?'

'No, it's just me,' he said quietly.

'Take a seat on the stairs behind you. I think we can get this sorted here.'

He rubbed at his sternum through his T-shirt. 'You what?'

'Sit on the stairs. It's there or the station. You decide.'

He backed away, reaching behind him with one hand and lowering himself slowly on to the third step up. 'Don't know what you're on about.'

Iona caught his look of defeat, rapidly getting the impression he was no ring leader in what had occurred the previous night. She stepped into the hall, careful to keep the door open. 'Shortly after eleven thirty last night, your works van was observed waiting on Hudcar Street. Were you the driver? Your boss said the keys are entrusted to you when he's up in Cumbria.'

He hung his head and started picking at the stubble on the back of his neck, playing for time.

Aware the person living in the ground-floor flat could be listening, she whispered, 'At the moment, he believes you might have been witness to an RTA at a junction somewhere in Bury. Answer my questions, he carries on believing that and you keep your job. Muck me around, Lee, and – given your previous convictions – losing your wage will be the least of your worries. Were you driving that vehicle?'

He raised his head and she could see he was trying to appraise the situation. That's right, Iona thought. I've just offered you a deal. 'Lee, if I was here just to haul you in, it would be with a couple of uniforms and a patrol car. I'm on my own.' She sensed the time was right to dangle him his get out. 'Now, I reckon you were dragged into driving for the other two. My witness says you played no part in the incident in that cut-through. I doubt you even wanted to be part of their plan.'

He dragged a hand down the side of his face, little finger catching on his bottom lip, peeling it down to reveal his lower teeth for a split second. 'Shit.'

'Names, Lee. Who were they?'

'I'm not sure.'

She got out her mobile. 'I don't have time to mess about. Do I call your boss first or my colleagues back at the station?'

Lee sagged sideways against the wall. 'I don't know who the headcase was, all right? Gary, that's what Martin called him.'

'Who's Martin?'

'I know him from when I was inside. He's not a mate – he just turns up every now and again. Usually trying to tap me for booze or whatever.'

'Where can I find him?'

'I don't know. He dosses about, no regular place.'

'Have you got a surname for him?'

'Rushton.'

Iona jotted it down. A check on the PNC would show up if he really was NFA. 'What about the other one?'

'Like I said, he was called Gary. Geordie accent, just out. Said he was inside for robbing a shop.'

'Out from where, Strangeways?'

Lee stayed slumped against the wall. 'Somewhere Newcastle way, for all I know. Martin just turned up with him. They wanted a ride. I didn't think they were really going to . . .'

'To what?'

'You know, go looking for Arabs or whatever.'

'That's what it was? An unprovoked attack? The first two poor sods you could find?'

'They weren't poor sods,' Lee said under his breath.

Iona let the comment pass. 'Where did you see them, the two men who were attacked?'

'On Woodhill Road. One was carrying a takeout. When they turned down the alley, Gary said to stop the van. He went after them, Martin followed. I didn't want to, I swear. Gary said to wait on the next street, where the alley came out.'

'Who's was the baseball bat?'

Lee picked at the skirting board. 'Mine.'

'What happened in the alley?'

'They didn't really say . . .'

'Something happened. Half the neighbours heard it going off. Who was it you had to help back into the van?'

He looked at her. 'The little one – has he said about stabbing Gary? I bet he left that bit out, didn't he?'

Iona kept her expression blank. 'Gary was stabbed?'

'Yeah – the little one with the shaved head did it.' He hauled himself up into a sitting position. 'He didn't mention that to you, did he? Vicious little fuck – you want to arrest him.'

He thinks the two people they attacked have made a report, Iona thought. She studied her notebook. 'Where did the knife come from?'

'He was carrying it – the shorter one. Don't let them act the poor little Pakis because that's bollocks.'

'You know the knife belonged to the shorter one with the shaved head?'

'That's what Martin said. The little one ran off to start, left the lanky one behind. Then he reappears to properly fuck Martin and Gary up. That Gary, he's got muscles jumping off him. The one with the knife smashed him, Martin said. Smashed both of them.'

'The lanky one and the shorter one; could you identify them if I were to show you a photograph?'

Lee's eyes shifted suspiciously. 'What? You going to charge them?'

Iona tilted her head, hinting it may be a possibility. 'Could you identify them?'

'The taller one, probably. The short one was on the other side of him as they went past. Didn't see him.'

'What about when you first saw them – on Woodhill Road, before they entered the alley?'

He shook his head. 'We were behind them. Only saw their backs.'

Iona wanted to stamp a foot in frustration. Is no one able to get a good look at the companion's face? 'What about Martin and Gary?'

'Not sure. They were closer, for sure. Had to have been if he stabbed Gary in the arse cheeks.'

Iona floated a glance to the top of the stairs. 'Where are they now?'

He shrugged again. 'Not a Scooby-Doo.'

'What do you mean?'

'I dropped them off on the other side of town. Fucking glad to get rid and all.'

'Didn't they need treatment at a hospital?'

'Gary wasn't going to A and E. Not for a stab in the arse.'

'So you dropped them off where?'

'On the Manchester Road, near Fishpool.'

'You don't know where they went?'

'No.'

She held eye contact until he looked down.

'Believe what you want,' he said. 'But that's what happened.'

Iona cursed to herself. The pair would be lying low, that's if they were still in the area. Two more people who could potentially identify Ranjit Bhujun really was in the country – and both wanting to avoid the police. Damn it! She closed her notebook. 'Keep your phone on, Lee.'

He raised his eyebrows. 'Is that it?'

'For the moment, it is.' She stepped back outside and pulled his front door shut.

THIRTY-ONE

Speeding round the M60 on the way back to Orion House, Iona found herself switching to Radio 5 Live. She glanced at herself in the rear-view mirror. Why are you doing that? You never listen to this station. A studio discussion was underway, several commentators dissecting the essence of the latest speech made at the conference. Are you, she wondered, expecting the programme to be suddenly interrupted? A voice to announce that, due to unknown developments in the city centre, coverage is suspended?

The panel concluded their analysis and the presenter began to talk about upcoming highlights – tomorrow's being the most talked-about. Tony Blair, Gordon Brown and – according to unconfirmed reports, the new Labour leader himself, Daniel Tevland – all on stage together. To Iona, the announcement seemed more like a portent. She sped up, anxious to be back at her desk.

Up in the main office, the atmosphere was noticeably tenser, even with half the desks empty. Euan had told her it was always like this once a major operation got underway – everyone praying that, if anything happened, it wasn't while they were on shift. Things wouldn't relax until the event was officially over.

She approached her desk with a mounting sense of discomfort. There was the yellow Post-it note stuck to her screen. Abruptly, she found Wallace's intrusive, yet impersonal, way of communicating annoying.

Why can't he leave a voicemail or an email like anyone else? Why this ridiculous little system of paper notes? Part of her suspected the answer; it got him out of his office on the floor above, allowing him to prowl around, monitoring those below him.

Call by when you get in. P.

She wanted to scrunch the square of paper up, throw it in her bin and claim, when asked, that it must have detached itself and drifted to the floor. Still, she consoled herself, at least the clipping of Baby wasn't back. Turning on her heel, she set off for the stairs.

'Enter.'

She pushed open the door and stepped into his office. 'Just got back, sir.'

'Close the door, Detective.'

After doing as he asked, she turned to see him gesturing at the chair beyond his desk. What Jim had revealed to her the previous night came flooding back and she couldn't look at him as she crossed the room.

'So, take me through the delights of Bury on a Sunday morning.' He leaned back.

'Pretty quiet to be honest, sir.'

'Figures. What was the score?'

'Sir?'

'The football match. Who won?'

'Oh, I crept away at half time. Once I knew neither Bhujun was there.'

'Anyone score while you were there?'

'The Mauritian team got one.'

He looked disappointed. 'And the mosque?'

'Well, as I said, I only parked near it for a few minutes. I did observe two women leaving it via an entrance at the back. I think you're right that they have separate doors for males and females.'

'Probably.' He neatened a stack of papers, glancing at her from the corner of his eye. 'It could be very easy getting a visual confirmation if this cleric is in there.'

'The women I saw, they were wearing traditional dress. Their heads were covered.'

'Yes, you'd need to go togged-up. A hijab and long-sleeved dress would do. You wouldn't need to be peering out from one of those letterbox numbers some of them wear. Not unless you wanted to.' His lips twitched with a small smile. 'What I'm getting at, Detective, is you need to start approaching this more under your own initiative.'

'You're saying I should go in there alone and without back-up? Surely there are protocols—'

'There you go again, Detective. If you want your hand holding, you should have stayed in uniform. We don't mollycoddle our officers here, whoever they are.'

Whoever they are? Iona wasn't sure what he meant. That I'm female? That I'm mixed race? She looked questioningly at him but he was busy examining a sheet on his desk once again. The silence started to drag. 'Meaning what, sir?'

'Pardon?'

'You said, whoever they are. Do you think I expect to be treated differently? And if so, why?'

He was smiling again. 'I didn't say that.'

'You said . . . you implied that I was –'

'Do you expect to be treated differently, Detective?'

'Not at all.'

'Good, because that's not how things work here. The officers who get ahead here – in my team – they're not shy about stepping up to be counted. They don't need any encouragement.'

It was like he was speaking in riddles, she thought. Deliberately using vague language. Deciding to change tack, she said, 'On the day Vassen Bhujun and his accomplice were seen outside the Central Library, they showed up on CCTV footage at the tram terminal in Bury.'

He looked up sharply. 'Really?'

'On leaving the library, they caught a tram there.'

'To Bury?'

'Yes.'

He appeared to be surprised by the information. 'That's interesting.' Crossing his legs, he picked at the stitching of his shoe. 'All the more reason we get an assessment of what's going on in that mosque.'

'I've also learned that – when they caught the tram into Manchester in the morning, they were carrying a rucksack.'

'How did you discover that?'

'A contact in the control room,' she replied. 'He went through the morning footage for me.'

If Wallace was impressed at her show of initiative, it didn't show. 'Facial on this accomplice?'

Iona shook her head. 'My point is this: that's a four-hour gap. And when they show up outside the library, the rucksack is gone and Vassen is shaking his hair like he's getting dust out of it.' She looked at her boss. 'What if they've been in a tunnel during that time?'

Wallace rolled his eyes. 'Hang on. Vassen's shaking his hair, so they've been in a tunnel? What about he's arranging it after having been in the shower at his gym? Or he's been having it oiled or lacquered or whatever his type do? You're jumping to conclusions again, Detective.'

'There was an incident among the overnights in Bury. A violent altercation between two white males and two Asian males. All of them fled the scene. The description of the two Asian males fits our men. A witness heard a name very similar to Ranjit being called out.'

'Very similar to?'

'Yes.'

'But not exact?'

'Well, he was in his flat. It was through the glass—'

'Detective Khan? Admirable work, but the threats currently sat here on my desk are real, they're credible and they apply right now. Let me mention a few.' He placed a forefinger on one of the intelligence reports. 'The threat from Irish-related extremism is currently high, due to recent phone intercepts between three members of the Continuity IRA. We've got a few domestic single-issue groups causing concern.

Plane Stupid, according to a well-placed source within the group, are intending to obstruct ministers at the main entrance with some kind of stunt. Combat Eighteen are planning to gather in Albert Square tomorrow, no cameras there, so we don't expect them to stay in that location. Something just came in about Father's For Justice – one particular individual who's just gone off the radar. Those are our home-grown extremists. The threat from international terrorism is moderate; want the details?'

She opened her mouth but he spoke over her.

'Now, I've let you roam around looking for these two men, but I still say your focus should be—'

'Sir, if the witness I've found is correct, they're likely to be living within a stone's throw of last night's incident. They were carrying a takeaway curry when these two white—'

'If I may finish?'

'Sir.'

Wallace interlinked his fingers as he leaned forward. He started to speak slowly, clearly enunciating each word. 'This cleric; you might be of the opinion he doesn't represent much of a threat to the conference. Perhaps it all seems a little tedious to you. But I'd like to know what the likelihood is of him showing his ugly face in the city centre. If you are prepared – in principle – to go in, I need to know. We can work out the details at that point.'

She thought about Jim's comment: how Wallace liked to test the allegiance and loyalty of those below him – test it through perverse acts like having a child beaten to death. 'I . . . need to think about it. It seems to me we're so close to Vassen—'

'Go.' He waved impatiently at the door. 'There are a load of vehicle registrations we need to manually check against scans from the M60's ANPR cameras. I'll have them sent to your desk.'

She was reaching for the door when he spoke again. 'You need to decide what you are, Detective Khan. There can be no in between.'

There it was again, she thought. Vague assertions. Faint insinuations. It's like he thinks me visiting a mosque to report on those inside will somehow prove I'm . . . what? Worthy of his trust? 'I don't follow you, sir.'

'Think about it. You played hockey at school. Scored a few goals, I gather. You've been part of a team. It's the same thing here. We're a team. We work for each other. Together. As one. That's how we win. People who aren't committed to our cause end up on the substitutes' bench. Now shut the door on your way out.'

'I'll do it.'

He glanced up. 'What?'

'I said, I'll do it. I'll visit the mosque.'

His eyes narrowed. 'You're prepared to go in it?'

'I'll do it.'

'Wearing the appropriate attire?'

'Yes.'

He looked steadily at her. 'Good . . . that's good.' Lifting a hand, he glanced at his watch. 'The conference is pretty much over for the day. Tomorrow is when a lot of the big guns are on stage. How about you pay the place a visit first thing in the morning? See what the activity levels are at that point?'

'OK.'

He sat back and gave her the faintest of smiles. 'We'll need to sort you out some robes, then.'

As she left his office, Iona had to suck in air. Her hands were trembling as she walked unsteadily towards the stairs.

THIRTY-TWO

'I know what he is now. A bully. One who uses words, but that's what he is.'

Jim's face was set tight as he filled his wine glass. 'Sure you don't want any?'

She shook her head, wondering to herself how much he was now getting through. You never used to drink on a Sunday night, she thought. You were puking your guts up in the kitchen yesterday evening.

'He's not even a subtle one,' Jim replied, carefully putting the bottle down. 'Not out in Iraq, anyway. He'd slap and kick people out there. Would do here, if he could get away with it.'

Iona shook her head. 'How does someone like him get into a position of such power?'

Jim snorted. 'Because he does a job, Iona. He gets good results and no one's prepared to complain about him. In fact, I hear most of his team rate him highly.' He took a sip. 'Besides, you're assuming everyone who gets senior roles in the police are intelligent, balanced and reasonable individuals. Believe me, they are not.'

'Should I be the one?'

He gave her a questioning look.

'Who makes a complaint? Perhaps if I did, others may –'

'No. He's too clever, Iona. You'll come out worse.'

'But I can't . . .' She closed her eyes. 'I dread going into work. He . . . he's able to make me feel so small. And I hate that. I hate myself for allowing him to do that.'

Jim gazed at her with a pained expression. 'Don't stress about it. He won't send you into that mosque.'

'He had the clothing guys dig me out a hijab and proper dress.'

'He'll think up a bullshit excuse and call you back as you're about to go in. Mind games, Iona. That's what this is.'

'You reckon?'

'Yeah, it's what he does.'

Her eyes were still closed as a shiver went through her. He reached out a hand and was about to brush a strand of hair back from her face when she sat forward. His hand recoiled and he scratched at his ear.

Head down, she studied the laptop on the table. The CCTV footage was frozen on Vassen in the act of shaking out his hair. 'I agree – it's dust. The rucksack could have contained overalls – something to keep their clothes clean while they were below ground.'

'Which leaves us trying to figure out where.' From the table, he picked up a tourist street map of the city centre and unfolded it across his knees. 'They set off down Long Millgate. That leads into Fennel Street, which passes between the cathedral and Chetham's School of Music before joining Deansgate.'

'And we know there are loads of tunnels running out from beneath the cathedral.'

'Plus, you mentioned the one that's supposed to stretch the entire length of Deansgate itself. Though I really find that hard to believe.'

'Well,' Iona sat back, 'the bloke in the visitor centre in the Great Northern looked like he thought it existed.'

Jim was tracing his finger down the long, straight road. 'Which still doesn't get us anywhere near the convention centre itself. The thing is, what? A hundred metres away from the road?'

'What if they're digging their own tunnel?'

'A hundred metres long? That requires some serious engineering, surely.'

'The Sub-Urban Explorers said Manchester is built on a layer of sandstone, which is very easy to scoop out. It's why there are so many tunnels in the first place.'

'Talking of which, weren't they meant to be getting back to you?'

Iona sighed. 'The contact is avoiding my calls. Has been all day.'

'What about that constable with the keys? He mentioned a secret council map to you, didn't he? Something with the tunnels marked out on?'

'Yes – but I'm not convinced even that shows where they all are. The SUE guys alluded to ones that the council are completely unaware of.'

'So we need to get hold of them again. You have a mobile number for this contact, right?'

'And a Christian name. Toby. That's it.'

He rolled his eyes in response. 'Shit.'

'There's the owner of the takeaway place on Woodhill Road who served Vassen and his mate. He saw their faces.'

'But you can't lean on him to make an identity without revealing Vassen and his mate are who you're really interested in.'

'Which we can't afford to do.'

'And this pair from the alleyway –'

'One is no fixed abode. And the other one is a Geordie called Gary, who claimed to have been inside for some kind of robbery. It's a dead end.'

Jim sipped at his drink, moving his lips in and out before swallowing. 'I could try trawling council CCTV from around Bury. You never know, I might get lucky.'

'What are the chances, Jim? Really?'

He gave her a look. 'You're right. Waste of time. If I had a week to do it in, maybe . . .'

Iona took another file out of her carry case. It contained the printouts on Reginald Appleton, the murdered Law Lord. 'He's linked, somehow. Has to be. I don't believe Ranjit killed him for his cash. He may have needed the money to get over here, but something else is involved.'

'MI6 were happy to sign it off as a burglary.'

'Yes, but that was before all this stuff came to light.' She swept a hand at her files.

Jim rubbed the tips of his fingers across his forehead, saying nothing.

She glanced to her side. 'What?'

'Wallace ran the new information past them. And there's been no come back.'

'Meaning what?'

He let his hand drop. 'As things stand, they obviously don't believe this adds up to much. Nothing worth a response from them, anyway.'

She turned to look at him properly. 'Is that what you think as well?'

'No – I didn't say that. But what have we got? A foreign student who's outstayed his visa. There are legions of them.'

'And a graduate in chemical engineering.'

'OK, hundreds then.'

'With an interest in Manchester's tunnels.'

'All of which – in the vicinity of the conference site – have been checked and sealed. What else have we got? Possible sightings of that person with another person suspected of murdering an ex-Law Lord – over in Mauritius. It's not enough, Iona. Can you see that?'

She lifted her chin and stared up at the ceiling. 'I know . . . I know . . . Hidden Shadow, damn him. He's the only person who can confirm if it was really Ranjit outside the library.'

Jim was nodding. 'You're right. Get a positive ID on Ranjit, confirmation he's here in Manchester, and the whole thing changes. Wallace will have to take it seriously.'

She straightened her back, letting out a yawn as she did so. A thought caused her mouth to suddenly shut. 'Blair and Brown are on stage tomorrow. If you're talking terrorist targets, they must be the best on offer for the day.'

'What time are they on?'

'Late morning. Eleven, I think.' She felt her eyes being dragged back to the still of Vassen outside the library. Would it be the next day when they tried something?

Jim let out a short and bitter laugh. 'A big part of me wouldn't mind if their plan succeeded.'

She looked at him, horror-struck.

'If it was only those two who were in the firing line,' he hastily added. 'Blair took us into Iraq, remember? All that bullshit about

WMD. Brown kept the occupation going. So many people died as a result.'

'And so many people will die if the Bhujuns carry out an attack. I've seen the centre, Jim. It's not just politicians in there. There are thousands of people – charity workers, non-government organizations, kids! I saw a bunch of kids out the front, leafleting for some cause or other. And how many of our colleagues are there as part of Operation Protector? I can't believe you just said that.'

'You're right, sorry.' Jim drained his wine and put the empty glass on the table. 'We spoof it.'

'Spoof what?'

'This Toby character. You've been ringing him all day?'

She nodded.

'And his phone has been on?'

'Yes – it just gets diverted to answerphone.'

'Which means that – with the phone company's cooperation – you can triangulate the location of his mobile. It's a Sunday – chances are he's been at home at least some of the day.'

Iona looked confused. 'That thought had occurred. But the amount of paperwork to access that kind of information. Wallace would never sign if off, anyway.'

'Toby doesn't know that. You're CTU. Ring him again. Use the threat of anti-terror laws to put the shits up him. He'll call you back quick enough.'

She picked nervously at the corner of the laptop's keyboard. 'I'm not sure . . .'

'Iona, he'll fall for it. Make up something about how you'll be able to get the co-ordinates of his phone by midnight. If he doesn't call you –'

'I'm not sure about using the threat of the anti-terror law is what I meant.'

'Why? I don't understand.'

'I made a promise, Jim. I said that what they told me about Vassen and the tunnels was in confidence and it wouldn't be used against them.'

'So you break your promise. Tough.'

'And confirm all their fears.'

'What bloody fears?'

'That we represent some fascist surveillance state, that we lie, that we can never be trusted . . .'

'Iona, what are you on about? You just said: if they are planning an attack, God-knows-how-many people's lives are at risk. The guy isn't returning your calls. The nice and soft approach ain't working.'

She continued to pick at the plastic casing.

'I'll call him, if you want,' Jim announced. 'Doesn't bother me.'

'No,' she announced quietly. 'It has to be me.' Resignedly, she reached for her mobile just as it started to ring. Seeing the name on the screen caused her head to rock back with surprise. 'DC Khan, here.'

'Detective, it's Superintendent Harish Veerapan, from Mauritius.'

She could hear the weariness in his voice. 'Superin—'

'I hope you don't mind me calling; I realize it's late evening in Britain.'

'Not at all – what time is it over there?'

'One forty-three in the morning. I'm ringing because I have just found some very significant new information. It concerns the murder of Reginald Appleton.'

THIRTY-THREE

Iona's eyes widened. 'Significant new information about Appleton's murder?'

'Yes. There's a link . . . I'm still trying to work it out.'

She gestured at Jim, who quickly passed her the pen lying at the end of the table. 'Harish, can I put you on speakerphone? I'm with a colleague here, I get the feeling we'll need to note this down.'

'That's fine. I've been thinking about the case – your suspicions that Ranjit Bhujun is now in England. I don't suppose you've found him?'

'Not yet, but I think we're close.'

'I had another look at the items recovered from Mr Appleton's study, considering things from the angle that – maybe – it wasn't a burglary.'

Iona was now sitting on the edge of the sofa. 'And?'

'Have you heard of an outfit in London called Slattinger-Dell?'

She immediately started to write it down. 'No.'

'According to a very understated website, they're a brand

consultancy that also specialize in promoting their clients' interests within parliament.'

'Lobbyists,' Iona muttered.

'Sorry?' Harish said.

'Lobbyists,' Iona stated more strongly. 'People who try and sway government policy.'

'Well, they certainly appear to be capable of doing that.'

'Why?'

'After Daniel Tevland wrestled power from the previous leader, he appointed Slattinger-Dell to revamp the Labour Party's image; to present it as a viable government-in-waiting.'

Iona thought of the flurry of photo shoots Tevland had been in since his election. It had all been very slick. 'So how does this connect to Ranjit Bhujun?'

'Ah, that's the interesting bit, Detective. Are you ready?'

'All ears.'

'Slattinger-Dell is jointly owned by a man called Tristram Dell.'

'Sorry, what was the Christian name?'

'Tristram. My pronunciation may be out.'

'No, it's fine,' Iona frowned. It seemed faintly familiar.

'He was a senior civil servant in the Foreign Office for many, many years before retiring to establish Slattinger-Dell. The contacts he made have obviously served him well.'

'Probably, it seems to be how these things work.'

'Prior to joining the civil service, he was at Oxford University –'

Iona's shoulders flinched as the connection suddenly came together. 'He studied with Reginald Appleton. There's . . . there's something to do with their families . . . hang on.' She reached for Appleton's file once more.

'Appleton's daughter, Lucinda, married Dell's son, Nicholas,' Harish announced.

'That was it.' Iona got on to her knees and started spreading the printouts from Appleton's file across the floor.

'Now,' Harish continued. 'Among the items from Appleton's study was a letter from Dell. In it, and I quote here, "The project I outlined in my last email is progressing well – hopeful of continuing the party's rehabilitation at the coming conference. Essential we get the old guard to unite behind Daniel if he is to truly take the party forward as its new leader".'

Iona looked up at Jim.

Harish's voice carried on from the mobile propped up on the coffee table. 'The old guard. What do you think he means by the old guard?'

'Not what,' Jim said. 'Who.'

'Sorry?'

'Harish,' Iona cut in, 'that was my colleague, Jim, speaking.'

'Hello, Harish,' said Jim in a slightly overloud voice. 'The old guard – Labour's previous leadership. Once known as New Labour.'

'Ah,' Harish said. 'What I thought. Blair and Brown – those two.'

Iona was staring at Jim. She didn't need to say the two ex-Prime Ministers were due on stage the next day, possibly alongside Tevland himself. 'What else was in the letter?'

'That was it. So I went to Appleton's residence and spent some time trying to access his emails. The one he referred to in that letter is now on the screen in front of me.'

'You're there now, in Appleton's villa?' Iona asked.

'Much of it is irrelevant, but there is one part worth hearing. I quote, "Regarding the project, have now held discreet meetings with several key figures. Overall, it's very encouraging. Negotiations taking place to secure an audience with A.B. Will write to you properly as I can't stand communicating via email – but expect some headlines at the conference in September! Hope to make it over before Christmas. Yours as ever, Tristram".'

Iona was looking at Jim as she spoke. 'He said, "write to you properly". That means there's another letter.'

'My impression also,' Harish replied.

Jim nodded. 'Have you been able to find anything, Harish?'

'No. There are serious consequences, I think, if Ranjit was able to access this information.'

'Is the computer password-protected?' Iona asked.

'Yes – but it was only the daughter's name and date of birth. Besides, Appleton may have had it forced out of him by Ranjit.'

Jim puffed his cheeks out. 'Shit.'

Iona sat back on her heels. 'How would Ranjit know that Reginald Appleton and Tristram Dell were friends?'

'Easily,' Harish replied. 'I've looked into how often Tristram Dell has visited Mauritius. Seven times since Appleton bought his retirement home here. Ranjit could have contacts anywhere – taxi drivers, luggage handlers at the airport, the gardener at this place; often Creoles carry out these kinds of jobs.'

'That's what he is?' Iona asked, sitting back on the sofa. 'A Creole?'
'Yes.'

'And what exactly is that?' Jim asked.

'Mauritius is a mixing-pot of people and religions,' Harish responded. 'Most of us can trace our ancestry back to present-day India and Pakistan. So we are mostly Hindu or Muslim. But there are also many Buddhists, originally from China. And the Creoles were first brought here from Africa as slaves.'

'And they're the ones in the lowest-paid jobs?' asked Iona.

'That is correct. I am not going to try and justify why, it is merely the reality.'

Iona toyed with the pen. 'Which religion would you say most Creoles are?'

'Overwhelmingly Christian. Roman Catholic, to be precise. Some have stuck to their original beliefs, Voodoo stuff. Some are nothing at all.'

'Are you aware of any extreme religious views there, Harish?'

'You mean are we harbouring al-Qaeda plotters?'

She could hear his smile.

'Detective, there has never been any type of Muslim extremism unearthed here. Now, I'll search the evidence bags back at my office for this other letter Dell refers to. The one which goes into more detail about what's being planned for the conference. But I need to sleep at some point. My eyes can hardly focus; I've been staring at this screen so long.'

Iona remembered how late it was in Mauritius. 'You must be exhausted.'

'I am.'

'Get some rest and call me after.'

'Very well. Good night to you.'

The line went dead and Iona turned to Jim. 'This . . . changes things.'

Jim was gazing into his glass. 'You could say that.'

'I'm going to have to bring Wallace up to speed,' she said apprehensively.

'When?'

She glanced at her watch. Just after ten. She suppressed a sudden yawn, realizing she'd been on the go all day – and that was after just a few hours sleep on the sofa the previous night. 'Now, I suppose. He's probably still in the office.'

Jim's eyes stayed on his drink. 'You sure?'

'He was there when I left. I don't think he was going anywhere for a while.'

'No, I mean are you sure about letting him know about these developments now?'

'Surely I have to.'

'I'd go to see him first thing in the morning.'

Iona looked surprised. 'How come?'

'Because that gives Harish a chance to get back to you about this other letter. Plus, you could try and contact this Tristram Dell beforehand, too. Get some solid answers out of him, assuming he's prepared to talk. I doubt he'll like the fact you know all about his big project.'

Iona looked unconvinced. 'You sure I shouldn't ring Wallace now?'

'Iona, nothing's solid at this point. It's just stuff we suspect. Besides, lift your hand a second.'

She shot him a quizzical glance and then slowly raised her hand.

'See? Your fingers are trembling. You need to break off from this. Like you just said to Harish, get some rest.'

She tucked her hand back under her armpit, knees pressed together. 'You know what? I could be dropped in the middle of an ocean and still not feel as out of my depth as I do now.'

'Hey, you're doing brilliantly. Better than I'd be doing in your position. But you can't keep going non-stop. That's when mistakes get made. Grab some sleep, even just a couple of hours.'

She took a huge breath in. 'You're right.' Getting down on one knee, she began to gather her things together.

As she did so, Jim stared at the back of her head, thoughts clouding his eyes. One of his fingers began to bounce rapidly up and down on the base of his wine glass.

'Are you on shift tomorrow?' she asked.

'Not until noon.'

'Lucky you.' She climbed laboriously to her feet. 'Jim? Thanks for . . . I don't know: everything.'

His smile was tinged with sadness as he also stood. 'Iona, that message I left on your answerphone. It might have been a bit drunken, but I meant what I said – I will always be there for you.'

She nodded once. 'Thank you.'

They looked at each other for a long second and then she turned for the door. 'OK to call you in the morning?'

'Whenever you like.' He followed her out into the corridor and watched as she opened the front door.

She paused on his front step, cold air flowing into the hallway. 'You'll be OK?'

He raised his eyebrows in question.

'With . . . you know . . . everything you told me last night. You're dealing with it OK?'

Stretching out a hand, he brushed his fingers across the handle bars of his mountain bike. 'Yeah. It was a relief to finally, to finally . . .'

'A problem shared and all that?'

He looked up at her. 'Yes. It's true.'

'Once this is over, we need to talk. What he was responsible for out there – something like that cannot be allowed—'

'I know.' The words came out too loud and he repeated them more softly. 'I know. He's been allowed to go unchallenged too long.' He made a shooing motion with his hand. 'Now go. Away to your bed, you hear?'

She smiled. 'OK, OK, I'm off.'

Once his front door had clicked shut, Jim marched straight into the front room. He stood staring at the bottle of wine, still two thirds full. Clenching and unclenching his fingers, he told himself no. Not yet. Not until you've done what needs to be done.

The keys to his car were on the shelf beside the photo of him and Iona in Manchester's big wheel. He dwelled on her face, those incredible turquoise eyes wide with mock-fright, her perfectly formed teeth exposed in a cheesy grimace. She's so beautiful, he thought. Even when she doesn't mean to be. One of his arms was round her, the other raised to the camera, thumb jutting up. He saw the look of sheer happiness on his own face and had to close his eyes.

Wallace must be stopped, he thought. It was simple. He looked at Iona's smiling face once again. I'm going to make him stop what he's doing to you. He focused on her eyes, so bright, intelligent and full of life. He will not rob you of that sparkle. He will not do to you what he did to me.

With another glance at the wine, he slid the car keys off the shelf, thinking about what Iona had just said. Wallace was in his office and didn't look like he was going anywhere.

THIRTY-FOUR

Wallace could only stare as the door to his office swung open. He regarded the figure standing in the corridor with bewilderment.

'Thought I'd find you here,' Jim said, stepping inside.

Wallace tilted his head, searching for anyone standing behind his former comrade.

Catching the look, Jim pushed the door closed. 'I'm on my own.'

Wallace put his pen down. 'How come you're here?'

Jim shrugged before glancing around. The office was characterized by what was absent from it. No family photos. No souvenirs or mementoes. Bare walls, aside from a few certificates. Nothing personal, no insight into the man. Barren, Jim thought. Just like his soul.

'What are you doing?' Wallace's voice was curt and impatient.

Jim looked at him and sniffed. He closed in on Wallace's desk, still saying nothing.

Wallace seemed to acknowledge something. He sat back, a trace of a smile playing on his thin lips. 'I'm surprised they even let you in.'

Jim was now looking towards the window. 'It's not like there are many people about. Fuck all on this floor, as far as I could tell.'

Wallace raised himself slightly straighter, the mocking tone gone from his voice. 'What do you want, Stephens?'

Jim scrutinized his old commanding officer. 'You want to know what I want?'

Wallace sighed. 'Yes. If you can get it out without choking. Still struggling with your . . . emotional issues? Smells like you are.' He tilted an imaginary glass to his lips.

Jim went still.

'Your scars look like they've healed nicely.' The mocking tone had returned. He pushed his chair back so he could cross his legs.

'Show up a bit though, when your face goes pale. What is that? Righteous indignation? Unresolved anger?' He nodded. 'Have a seat. Let's talk about it.'

Jim shook his head and gave a tired laugh.

'Oh, come on, Sergeant. You came here, don't clam up now you've got this far. Deep breath, isn't that what they advise in counselling sessions for emotional fuck-ups?'

'Say whatever you want, Wallace, you piece of shit. I could not give a fuck.' He stared into the superintendent's face and saw a flicker of uncertainty in the other man's eyes.

Wallace licked his lips. 'What's this about?'

'Detective Constable Iona Khan.'

The super's eyes suddenly turned to slits. 'Khan?'

'This gets said only once, so listen. Any more of your shit occurs after this conversation and I will destroy you.'

Wallace burst out laughing. 'You'll destroy me? Me?' He laid a forearm over the armrest of his chair, hand dangling loosely in the air. 'I'm all ears.'

Jim took another step closer to the desk. 'The mind games stop. All your shitty, sick little tactics. Your tests, your snide comments, the whispers you've been putting round the office. All of it stops.'

Wallace cocked his head, as if his hearing was playing tricks. 'You come in here accusing me of . . . what was it again?' He reached for a pen. 'Repeat what you just said, I want this word for word.'

Jim placed both hands on Wallace's desk and leaned forward. He spoke slowly. 'I said your mind games stop right now. The newspaper cutting on her computer. The joke with the toilet rolls. Sending her into that mosque to gather intelligence.'

Wallace had stopped taking notes when Jim mentioned the newspaper cutting. 'Who's been . . . was it her? Has she been discussing an operation with you?' He looked Jim up and down. 'Why the hell has she . . . hang on . . .' His lips peeled back. 'Are you fucking her?'

Jim's eyes dropped, just for a moment.

Wallace placed his pen on the desk and grinned. 'You're fucking her, aren't you? You're slipping it to our little Iona. Christ, Jim, she's only just out of school uniform. Mind you, you always seemed a bit too keen on the school kids in Iraq. Handing out sweets, letting them play with bits of your kit. Teaching them English. Classic kiddy-fiddler stuff, now I think—'

Jim slammed both palms down on the table. 'Shut the fuck up!' He stood back and raised a hand, pressing the ends of his fingers against his temple. 'You're so wrong, aren't you? Up here? I forgot about the stuff that comes out of your mouth.'

Wallace sneered. 'I'm bored by this, Stephens. Now, fuck knows what you were thinking about coming in here, but you've just kissed goodbye to what remains of your police career. And Khan? Don't worry, I'll be looking out for her, all right.' He reached for his pen. 'Who's your boss over in . . . what godforsaken little station do you work out of, again? I know we didn't want you here.'

Jim lowered his hand, saying nothing.

Wallace seemed to gain encouragement from his silence. 'You know why I scratched your application to this unit? Same reason I kept you down in the army. Can't trust you, mate. Never quite sure where your loyalties lie.'

'My loyalties?' Jim asked quietly.

Wallace nodded. 'That's right. Loyalty. I'm just glad you were never watching my back on any patrol. Now, Sergeant, give me the name of your senior officer and start hoping I have a change of heart and decide not to take this any further.'

Jim started to smile.

Wallace frowned impatiently. 'I said, the name of—'

A low chuckle rose up from Jim's throat and the flicker of uncertainty reappeared in Wallace's eyes. He tapped the point of his pen up and down on the piece of paper, creating a cluster of little dots.

Finally Jim's low laughter died down and he sighed. 'You think that will work?'

'Letting whoever has to manage you know just how unhinged you are?' Uncertainty had crept into Wallace's voice. 'Your chances of promotion will hardly look rosy.'

'I have no career, you prick. I have nothing. No girlfriend, no family, nothing. All I have is a sense of fucking shame.'

At the mention of shame, Wallace blinked.

'Yeah.' Jim nodded. 'You know what I'm talking about. I can carry on doing what I'm doing until retirement or they can kick me out. Doesn't bother me.'

Wallace let out a derisive snort.

'You don't believe me?' He leaned forward again. 'Then look into my eyes. I do not fucking care what happens to me.'

Wallace swallowed nervously. 'What do you want?'

'Keep away from Iona. Assign her to a different team in the CTU and never go near her again. I'll be watching. Any of your shit carries on and I'll go on record about what you did in Iraq. I'll bring both of us down.'

Wallace checked the door was closed. 'I have no idea what you are referring to,' he stated deliberately, eyes now sweeping across Jim's shirt.

Spotting the direction of Wallace's glance, Jim undid the top buttons of his shirt and yanked it over his head. 'No wire. Nothing recording this.'

Wallace stared at the rivulets of scars running across Jim's chest.

'When they dragged that kid off the street and into our compound, you should have ordered them off him,' Jim said, his voice raw with emotion. 'You should have pushed him back out through the gates and told him to run home. But you didn't.' A finger was thrust towards Wallace's face. 'You hooded him and you told them to take him down into that cellar.'

'I have no idea—'

'Shut up! Shut your lying fucking mouth. You let the boys crack into some booze, you got them angry, you goaded them –'

'Our base was coming under mortar attacks. Every single day!'

'That kid had nothing to do with that. He'd thrown a few stones. He was about ten.'

'He was a terrorist – he had a knife on him. I'm not getting into—'

'You planted that knife on him,' Jim whispered. 'You put it in his hand after he was dead. After they'd kicked him around like a fucking rag doll. Jonesy had stolen that knife from a house we'd searched the day before. You told him to go and get it when you realized the kid was dead.'

Wallace shook his head.

'Know what Jonesy is doing now?' Jim sat heavily in the chair opposite Wallace. 'He lasted a while as a security guard in some discount supermarket in Gorton. When he lost that job, he started selling *The Big Issue*. Now he sniffs aerosols. I spoke to him the other week. He still remembers running across the courtyard to fetch that knife. Following your orders.'

Once again, Wallace put his pen down. 'That incident was fully investigated by the military police. They concurred with the events as reported.'

Jim's laugh was bitter. 'Fuck off, Wallace. That report was a pack of lies. You knew it, we knew it, the whole fucking town knew it. Jonesy will back me up on that.'

'This is all—'

'Things were never the same after that, were they? Hearts and minds, that's what we were meant to be winning. Getting the locals onside. Digging wells and irrigation ditches. You lost us any sympathy or support we might have earned that day.'

Wallace uncrossed his legs in readiness to stand, freezing when Jim slapped his hand against the disfigured skin of his chest.

'We were never petrol-bombed before that kid! But we were after. They fucking hated us being in their town after.' A tear spilled from Jim's eye. 'And Ade dying? Ade burning to death in that Land Rover? That was because of you, you bastard. You're to blame.'

Wallace lowered his head and the only sound was Jim's ragged breathing. Head still hanging forward, Wallace eventually spoke. 'You were in that cellar, too.'

Jim winced and fresh tears squeezed from his eyes. 'I know I was. Every day I ask myself why I just stood there and watched. Every fucking day.' He raised his hands and pressed his palms against the sockets of his eyes. 'I can still see it, still hear their screams. That kid down in the cellar. Ade trying to get the door of the Land Rover open. Do you still hear their screams?'

Wallace said nothing.

Jim wiped at his cheeks with both hands and cleared his throat. 'Right,' he announced. 'Now you know: fuck with Iona and I will take you apart, Wallace. You understand?'

Chin on his chest, the other man could have been asleep.

'Look up!' Jim bellowed.

Wallace raised his eyes to see Jim straining forward in his chair, cords in his neck standing out. 'Do you understand?'

'Yes.'

Jim stared at him for a moment longer, then the tension left him. He got to his feet and started pulling on his shirt. 'She'll be in first thing tomorrow with some news. Word has come from Mauritius – more information on Appleton's murder.' He paused at the door, tucking in his shirt. 'You'll treat her report like you would any other detective's, is that clear?'

He waited for Wallace's nod before opening the door and walking out.

Wallace remained at his desk, arms quivering slightly as he went over what had just occurred. There was, he quickly realized, no room for manoeuvre. Jim had him trapped. The bloke was clearly teetering on the brink and there was no doubting he'd happily blow the lid on the Iraq thing. Human rights lawyers had sniffed around for years, making enquiries, trying to find a crack in the official version of events. If Jim picked up the phone, all their files would come back out in a flash.

He banged his hands down on the armrests of his chair. My office. The bloke walks into my office and gives me instructions.

An image of Iona began to burn in his mind. The little Paki bitch would be moving teams, all right. No way she was staying in his. I never wanted her anyway. He looked at the piles of paper covering his desk, musing that he never did pass on her report to MI6.

He wondered whether he should cover himself by sending it on now. That was if he could even remember where he'd put it. No, he decided. Better wait until tomorrow and see what the uppity little whore reckons she's unearthed. Probably will turn out to be a load of bollocks, anyway.

THIRTY-FIVE

Iona gave up on sleep and reached for her bedside radio. The presenter was discussing the likely impact of Blair and Brown's joint appearance later that morning at the Labour Party conference in Manchester.

Fresh anxiety washed through her and she threw the covers back, wondering how much of the night she'd been awake. It felt like most of it had been spent with her eyes fixed on the cream-coloured hijab hanging from the back of her door.

The tunnels, the damn tunnels. There had to be one the council didn't know about, she thought. Her mind had repeatedly jumped to the constable in the CTU who'd shown up with the keys to the one beneath the Great Northern Warehouse. The council map he mentioned. Before setting off for the mosque, was it worth ringing him again? The fact she still hadn't spoken to Toby especially irritated her. Jim was right; the guy would need to be frightened into co-operating. Nothing else was working. Every time she thought of Jim, his advice replayed in her head. Get in touch with Tristram Dell, the friend of the murdered Law Lord. Find out exactly what might have been divulged about the conference in that letter. Then would come Wallace – presenting him with the latest developments, trying to make him take it all seriously.

She scrunched her toes against the carpet. Too much needed to be done. Too much for one person.

Needing to do something just to force her thoughts on to another track, she slid her towel off the radiator and set off for the bathroom at the end of the corridor.

She felt slightly better after a brief shower, glad of the fact her three housemates were still all slumbering in their beds. After drying her hair and dressing in faded jeans and a fleece top, she trotted softly down the stairs to the kitchen.

After turning on the television, she turned to a breakfast show where the guest was flicking through that morning's papers. The *Independent* had devoted the lower half of its front page to further revelations about America's extraordinary rendition programme that were emerging as a result of WikiLeaks. The focus was now on a series of flights that had stopped at a remote US airbase on a British territory far out in the Indian Ocean.

By the time Iona had forced down some toast, there were sounds of movement on the floor above. The bathroom door banged shut and the boiler ignited just as her phone went off.

Mum, she thought, looking at the screen. What's she doing phoning me this time in the morning? Fenella, she thought, a mental picture of her pregnant older sister suddenly before her. She hit the mute button for the telly. 'Hi, Mum, everything OK?'

'Yes, sorry to ring early, hen – but I thought you'd be up.'

'I am. Did you see Fenella over the weekend?'

'We did. She stopped by on Sunday. She had a printout from the scan. Iona, she's going to be so big. I didn't dare say, but it made my eyes water just thinking about it, poor lass. Anyway, she was asking after you. Are you getting enough rest with all this conference business going on?'

'More or less. There's been a few late nights, but it's all over soon.'

'Well, talking of the conference, we had some exciting news last night.'

Iona frowned. How could the conference possibly involve exciting news for mum and dad. 'How do you mean?'

'You know your father's colleague in his department at the university? Andrew Trilling?'

'Vaguely. He's come to the occasional party you've thrown?'

'Yes. Well, he was due to be speaking at a debate they're having. Middle Eastern foreign policy. But he got something in his eye fitting some shelves. Bit of wood flew in. That's not the good news, obviously. He has to go back to the Royal Eye Hospital this morning.'

'Mum, you've lost me here. Who's having a debate?'

'Sorry, hen. They are, at the conference. People from all sorts of organizations. Not in the big hall. A side bit, but the conference all the same. Your father's had to go to do all the security clearance stuff.'

Iona felt her back stiffen. 'He's what?'

'Filling in for Professor Trilling. But he needs one of those security passes – you must know what I mean. Andrew was describing it when he rang. It has his photo on and other details.'

'Dad's going to be at the conference centre?'

'He's already there, Iona. Isn't it exciting? You might cross paths, if you get the chance to go down. His event starts at half past nine.'

Iona was on her feet, her free hand gripping the top of her head. 'When did he set off?'

Muriel's voice faltered slightly. 'About half an hour ago? Iona? What's wrong?'

She lowered her hand. 'Nothing . . .'

'You sounded shocked.'

'Surprised, Mum. That's all. I'll ring him – see where he is.'

'He's at the conference centre—'

'No, I mean if he's inside yet. Maybe he's stuck in a queue, doing the checks. I . . . I could see if he is.'

Muriel sounded baffled. 'You mean to say hello?'

Iona nodded. 'Yeah, I suppose. Let me ring him, OK? I'll speak to you later.'

'Just when you have a minute. I know how busy you are.'

'Thanks, Mum, bye.'

She cut the call and sat back down, only aware that Jo was in the room when she heard her voice.

'That didn't sound so good.'

'What?' Iona's gaze skittered across to the television. A sweeping shot of the conference centre's plaza. Text at the bottom of the screen said live coverage would resume in forty minutes' time.

'The phone call.' Jo nodded at the mobile clutched tightly in Iona's hand. 'Wasn't bad news, was it?'

'No . . . not bad,' Iona murmured distractedly, heading quickly for the stairs. 'Just need to ring my dad.'

She had selected Wasim's number from her address book before she reached her bedroom. Closing the door, she listened to it ring. Come on, come on, Dad, answer your phone, come on.

'Hello, I can't speak right now. Leave me a message, please.'

Damn it! As the beep sounded Iona was suddenly unsure what to say. 'Dad, hi, it's me, Iona. Call me, please – soon as you can.'

She sat down on the edge of her bed, phone bouncing in her cupped palms as she jiggled her knees up and down. What do I do? Go down there and drag him out? What do I say? Mum's been taken ill? Should I say anything? He won't leave without a good reason. Do I say there could be some kind of an attack? He'll want to know why he's the only one leaving.

She let out a sigh of anguish. OK, OK, calm down. The thing hasn't even started. Blair and Brown aren't due on stage until later this morning. There's no need to rush down there – yet. She looked at her phone once again. That bloody Toby from the Sub-Urban Explorers. Anger blazed at how he was ignoring her calls.

She brought his number up. Try and ignore this, she thought, jaw set tight.

THIRTY-SIX

'Toby, it's Detective Khan from the Counter Terrorism Unit. This is the last message I leave you. The position of your mobile has now been triangulated. If I haven't heard from you by nine o'clock this morning, I'll be paying you a visit. Not to your home address. I will arrive at your workplace with a snatch squad in full protective gear. You will be arrested under the Counter Terrorism Act, 2006. You will be held for twenty-eight days without charge. Your home will be like a building site when you get to see it again. Every single one of your friends and family will be dragged in and questioned. We will tear your life apart unless you call me.'

She hit red and took a deep breath. Am I, she asked herself, bad at my job? Last night I didn't want to make that call. Now Dad's at risk it was easy. So damn easy.

For a moment she wondered what the young man's reactions would be when he heard the message. Anger? Fear? Resignation? Think what you like, she concluded, getting to her feet. I don't really care.

Next, she called Harish Veerapan. Four hours ahead. That meant it was noon over there. Her call was answered on its third ring. 'Harish? It's Iona Khan.'

'Morning, Iona. I was about to ring but it seemed too early—'

'Any luck?'

He groaned. 'I am surrounded by a sea of paper, Detective. But no other letters from Tristram Dell – not written after the email I found yesterday, anyway.'

'Have you searched through all his stuff?'

'Yes, everything. It's not here, I'm sure. My concern is the letter is now in the possession of the wrong person.'

'Mine, too, Harish. OK, thanks, anyway.' She dropped the phone on her bed, turned the computer on and began to pace up and down, willing it to boot-up faster. Finally it was ready for her to go online. The website for Slattinger-Dell, as Harish had mentioned, wasn't trying to impress. In fact, it was so understated to appear almost empty. She went straight to the unobtrusive bar of tabs at the bottom and selected, contact.

An address in Parliament Square, nearest tube stop Westminster. Appropriate enough for the type of work the company specialized in, Iona thought, dialling the office number.

A woman who sounded like she was into her fifties answered the phone. Clipped, Home Counties accent. An image of Miss Moneypenny sprang up in Iona's mind. 'Good morning, this is Detective Constable Khan from Greater Manchester Police. Could I speak to Tristram Dell, please. It's extremely urgent.'

'Mr Dell is not in the office today, I am afraid.'

'Would you have a mobile phone number for him? As I said, it's extremely urgent.'

'He . . . Sorry, could you identify yourself again?'

'Detective Constable Khan. I work for the Counter Terrorism Unit up here in Manchester.'

'That's where he is . . . at the Labour Party conference.'

Of course, Iona thought. Where else would he be? 'Does he have a number I could contact him on?'

'It would be preferable if I took yours and ask him to call you at his earliest convenience.'

No, Iona thought. I'm not leaving any more messages with people. 'I can't wait for him to ring me.' She said nothing more, letting her silence force the other woman to speak again.

She eventually gave a small cough. 'I see. I'd better warn you, he has a very busy schedule.'

The first thing Iona heard when her call was picked up was a mass of voices punctuated by the clink of cutlery. Someone nearby let out a loud guffaw.

'Tristram Dell speaking.' His voice was deep and authoritative.

'Mr Dell, my name is Iona Khan. I'm a detective with Greater Manchester Police.'

'How did you get this number?'

'The lady in your London office gave it to me.'

'Did she? How can I help you, Detective?'

'I need to speak to you in person, Mr Dell.'

'In relation to?' He sounded faintly intrigued by the suggestion.

'A very sensitive matter. It concerns Reginald Appleton.' The background noise took over once more as Iona waited for a reply.

'Reginald?' he asked warily.

'That's correct. Could I come to see you now?'

'Impossible. It's almost nine. I'm about to go into the convention centre. The day's proceedings are about to begin.'

'Where are you now, sir?'

'In the Midland Hotel – why?'

'You were in regular contact with Mr Appleton in the run up to his murder. Some of that contact was about the conference here in Manchester.'

He spoke away from the phone. 'Yvette! So good to see you. Yes, I'll be along. Catch up later, yes. Bye.' There was a pause before he said quietly, 'What leads you to assert that?'

'A personal letter found from you in Mr Appleton's study. Emails on his computer.'

Silence again. The background noises were now fainter and Iona guessed the man had moved away from the throng. 'I would be prepared to talk in a couple of days' time.'

'Sorry, sir. There isn't time for that.'

'Well, that's . . . regrettable.' His voice had the formality of someone delivering a statement. 'However, I am unable to comment further without my lawyer being party to proceedings.'

'Sir, we're concerned there has been a security breach. There was a particular letter we think you wrote to Reginald Appleton. In it, you may have mentioned certain details about the conference. Tony Blair and Gordon Brown are due to appear with Daniel Tevland –' Her sentence ground to a halt. I'm talking, she realized, to the person who arranged the whole thing. 'They will be on stage together very soon.'

'Who are you again?'

'Detective Constable Khan, I'm with the Counter Terrorism Unit.'

'Detective Constable? Forgive me, but why isn't someone of a senior rank contacting me about these concerns?'

Iona pursed her lips. 'I'm sure they will, in due course –'

'I sincerely hope they do, Constable.'

She heard voices and some laughter getting louder. He's on the move, she thought. 'Who is A.B., sir? What are your plans in regard to the movements of Mr Blair –'

'Morning, Michael. Did you get my—' The line went dead.

'Mr Dell? Sir?' She looked at the screen of her handset. Did he just cut the call? She dialled his number again and got an answerphone message. He hung up on me. Unbelievable. Taking several deep breaths, she put her phone down and tried to calm her thoughts.

Whatever information Ranjit may have gleaned was, she realized, now of secondary importance. The priority had to be finding him and Vassen before they carried out their plan. Think, she said to herself, getting to her feet and beginning to pace again. Tunnels. You need to know about any tunnels. She went through her carry case and retrieved the card given to her by the constable who'd arrived with the keys to the tunnel beneath the Great Northern Warehouse.

'Constable Davis, this is Detective Constable Khan. You escorted me down—'

'Iona. Morning.'

'Hi. Um . . . Mark. Are you on duty?'

'Yeah, over at Silver Command. Things are completely manic. You?'

'Yes – I'm not in the office, though. Listen, I'm still looking into any tunnels that might be in the vicinity of the convention centre.'

'Still?' He sounded vaguely amused. 'The conference has already started, you realize?'

'I know. But new information has come to light. Mark, when we were in the visitor centre, there was mention of a map. A council one with the whereabouts of all known tunnels beneath the city.'

'Iona, you do know about the step-up in security?'

She hesitated. 'No. As I said, I'm not at my desk –'

'The announcement?'

'What announcement?'

'Doesn't matter.'

'What announcement?'

'You wanted to know about the council's schematic, yeah?'

She tapped a finger uneasily, the feeling of not being part of things suddenly back. 'Yeah. I need to know what else is on it. The guy in the visitor centre mentioned the possibility of a tunnel running under Deansgate. Were there others? Maybe another encroaching beneath the ring of steel. Under the Midland, perhaps?'

'You didn't hear this from me, but – yes, there's one under the Midland.'

'There is?'

'Approaches from the south-east, possibly once went to where the Bishopsgate Centre now stands. Inspected and the sole entrance sealed. Deansgate tunnel?'

She felt her eyebrows arch. 'It exists?'

'It exists, all right. But now only in parts. The tunnel's most intact at the cathedral end of Deansgate. As you go further along, more and more of it has been back-filled. Sections have also collapsed. Last decent stretch you can actually walk along for any distance ends roughly where Saint John Street joins Deansgate. That's a long, long way from the conference centre. Over one hundred and fifty metres. It's not deemed as a threat.'

She glanced at the view of the conference centre on her TV. Vassen and his companion were planning something, she was certain. It had to involve a tunnel. 'That's really it? Nothing else?'

'Not a thing. Now, I've got to go. Whoever's got you chasing this tunnel angle needs to find something better for you to do. Get yourself into the office, Iona. You're off the pace.'

Once more, she found herself staring at her handset. Off the pace? What did he mean by that?

THIRTY-SEVEN

anjit Bhujun flexed his head from side to side, unable to keep still. For the fourth time in as many minutes, he pulled the curtain back a few inches and peered down at the quiet street below. He searched for any new vehicles parked nearby. Vans or similar. Anything with a rear compartment where someone could be concealed. He searched for any workmen – technicians fixing cables, labourers digging up the pavement, council employees mending a streetlight. He scanned any window in the houses opposite that had net curtains drawn. Satisfied everything was fine, he turned to Vassen.

The younger man was kneeling at the foot of the bed. The bruises on his face seemed to have expanded and grown darker in colour. The briefcase he'd just slid out from beneath the bed was open. Vassen was staring at the row of four small Perspex vials in the tin. Each was full of dirty-looking powder.

On the floor next to it was the piece of equipment Vassen had taken from the laboratory at the university. Twin plastic tubes curved out of the top, trailed down and re-entered the grey casing at its base. A stainless-steel panel was inscribed with the words, GE Healthcare Frac-900.

Vassen was mumbling to himself, sweat standing out on his forehead.

'What are you doing?' Ranjit asked.

Vassen's eyes were closed.

'Are you praying?'

The younger man's near-silent recitation came to a finish. 'Yes,' he answered in a soft voice.

'Do you go to church?'

'No.'

'Did you? Back on Mauritius?'

'No.'

'But you believe? In God?'

'I don't know. I didn't. But . . .' He looked at the vials again.

'Let me show you something, cousin.' Ranjit crossed the bedroom, lifted a small hold-all from the floor and placed it on the bed. 'Sit next to me.'

Face pale, Vassen did as he was asked. Ranjit had taken a small photo album from among his meagre possessions. The cover was made of a cardboard-like material. Mounted on the first stiff page were a couple of faded black and white photographs, the corners slightly buckled.

'Home.' Ranjit stated.

'Where did you get these?' Vassen whispered, wonder filling his voice.

The top image showed a group of small children waving to the camera from the veranda of a crudely built wooden building. All the girls were wearing floral dresses and white, sleeveless shirts. Each boy was wearing white shorts and a shirt. Their black hair was thick, like Vassen's. Some were hanging from the wooden railings, laughter lighting up their faces.

'That was the schoolhouse,' Ranjit said quietly.

The image below it was of a wide clearing, dense palm trees forming a perimeter. Pathways had been worn across the thin grass, one leading towards a cluster of huts. A small fishing boat lay in the shadow of each building.

Another path branched off to a larger building with a cross jutting up from the apex of the roof. Adults were gathered in front of its open doors. Out on the grass, several children were playing with a couple of dogs, whose legs – captured in the act of running – were slightly blurred.

'These photos were Aunty Lizette's,' Ranjit announced. 'She was sent them by someone from the Colonial Office – he came to make a film about our lives.'

Vassen's face was sombre. 'When?'

'Sometime during the fifties.'

'Before –'

'Yes. Before they removed us. The people who did this to us claimed to be Christians. How could a Christian do what they did?' He paused. 'I wonder if the church is still standing. Aunty Lizette said they killed our dogs, once we were all in the naval boats. Rounded them up and clubbed them to death.'

The younger man cleared his throat and Ranjit saw there were tears in his eyes. He closed the book. 'Aunty Lizette died earlier this year. How many of the older generation are now left? Fewer and fewer. It's for them, Vassen. That's why we must do this.'

The younger man gave a nod.

'Now,' Ranjit continued. 'We need supplies – water, some food. There's no way to tell how long we'll have to hide afterwards. I think it best we stay below ground for as long as we can. Look at the pictures, cousin. Look and remember. We wouldn't be here if they hadn't done what they did. They are the guilty ones in this, not us. When I get back from the shop, you need to be ready to go.'

THIRTY-EIGHT

Iona had scrolled down to Paul Wallace's number when her phone's screen lit up. A split second later, it started to ring. She looked at the number, hoping desperately it was her dad. The name on the screen was Toby. Finally, she said to herself, accepting the call.

'Hello, Toby.'

'You leave a message like that and then, every time I ring, your phone's fucking engaged?' he whispered. 'Are they on the way here?'

Iona glanced at her watch. Almost nine. The poor guy was already at work and under the impression he was about to be lifted. 'No, they're not.'

'You're out-of-fucking-order, you know that? Yeah, course you do. Not that you give a shit – you're a fucking pig. All pigs are the fucking—'

'Toby, shut up.'

'Yeah, that's right. True colours and all that. Happy to drop the nicey-nice shit now aren't—'

'Shut up and listen to me. Please.'

There was a slight pause. 'What?'

'Things are serious, Toby. I need to speak to Hidden Shadow. Right now. Let me have his address and phone number.'

'We had an agreement. You promised, for what that's worth.'

'That was then. Now it's different. How do I get hold of—'

'What'll you do? Threaten him with the full treatment, too? Throw in the option of extraordinary rendition? You lot like that, don't you? Passing on innocent people for a bit of harsh interrog—'

'The snatch squad are still here, Toby.' Iona was imagining her father, queuing to get through the security check at the perimeter. 'You want to discuss this in a cell? We can do it that way.'

'You can't contact Hidden Shadow.'

'Why?'

Toby now sounded like he was relishing the conversation. 'There's no phone signal where he is.'

'What do you mean?'

'He's potholing. Out in the Peak District, somewhere near Castleton. No phone signal underground.'

Iona sat back on the bed. She could not believe this. 'Where near Castleton?'

'I don't know. There are dozens of spots around there. He could pop up from any of them.'

'Well . . . when's he back? It's Monday morning. Hasn't he got work?'

'He's taken today off. Could be tonight. Could be earlier. You might get lucky – it was raining in the night.'

'What?'

'In the night – there was rain. Not good for potholing. Floods?'

Iona felt a glimmer of hope. 'So he might be heading back to Manchester early? How's he travelling?'

'Train. Hathersage station.'

'Where does he stay when he's there?'

'He'll have a tent. They'll either sleep out or stay the night underground.'

'Who's they?'

'Him and Thompski, they always go together.'

'Thompski?'

'You know, you met him down in the . . .'

So that's his name, Iona thought, an image of the taciturn companion from the Temple of Convenience in her mind. She wrote the name down. 'I need their mobile numbers, Toby.'

'Shitting hell.'

'Their numbers.'

'What if I ring them and leave a—'

'There's no wriggle-room here. Their numbers, please.' He read them out and she noted them both down before repeating them back. 'OK, I'm going to call them now and I'll keep calling them until I get an answer. If either contact you in the meantime, you must get them to ring me immediately. Is that clear?'

'Yes, sir.'

'And make sure you answer your phone, Toby. No voicemail.'

'But I might be in a meeting. I can't—'

'No negotiating! Put it on vibrate or something. You have to answer it if I call.' She pressed red and keyed in the numbers for Hidden Shadow's phone. Her call went unanswered. Same for Thompski's phone. In an attempt to quell a rising sense of panic, she had to start sucking in air through her nose and blowing it out through her mouth.

An urge to see what was happening at the conference centre took her. She turned to her little telly. Some kind of interview. The camera was trained on a politician in full flow. Iona found her eyes wandering to the view through the plate-glass windows behind him. Below the grey and featureless sky, she could see the massed buildings of Manchester in the foreground, rolling countryside and the faintest suggestion of hills in the far distance. They're filming in the Sky Bar, she thought. Halfway up Beetham Tower. She recalled that was where the BBC conducted its interviews during the yearly conferences.

If the camera moved towards the windows and then angled down, the view, she realized, would be of the conference centre itself. Wasim would be down there, maybe even in sight as he crossed the plaza to the conference centre steps. She bit at her lower lip, wondering what to do.

They should be flooding the whole of Bury with plain-clothes officers, she thought bitterly. Every available person from Bury's station should be out looking, too. People at the Metro stop, people walking the streets. The entire CCTV control room should have Vassen and Ranjit's mugshots in front of them. As should every officer on the perimeter of the secure zone. She groaned with frustration as it dawned on her that all those measures depended on the two Mauritians not being down in the tunnels already. If they were, every single camera was useless. Every officer checking faces would be wasting time.

I can't wait, she decided. I've got to go to Wallace with what I've got. He must see the threat, surely? He must contact Gold Command and get them to issue a yellow site alert.

She was down the stairs and almost out the front door when her phone's ring tone stopped her in her tracks. Dropping her carry case on the mat, she looked at the screen. Unknown number. 'Detective Constable Khan speaking.'

'Good morning, Iona. It's your observation post out in Bury reporting in.'

A split-second of confusion and then the penny dropped. 'Mr Cooper?'

'Correct.'

'Has something happened?'

'It certainly has. I just had an eyeball of one of your suspects. The shorter one with the shaved head.'

'You've seen him?' Her heart felt like a bird, trying to flutter free of her chest.

'He just passed by with an empty carrier bag dangling from one hand. He went down the same alley, on the way to the mini-mart on Woodhill Road, I should imagine.'

Iona was fumbling for her car keys. 'Was it him? The one whose picture I showed you?'

'I'd say it was. Hurry and you can see for yourself – my guess is he'll soon be returning this way with his shopping.'

Iona slammed the door and started running down the front path.

THIRTY-NINE

Iona glimpsed Mr Cooper up in his window as she swung her car on to the forecourt of his block of flats.

She strode quickly up to the front entrance, relieved to hear his voice coming from the little panel as she neared the door.

'Come straight in, it's open.'

Out of sight of the road, she was able to run up the stairs to Cooper's flat on the first floor. Once more, he was waiting for her in the corridor. 'Any sign?' she asked, slightly out of breath as she jogged towards him.

He shook his head as he waved her in. When the door was closed, he said, 'Under twenty-five minutes. You must have motored.'

'Yes,' she responded, recalling her mad dash round the outside lane of the M60. 'I haven't missed him?'

'He hasn't been back this way, that's for sure.'

'You said he had a carrier bag?'

'That's right. A reusable one – made from canvas or some kind of cloth.'

'Baseball cap on his head?'

'Not this time.'

Iona sent up a silent thanks. In the dim front room, she could see that Cooper had positioned the fold-out chair next to the armchair. Both were several feet back from the window.

'I've been keeping the lights off. The chairs are as far back as possible without losing the view down on to the road,' Cooper announced, closing the door behind them and rubbing his hands. 'Forgot the feeling you get from doing this type of stuff.'

'That's great, Mr Coop—'

'Come on, it's Bob. First-name terms if we're surveilling.'

'Bob,' she said, smiling briefly.

'I didn't think you'd be showing up on your own. Or is your support positioned nearby?'

'No – it's just me. For now.'

He looked mildly perplexed. 'Is that so? What about optics? A camera?' he asked, glancing at her carry case.

She realized she'd turned up without anything. 'No . . . as a matter of fact, I haven't.'

He gestured at the small pair of binoculars on the window sill. Green rubberized casing, the sort birdwatchers favoured. 'You're welcome to use mine.'

Feeling like a complete amateur, she thanked him and got her phone out, eyes on the entrance to the alley. 'Once I can confirm he's our man, I'm sure things will happen very quickly.'

'Sit yourself down. Tea or coffee?'

'No, I'm fine, thanks.' She perched on the edge of the wooden chair, phone cradled in her hands.

He leaned his forearms on the back of the armchair. 'I'm dying to know what type of threat this man poses.'

She didn't turn her head. 'Sorry, I can't say.'

'I understand. He's dark-skinned, so I'm assuming it's al-Qaeda or related. He looks like he could have had training – the way he carried himself. You'll want that support when it comes to taking him down.'

Iona thought about the events in the alley. Two young men, both armed. One ended up being stabbed, the other injured. 'I certainly don't intend to do it alone.'

Cooper straightened up. 'I'll put the kettle on. Sure I can't make you a drink?'

Iona thought about the prospect of being in the loo when Ranjit reappeared. 'No, thanks.'

Once he was out of the room, she lifted her mobile and, between quick glances across the road, tried her father's number once again. Answerphone. Well, she tried to reassure herself, if Ranjit's here, no attack on the centre is about to take place. She stole a swift look at the books lining the shelves to her left.

Her phone rang and she almost dropped it in her rush to examine the screen. Toby. 'DC Khan here.'

'Yeah, I know that. They just got the nine twenty-eight from Hathersage. Arrives in Manchester Piccadilly at ten twenty-two.'

She looked at her watch. That was in three quarters of an hour's time. Blair and Brown were due to take the stage just over half an hour after that. Time was slipping by so fast. 'Why didn't they call me?'

'No idea. They were piss-wet-through and cold? Preferred to get on a warm train than speak to you? Who knows?'

Damn it, she said to herself, trying to gauge the quickest way to get to them. It was all little rural stops from Hathersage, right until the train reached Stockport. By then it was only another ten minutes into Manchester itself. 'They should have called me.'

'I'm sure they're gutted they didn't. Probably they're looking forward to the reception committee you'll have waiting for them at Piccadilly.'

Iona was trying to think. There was no way she could abandon her watch for Ranjit – as things stood, it was the best bet she had of confirming he really was Vassen's companion.

'Can I go now?'

'Pardon?'

'I said, can I go now?'

His attitude was really beginning to grate. 'Will they have gear with them? Kit bags, for instance?'

'Yeah, them. Coils of rope, helmets as well.'

'OK, you can go Toby. Same arrangement applies, though. I call, you answer.' She cut the call and brought up Jim's number. The phone reached its fifth ring before he picked up. 'Jim, it's me. Listen, what time are you on duty – noon, wasn't it? I need you to do something—'

'Hey . . . slow down, for Christ's sake. Say all that again.'

He sounded groggy with sleep. How much more, she wondered, did you drink after I left last night? 'I need a favour, Jim. I don't know who else I can ask.'

'Right, OK.'

She could hear a rustling sound and pictured him sitting up in bed, rubbing at his dishevelled hair.

'What is it?' he asked.

'The Sub-Urban Explorer who can identify Ranjit from his mugshot. He's arriving at Piccadilly station at ten twenty-two. That's in about forty-five minutes' time. He uses the name Hidden Shadow and he's with another male, also twenty or thereabouts, called Thompski. They'll be carrying potholing stuff: kitbags, rope and helmets – should be easy to spot. Can you meet them off the train? You've got a copy of Ranjit's photo – on your computer from when you printed it off before. We need this bloke – Hidden Shadow – to confirm it really was Ranjit outside the library and we need to know if any tunnels the council are unaware of exist in the vicinity of the conference centre. Got that?'

'Yeah. Confirm identity of Ranjit, ask about existence of any tunnels near the conference centre the council are unaware of. What time are they getting to Piccadilly again?'

'Ten twenty-two.'

'So where are you now?'

'Bury. There's been a probable sighting of Ranjit out here. I'm waiting to see if he returns this way.'

'Wallace sent you out with a team, then?'

'No. Why would he?'

'Well, why else would you . . .' His words stumbled to a halt. 'You've been to see him this morning?'

'No, I came straight from mine when I got the call.'

'So you haven't . . .' He was silent for a moment. 'Who are you with?'

'It's just me.'

'You've gone out there on your own?'

'Yeah. Once I can say without doubt it's Ranjit, I'll ring Wallace.'

'Iona, you can't be out there all alone—'

'Jim, it's fine. I'm up in a flat. Listen, there's something else: my dad's in the conference centre for a debate. He's there right now.'

'Say that again.'

'Dad's been invited to take part in some kind of debate in the conference centre.'

'Wasim is there?'

'Yes.'

'Shit. Can't you ring him?'

'I've been trying. He's probably turned it off. He usually does.'

'Jesus.'

'You have to find Hidden Shadow and get confirmation it really is Ranjit. It's the only way to make Wallace take this seriously.'

'OK, I'm leaving now.'

The line went dead and she took a huge juddering breath in. What if Jim missed them? He wouldn't miss them, would he? Two young guys carrying potholing gear. He won't miss them. Nervously, she looked at the military-type books lining the shelves once again before focusing back on the mouth of the alleyway. 'Where did you serve, Bob?' she asked over her shoulder.

'All over,' he replied from the kitchen. 'Much of it unofficial. Covert stuff. All ancient history now, though.'

She couldn't help making a comparison to Jim in her head. Both ex-soldiers, both had served abroad – though the contrast between their states of mind was stark. 'Did you,' she said hesitantly, 'ever have to do stuff you've come to regret?'

There was a long silence. She watched the deserted street, assuming that he'd chosen to avoid the question.

'Yes.'

He was so close, she jumped. 'My God.' She reached a hand up to the base of her throat. 'I didn't hear you come in.'

Slowly, he lowered himself into the seat beside her, a cup of tea in one hand. Watching him, she wondered if the stiffness in his posture was his military bearing or simply old age.

'Of course, over the years, I've come to realize that much of what they told us simply wasn't true.'

Her gaze wavered briefly between him and the street below. 'How do you mean?'

'The people we were fighting. Why we were there.' A wistful

note had entered his voice. 'The Great Game. We were just pieces deployed in it.'

'Great Game?' Iona asked, stealing a proper look at his face. He was turned towards the window, a distant look in his eyes.

'A phrase used to describe the jostling for control of Afghanistan during the eighteen hundreds. The British and Russian empires. Nowadays, more players have joined in – America, China, NATO countries like France. There's also Pakistan and Turkey. And the area of play is also much larger. Central Asia and all around.'

'Including Iraq?'

'The entire region. Iraq, Iran, Saudi Arabia, Bahrain, Afghanistan. Libya most recently. Anywhere with oil supplies, tanker routes, pipelines and ports. Territories of strategic importance.' He continued to speak at his reflection. 'I don't oppose what goes on, but I do feel for the people of those countries we squabble over.'

Iona shifted in her seat. This wasn't the kind of thing she'd expected to hear coming from an ex-member of the SAS.

'We did some terrible things,' he stated quietly. 'And against people who were completely innocent.'

She swallowed, unable to keep Jim's words about what had happened in Iraq from echoing in her head. Deciding to remain quiet, she concentrated on the view outside. Movement in the alleyway. A figure started to emerge from the shadowy space between the concrete panels. Iona craned her head: it was a woman, pushing a buggy with a shopping bag hooked over each handle.

They both sank back slightly.

Cooper took a sip of his tea. 'I was sent to Malaya in the late fifties,' he announced matter-of-factly. 'Are you familiar with it?'

'No,' Iona replied, feeling slightly apprehensive about what was to come.

'I was flown there to help in the counter-insurgency. Going out into the jungle to deal with the communist terrorists – or CTs, as we called them. It was brutal stuff.'

Iona nodded. 'I bet.'

'You need to understand, Iona, at that time British companies effectively owned many nations, including their considerable natural resources. In Malaya, it was rubber plantations. I didn't really realize this at the time, but the real reason we were sent there was to protect those commercial interests. But who were we protecting them from?'

She gave a small shake of her head. 'CTs? Terrorists.'

'But who were the CTs, these people we were sent to eliminate?' There was a tremor in his voice. 'Sorry.' He cleared his throat. 'It took me a great many years to admit that many of the people I helped to kill were not terrorists. They were just plantation workers who had joined the trade union movement. Yes, they were communists. I think I'd have joined too if I was being exploited as ruthlessly as they were.' He sighed. 'But our government couldn't let that country's inhabitants wrest control of such a lucrative industry from us. Do you know how many air strikes we carried out during the so-called emergency? Four-and-a-half thousand. Tens upon tens of thousands of pounds of bombs were dropped to protect, it was claimed, a civilian population from dangerous fanatics.' He looked at her. 'We always seem to be invading other countries to protect their people from dangerous fanatics, don't we?'

She wasn't sure what to say. It was, she thought, more like the kind of rhetoric her father used when talking about Britain's foreign policy in the Middle East.

'I don't envy you,' he added.

She turned to examine his profile. The sadness had vanished from his voice.

'Our battles were fought thousands of miles away. Mostly against minor, poorly organized resistance. But you? It looks like you have a real problem. And it's not in some other country. It's right here.' He nodded at the window.

Iona turned to the view outside. There was a figure at the end of the alleyway.

FORTY

'Professor Khan?' The young woman's face held an earnest, slightly anxious, expression.

'Yes,' Wasim replied.

She smiled with relief. 'Oh, good. Sorry to keep you – and sorry about meeting in such hectic surroundings.'

He looked at the throng of people queuing to get into the security check between the Midland Hotel and neighbouring office block. 'It's certainly far busier than I expected.'

Nodding in agreement, she looked about. 'Word has spread like wildfire. Everyone wants to be in the main hall, now.'

Unsure what she meant, Wasim looked at the mass of delegates edging their way forward. Men in suits, women in jackets and skirts. Some had briefcases like his, others were clutching files or folders. They could have been rush-hour commuters at any train station – except that rather than being silent, most were engaged in lively conversations.

Beyond, he could see the people out on the main road shouting their various causes. He looked again at the mass of leaflets that had been pressed into his hand as he'd passed them. Kids Count charity. Oxfam. Campaign for a Referendum. Remploy. Sure Start.

On entering the security-check building, most people were shoving the pieces of paper into clear bin bags that had been hung at each side of the doors. Wasim lifted the flap of his briefcase and slid his safely inside.

'I have your pass,' the young lady announced. 'Thank you so much for agreeing to stand in at such short notice.' She produced one of the plastic cards and red lanyards everyone else had round their necks. 'Here you are.'

He examined it. Next to a panel containing his details was his passport photo and, below that, a barcode. 'Thanks. Sorry, you didn't mention your . . .'

'Oh, gosh! Sorry! It's Fiona Wallis. I work as a researcher for the Labour Party. If you follow me, we can hopefully get round some of the waiting.' She led him up the gently sloping ramp into the building. 'Excuse me, please!' She beckoned him to the end of a row of monitors.

Sitting beside each one was a man in a uniform not unlike that of a customs officer.

'I just need to cut in here.' Fiona held up some kind of identity to the line of waiting people. Several looked round eagerly to see who was being whisked to the front.

Wasim gave an apologetic smile as their excited looks changed to ones of disappointment.

Fiona held up her own delegate's pass and the security officer swiped it with a hand-held reader. Wasim then offered his for inspection and the officer did the same, scrutinizing the monitor for a second before waving his hand. 'In you go, sir.'

A pair of archway metal detectors was next, each with a large X-ray machine beside it. More security officers were on the other side.

'Just like an airport,' Wasim commented, glad that he wasn't wearing a belt with his dun-green corduroys. After putting his briefcase in a grey tray, he removed his tweed jacket, folding it on top. Then, checking his phone was turned off, he placed it on his jacket along with his keys and loose change. 'No need to take off my shoes?'

Fiona shook her head, stepping through the archway with her low heels still on. Wasim followed her and they turned round to wait for his personal possessions to appear on the scanner's conveyor belt.

'It's a pain, I know,' Fiona stated.

'A sign of the times, sadly,' Wasim responded.

'True. But, considering this morning's announcement, you can see why.'

He looked at her. 'Which announcement was that?'

She seemed taken aback. 'You weren't aware? I'm afraid our event is definitely being overshadowed now. I think even Daniel's closing speech tomorrow might be.'

He lifted his eyebrows.

'Bill Clinton is due to appear on the main stage.'

Wasim felt his mouth open and close. 'Pardon?'

'They kept it quiet until now. I had no idea, either.'

'You said Bill Clinton? As in the ex-President of the United States?'

'Yes!' She was beaming from ear to ear. 'In the flesh.'

'That's . . . that's some coup, isn't it?'

'Absolutely!'

'When's—' He felt a tap on his arm and looked round.

'Your items, sir?' A security officer was pointing at the tray blocking the end of the conveyor belt.

'Sorry, yes.' He retrieved them, slipping his lifeless phone back in his jacket before turning to face Fiona once more. 'What time is he appearing?'

'Eleven o'clock this morning.'

'With . . . alongside Blair?'

'And Gordon. They are being joined on stage by Daniel Tevland.'

Two ex-Prime Ministers, an ex-President of America and Labour's new leader, Wasim thought. Quite a line-up.

'For Daniel's leadership, it's the ultimate . . .' She wiggled her fingers. 'There was a word in the press release . . .'

'Impramatur?' Wasim guessed.

'Yes,' she answered, looking impressed. 'Impramatur.'

Figures, Wasim thought. Labour's old rifts healed, everyone happily lining up behind a young, dynamic new leader. And all with the blessing of one of politics' ultimate showmen.

'Mr Clinton carries with him the Democrat Party's – unofficial – endorsement of Daniel,' Fiona said, continuing to the exit. 'They're already talking about him being Britain's Prime Minister in-waiting.'

As they descended the ramp, Wasim could feel it bounce slightly with each step. No wonder everyone seems to be walking on air, he thought, surveying the plaza area before him. Pristine white marquees had been erected at its edges, trembling bunches of red balloons by the entrances. The ornamental lamp posts dotting the plaza had vertical banners hanging from their upper parts, each one bearing the Labour Party's emblem. Troughs of red flowers lined the walkways.

Those not making their way up the steps and through the main doors were hurriedly finishing cigarettes or paper cups of coffee. As was his custom, Wasim looked beyond what was directly in front of him. There, in the background, police officers were dotted discreetly along the perimeter fence. He looked up to take in the structure of the Beetham Tower looming behind the curved roof of the conference centre. Just visible at the railings at the top, hardly more than dots against the dull sky, were several heads and shoulders. For a fleeting moment, he wondered if he was in the sights of a high-powered rifle.

I'm in the inner sanctum, he thought. The atmosphere almost crackled with anticipation.

'Now, sorry to be ushering you away from the main event,' Fiona said, setting off at an angle towards a flight of steps leading to the conference centre's annex. 'Obviously the news of Mr Clinton's appearance changes things a bit. The shadow foreign secretary can no longer attend the discussion – but a senior advisor from his team will be in his place. We still have speakers from several think-tanks and representatives from a few NGOs. The Bishop of London has also confirmed he will still be attending.'

'That's fine with me,' Wasim answered. 'I'm just grateful the issues are being aired.'

She gave him a quick smile. 'Absolutely.'

Wasim got the impression she'd be racing back to the main hall at the earliest opportunity.

FORTY-ONE

A dying mass of leaves dominated Iona's vision. Then a brief curve of red, followed by an expanse of white. A black line ran across a silhouette of a bike. The no-cycling sign, she realized, edging the binoculars slightly to the left. Suddenly she was staring into Ranjit Bhujun's face from what seemed like inches away. She let out a tiny gasp. Before stepping fully out of the alley, he looked up and down the street.

'It's him, is it not?' Cooper said quietly.

Iona lowered the binoculars and felt relief when the sense of proximity to her target vanished. He almost seemed to be sniffing the air, like an animal that sensed danger. Suddenly she was glad Cooper had kept the lights in his flat off. They would be all but invisible from outside.

The straps of the bag hanging from Ranjit's hand were tight and the bag itself bulged. 'Yeah, it's him,' Iona whispered. Her heart was pounding once more. This was the confirmation she needed. More than that, it meant her fears that some kind of plot was underway were justified.

He stepped out on to the pavement and started walking along the street.

'Now you'll call for that support?' Cooper asked.

'No time,' Iona replied, handing the binoculars to him. 'I'll see where he goes then call.'

Cooper looked at her doubtfully as she ran to the front door. 'Just be careful, for God's sake!'

She rushed down the stairs and out the doors, jogging round the side of the building before pausing to compose herself. Calmly, she walked out of the car park.

He was on the far side of the road, less than thirty metres ahead and moving with an air of purpose. Her hands felt empty and she wished she'd brought something from Cooper's flat to carry.

His angle changed, pace slowing as he veered to the kerb, checking for any traffic before starting to cross over. She fixed her eyes on the pavement at a point around five metres in front, just enough to keep him in the upper edge of her vision. She thought he might be looking her over as he reached the same side of the road as her.

Every movement felt forced and rigid, her entire body like that of a self-conscious teenager. A strand of hair had fallen forward across her face. Do I brush it back? Would a normal person look up as they brushed it back? If I don't brush it back, will that seem suspicious? Is he even looking at me?

He was moving forward again, now less than twenty metres ahead. Too close, she thought. To slow her step, she reached into the pocket of her jeans and brought out a handful of change, giving it a cursory glance over. He was turning right, into a narrower street of terraced houses. Parked cars lined its hundred or so metre length.

I have to follow him, she realized. There's no other choice.

The other end of the street ended at a T-junction and, on its far side, she could make out a shop. A salon of some sort, a poster of a tanned woman in the window. That's where I'm going, she said to herself. I'm just out getting my nails done.

She turned into the side street, eyes flicking to the sign on the low wall. Barrett Avenue. He continued for another forty metres then pushed open a gate and stepped on to the front path. Her excitement turned to horror as he stopped, turned round and stared at her.

She felt like her knees were turning to sludge. The skin of her scalp shrivelled beneath his gaze. He wasn't moving. She got to within a few metres and knew she'd have to look up at him. When she did, his eyes – dark and hostile – stayed on her. She skirted to the far side of the pavement. Head perfectly still, his eyes kept tracking her. She swept him up and down with a contemptuous look. As if the glance said, I'm way out of your league, you loser.

He blinked and she was past him. The gate clanged shut and she heard his footsteps on the path. Her breath seeped out from her nostrils and she tried not to quicken her pace. The house two doors along had the number thirty-three on it. Behind her, she could hear keys in a lock then a front door as it opened and closed. The next house she went past was numbered thirty-one. She got round the corner and immediately reached for her mobile.

'Detective Constable Khan, what is it?'

Wallace was sounding more than harassed. There were multiple

voices in the background. 'Sir, I'm in Bury,' she said in a low voice.
'I have a positive identification of Vassen Bhujun's companion. It's
Ranjit, sir. Prime suspect in the murder of Reginald Appleton. He's
here.'

She waited for some kind of exclamation from her senior officer.
Nothing.

'Sir?'

'They're where? Approaching from the direction of Piccadilly
Gardens?'

Iona started to say something then stopped, realizing he wasn't
even talking to her.

'Keep them on CCTV, OK? We need to get officers to intercept
them. Khan? I'm putting you on hold.'

The line went dead.

What's he doing? She looked around, uncomfortably aware of
how exposed she was. I don't believe this. Holding her phone to
her ear, she crossed the road and stepped into the dimly lit salon.
A Chinese-looking woman wearing a face mask was working on
the nails of an overweight Indian female. Under the harsh glare of
a table spotlight, the pale hands of the salon worker looked like two
crabs, scavenging for food between the other woman's pudgy fingers.

Iona lifted a price list from the counter and began to study it. It
was almost a minute before Wallace came back on the line. 'Ranjit
Bhujun is in Bury?' He sounded incredulous.

'I have the address,' she whispered. 'I also spoke with our
friend in Mauritius late last night. He believes Ranjit could have
gained sensitive information from a letter in Appleton's study.'

'About?'

She glanced over her shoulder, aware the other two women could
probably hear her. 'What's going on in town. Right now. Arrangements
relating to the movements of certain key figures.'

'Key figures? Who?'

'Household names. Architects of the old party.'

'Detective, are you not able to speak freely?'

'That is correct.'

'Then you need to come in and make a report. I don't have time
to play fucking guessing games.'

'I can't. They're here – in a property just along from me. You
need to send support.'

'Negative – that's not possible. Have you any idea of the activity levels we're currently dealing with? How can you be sure it's him, anyway?'

'It's him.'

'Did you get a photo? Something you can send?'

'No.'

'No photo? Where are they, anyway? In that mosque?'

She fought the urge to scream. 'There is someone due to make an appearance on stage in about an hour's time.'

'Is that so?' His voice was loaded with sarcasm.

'I believe Ranjit is fully aware of that fact.'

'That, Detective, is completely impossible. I wasn't aware of that fact until this morning. Only a few people in Gold Command were. Now, I want you back at Orion House.'

Iona shook her head. 'I think correspondence in Appleton's study referred directly to his appearance. Gordon Brown's, too.'

'Whose appearance?'

'Tony Blair's.'

'Detective, I'm not talking about Blair. I'm talking about Clinton.'

Iona put the price list down and raised her hand to the side of her face, trying to shield her voice from the women. 'Who?'

'Bill Clinton. Plays the saxophone. Used to be in charge of America. Heard of him?'

'He's here?'

'He's on stage – alongside Tevland – in approximately fifty minutes' time.'

Iona dropped her hand to see a figure emerge from the gate Ranjit Bhujun had gone through. The person's head was bowed, face concealed beneath the rim of a flat cap. He seemed bulkier than Ranjit and not tall enough to be Vassen. The way he walked, too. It was slow, like an old person.

'Detective,' Wallace spoke again. 'Get back here and explain exactly what's going on.'

As the figure turned to cross the road, he looked up. It's the old guy, Iona thought. The one who was watching the football match in the park. The team made up of Mauritians. As he made his way over the road, Iona saw he had a bulging backpack slung over one shoulder. 'Sir?'

But Wallace had gone. The line was dead.

Sliding her phone back into her pocket, she placed a hand on the door, ready to follow once again.

FORTY-TWO

As they passed out of the tight cluster of residential streets, the old man kept his head down. It made following him easy. Almost too easy, Iona began to think, checking over her shoulder to make sure no one was shadowing her. The street behind was empty.

The fact he seemed so wrapped up in his thoughts started to cause her an increasing sense of alarm. She cast her mind back to the training session on how to spot the telltale signs of a bomb carrier. Profuse or abnormal sweating. Mumbling or praying to self. Bulky clothing. Trance-like state. Tunnel vision. Agitation or looking anxious. Suspect baggage.

He ticked at least three of those boxes.

A few minutes later they reached a main road. A drop opened up beyond the railings on the left and Iona was able to see down on to a set of train tracks. Old-fashioned signals stood like sentries before the platform where what appeared to be a steam train was sitting.

He turned left and Iona thought the road they were now on seemed familiar. There was a church up ahead and she realized it was the same one she'd seen him on the steps of the previous day. He continued past it before turning right down a narrow street which ran between the library and a modern building with a sign that said, The Fusilier Museum. She had time to mentally note they were on Moss Street before she saw the line of bus ranks up ahead.

Barely bothering to check for traffic, the old man crossed the road and made his way past the shelters. Iona looked with trepidation at the letters above the entrance of the building he was heading for. Bury Interchange for buses and Metrolink trams. There was only one direction the trams went from here: Manchester.

He continued along the covered walkway to a set of stairs and started down them. There was a tram waiting on the platform and he climbed straight onboard. Iona made her way down the stairs and hovered near a map of the Metrolink system. Do I stay with him? What about Ranjit? He's back at the house on Barrett Avenue, probably with Vassen.

A rapid beeping noise started from inside the half-empty carriages. Stay, she decided, watching the tram doors slide shut. The whine of the engine increased and, as the tram pulled away, she rechecked the map, looking for journey times. The city centre was twenty-eight minutes away.

She brought up Wallace's number and started jogging back towards Barrett Avenue. When her senior officer allowed her call to go through to his answerphone, her step faltered. He knows it's me calling, she thought. He has the number for everyone in his team. 'Sir, it's DC Khan.'

She had to dodge sideways as a bearded man in flowing robes opened the rear door of an old Datsun parked half on the pavement. Its back seats were piled high with trays of aubergines.

'I've just followed an elderly male – approximately sixty years old – to the tram station in Bury. He's boarded a tram and is currently en route to Manchester. He's of Asian or possibly Middle Eastern appearance and is wearing a flat cap, beige overcoat, grey trousers and black shoes. He also has with him a backpack that appears to be quite full. I repeat, a backpack that appears to be quite full. I'm returning to my previous location to keep watch on thirty-seven Barrett Avenue where Ranjit Bhujun is currently located. Sir? I need help, please.'

As soon as she cut the connection her phone started to ring. Jim. 'Hello.'

'It's me. They're with me now, just off the train.'

She dropped her pace to a quick walk. 'Have you asked—'

'It's him, Iona. No doubt. I got that mugshot of Ranjit out and—'

'I know. He went past where I was watching.'

'Is support on the way?'

At his end of the line she could hear a tannoy announcement starting up. 'No.'

'No? Where are you? Sounds like you're on the move.'

'I am. I just followed an elderly male from the house Ranjit entered. The old guy was wearing a backpack, Jim. He got on a tram to Manchester.'

'Hang on. You followed Ranjit on foot?'

'Yes. I'm going back to the house now. I figured officers can intercept the old man when the tram reaches Manchester.'

'You figured . . . I don't understand this. Why do you reckon? What the hell is going on?'

'I'm still out here on my own, Jim.'

'Jesus Christ! What did Wallace say? You have reported in, haven't you?'

'Of course! He thinks I'm chasing shadows. Wanted me to come in, report what I'd found to him in person. I just don't get it. The guy will not take this seriously.'

'I will fucking have him.'

'Sorry?'

'I can't believe you're on your own out there.'

'I can handle it. I'll try Wallace again in a minute, but I don't care what he says. I'm not leaving here. We know where Ranjit is, and as long as that's the case, he can't do whatever they're planning.'

'I do not like this at all.'

'Did you ask about the tunnels? Any near the convention centre the council don't know about?'

'Yeah, they mentioned a possible one. Hang on.' His voice grew muffled. 'Where did you say it was? Right. Iona? There's one going from somewhere near Barbirolli Square. But it's only an old storm drain.'

'Which square?'

'Barbirolli. It's near the Bridgewater Hall.'

'OK. And does it go towards the convention centre?'

'Not to the main building. More to the edge of the site, where the annex is.'

She came to an abrupt halt. 'Jim? I think that's where my dad is.' She ran a hand through her hair. 'I have to get him out.'

'You have to do what?'

'I . . . I don't know what to do.' She looked up the street, knowing her best option was to keep watch on the house.

'Iona, don't worry, we're going to check the tunnel out now.'

'Please hurry.'

She was back on the road which cut across the top of Barrett Avenue a couple of minutes later. The nail salon didn't give a good view of the property Ranjit had entered and she looked around anxiously, fighting the temptation to just carry on back to her car, race over to the convention centre and get her dad out. No, she told herself. You must stay with Ranjit.

She set off down the opposite side of Barrett Avenue to number thirty-seven, scanning the houses on her side of the road.

They all looked dark and quiet, their owners probably at work. Praying for a light to be on in one of them, she kept walking, aware she was now in full view of the property Ranjit had disappeared inside.

Something colourful on a front step caught her eye. A pair of kid's wellies. The steel-blue light in the front window flickered slightly. There's a television on inside, Iona thought, walking swiftly up the garden path. Knocking gently on the door, she removed her warrant card from the pouch pocket of her fleece as subtly as she could.

A woman of about thirty opened the door. 'Yes?' she asked cautiously.

Holding her identification close to her chest, Iona gave the woman a big smile. 'Madam, please don't look alarmed, but I need to come in.'

'Sorry?' she said, frowning as she saw what was in Iona's hand.

Wishing she was tall enough to block the view of the house-owner from anyone watching behind, Iona kept smiling. 'Just move back a step, Madam.'

The woman was obviously unsure about obeying the instruction.

'It's fine,' Iona said, moving on to the front step. 'Just do as I say, please.'

Warily, the woman retreated a step. 'What's going on?'

'I'll tell you,' Iona said, slipping through the door and immediately closing it. Breathing out, she tried to sound reassuring. 'I need to keep an eye on a house over the road, that's all. Here,' she slid a card out from behind her police badge. 'Call the main switchboard, they'll confirm who I am, OK?'

Looking troubled, the woman gestured at the hallway phone. 'I don't know. I'm calling my husband. He works nearby.' She shot a glance at the doorway of the telly room. 'Are we in danger?'

Iona could hear the tinkling sounds of a kids' programme. 'No. Absolutely not. Just carry on with what you were doing. Call your husband, by all means. But please don't ask him to come home. Don't look out the window, either.' Handing her the card, she set off up the stairs. 'Whose is the room that overlooks the road?'

'Mine. Ours. Mine and Richard's.' She was looking up through the banister's spindles with a fearful expression.

'Net curtains?'

'Yes.'

'I'll need to keep all the upstairs lights off. Don't worry, I'll be out of your hair very soon.'

Their bedroom was large and untidy. On a chest of drawers in the corner was a small television and DVD player. Children's books formed a precarious tower beside it. A cream-coloured duvet lay askew on the double bed. Iona spotted a bra and knickers lying across the sheet and she pulled the corner of the duvet over them to spare the woman downstairs any embarrassment.

The room gave a good view of the road. Iona moved the wicker stool from in front of a make-up table and sat down facing the window. A line of little socks were drying on the radiator barely beneath her nose. Curtains or blinds were drawn across almost all the windows of number thirty-seven. A light appeared to be on in one of the upstairs rooms and she thought she glimpsed movement there. The woman's footsteps were coming up the stairs.

'I rang the number,' she hesitantly announced. 'You seem genuine.'

Iona didn't turn round. 'I am. My name's Iona, by the way.'

'Oh – Sarah.'

'How old is your little one?'

'Evie? She's two. Sorry, it's a right mess in here.'

'I honestly didn't notice,' Iona said, glancing back.

The woman was straightening the bed and plumping the pillows. 'Erm . . . do I offer you a drink? Who is it you're watching?'

'A suspect in a fraud case.'

'Benefit fraud, you mean?'

Iona nodded, happy if the woman was satisfied with that explanation.

'Which number house?'

Not wanting to reveal the exact property, Iona said, 'Actually, a cup of tea would be brilliant. I haven't stopped all morning.'

'Right. Give me two minutes.'

'And I know this is odd, but would you mind putting the telly on? Any news channel will do.'

'Yes,' Sarah answered, sounding confused. 'Richard has it on BBC News 24, if that's OK.'

'Perfect.'

The screen came to life. A female presenter was talking excitedly to camera from outside the conference centre's main entrance. The text across the band at the base of the screen read, Clinton due to appear.

'. . . official confirmation – yes, Kirsty. He's here. Touched down at Manchester Airport just after nine, we understand. Now, the press office wouldn't give details of any speech or, indeed, if he'll even make one. But the symbolism of his appearance is plain; we, the Democrat Party, can do business with Daniel Tevland. And the fact he'll be walking out on stage with Tony Blair and Gordon Brown also means that the Labour Party's old warring factions are happy to move on, united behind their new leader. Even Manchester's grey weather cannot dampen spirits around the venue. Political conference? More like a pop concert!'

FORTY-THREE

J im squatted down to examine the padlock. Strands of old spider web stretched across its keyhole. Flakes of rust lay across its top, fallen from the bars of the grille it secured. The opening behind it was pitch-black. He looked up at Hidden Shadow.

When the two Sub-Urban Explorers had alighted from the train at Piccadilly station, the first thing Jim asked, after showing his badge, was their real names.

The one who Iona had referred to as Hidden Shadow looked at his companion, who was glaring defiantly at Jim.

'Don't you think it's time we dropped the tags?' Jim had said wearily. 'Come on, a Christian name. It's all I'm asking. Mine's Jim.'

Hidden Shadow ran his tongue across his teeth. 'Chas.'

'Thank you, Chas.' Jim looked expectantly at the companion. 'Fraser.'

'Right, Chas and Fraser, let's drop your stuff off in the Transport Police's office round the corner. The sooner we get this sorted, the sooner you two can go home and have a warm shower.'

From his position by the grille, Jim placed his hands on his knees. 'When did you last access this, Chas?'

'Two years ago?'

Jim stood. 'Looks like you were the last to have done that.'

Chas lifted a grubby hand and examined a nasty scrape running across his knuckles. His hair was matted and he smelled of damp earth. 'I'd agree.'

'And you got in here?'

'Yeah, the padlock that used to be there was very basic.'

You mean easy to pick, Jim thought. 'How far does it go?'

'Seventy-five metres at the most.'

Jim stepped over the low shrubs forming a screen round the narrow opening. The curving white expanse of the convention centre's roof was visible between the buildings to either side of him. A few office workers looked down from upper windows. Jim realized that the passageway would be impossible to access during daylight hours without arousing suspicion. He wandered across the strip of grass, back to where Fraser stood smoking a roll-up. 'And it doesn't have an entrance at the other end?'

'Nope,' Fraser replied sulkily.

'Bricked-up,' Chas announced, joining them. 'It was probably once an overflow from the underground canal, who knows?'

Iona answered his call after half a ring. She sounded sick with worry.

'It's secure,' Jim said emphatically. 'And it hasn't been accessed in a very long time.'

'Jim, they've overlooked something. They must have. Something's going to happen, I know it.'

'Are you back at the property where our friends are?'

'Yes, opposite it.'

'Not on the street?'

'No, in a house. It's OK, I'm safe.'

'What's the score with Wallace?'

'I left another message to ring me. This time with the office manager.'

'What did he say?'

'That Wallace is up to his eyeballs, but he'd pass my message to him in person.'

Jim looked at his watch. Ten twenty-one. 'OK, he'll get back to you soon. He has to. Let me know when he does.'

'I'm worried about the old guy. His tram will get into Manchester soon. What if Wallace puts my message to one side?'

'Leave that with me. I can call the Bootle Street nick and get them to let officers on the platforms know. He's an old guy, you said, Middle Eastern appearance and wearing a backpack?'

'Yes, and a flat cap.'

'OK.' He closed his phone and sent a despairing look up at the sky. The fact she was still out there on her own, trying to keep tabs on a terror cell infuriated him. What was Wallace trying to prove? That he still had power over Iona? Or did he know something they didn't? Something to convince him Iona hadn't really stumbled over anything to worry about. It didn't add up. Something wasn't right.

The familiar black half-spheres mounted on the corners of the office buildings caught his attention. CCTV cameras. A thought hit him and he turned to the pair of Sub-Urban Explorers. 'You're firm believers in the Big Brother state?' He gestured up at the camera units.

Chas shrugged. 'What's to debate?'

'Come on,' Jim replied. 'I'll show you something that will really freak you out.'

They were in the lobby of the CCTV control room a few minutes later. As Jim waited for Colin Wray to appear, he walked back and forth, speaking to the bedraggled-looking pair. 'This is where it all happens. Inside there,' he pointed to the inner door, 'is where all the views from all the cameras round town connect. Seventy-six of them covering the city centre alone.'

The pair regarded the door with a mixture of awe and mistrust, both flinching slightly when it suddenly opened. Colin Wray stepped out. Nose wrinkling, he glanced briefly at Chas and Fraser then looked at Jim. 'You better make this brief, mate.'

Jim pointed at the pair. 'Any chance they can accompany me inside? I need a quick word with someone in there.'

Colin looked sceptical. 'Are you two police?'

They looked at Jim for an answer.

'Would you believe me if I said they were working undercover?' Jim asked.

Colin sighed. 'They're not even police, are they?'

'How about if they're assisting me with an enquiry? They'll be quiet as mice.'

'Jim, you really take the biscuit bringing them in here.'

'Yeah, sorry. Listen, lads, sit here and I'll be back in a few minutes. We're nearly done, I promise.'

Colin turned round and swiped the card reader of the inner door. They entered the main room to a buzz of voices. Blinking as his eyes adjusted to the gloom, Jim hoped he wouldn't see Wallace among the many people standing behind the row of camera operators. The nearest of the watching group had American accents. 'Why the yanks?' he whispered.

'They're with Clinton's security detail,' Colin replied.

Jim's head turned. 'Who's?'

'Clinton's?'

'Bill Clinton?'

'That's the one.'

Jim wasn't sure he'd heard correctly. 'Clinton's here?'

'Appearing on stage with the Labour Party big-hitters, any minute now.'

Ignoring the images filling the Barco screens, Jim looked over the other clusters of observers. Most were neat-haired men wearing dark, sober suits. He set off down the narrow room, head-cocked for any southern accents. Halfway along, he heard one. A tall man, late forties with grey-flecked hair. He was talking to a colleague who seemed a good fifteen years younger.

'Excuse me,' Jim said, addressing the older of the two. 'Are you with MI6?'

He looked round. 'Sorry?'

Jim held up his warrant card. 'Are you with MI6?'

He studied Jim's face. 'Yes.'

'Could I have a word? I'm with the GMP. Sergeant James Stephens.'

The man hesitated. 'You need a word with me?'

'Yes, it's really urgent.'

He whispered briefly to his companion. 'Right.' He turned fully to Jim, light from the Barco screens creating a halo round his hair. 'How can I help?'

'A colleague of mine in the Counter Terrorism Unit is shadowing two suspects out in Bury, just to the north of here. One is the prime suspect in the murder of an ex-Law Lord at his retirement home out in Mauritius. This man has now entered the country illegally, we're not sure how recently. We think he has sensitive knowledge about the conference gained from personal correspondence in the study of the person he killed.'

The MI6 officer looked like he was struggling to take it all in. 'You are with the Greater Manchester Police?'

'Yes.'

'This colleague you mentioned is in the CTU?'

Jim could see doubts creeping into the other man's eyes. 'I know this isn't following the expected channels, but my colleague's lines of communication are down. The suspect – a Ranjit Bhujun – is here. He is wanted by the Mauritian police for the ex-Law Lord's murder.'

'Are you talking about Reginald Appleton?'

So you're familiar with the case, Jim thought. 'Yes.'

The man considered the comment. 'What is your involvement in this?'

'I have been assisting my colleague. My point is, this should have all been flagged in a report. Can you check your lot in London were made aware of it? I'm afraid it's fallen between the cracks somehow.'

'Be more specific. What was the nature of this material in Appleton's study?'

'Details about the movements of Tony Blair and, possibly, other high-profile figures. They were sent to Appleton by a senior person at a firm of lobbyists in London.'

The man's hawk-like eyes were now fixed on Jim. 'Who is this lobbying firm?'

'Slattinger-Dell. Tristram Dell is an old acquaintance of Reginald Appleton's. Slattinger-Dell has been conducting some kind of branding exercise for the Labour Party.'

With a knowing nod, the man removed a mobile phone from his jacket and, edging away from Jim, made a call. He spoke quietly, eyes staying on Jim the entire time. After a few second's wait, he lowered the phone and asked sharply, 'Where in the CTU was this report supposed to have come from?'

'The officer out in the field is a Detective Constable Khan,' Jim responded. 'Her report should have gone via her senior officer, a Superintendent Paul Wallace.'

FORTY-FOUR

Iona's sense of isolation was mounting by the minute. The house opposite was still. Not daring to take her eyes off it, she could only listen to the commentary coming from the little television. The discussion refused to budge from Bill Clinton's imminent appearance. Mind on where her father was, Iona half-listened to the phrases being bandied about the studio.

One of the world's great political showmen.

Audiences eat out of his hand.

Charisma and charm.

A supreme speaker.

Her phone went off and she lifted it to see the screen. Jim. Just the sight of his name made her feel better.

'Where are you?' he asked, voice tight with something that sounded like excitement.

'Still opposite where Ranjit is holed-up.'

'What number is the house you're in?'

She had to think for a second. 'Thirty-four, why?' She heard him call the number to someone else before his voice came back on the line. 'Expect a quiet knock on the back door, any minute now.'

'What? Why?'

'They're clearing the street.'

'Who is?'

'The cavalry, my beauty. They're almost with you.'

She risked a swift look over her shoulder. 'I don't follow you.'

'Your support, Iona. They're sealing off the street at each end. All residents in the vicinity of thirty-seven are being escorted away. Tell me that is the right number, please.'

She stood up, craning her neck, trying to see to the end of the road. Everything appeared normal. 'Who? Who is, Jim?'

'The works.'

'I . . . Why are you ringing me with this?'

'Wallace hadn't filed your report. The fucker did absolutely nothing with it. He's been letting you run round Bury on your own.'

She sank back on to the wicker stool. 'What do you mean?'

'I double-checked. MI6 had no idea.'

Her mind was trying to leap in several directions. 'You went to MI6?'

'Too right. And bloody glad I did.'

'Does Wallace know what's going on?'

'Maybe by now, he does. Listen, Iona, they're asking me to get off the line. The guy co-ordinating this is about to call. His name is Alex.'

Jim's call ended and a second later her phone lit up again. 'Iona, it's Alex. You were just speaking with Sergeant Stephens.'

She gave a single nod. Everything was moving so fast.

'How are you doing, anyway? Got things under control there?'

He sounded so calm and at ease, she couldn't help feel reassured. 'I've not taken my eyes off the house, if that's what you mean.'

'Good on you. Who do you think is in number thirty-seven?'

'Two adult males.'

'Vassen and Rhanjit Bhujun?'

'That's right.' The fact help had arrived was beginning to sink in. The danger to her father was over. She wanted to cry.

'No one else?'

'As far as I'm aware, no.'

'The house number you're in and location within the house, please.'

'Thirty-four, first floor, bedroom overlooking the street.'

'OK. My two planners will be with you any second. Good lads, the both of them. They're about two properties away, coming along the back alley.'

'You're here?'

'No, I'm in the CCTV control room in Manchester. There's a helicopter above you. Live images are being relayed from it. Don't worry, it's too high for anyone on the ground to know it's there.'

'Do I stay where I am?'

'For the moment. How much charge is on your phone?'

She held it away from her face. 'Down to one bar.'

'Stay on the line. One moment.' She could hear vague voices in the earpiece. From downstairs came three quiet knocks. 'That's them.'

'Sarah!' Iona called over her shoulder. 'Can you let them in? It's fine, they're police.'

Alex spoke. 'Are they with you?'

'The owner is letting them in.'

'Great. Well done, Detective, I hear you've been doing this on your own. I'm hanging up, OK?'

Footsteps were coming up the stairs. She glanced round. Two scruffy-looking blokes in civilian clothes were approaching the doorway. The taller one was carrying a large green kit bag.

'Yes, she's here,' the other one said into his earpiece, removing a laptop from his jacket. 'OK, will do.'

The taller one was unzipping the kit bag. After removing a shotgun from inside, he held up a packet of sandwiches and a can of drink to Iona. 'Brought you some scoff. Now, which house is it?'

Iona pointed to thirty-seven.

FORTY-FIVE

Jim stepped back out into the lobby of the CCTV control centre. To his relief, the two Sub-Urban Explorers were still there. Both looked bored and pissed off. 'Sorry, lads, that took a minute or two longer than I thought.'

He went over to the main door and pulled it open. The knowledge that Iona was safe and the situation under control filled him with a sense of exhilaration. He wanted to skip off to the nearest pub and have a drink. Only the fact that the MI6 officer wanted to question him further stopped him from giving in to the urge. One thing seemed certain: Wallace was well and truly screwed.

'Thanks for your help in this. Sorry if it got heavy-handed.' He stepped aside. 'You better know that there's every chance you'll be contacted again about this.'

'That's it, then?' Fraser scowled, getting off the sofa.

'Yup. Free to go.'

They moved past him and out into the cold of the NCP car park. An uneasy glance passed between them. Jim stopped the door from fully closing and poked his head out. 'What's up?'

Chas' lips twisted as if he was trying to remove something unsavoury from his mouth.

Fraser started to step away. 'Doesn't matter. Come on, let's do one.'

Jim looked from one to the other. 'Hey, may as well say it – if you reckon it's important.'

Chas shrugged. 'We were thinking about the tunnels – any near the convention centre that might have been overlooked.'

'And?'

'That bloke from Sri Lanka or wherever he's really from. There's this one location. We're pretty sure it was talked about in front of him. He could have gone looking for it himself.'

Jim pulled the door fully open. 'Come in,' he announced resignedly. 'You'd better give me the details.'

They re-entered the lobby and Jim gestured to the sofa. 'Have a seat.' He was sinking into the armchair when a call came in from Iona. Pushing himself back up, he turned to face the wall. The clock on it read ten thirty-eight. Seeing the time made Jim feel uncomfortable, but he couldn't put his finger on why. 'You OK?'

'Fine. I've had no word from Wallace yet.'

'I wouldn't worry about him,' Jim replied, thinking he would probably have packed his things and left Orion House before Iona got back.

'The crew who showed up here – it's more like a military operation. People are now in the houses on each side of number thirty-seven. They've got those devices up against the walls, the ones for detecting sounds and thermal images.'

'Where are you?'

'Still in the house opposite.'

'No sign of them?'

'Not as yet. How about the old guy?'

Jim felt his spirits drop like a stone. Oh, shit. His eyes went back to the clock. The tram would have arrived in town over ten minutes ago. Plenty of time for him to have got into the convention centre.

'Did they lift him as he came off the tram?' Iona asked. 'What was in the backpack?'

'I don't know,' he replied, walking towards the inner door. No means of calling the main room.

'But they did pick him up?'

Now pulling open the main door, Jim held down the buzzer outside as Chas and Fraser watched him intently.

'Jim?' Iona asked. 'What are you up to?'

He kept his finger on the buzzer.

Wray's voice sounded from the speaker. 'All right, Jim! Bloody hell—'

He cut across the team leader's complaint. 'Let me back in, Colin. Now!'

'OK.'

Iona was speaking again. 'What's going on?'

'I'll call you back.' He pressed red and pointed his mobile at Chas and Fraser. 'You two, stay here.'

'Don't worry,' Fraser smirked. 'We will.'

The inner door opened a crack and Jim practically shoved Wray back into the corridor beyond. 'We need to send out an alert to officers at the secure zone!'

Iona found herself staring at her phone. Oh my God, had the old man with the backpack been missed? He could be inside the convention centre by now. Was he the one really carrying out the attack? Were they all in the wrong place? She looked at the little TV. The sound had been turned down, but it was still tuned into BBC News 24.

The view was of the main plaza. It was now largely empty, just a few catering staff in white suits carrying crates of glasses. Police officers at the edges were looking out through the perimeter fence. A pair of delegates were jogging up the steps to the main entrance where more security personnel stood. Text appeared at the bottom of the screen. Clinton due on main stage.

The officer with the laptop was clicking his fingers at Iona. 'They're not picking up any movement in number thirty-seven. You're sure the targets are inside?'

'As sure as I can be. I . . . left my position for about twelve minutes to follow a third suspect as far as the tram station.'

He lowered his radio and gave her a disbelieving look. 'No one had eyesight of the house for almost quarter of an hour?'

His outraged tone caused a stab of anger. 'It was me, OK? Just me, I had no support. What was I meant to do?'

He looked away, speaking into the radio as he did so. 'We need to go in. Move the teams into position.'

Iona turned back to the television. Coverage had now cut to inside the building. The main hall was rammed with people – every seat taken, thousands of faces looking expectantly in one direction. The camera swung through one hundred and eighty degrees to focus on the enormous stage. Spot lights angled up from the front edge swept slowly back and forth across the Labour Party emblem dominating the back wall. A figure was crouched before one of the podiums, busily adjusting something at its base.

Iona's mouth felt dry as she thought of her father in a room just seconds away from the main hall. Get out, she wanted to scream at the telly. Just get out of there! Her phone started to ring and she could only just summon the will to look down at it. A number with the Manchester prefix was on the screen. 'Hello?'

'DC Khan?'

She thought she recognized the voice. Softly spoken, but confident. 'Yes.'

'It's Professor Coe. You came to see me at the university? Vassen Bhujun was one of my tutees.'

'Yes, I remember. Professor, can I call you back?'

'Well – I think you need to hear this. I've put my finger on something very disturbing.'

She hunched forward, still watching the screen. 'I'm listening.'

'There they are,' whispered the officer at the window. Iona glanced down. Black-clad officers were in the garden of number thirty-seven, crawling along the base of the wall towards its front door.

'It relates to the piece of equipment I suspected Bhujun of taking. The fraction collector.'

'OK.' The footage on the TV had returned to the make-shift studio in the Sky Bar from earlier on. Iona suddenly wondered if the view across Manchester beyond the plate-glass windows was actually some kind of special effect. A computer image beamed on to giant screens in a studio that was really down in London.

'His thesis was about manufacturing a less expensive alternative to cocoa butter.'

'Yes, I recall.'

'The raw product he was using was a processed form of mamona oil. I didn't even question what mamona oil was – to me it was just some kind of cash-crop they grow on Mauritius.'

The presenter on the screen paused in his questioning of a politician that Iona had seen countless times on the TV. He glanced at his watch and turned to camera. She was able to lip read him say, about ten minutes. 'Please, Professor, get to the point.'

'Mamona oil is known as castor oil in other parts of the world. There's an aqueous phase which is left once the oil is extracted from the castor beans—'

'Aqueous phase?'

'The waste. A dark, syrupy sludge. That, Detective, is very toxic. Processed castor oil is known as PGPR. Polyglycerol polyricinoleate. Do you follow?'

'No, I don't.'

'Ricin, Detective. The aqueous phase contains ten per cent ricin. Separate it with a fraction collector and you can obtain the poison in its pure form.'

Iona turned to the window. The team were now crouched below the ground-floor windows and to either side of the front door. 'Call them off!'

The officer's head whipped round. 'What?'

'Call your team back! The house. They've been using it to make ricin.'

Jim crashed back out into the lobby. Chas and Fraser were sitting on the sofa like audience members of a show.

'You've got a big problem, haven't you?' Chas asked cautiously.

'Fuck, yes. You were mentioning a tunnel just before. Where is it?'

'It's more of an access point. Part of the Deansgate tunnel.'

'Deansgate tunnel?'

Chas nodded. 'I made it down there, just the once. I told your colleague, the one in the Counter Terrorism Unit.'

'Tell me.'

'It was when they were building the new offices and stuff in front of the law courts a few years ago. Where the *Manchester Evening Chronicle* is based.'

Jim knew where he was talking about – the new complex contained a Wagamama noodle bar and Armani shop on its ground floor.

'To build it, they had to dig up a big section right on the edge of Deansgate itself.'

'And that's where you found the tunnel?'

'Just a section of it. I made it down there during one lunch hour. Only had time for a quick look about. The section was about sixty, seventy metres long, bricked up at both ends. Fucking big it was, once. There was loads of silt and rubble on the floor, though. Some places almost to the roof. My guess was—'

'Chas, get to the point.'

He blinked. 'Yeah, sorry. Right, I followed it in the direction of the cathedral. Just before it ended at the bricked off part, I spotted this little door. Wooden – well knackered. The lock was half-hanging off. I got it open and there was this passageway sloping up. Very narrow, not much more than shoulder width. Stone floor, like cobbles, but flatter. So I walk along it for about twenty steps, using the light from my mobile phone. It ends at another door, this one metal and newer. Much newer. No way I could get that open – but there was a key hole in it. So I look through it. Some of the view was blocked by boxes or something, but through the cracks I could see this narrow room on the other side. The walls were lined with these glass-fronted cabinets. Narrow metal frames to them. Inside were loads of old books, some of them—'

'How far did the Deansgate tunnel go in the other direction – towards the conference centre?' Jim interrupted.

'As far as Saint John Street, maybe a bit further.'

'How far – roughly – is that from the centre?'

'A long way,' Fraser said. 'Well over a hundred metres.'

Jim couldn't see how two men – maybe assisted by an old man – could dig a tunnel that length. And besides, what would it join? The subterranean canal Iona had inspected only a couple of days before?'

'Only possibility is if this Muttiah bloke knocked through the brick partition sealing the tunnel off below Saint John Street,' Chas continued. 'Say he did and there's another navigable stretch beyond. Say then there's a side tunnel off that bit going in an easterly direction. It would be getting you very close to the conference centre. Chance is miniscule, but you never know with these tunnels . . .'

Jim's mind was back on the CCTV footage from outside the Central Library. Vassen shaking dust from his thick mop of hair. The missing rucksack. They'd deposited that thing somewhere. 'But this way in you found on the construction site. That building was finished ages ago.'

'You're right,' Chas replied. 'Next time I tried to go back, it had all been back-filled with concrete. Then the new building went up over the top of it.'

'So how could anyone –' Jim paused. 'The metal door looking in on that store room?'

They both nodded.

'The room was lit by this single bulb up in the ceiling,' Chas said. 'The fitting was really distinctive.'

'Why?'

'It was like a metal tube. The thing went up and then ran all the way across the ceiling and out through the wall. We worked it out eventually. The place was closed for about four years. Big heritage project. We've been back since it re-opened. The security on the doors getting you out of the public areas was way beyond us. But Vassen? We know he's good with locks. He got up the clock tower of the town hall one time.'

Jim scratched at the back of his neck. 'You're ahead of me here. Which building was this storeroom in?'

'Heard of the John Rylands Library?'

Jim had. The old Victorian building with its Gothic architecture and bricks the colour of dry blood had stood at the mid-point of Deansgate for well over a hundred years.

FORTY-SIX

Iona was on her feet and staring across at the house. Beside her, the man with the laptop continued speaking into his radio. 'Yes, it has to be Silver Commander. Negative, we are not located in the Outer Zone.' He listened for a second. 'It's code three – chemical. Silver Commander needs to call it. The elderly male seen leaving the house will have arrived in the city centre over quarter of an hour ago. If he's entered the secure zone via an official entry point, ricin will not have shown up as part of the standard security checks.'

'What's he talking about?' Iona asked the colleague.

'Whether to declare Operation Lock-In at the secure zone. Problem is, if you do that you could trap everyone on the site with a terrorist carrying ricin.'

The words caused Iona's head to jerk round. Wasim. He won't be able to get out. She sat on the end of the bed, hands clutched between her knees.

The officer spoke again. 'No, we did not come with CBRN suits. This entire area will need to be evacuated. We think two suspects, possibly more.'

Iona spotted something happening on the television. People in the audience at the convention centre were looking round. Several near the front had stood and were looking off to the side with bemused or angry expressions. The camera moved round, catching fluttering movement in the far distance. The picture blurred as the cameraman tried to refocus.

Iona felt like the floor had turned to sponge as she crossed the room and turned the sound up.

'. . . kind of a disturbance to the rear of the hall. Yes, I can see a man on the balcony. He's throwing something down on to the audience below him.'

Iona stepped away from the television and bumped into the end of the bed. Her legs didn't belong to her. Everything seemed disconnected and unreal.

The commentator began to talk again. 'It's . . . I'm not sure . . . Handfuls . . . handfuls of what appears to be paper. Are they leaflets? They look like leaflets.'

Now the picture homed in on a single figure. He was leaning against the balcony railing, reaching down and flinging his arm outwards, squares of paper drifting through the air.

'He's shouting. I'm not sure if our microphones are picking this up, but he's shouting about Sagossia. Oh, that's a relief. Security staff are now on the scene. They're making their way towards him.'

The camera had closed right in on the person and Iona felt her mouth drop open. 'It's him! The one who got on the tram!'

The officer near the window looked round at her.

'There!' Iona pointed at the screen. 'He's in the main hall!'

'Hold the line.' The man at the laptop cupped a hand over his mouthpiece. 'What the fuck are you on about?'

'The one who I saw get on the tram. That's him, on the TV!'

Now looking completely bewildered, the planner turned to the screen. The elderly man was moving along the balcony in order to keep ahead of the nearest security guard hurrying in his direction. Two more were at the other end of the balcony and closing in from that side.

'Return Sagossia!' the man bellowed. 'Return Sagossia to its rightful people!'

He threw out his arm again and another handful of flyers were released into the air. 'Return Sagossia!'

'Are you sure that's him?' the officer with the laptop asked. 'Yes!'

The nearest security guard lunged at the old man, catching him by the neck and forcing him into a headlock. Gasps of concern rose up from the watching crowd. The old man continued trying to shout as the other two security guards reached him. One twisted his arm back as the other yanked the rucksack out of his hands. They started bundling him along the balcony. A wave of talking was breaking out as the camera continued to track the old man's removal.

'There we have it,' the announcer faltered. 'It, it seems some kind of protestor has chosen this precise moment to make his views be known. What those views were, I'm not entirely sure. We'll keep you informed as more details emerge, but for now, it seems all attention is turning back to the main stage.'

The officer with the laptop was speaking again. 'Did you get that? The person just removed from the main conference hall was the same person who boarded the tram from here. Correct, the same person. Yes, he left the property we're currently surveilling.' He nodded his head a few times. 'Understood.' Looking up, he spoke to Iona and his colleague. 'We're pulling back. An engineer has patched into the phone line for thirty-seven. A negotiator will try to make contact. We're out of here.'

Iona took another look at the television. The old man was no longer in view. 'Someone needs to get hold of one of the leaflets he threw. We need to know what it's about.'

The planner with the laptop had now closed it and was setting off out of the room. 'They'll be interrogating him, don't worry. Come on, let's go.'

Iona followed the two officers down the stairs, through the kitchen and out the back door. Uniformed officers were emerging from the backyards on either side of the alley, herding residents towards each end. She saw a police van reversing round the corner, its hazard lights flashing.

As they strode past clusters of blue and green wheelie bins, Iona took her phone out and started scrolling through her address book. Other officers were out on the road directing everyone away from Barrett Avenue. The two planners made a beeline for an unmarked car that was parked with its front doors open.

'Hugh!' the one carrying the laptop barked. 'We need the obs points at the rear to stay in place. We don't want these guys going anywhere.'

Iona found the number she was looking for and pressed green.

'Madam, you can't stay here.' A hand gently took hold of her upper arm and she tried to shrug it off. 'Madam, you can make your call where it's safe to do so. Now I need you—'

She produced her identification and held it up to the uniformed officer. 'I'm with the CTU.'

The female officer let go of her arm.

'Ayo, it's Detective Constable Khan.'

'Detective! I was just looking for your number. Have you seen the television?'

'Where is Sagossia, Ayo? Have you heard of it?'

'Yes, it was one of Lord Appleton's final rulings. Sagossia is an island—'

The driver of the police van revved the engine, obliterating Ayo's words. 'One of Appleton's rulings?'

'Practically his last.'

'Where is Sagossia?'

'The Indian Ocean.'

A memory hit home. A recent item in the news. Something to do with extraordinary rendition. Was it an American military facility? Somewhere flights carrying terror suspects had been landing? 'Did Appleton rule on someone who was tortured there?'

'No – the ruling related to events going back some fifty years. The island's inhabitants were forcibly removed by the British Government back in the sixties and relocated to Mauritius.'

The people filing past Iona looked scared and confused. She heard one asking about how long before she could go back to her house: her cat was still inside the property. Officers were aggressively calling out, beckoning them to a line of barriers further down the road. 'Why were they removed?'

'To make way for an American airbase.'

That's it, thought Iona. It's an airbase.

'The inhabitants have been fighting for the right to return ever since. Our government resisted and resisted, despite several rulings going in the islanders' favour. It finally went to the Law Lords in 2008.'

Iona heard a voice calling out the word, sir. She glanced to her side to see a young constable leading a woman of about fifty towards the vehicle with the front doors open. The taller of the two planners had an elbow on its roof, busily talking into his radio.

'Sir!' the young officer called again.

'What was Appleton's role?' asked Iona.

'He was the lead Law Lord on the case. It was Reginald who wrote up the final judgement.'

The uniformed officer was now at the unmarked car. 'Sir! This lady has information about number thirty-seven.'

The planner looked round. 'What is it?'

'She lives on Hacking Street, the one on the other side of Barrett. The rear of her house faces the rear of thirty-seven.' He nodded at her. 'Go on.'

'Ayo, one moment.' Iona turned to listen.

'Well,' she said nervously, 'it's the two younger men who've been staying with Navin.'

Iona moved closer to the car.

'Navin being the house owner?' the young uniform prompted.

'Yes,' the woman replied. 'He works for the council and has done for years. Lovely man.'

'Does he wear a flat cap?' Iona asked.

She nodded. 'Yes, he does.'

'What about the two younger men?' the planner demanded.

'They were blocking the alley. I was going to say something.'

'Blocking the alley?' he said warily.

'With Navin's car. He keeps it in a lock-up on Canning Crescent, round the corner. Anyway, I didn't need to in the end because they left.'

The planner shot a concerned glance at Iona. 'When?'

'Just after ten.'

Iona looked at her watch. Almost three minutes past eleven. She felt sick.

'I think they were going away for a while,' the woman added. 'They had rucksacks and everything.'

Dad, Iona thought. She whirled round and started sprinting back to where her car was parked.

FORTY-SEVEN

Iona had passed over the M60 and was approaching the outskirts of Manchester when her phone started to ring. She put it on speakerphone and wedged it into the holder on the dashboard. 'Ayo, can you hear me?'

'Yes. It sounds like you're in a car.'

'I am.'

'Is it safe for you to talk?'

She checked the speedometer. Sixty-four miles an hour in a forty zone. Her attention went back to the road ahead. At least there weren't too many cars about. 'You were saying about this case involving Sagossia.'

'Are you sure it's safe? I can ring you back . . .'

'No, I need to know.'

'You sound upset, Iona. Is everything OK?'

'Ayo, please. I'm just . . . I'll just listen, OK? You talk.'

'Very well. I've accessed the notes and I was correct. It was one of Reginald's last rulings – and possibly his hardest. I remember how much it troubled him at the time.'

'Why?'

'The Sagossians were treated appallingly, and still are, I suppose. Back then, it was the days of the Cold War. Russia's influence was growing in Asia and the Americans needed an airbase in the region. They settled on Sagossia – which was owned by the British. The problem was the island was inhabited by around two thousand or so people. The British agreed to clear them from their homes. They were rounded up, shipped over one thousand miles to Mauritius – also owned by the British at the time – and simply dumped there. Many died in the slums of Port Louis from starvation or disease. Others, apparently, committed suicide.'

Iona braked and swung out on to the white lines to avoid a moped rider emerging from a side street. The lights at a pedestrian crossing up ahead were turning to orange and she held her hand on the horn to deter an old couple from stepping out. They looked in astonishment as she shot past.

'Iona? Can you hear me?'

'Yes. Carry on.' She eased her speed back up into the fifties.

'The British Government then leased the island to America and embarked on a campaign of, frankly, deception. This was maintained by successive administrations for the next fifty years. You see, they couldn't acknowledge the existence of the Sagossians, especially since – technically – they were British citizens.'

'How do you mean not acknowledge they existed?'

'Proper residents would have democratic rights. So they were made out to be transient workers, not an indigenous population.'

'Like gypsies or something?'

'A few Man Fridays was the unfortunate term one British diplomat used to describe them in a recently released private memo from the time.'

It was the first occasion in any of their conversations that Iona had heard anger in Ayo's voice. The turn-off flashed by for Sedgley Park, where Gold Command was located. She pictured the chaos that would currently be breaking out in that place. Another half a mile and she'd reach the cathedral where the road merged with the end of Deansgate. 'So who is the grievance with now if this all happened decades ago?'

'Every government since has been complicit in the cover-up,' Ayo replied. 'That includes three prime ministers – starting with Harold Wilson – and over a dozen cabinet ministers.'

'What about Blair's government?'

She sighed. 'Iona, Tony Blair used the royal pejorative to circumvent a high court judgement finding in favour of the islanders' right to return. That means he resorted to the divine right of kings. Then there's Lord Appleton's ruling, when he found in favour of the Secretary of State for Foreign and Commonwealth Affairs. That was the islanders' final chance gone. Secretary of State at that time –'

Iona could see the dark outline of the cathedral up ahead. It seemed to be crouching on its elevated piece of land. To her right was the River Irwell. She was now on Deansgate itself. 'Ayo, I didn't catch that. Who was in charge at the Foreign Office?'

There was no reply.

Iona risked a quick look at her mobile, hoping the call hadn't been lost. The screen was blank. She reached forward and pressed the green button. No! Oh, damn it, no!

The phone's battery had run out.

Jim was going to start marching along Cross Street towards the town hall when Fraser called out to him. 'Quicker to cut through here.'

He followed the two younger men across St Anne's Square, passing the old church with its paving slabs made of grave stones.

'Good little tunnel under there,' Chas nodded. 'Leads into an old crypt. Skeletons and everything.'

Jim could only shake his head as he trailed the men who, suddenly, looked at ease in their surroundings. They rounded the corner on to Deansgate and there, a short distance further down, was the John

Rylands library. The Gothic architecture of the place stood in stark contrast to the modern buildings on either side. Intricate stone carvings were etched into the frames of the church-like windows, ornate balconies protruded higher up and, above them, battlements ran along the top.

Sirens were ringing out from the direction of the convention centre and, as they walked, Fraser was flicking through screens on his iPhone. 'Been an arrest in the main hall.'

Jim looked sharply to his left. 'What does it say?'

'Just breaking now. Lone protestor, up on the balcony, chucking leaflets about something down on to the audience.'

'Elderly male, was he?'

'Doesn't say.'

He reached for his own phone and tried to ring Iona. Engaged. As they jogged over a pedestrian crossing Jim looked up at the imposing building.

'This was all slums, beerhouses and factories when it was built,' Chas said. 'A bit of civilization amid the chaos.'

Jim had the abrupt impression of the city as something that evolved, continually putting down layer on layer in a never-ending process of change. He went to mount the shallow steps leading up to doors that looked more suited to a castle.

'Shut,' Chas called. 'After they did the big refurb. You get in through the visitor centre down the side.'

They scooted round the corner on to a wide plaza. To the left, beyond a line of young trees, the signage in the windows of the Armani shop shone gaudily out. They headed towards a low, white-walled structure that jutted out from the dark and sombre stone of the library's rear.

Chas shuffled through the revolving door and into the brightly lit space beyond. As Jim followed, he glimpsed a cafe area at the far end. He approached the front counter, badge at the ready. There was an attractive, dark-haired woman typing away behind the counter. 'Hello, I'm with the police. Is there a basement to this building?'

She nodded calmly, taking her hands of the keyboard and crossing one over the other.

'We need to go down there,' Jim said, voice low and urgent.

'I beg your pardon?' Her words carried the trace of an American accent.

'Can someone in your maintenance or facilities department take us down? We urgently need to look around it.'

'Oh . . . all right. One moment.'

She picked up her phone and pressed a couple of buttons. Jim turned round, watching as two men – both carrying bags over their shoulders – strolled straight past the front desk into the library's main part.

'Someone's on the way,' she said.

'Can anyone just wander in?'

'Of course. We are a public library. Anyone is welcome to use the Historic Reading Room up on the first floor.'

'You don't need to be a member?'

'Only if you're borrowing books.'

'What about bag inspections. Is there nothing like that?'

'Anything of value has to be signed out. Rare books and manuscripts cannot be taken from the Elsevier Reading Room, if that's what you mean.'

I was thinking about monitoring what people were bringing in, Jim thought, crossing his arms. Ranjit and Vassen could have been passing in and out of here pretty much as they pleased.

'Erika,' a voice said. 'Are these . . .?'

'Yes. Um, Officer?'

Jim turned to see a man of about twenty. His shirt, trousers and shoes were black and his hair was tied back in a ponytail. There was something apologetic about his demeanour. Trainee, Jim thought. 'Hello.' He extended a hand. 'We need to take a look round your basement area, please.'

'Certainly. Is there something amiss?' He led them along the counter to a set of spotless steps. Halogen lights shone down from the white ceiling.

'We're not sure,' Jim replied, checking Chas and Fraser were behind.

'Because the security is very robust,' he replied, pointing to the ubiquitous black half-sphere above. 'It's all monitored.'

'What's exactly down here?' Jim asked.

'Toilets, baby changing and a locker area. Through here are the storage facilities for the parts of the library's collection we don't keep out on display. Two of the world's twelve remaining complete Gutenberg Bibles are in here.' He unlocked a door marked, No Access. Immediately beyond was a second door with a camera mounted above it. He swiped a card attached to his belt by a looped cord. They entered a wide area dissected by row after row of locked shelving units. Books of every shape and size were lined up behind the thick Perspex fronts. Jim saw digital panels with temperature and what he guessed were humidity levels on the end of each unit.

'Is this the area you wanted to inspect?' the library employee said, stepping aside.

Jim looked at Chas for confirmation. The Sub-Urban Explorer was peering about. The more he looked, the less happy he appeared. 'Are there side rooms? Something with a door set into the wall?'

'Not as such,' their guide replied. 'There are doors in the partition walls to stop the spread of fire.' He continued down the central aisle, using his swipe card to open one so they could look into an identical area beyond.

Chas was shaking his head. 'It's all too . . . new. What I saw, it was old. The walls weren't white. The cabinets weren't these new things. They had thin metal frames, glass that looked warped.'

Jim addressed the library employee. 'This area was dug out recently?'

'Yes.'

'We need to be in the old part. A cellar or basement that's below the original building.'

'Nothing of value is stored there any more. All the rare manuscripts, the original—'

'We're not interested in the library's collection,' Jim interrupted.

Chas clicked his fingers, the sound quickly snuffed out by the confined space. 'And the light. It had this weird tube thing for the wires.'

'That's definitely the old basement,' the staff member replied. 'When it was built, the library was one of the first in Manchester to use electric light. All the wiring had to be done by plumbers and they used pipes to run the cables through.'

'That's where we need to be,' Jim said. 'The old basement.'

They retraced their steps to the ground floor. At the top of the stairs, the staff member opened a door marked Private and led them along a narrow corridor with a stone, not polished concrete, floor. Door after door was set into the old brickwork on their left, silver-clad pipes ran along the low ceiling just above their heads. He unlocked another door at the far end and they stepped on to a landing halfway up a curling set of stone stairs.

'Cool,' Chas whispered.

'This is the front of the building,' the library employee announced. 'We're on the staircase leading up from the old entrance out on to Deansgate.'

'Deansgate?' Jim asked, stopped dead by the incredible architecture. Stone pillars shot up all around him, each one bursting out in a fan of struts to form multiple vaulted ceilings, the centre of each studded with carvings of oak leaves, dragons or gargoyles. Mullioned windows let in light, but not enough to banish the shadows clinging to the swirling grooves of the stone banisters.

'That's right,' he replied, descending the flight of steps to the lobby area before the old doors. 'These are permanently locked, now.' He turned back on himself to gesture at another, narrower set of stairs.

At their top, Jim saw a sign that read, Men Only. Please Note: These Are Working Toilets. Photography Is Not Permitted From This Point. Thank You.

'The door to the dust store, as we call it, is down here,' the library employee said.

Jim scanned the ornate archway at the top. 'No CCTV?'

'Not down here, for obvious reasons.'

In the gloom at the bottom of the stairs were two doors. The one on their left was slightly ajar and Jim could see a white-tiled toilet area that looked unchanged in over a century. The door on the right was plain wood with painted lettering in its centre reading, Private.

'In here?' their guide asked, sounding unsure.

'Please,' Jim replied.

He used a key to open it up and flicked the light switch just inside. A row of single ceiling bulbs came to life, each one connected by a dark pipe which was bolted to the curved ceiling. The place smelled of sawdust.

'This is it,' Chas said from the doorway behind Jim.

The library employee led the way once more. 'This passage goes the entire length of the building. To the right are the old storage bays.' He stopped at the first recess, which was barred by a metal gate.

Like a dungeon, Jim thought, looking in. Behind it were empty cabinets and stacks of wooden chairs. Right at the back a pale face was staring in his direction. He felt a brief jolt of alarm before realizing it was just a stone bust.

'I'm not sure what would be of interest . . . the bays housing the old generators are further along . . .'

'We're going the wrong way,' Chas called out from behind them. 'You're leading us away from Deansgate.'

He's right, thought Jim, turning on his heel.

Chas was standing at the end of the corridor, thumb gesturing to an unmarked wooden door behind him. 'What's through here?'

The library employee frowned. 'I'm not sure.'

'Have you got a key?' Jim asked.

He examined his set. 'No. I've . . . you know? I've never had cause to open it.'

Jim waved a hand at Chas. 'Step aside, mate, you're cutting off the light.'

The two Sub-Urban Explorers pressed themselves up against the wall. Jim looked up to the ceiling, immediately spotting that the metal tube carrying the light cabling went through the stone above the door. Directing his gaze to the floor, he could see scuff marks on the dusty floor. He craned his neck to look more closely at the scrolled metal of the door's small handle. Sticking to its side was a small smear of dry soil. 'Did you touch this, Chas?'

'No.'

'We'll need the key,' Jim said, looking back at the library employee.

'The key,' he murmured. 'Yes. I can fetch Ian, he's my boss.'

Jim straightened up. 'While you do that, I need to make a call.' He took his mobile out and immediately saw the light was blinking red. No signal down here, he realized, setting off back up the stairs.

By the time Iona had weaved her way through the traffic clogging Deansgate she was almost weeping with frustration. It had gone quarter past eleven when she reached the junction with Peter Street. She turned into it and accelerated briefly before screeching to a halt in front of the yellow barrier blocking the road. She leaped out of her car, warrant card raised. 'DC Khan, CTU! I need to get into the conference centre.'

The pair of officers held their arms out to block her path. 'Hey! You cannot abandon a vehicle here!'

She tried to push past but they shoved her back. 'The keys are in the ignition, you move it. I have to get into the conference centre.'

Three other officers set off towards them from their position on the far side of the road.

'Wait up!' said one of the officers manning the barrier. 'Just wait up, OK? Let me see that ID again.'

She held it up to him. After taking a proper look, the officer started speaking into the handset of his radio.

Iona stepped away from them. The stretch of road beyond the girder-like barrier was still fairly crowded with people leafleting and others who obviously didn't possess passes into the centre itself. In the walkway between the outer and inner perimeter fence were two more officers. Both were watching her suspiciously. Further down the road, before the Midland Hotel, was the opening for the main entry point into the secure zone. It was about thirty metres away. Pretending that she was about to lean her forearms on the metal barrier, she ducked under it and started sprinting for the entry point.

The three officers crossing the road broke into a run, trying to cut her off. She headed straight for them, forcing them to check their step before jinking sharply to the right. Outstretched fingers brushed her sleeve, failing to get a firm hold. They started yelling at her to stop as she raced into the fenced-in corridor which led to the security check.

Standing in front of its entrance were two officers in black vests and black baseball caps. They raised their automatic weapons at her. 'Armed police! Get down! Fucking get on the floor!'

She stopped as if a cliff had opened up before her and raised her warrant card towards them. 'I'm police.'

'Get on the floor!'

They kept their weapons on her as footsteps approached rapidly from behind. Iona half-turned, directing her identification at the men she had just dodged. 'Detective Constable Khan, CTU!'

The first to arrive snatched her warrant card before shoving a knee into her back. She slammed into the tarmac and lay still, arms out by her sides.

A moment later, she heard someone call, 'She genuine?'

'Looks like it.'

'What the fuck are you playing at?'

She looked up. They had surrounded her, a ring of furious faces looking down. 'Can I get up?'

They stepped back and she climbed to her feet. 'I have to get in,' she said breathlessly, glancing between them towards the security check. The armed officer's weapons were still half-raised.

The one holding her ID handed it to a colleague who began to scrutinize it. 'No one gets in or out.'

She looked up into his puce face. 'Listen, I know I don't have a pass—'

'No one goes in or out. Pass or not, it doesn't matter.' He crossed his arms and stared down at her.

Iona took a breath in, about to try again.

'Operation Lock-In,' someone said to her side.

Her eyes bounced along the line of angry faces. 'Operation Lock-In?'

'We're on yellow alert – you're bloody lucky not to have got yourself shot.'

'Who is she, Sarge?' One of the armed officers stepped into view, weapon now lowered.

'A detective in the CTU,' the man holding Iona's warrant card responded, handing it back to her. 'What's this about?'

'Why aren't they evacuating?'

The sergeant shrugged. 'We're on standby for further instructions. Why?'

Iona bit her lip, wondering how much to say. 'It was me . . . I'd been following two suspects. You haven't picked anyone up at the perimeter?'

'Two males, Asian appearance? One shorter with a shaved head, late twenties?'

'Yes.' She nodded eagerly, suddenly hopeful.

He shook his head. 'That's who we've been briefed on.'

She couldn't help looking between the shoulders of the officers hemming her in. The roof of the conference centre rose up behind them all. 'Things are carrying on inside?'

The armed officer spoke. 'They're on stage right now.'

Iona needed space to breath. They were all staring at her, some with curiosity, others with irritation. 'You've got the suspects' descriptions,' she said. 'I didn't know.'

A few nodded.

'Sorry to have caused any hassle; my mobile gave up the ghost. I didn't know.'

Several stepped back again, a few murmuring quietly.

'I'll . . .' She pointed to the street. 'I'd better get my car. Sorry, guys.' Someone at the back said, *stupid bitch* under his breath.

'This is going in a report, you realize?' the sergeant stated. 'No bloody way it isn't.'

Iona gave a nod. 'Of course. My fault, my mistake.'

She made her way back out of the fenced corridor and on to Peter Street, aware dozens of eyes were upon her. Fighting back tears, she set off towards her vehicle. They're here, she thought. I know they're here. And no one has seen them because they're not above the ground. Her eyes dropped to the pavement and she pictured black and dripping tunnels beneath her feet.

Back in her car, she executed a three-point turn and drove slowly to the junction. An overwhelming sense of helplessness washed through her. She looked at her dashboard clock. Eleven twenty-two. Not knowing what to do, she turned left. They've found something nearby, she thought. They must have. Some way below ground we've all overlooked. She scanned the front of the shops lining the road. Not here. These places are too busy. They'd have needed somewhere quiet. An isolated building.

She reached the turn-off for Great Bridgewater Street. Rearing up out of the ground on its far side was the sheer glass walls of the Beetham Tower. The Sky Bar, she thought. It's halfway up the tower, before it turns into private apartments. I'll have a decent view of the entire area from up there.

Seeing the forecourt in front of the tower was empty of vehicles, she pulled up on it, put her hazards on and got out. 'Police,' she said, showing her warrant card to the approaching security guard.

He pointed towards the lobby. 'We're under strict instructions not to allow any parking here. Anti-terrorism precautions.'

'I'm Counter Terrorism Unit,' Iona replied. 'Detective Constable Khan, it's OK.'

He looked unsure. 'I don't know, we've been . . .'

'Then catch.' She threw him the keys and continued swiftly into the lobby of the tower. The reception desk was up ahead, lift doors to her left. Two police officers stood before them.

She approached them with her warrant card out. 'Is the Sky Bar open?'

'Not to the public, it isn't.'

'But these lifts will take me up there?'

They checked her identification before nodding. One pressed the button and the right-hand doors parted. An anxious flutter in her chest as she regarded the small space. Picturing her dad caused the feeling to vanish and she stepped inside. There was only one button.

As soon as the doors closed, the lift started to rapidly rise.

Jim stood at the locked main doors of the library, listening to the sound of traffic moving along Deansgate. The armed response officers he'd requested were on their way but, maddeningly, were having to come in via the visitor's centre entrance at the far end of the building. Ian, manager of the facilities department, had gone to meet them almost four minutes ago.

In the silence of the deserted lobby, it suddenly seemed so easy for the two Mauritians. A rarely used part of the building, CCTV coverage not permitted because of the proximity of the toilets, old doors which – presumably – were relatively easy to open.

He looked back at the three stone figures forming a tableau on the landing of the main stairs. The female in the middle looked like the Virgin Mary, flowing robes almost brushing the two male figures seated at her feet. He tried Iona's phone once more and, this time, got a number unavailable message.

Fraser spoke up from the shadows to the side of the doors, face made ghostly by the glow of his iPhone's screen. 'Crowd's already on their feet. Blair and Brown are on stage. Big grins and back slaps all round. I expect the women in the front rows are saving their knickers for when Clinton makes his appearance.'

'Yeah,' sniggered Chas. 'You, you and you. Why don't y'all come join me backstage for a bit of a party?'

Fraser giggled in response. 'I'll get my saxophone out. Who enjoys blowing on a—'

'Fuck's sake, lads,' Jim snapped. 'Give it a rest, will you?'

They glanced at him then at each other. As a sullen silence fell over them, Jim heard the sound of heavy footsteps. The noise floated out, echoing lightly off the arched spaces above them, making it impossible to pinpoint where the sound was coming from.

Ian re-appeared at the top of the steps – a stoutly built man in his forties, bald head, goatee beard and tattoos on each forearm. Behind him were two armed officers, G36c carbines slung across their chests.

'Down here, gents,' Ian said, leading them towards where Jim was standing with his badge raised.

'Glad to see you two.'

'You were lucky to get us – it's all kicking-off at the secure zone.'

The man had a Scouse accent. Drafted over from Liverpool, Jim thought. 'Why's it kicking-off?'

He shrugged. 'Word from the top. Whatever it is, they're shitting themselves. It just went to yellow alert as we came in here.'

A sudden chill went through Jim. 'Not something linked to events in Bury, was it?'

'No idea.' He turned back to the other officer. 'Steve, what was it?'

'An alert on two males. Asian appearance, one six-two or so, the other a foot shorter with a shaved head. The boys at the perimeter got a proper briefing.'

It's them, Jim thought. That must mean they weren't in Bury after all. As he glanced down the stone steps, he thought of something else. Iona. Oh my God, if the Mauritians are still free, there's no way she'll have stayed in Bury. Not with her dad in the conference centre. He looked over his shoulder. 'Fraser, what's going on in the main hall now?'

'Blah, blah, blah, blah, blah. Tevland, telling us all how thing's are going to be different.'

Christ, thought Jim. If something's going to happen, it's going to be any minute.

'What is this place, anyway, Hogwarts?' Steve asked, craning his head back.

His colleague was eying Chas and Fraser mistrustfully. 'And you are?'

Jim waved a hand in their direction. 'It's OK, they've been helping me. My name's Jim, by the way.'

'Tony. So, what have we got here, Jim?'

'Not sure to be honest. Looks like a tunnel has been illegally accessed from the basement down here. There's a chance the two suspects you just heard about are responsible.'

'Tunnel?' Tony's demeanour was suddenly serious. 'What kind of a tunnel?'

'A very old one,' Jim replied.

'Where does it go?'

'Could be towards the conference centre.'

The man's throat bobbed and he looked at his colleague. 'I'm not happy about going into some tunnel.'

Steve nodded in agreement.

Jim looked from one to the other, trying to hide his dismay. 'Let's just take a look at the opening, shall we? I may be wrong.'

Tony gestured reluctantly. 'Lead the way then.'

Ian stepped forward, a giant set of keys in his hand. 'I'll get the door open for you.'

As he set off down the steps to the basement, Jim beckoned to Chas. 'I'll need you to confirm it's the room you saw.'

The others waited on the bottom steps while Jim and Ian stepped through the basement door and into the narrow corridor. Ian searched through his keys. 'Reckon it has to be this one.' It turned surprisingly easily in the lock and he pushed it open.

Jim looked over the man's shoulder. Its dimensions made the room beyond no more than a short extension of the corridor; it ran for about twelve feet before ending at a solid stone wall, partly obscured by a stack of dusty crates bearing the word, Fragile. A single bulb hanging from the ceiling provided poor light. 'What is this room?' Jim asked.

'Just used for storage, by the looks of it.'

Jim examined the ancient-looking glass cabinets lining the side walls. Most of the shelves were empty, just a few leather-bound books lying on their sides. The piles of crates at the end had been moved aside to give access to a faded-green metal door set deep in the wall.

'Well, I'll be . . .' Ian whispered. 'I never knew that was there.'

Chas' voice sounded from the doorway behind them. 'This is it. I had to crouch down to see through the keyhole.'

The facilities manager looked dumbfounded. 'See through which bloody keyhole? This area is out-of-bounds to the public.'

Jim approached the metal door. At its centre was an embossed crest. Above the shield-like shape was the word, Chatwoods, below it the word, Patent. The keyhole was huge.

'What's the biggest thing on your key ring?' Jim whispered.

The facilities manager shook his head. 'Nothing to fit that. I'd have to go through the key store, see what's on the hooks in there.'

Jim pointed to the floor in front of it. 'Someone's opened it recently. Those scratches in the stone look new.'

'Well, you lot have got me scratching my head,' the manager said, looking back at Chas. 'What did you mean about looking through the keyhole?'

Jim reached out and tried the lever-handle. It turned stiffly under the pressure of his hand.

*   *   *

Iona emerged into the Sky Bar.

The slate-coloured floor immediately in front of the lift gave way to wood after a few metres. The front part of the bar was dominated by high tables surrounded by minimalist stools. Beyond them were clusters of low-slung chairs, most facing the floor-to-ceiling glass that formed the walls. There was a lot of excited talking coming from round the corner and she stepped forward to see what was going on.

Several lamps, a fair-size bigger than the ones they used to illuminate crime scenes, were casting their glare on to an arrangement of armchairs and a sofa at the far end of the bar. Cameras on moveable stands were positioned between the lights.

A mass of cabling ran towards a desk on which were several monitors and what she guessed was recording equipment. Some of the people who were gathered round the screens called for quiet. The remaining people also crowded round the desk and a hush descended.

Of course, she thought, this is where the BBC stage their interviews. The view across Manchester on the television was a genuine one. Unnoticed, she crossed the bar to the vast windows.

As she hoped, she had a bird's-eye view of the conference centre and the entire secure zone. She immediately picked out the annex to the main building. Dad, she thought. Dad. Her eye travelled the short distance to the main building. Would it be enough? Was he far enough away if Vassen and his accomplice somehow released ricin into the main hall? She felt a sharp spasm of guilt at how her concern was focused on just one man. There were thousands of innocent members of the public down there. Not to mention loads of her colleagues.

She watched two officers in high-visibility jackets crossing the plaza area. They're jogging, she realized. From this high up, they really do look like ants. Each section making up the white curved roof of the main hall seemed unnaturally bright. A tram was crawling slowly along Mosley Street and she realized the thick glass in front of her face cut out all sound from the city below.

Her remoteness from the scene made her feel like, somehow, it wasn't real. Like it was all some kind of show. One where the good guys would sweep in and save everyone. To her side, she could just hear the American accent of someone talking on the screen. Clinton, she realized. He's down there, on stage right now. This will be when something happens, surely. And I'm too late. Too late to stop it.

Pressing her hands against the cool glass, she examined the streets beyond the perimeter fence. *Where are you hiding? Where the hell are you hiding? You're down there, somewhere none of us can see.*

An image hit her: streams of people pouring out of the main doors. A panicked stampede of humanity, bodies falling down the steps. People vomiting and collapsing by the hundred, countless more trapped inside, crushed by the numbers fighting to flee.

The roof of the Great Northern Warehouse was a mass of masts. There were four figures at the side overlooking the plaza. Two snipers and their spotters. She could see the spotters sweeping their high-powered binoculars back and forth.

Applause broke out on the monitor and the people who'd been silently watching all began to speak.

'OK, we've got about ten minutes.'

Wondering what was going on, Iona looked in their direction. The clapping she could hear was obviously being transmitted from the main hall. Was it over? Had the speeches finished? Were her suspicions wrong? The thought thudded into her like a blow to the stomach. *If I was wrong about this . . .*

'Can we do something about those spotlights behind the bar? Camera two is picking them up.'

'Someone sort Angus's tie out, please!'

'Tristram, you've got a call from the London office.'

The bright lights shining down on the interview area made it hard to see the people beyond their harsh glare. A thin, angular figure stepped out from the shadows. The interviewer, Iona thought. Angus something or other. The one always on the TV.

'Tristram?' the same voice asked.

A tall man with tufts of hair sprouting out from behind his ears took off his glasses. 'Tell her I'll ring back later, for God's sake.'

'She says it's urgent.'

'Once this is over,' he snapped irritably.

Iona moved round the low glass tables and cream-leather loungers, eyes now fixed on the man.

'We need another glass on the table. There'll be four of them, remember. Come on, now, let's not drop a bullock.'

Iona continued towards the one called Tristram. He was now cleaning his glasses, fingers moving in small, tight circles.

A young woman in jeans, a puffer jacket and a pair of headphones stepped in front of her. 'Can I help you?'

Iona raised her warrant card. 'Detective Khan, Greater Manchester Police.'

Tristram's fingers stopped moving.

'Mr Dell?' Iona asked.

His head swivelled but he said nothing.

'You hung up on me earlier on.'

He replaced his glasses and peered down his nose at her. 'What are you doing here?'

She cocked her head. 'What are *you* doing here?'

He nodded in the direction of the cameras. 'My job.'

You're in PR, Iona thought, her conversation with Harish Veerapen coming back. The groundwork Slattinger-Dell had been doing for the Labour Party. Something about expecting headlines at the forthcoming convention. 'You told Reginald Appleton about the plans you were putting in place. Something in a letter. You told him—'

'Detective Constable, isn't it?' His appeasing tone failed to mask a certain degree of tension.

'Correct.'

'I will gladly furnish you with the information you require. If you'd speak to my assistant over there, she can arrange a time for me to see you before I return—'

'You're not listening!' Iona saw several heads turn and she realized that she'd shouted. She stepped closer and lowered her voice. 'Mr Dell, we have no time. Whatever the threat is, I believe it concerns the very people you represent.'

'They're leaving now,' someone called out. 'We've got eight minutes, maximum.'

'Detective, I fully appreciate the urgency of your work. But this really is not an opportune moment—'

'You realize,' she said, raising her voice enough for those nearby to hear, 'we're on a yellow alert? There is credible evidence of an attack being planned.'

The corners of his mouth twitched down in an involuntary grimace. 'I . . . I have complete faith in the security measures that are in place . . .'

'You told Appleton something. You breached that security. If anything happens, it will all be down to you!'

Dell's eyes slid to the sofa area. Iona followed his glance. The interviewer was bent forward, intently going over his notes. Iona felt a rush of dizziness as his name popped up. Angus Barr. Oh my

God. In his email to the ex-Law Lord, Tristram Dell had mentioned an audience with A.B. 'Is this . . .' She turned to the cluster of watching people. 'Who is coming here? Who is on their way?'

They looked at her with quizzical expressions.

Iona turned back to Dell. His face was pale and he was mumbling something.

She brushed past him, closer to the group. 'Who is arriving?'

A man lowered his clipboard. 'Tevland, of course.'

Iona's gaze shifted to the seats alongside Angus Barr. Four glasses on the table. 'Who else?'

'Blair, Brown and Clinton.'

Tristram Dell started to speak. 'How can there be a threat? The ring of steel – you call it a ring of steel. The site is secure.'

'Did you tell Reginald Appleton about the plans for this interview? In that letter to him?'

He blinked rapidly. 'I do not recall—'

Iona felt sick. 'We're not in the ring of steel. This building is outside the secure zone.' The convention centre was never the target, she thought, looking around her with wild eyes. This was.

The air in the pitch-black passage smelled of mould.

'Where the bloody hell does that go?' the facilities manager murmured.

'Got a decent torch?' Jim asked.

The manager pushed past Chas and Fraser angrily. A few seconds later, he stomped back in to the tiny room with a powerful-looking flashlight. 'From my little store cupboard.'

Feeling the weight of its metal casing in his hand, Jim switched it on. The narrow passage was instantly bathed in its brilliant beam.

'Fuck me,' the manager stated.

Walls of roughly hewn sandstone. A floor that sloped gently downwards and, at the far end, another door just visible. It was slightly ajar. More darkness was on its far side.

'What the heck is down there?' the manager asked with a fearful glance at Jim.

'The Deansgate tunnel,' Chas said quietly. 'Legend.'

'Deansgate tunnel?' The manager was still looking at Jim, seeking clarification.

'He's right. Tony? Can you come in here?'

The others moved aside to let the armed officer through.

'No way,' he immediately said. 'That is not happening. Not without support, detailed plans of what we're going into and ballistic shields.'

'Tony,' Jim hissed. 'You realize what this is about? Where that might lead?'

He shook his head, hands not moving off his weapon. 'I'm armed response. You want to go chasing al-Qaeda down there? Call the frigging SAS.'

Jim blinked slowly in an effort to keep calm. The nagging suspicion Iona was in the city centre wouldn't leave him. 'Tony, we have to do something. Now.'

'Yeah, we call my boss and dump this all on him. That's what bosses are for.' He unhooked his handset from the shoulder strap of his body armour, frowning when he realized the channel was silent.

Jim sneaked a quick look at Tony's sidearm. A Glock 17, sitting in a drop-holster that incorporated three anti-snatch features. Any armed officer who valued his job would fight to a standstill before losing his weapon.

'You're right.' Standing up, Jim started shooing Chas and Fraser towards the doors. 'Out! Everyone out! We leave this to the specialists.'

Chas and Fraser started backing away, Ian cursing when one of them stood on his foot. The retreating press of bodies forced the other armed officer out of the door.

Jim gestured for Tony to go in front of him, the heavy metal torch held at his side. He focused on the back of the man's head, the curve of bone just behind his ear. Now, he thought. He lifted the torch up and brought it down in a sharp chopping movement, knowing the impact would cause the officer to blackout for a few seconds.

Tony's legs buckled and he fell forward on to his knees. With one hand, Jim reached out to the door and shut them both in. The Glock was free an instant later, Tony toppling senselessly into a cabinet, the glass immediately splintering. From the other side of the door came a shout.

'Tony! What's going on! Tony!'

Jim pulled Tony by the straps of his vest away from the cabinet and carefully lay him down across the base of the door.

'Tony!' his colleague shouted from outside. 'You OK in there!'

Jim plunged into the dark opening at the other end of the room and turned the torch back on.

*　　*　　*

The lift doors to the hotel lobby opened on a wall of backs. Among the police uniforms were people in civilian clothes. She spotted curling wires emerging from earpieces to vanish down collars. Security personnel, she thought, from any number of organizations.

'Excuse me,' she said. None of them reacted; all their attention was focused towards the hotel entrance. 'Excuse me!'

Several turned their heads to examine her with indifferent expressions. Their unwillingness to move suddenly made her feel trapped inside the lift. Anxiety surged up from her stomach.

'I need to get past!'

A ripple of movement and she squeezed through a gap. Out on Deansgate she could see unmarked vehicles blocking off the road, lights silently flickering behind their radiator grilles. Her own vehicle had vanished.

A police motorbike swept into view from the direction of Great Bridgewater Street. They're on their way, Iona thought. They're coming.

Immaculately dressed hotel staff were lined up behind the front desk. Iona crossed the lobby as quickly as she could without actually running. 'Who is in charge of the building's utilities?'

A smartly turned out lady of about forty, black hair scraped back in a tight ponytail, inclined her head. 'My name's Georgina and I'm the assistant duty manager. Is there a problem?'

Iona nodded. 'I need a caretaker or whatever the title is.'

'We do have a maintenance department. But if it's just a problem with your air conditioning or hot water, it's normally possible to get—'

'Air conditioning?' Unobtrusively, Iona placed her identity on the counter. 'Where is the air conditioning controlled from?'

More police and plain-clothes officers were filing in through the main doors.

'There's a plant in the basement. The units are located down there.'

'For the entire building?'

'Yes.'

'Including the Sky Bar?'

'Yes.'

'I need access, right now.'

The woman leaned forward. 'You do realize the whole building has been searched?' she whispered. 'I think they even put security tape on the door to the plant room.'

They won't have entered through the doors, Iona thought. They'll have come up from below. 'Please, get whoever it is immediately.'

The employee lifted the phone and pressed a button. 'Is Walter still on duty? Please send him to front reception. Yes, right now.' She replaced the phone. 'He's coming. As I said, your colleagues were very thorough; they are every year. The building's residents have to hand in their key fobs for the underground car park weeks before the conference starts. The concierge buzzes each person through in person.'

Iona was transferring her weight from foot to foot, arms tightly crossed. 'How many people live here?'

'In the apartments above the Sky Bar? About two hundred and twenty.'

'And the hotel part?'

'There are two hundred and eighty-five rooms.'

'Fully booked?'

'Always when the conference is on. But everyone is vetted.'

'So right now, in this building, how many people are here?'

'I don't know – including staff, about one thousand.'

Iona was thinking about the exact location of the huge tower. It stood between the wide lanes of Deansgate and the site of the conference centre. There was no need for any tunnel to branch out far from beneath the road – not if the tower was the target.

'Ah, Walter. Could you show this police officer the basement?'

A grey-haired man with a bulbous red nose was approaching from the direction of a Staff Only door at the end of the counter. He wore white overalls. 'Morning.'

Iona stepped towards him then halted. She looked over at the lifts. There were now about ten uniformed officers gathered there. Several looked like they were Tactical Aid Group – massive great blokes trained for dealing with crowd disorder. She veered off in their direction. 'Can I borrow a couple of you, please?'

They regarded her in the usual assessing way. 'You what, love?'

She raised her badge. 'We need to check the plant room down in the basement.' She dropped her voice for emphasis. 'It's very urgent.'

A dubious look passed along the line before one stepped forward. 'Always happy to accompany a lady in distress. I'm Marcus.'

'Cheers, Marcus. And who's coming with you?'

He beckoned to a colleague. 'Come on, Stewart.'

'Thanks,' Iona said as another left the line. She gestured at Walter. 'Let's go. Quick as you can.'

He led them back to the door he'd come through. A couple of steps down and they entered a long corridor, one side of which was clogged with cardboard boxes. 'I've told them that's a fire hazard,' Walter said, pointing down. 'They don't listen.'

After turning left, they passed two more sets of doors before reaching a stairwell. 'You want the plant room? Incoming services? Gas, water, electricity? Boilers?'

'Wherever the air conditioning units are,' Iona responded.

'Same place. It's two flights down. The plant room is located at the end of the lower one.'

'On which side of the building?' Iona trailed him down the bare concrete steps, the uniformed officers' utility belts clinking behind her. 'Is it the side nearest to Deansgate?'

'Yes, side nearest Deansgate.'

Not much more than the width of the pavement away, she thought. 'You worked here long, Walter?'

'Me? Since it opened.'

'What was here before this thing went up?'

'Well, the building's footprint was dictated by the arches and buttresses supporting the railway going into the Great Northern Warehouse. All of it was swept away when they dug the foundations – which were far easier to lay than planned.'

'Because?'

'They hit load-bearing rock much sooner than anticipated. So they did away with the deepest pilings and just sat the building directly on it.'

'Would that have been sandstone?'

'Very good,' he said, sounding impressed at her knowledge.

At the bottom of the stairs, Walter pushed through another door and into a starkly lit passageway. 'That way into the car park,' he said, setting off in the opposite direction. 'And this is us.'

He stopped at a stainless-steel door marked, No Access. Below that was a black and yellow graphic of a man being speared by a jagged line. Electricity. Danger of Death. From beyond it came a low humming noise, like a small aircraft preparing for take-off. The same type of tape she'd seen in the visitor centre in the Great Northern Warehouse had been stretched across the door and surrounding frame.

'No one's been inside,' he said, running his forefinger across it. 'See? They were down here inspecting it again first thing this morning.'

'What will we see on the other side?' Iona asked quietly. Her head felt light and a tingling sensation was going through her legs.

'A lot of machinery.'

'Including the air conditioning?'

'No. Boilers first. Air-con units are housed inside a smaller room at the other end.'

'Will it be locked?'

'No, shouldn't be.'

'OK. We need to check inside.'

'You'll vouch for me breaking this tape?'

'Yes. Please hurry.' She turned to the pair of officers. 'You got CS spray?'

They nodded, both removing small canisters from the pouches on their utility belts.

'What is this about?' the one called Stewart asked.

'We're after two male suspects. Shorter one could be a handful. Possibly armed.'

Next to her, Walter was peeling the tape off the door.

'Armed with what?' Marcus asked uneasily.

'Knife.'

'Hang on,' Stewart said, 'if they've got weapons, we should call for armed response, shouldn't we?'

'If there was time,' Iona shot back.

'Bloody hell.'

He closed up the zip of his stab-proof vest before removing his telescopic truncheon and extending it out. His colleague did the same.

'Quick as you can, Walter,' Iona whispered.

He slid a thick key into the lock, turned it through three-hundred-and-sixty degrees, took it out and stood back. 'It's open.'

Entire sections of the wooden door at the end of the narrow passage had rotted away. Aware he didn't have much time, Jim turned the torch off and stared at the gaps. The darkness beyond was absolute. He flicked the torch on again and swung the door back on its warped and rusted hinges.

Voices carried down from the storage room he'd just left behind. 'Tony? Tony? Shit, mate, what . . .'

'Where is he? He took my fucking gun!'

A small step down and then damp earth. Multiple sets of foot-prints led off to the side. He lifted the torch beam and a wide tunnel with an arched roof jumped into view. The ceiling was furred with thousands of stubby white stalactites. He shone the torch off to the right and, across the mounds of earth rising up from the floor, he could just make out a brick wall blocking off the tunnel. It was about thirty metres away.

He looked back. Shadows were moving in the storage room at the other end of the passageway. A voice called out.

'You are fucked, mate? You hear me?' It was Tony, shouting. 'I will fucking fill you in, you mad fuck! You hear me?'

Satisfied they weren't coming after him, Jim turned and started to follow the tracks, quickly becoming aware of the temperature. It was like being in a giant fridge. He'd got to within ten metres of the tunnel's end when he spotted smashed bricks scattered round an opening at one side. The footprints led straight to it.

Marcus put a hand on Iona's shoulder. 'I think we'd better go first, don't you?'

'Why?' she replied, irked by the tone in his voice.

'For a start, we're armed. And I don't think you've got body armour on under that fleece.'

Begrudgingly, she stepped aside.

As he pushed the handle down it squeaked slightly. Bringing up his truncheon, he pushed the door open. A concrete floor and a forest of pipes wrapped in foil. The thrum of electrical equipment picked up and a wave of heat washed over them. White metal panelling encased a row of six machines that were far taller than Iona. Fat pipes rose up from their tops and went straight through the ceiling.

'Air-con units are the other end,' Walter whispered behind them.

The uniformed officers looked round at Iona, eyebrows raised.

'You sure about this?' Marcus sounded uncertain.

'I'll go first, if you want,' she murmured back.

A glance bounced between the two men and they stepped through the door. The room was about thirty feet long and a shade less in width. The ceiling was made to feel even lower by the intricate arrangement of pipes running across it. To their right, squat metal objects resembling fire hydrants lined the floor, each one with solid-looking pipes running off them. Gas or water, Iona guessed, shadowing the officers as they moved down the aisle towards a wooden door at the far end.

A triple beep sounded somewhere off to their side and the hum coming from one of the white machines dropped away. A second set of beeps and another machine fell slowly silent. From behind the door at the end of the room, they heard a metallic clink as something dropped on the floor. A blurred and indistinct voice spoke inside.

Marcus held up a hand with three fingers outstretched. His colleague nodded, canister of CS spray ready. Marcus flexed his shoulders then dropped his fingers one by one to form a fist. He raised up a boot and kicked at the spot just below the door handle.

It flew open and Iona glimpsed Vassen and Ranjit kneeling before a grey cabinet set against the side wall. The controls for the air conditioning, she thought. Next to the pair was a jagged hole in the concrete floor. Both men were covered in reddish dust and pale fragments of stone. There was a bang as the door hit the wall. It swung back, cutting off their view.

'It's them! Go, go, go!' Iona yelled.

Suddenly coming to life, the two officers barged through the door, both shouting. 'Police! Police! Get down! Police! Down!'

Vassen scrabbled backwards, arms raised in surrender.

Ranjit jumped into a crouch, one hand flat on the floor. His eyes darted about.

'Get on your front!' Marcus roared, raising his baton up. 'Now! On your stomach, now!'

Vassen fell into a prone position, arms out at his sides. He appeared to be crying.

Stewart was moving to the side, can of CS spray held towards Ranjit, whose entire body was rigid. Like a cornered animal, Iona thought, registering the briefcase on the floor. Inside was a row of powder-filled vials and a pair of face masks. The casing below the controls for air conditioning had been removed.

Marcus advanced another step closer to Ranjit. 'Do as I say! On your front!'

The only parts of Ranjit that moved were his eyes: they skittered about, settling on Iona for a moment before moving on once more.

He's going to do something, she thought, wishing for some kind of weapon.

'Spray him,' Marcus ordered his colleague. 'Give him a face-full, the fucker isn't listening.'

But then Ranjit went down on his knees. Slowly he bent forward, and placed both hands on the ground. As Stewart started unhooking the quick-cuffs from his belt, Iona spotted a slight movement of Ranjit's head. She realized he was looking at the hole in the floor.

With amazing speed, he moved sideways. One moment he was above the opening, the next he was dropping into it. Iona leaped forward, trying to catch hold of him as he vanished from sight. She peered into the dark hole and then up at the nonplussed officers. 'We've got to go after him!'

Marcus took a step forward and looked in. 'You're joking.'

Shaking his head, Stewart continued to restrain Vassen. 'What does it join? Get him at the other end.'

'It's a network,' Iona stated. 'If no one follows, we'll lose him!'

Stewart was kneeling beside Vassen. 'You think either of us could fit into that? Listen, whatever they were planning, it's—'

Iona had turned to Marcus. 'Then give me your belt.'

'What?'

'Your utility belt, come on, quick.'

'You're seriously going after him?' Looking bewildered, he started undoing it.

'Someone has to,' she said, pulling it out of his hands.

'That's a really bad move,' Stewart muttered, removing his knee from the small of Vassen's back.

After securing the belt round her waist, she unclipped the small torch and looked into the dark hole once again. Do not think about this, she said to herself. Just do it. Don't pause. If you pause, you'll back out. She shone the torch into the small opening. The layer of concrete had been chipped away and, below it, she could see reddish stone. A smooth, narrow tunnel branched off at ninety degrees.

Sitting down, she dangled her legs into the opening, part of her expecting a pair of hands to grab her by the ankles and drag her in. Come on, Iona. Come on, Iona.

'You're really doing this? Stewart asked.

Vassen, now handcuffed shook his head, as if warning her not to.

'Don't touch that suitcase. I think that's ricin in the vials.' She began to lower herself down.

*   *   *

Emerging on the other side of the opening knocked through the partition wall, Jim found another section of tunnel. His forearms were covered in reddish brick dust and he raised the Glock to blow the coating from its metallic surface.

The tunnel in front was almost completely blocked by a massive pile of mortar chunks welded together by concrete. He could see cloth sacking in the rubble at its edges and, shining the torch up, he saw the mound rose up to plug a hole in the ceiling. No doubt where workmen on a building site above had accidentally broken through.

Following the footprints, he skirted round the obstruction and splashed through a shallow expanse of black water on the other side.

The tunnel ended at another partition comprised of bricks that were uniform in size and shape. Manufactured, he realized, in a modern kiln. He swept the torch back and forth, looking for tell-tale debris. The wall was intact.

Directing the beam straight down, he searched for footprints. The earth all around him seemed to be undisturbed. That couldn't be right. He walked slowly along the partition, examining the mortar for any that had been chipped away. Every brick was cemented firmly in place. The trail of footprints had vanished.

Totally confused, he shone the torch behind him, light catching on the ripples he'd created just before. A feeling of utter desolation hit him as he realized he'd been wrong. The two brothers had explored this section of tunnel, he was sure of that. But they'd given up on it. The implications of his mistake started to reverberate in his head. He looked at the Glock in his hand. What was I thinking? They'll lock me up for this. Iona. He closed his eyes. I failed her. She's up there somewhere. And so are the Bhujuns, free to launch their attack.

He stepped into the freezing water, oblivious to it sloshing over his feet as he began the slow trudge back.

FORTY-EIGHT

H er toes made contact with the tunnel when the floor of the plant room was level with her face. Sucking in air as if she was about to go under water, she dropped to her knees and looked along the thin passage.

A light was bobbling about, no more than twelve metres in front. Ranjit. Iona started crawling after him. The dark stone of the tunnel seemed to suck away what little light the torch threw out. To her sides, she could see the grooves and ruts where the soft stone had been dug out. The light ahead winked and then disappeared.

Now all she could see was its faint glow and that was quickly getting weaker. She tried to speed up, jarring the top of her head against some kind of protrusion in the tunnel's roof. The pain seemed trivial, dulled by the adrenaline coursing through her. Every time she lifted the hand holding the torch, the tunnel felt like it was lurching from side to side. Her breathing and the scrape of her jeans against stone were the only sounds.

Just as her resolve begin to waver, she felt brick beneath her hands. A ledge. She poked her head out into what seemed like a cavern. The torch picked out walls, curving inward to form a roof some eight feet above that was thick with pale and spindly stalactites. Deansgate tunnel, she thought. This must be the Deansgate tunnel. Just wide enough for a horse and carriage, like Hidden Shadow had said.

The bobble of light was off to her right and the sound of Ranjit's heavy breathing filled the dank, cold space. Iona swung her legs and was about to jump down when she registered how the floor beneath her glimmered and shifted. A puddle, she said to herself. Just a puddle. Keeping one elbow hooked on the ledge, she slid down into ice-cold, ankle-deep water. She splashed her way out of it, aware Ranjit's light had disappeared from view once again. The water ended and she found herself stumbling over an earthy surface made bumpy by deposits of silt. A mound of broken bricks and red chunks of stone at her side. What they must have removed when they burrowed out in the direction of the Beetham Tower. Next to them, she glimpsed some tools – crowbars, short-handled spades, a stack of empty water bottles. Rucksacks.

The floor was rising, white fragments of broken stalactites strewn across it. Her foot went into a dip and she staggered to the right. Stalactites snapped against her head and fell to the ground. Lifting the torch, she realized the two men had cleared a corridor of them from the ceiling: an upside-down path revealing their route. She started forward once more and by the time a bricked-off section loomed ahead, she was bent almost double.

Spotting an opening in the partition, she looked into it. Ranjit's light on the other side allowed her to gauge the thickness of the wall. Two metres, maximum. She clambered through and into the next section of tunnel. How far, she wondered, have I now come? Thirty, forty metres?

Ranjit's shadowy form was scrabbling up some kind of slope further along the passage. Loose stones were shifting beneath his feet, the noise reverberating all around her. Abruptly, his light contracted down to a small rectangle and, as she set off in its direction, she realized he'd crawled into another opening.

Something dry and fibrous raked across her forehead. Another step and it began to snag in her hair. Shuddering, she tried to duck clear. More of it, these strands longer and thicker. It was now all around her face, tendrils of it brushing against her lips. Wanting to scream, she fell to the floor and pointed the torch up. A curtain of dusty tree roots hanging down. She crawled out from beneath them, ran forward and started climbing the loose fragments of stone up to an opening just below the ceiling.

Not much bigger than an oven door, she thought. It veered off on a diagonal angle. She could see Ranjit, hear his grunts as he struggled to get out the other end. Five, six metres, she told herself, briefly closing her eyes. That's all. You can do it. There was a scraping noise and she looked in again. Now only Ranjit's feet were visible. They slid downwards from sight.

She clamped the torch between her teeth, got her head and shoulders in and started forward on her elbows. When her legs were also inside, she was able to half-crawl, half-shuffle herself along. Midway, she started to feel the roof of the passage making contact with the curve of her shoulders. It was getting lower. She went on to her stomach and dragged herself on using her forearms. The other end wasn't much more than an arm's length away but she realized it was horribly narrow. Fighting back another urge to stop, she stretched out a hand and hooked her fingers over the lower part of the opening. Now she was able to pull herself across the remaining distance.

Freeing one arm, she directed the torch about. The opening she was looking out from was about a metre and a half above a floor made of tiny bricks. It was some kind of room. The stone walls had been rubbed smooth and, at some point long ago, painted white. Now they were peeling and she could see the remnants of black wedge shapes staining the surfaces. Smoke marks, she guessed, from where candles had once burned. Ranjit's escape route was given away by the glow coming from an archway in the opposite wall.

Sensing she was close to the point where he must have entered the tunnel network, she squirmed her way forward, leaning to the side in order to drag her other arm free. Now she could reach down to the cold floor and start walking herself forward on her hands. Her torso was almost out when she came to a halt. Something was catching at her waist. By wriggling from side to side and using the weight of her upper body, she advanced another few inches. But the pressure across the base of her back grew too painful. The utility belt, she realized with dismay. The one I put on back in the basement of the Beetham Tower.

She arched her body, reached back and tried to seek out the belt's buckle. But it was pressing into her stomach which, in turn, was jammed tight against the edge of the opening. She tried to rock her hips but it was no good: her waist was trapped.

Panic fluttered across the back of her neck like a moth trying to land. No! Do not lose control, she told herself. Breathe. Keep breathing. Now, take your weight on your arms and walk yourself back into the opening. She had just straightened her elbows when the glow filling the archway seemed to alter.

She stopped moving and stared. Had it? Did it really change? She turned her own torch off. Blackness immediately engulfed her and she blinked her eyes, focusing on the dimly lit arch. The weak shine coming from beyond it could only be caused by Ranjit's light. It was getting stronger. Oh, no, she thought. He's coming back.

She turned her torch back on and started kicking frantically with her legs. She could hear soft footsteps now. Scrabbling desperately at the floor, she felt her nails beginning to splinter and snap. The muscles in her shoulders and arms were screaming out and she stopped for a moment to listen. She could hear his breathing. She pushed back with all her might and the leather belt began to squeak. But still it refused to budge.

And then she heard the scrape of a shoe. Fearfully, she lifted her chin. He was standing in the doorway, a torch in one hand and a knife in the other.

FORTY-NINE

Blotches of red broke out, merging with each other to cloud the sight of him as he stepped into the small room. She started bucking her torso up and down while thrashing her legs. The base of her spine popped and creaked, sending darts of white pain down the backs of her knees. 'No,' she said through gritted teeth. 'No! No! No!'

Her heart was racing so fast, sounds were now being drowned out. Her scream of frustration seemed to come from so far away.

Then his wet trainers appeared before her. Their edges were clogged with damp soil. Gasping for breath, she sagged on to her elbows, too exhausted to support her body weight any longer. She knew the back of her neck was exposed and, crying tears of anger, she wondered if he would jam the knife in there. Would it be quick, to die like that?

One of the trainers slid closer and she saw that a section of lace was twisted where it came out of an eyelet. The wet and grimy canvas buckled slightly as his toes flexed. This is it, a voice inside her calmly said. She saw her father's face; safe now. Everyone is safe. Her mum's twinkling eyes. Her sister and the babies she would never see. Everyone is safe.

A sense of peace was settling over her. For a moment, she thought, maybe the knife's gone through the top of my spine already. No pain, just a gradual numbness. A gentle drift into sleep.

She could hear him breathing. Sounds, she realized, were coming back. I can hear again. Why isn't he doing something? She wished she was able to look up at his face. Is he changing his mind? Hope, like a candle in the dark. If I could make eye contact and say something, maybe he would . . .

A hand roughly cupped her chin and started to lift her head. She could see his shins, then his knees, then the hand holding the knife. Still he forced her head back, pressing her lower teeth against her uppers, constricting her airway, making it harder to breathe. My throat, she realized. He's going to cut my throat. She tried to say something but, unable to open her mouth, only a strangled moan came out.

At the lower edge of her vision she could see him reaching below her chin with the knife and, as she closed her eyes, a voice began to bellow.

'Put it down! Put it down or I will shoot you in the fucking head!'

EPILOGUE

'I feel like one of those dogs. When they've been to the vet and had a plastic cone shoved over their head,' Iona mumbled, probing at the neck brace.

Wasim and Fenella smiled at her from the side of the hospital bed. Iona could see the distress still lingering in her father's eyes.

'Dad? Stop looking at me like that. I feel fine.'

He nodded and tore his eyes away.

'So that's it, then?' Muriel said, adjusting the small row of cards on the window sill. 'You cricked your neck falling off a mountain bike?' She turned round, feigning outrage. 'That's the best they can come up with? My daughter practically saves the country and I have to keep my trap shut about what really happened? Oh, hen.' Her hands twisted in a knot. 'I can't bear this.'

Iona suppressed a giggle. 'I didn't save the country. And don't make me laugh, it hurts.'

Wasim took her hand gently between his. 'We know the truth. That's enough.'

Not everything, she thought. Not how close Ranjit came to cutting my . . .

'Her bosses know too,' Muriel corrected him. 'Big gold star. Big, big, big bloody gold star.' She moved Wasim's copy of the *Guardian* so she could sit down.

Iona took in the front page headline yet again. Terror Plot Foiled. She knew the official line without reading the story below: Vassen and Rhanjit Bhujun had been intercepted the moment they tried to access the plant room of the Beetham Tower via the exterior door from the underground car park. Security forces had been aware of their movements all along. A quantity of suspicious materials had been seized from an address in Bury that had been under surveillance for weeks. There were no tunnels involved in the plot.

Wasim lifted the newspaper off the bed. 'The leaflets the elderly man was throwing down from the gallery get a brief mention on page seven. Red faces all round, it seems.'

Iona had been unable to elicit any clear answers from the senior officers in the CTU who'd debriefed her first thing that morning. 'What do you mean, red faces all round?'

He opened the paper at the modest article. 'Tory and Labour – they were all complicit in the scandal. Decades of systematic deception about the islanders and their rights.'

'Wasim,' Muriel cut in. 'Now is not the time to talk about those people.'

'No,' Iona said. 'I have to know. Who were they really after then? Was it Blair?'

'More likely Tevland,' Wasim responded, sending an uneasy glance at Muriel, who had now crossed her legs and looked away. 'When the Law Lords made their final ruling, Labour was in power and he was in charge at the Foreign Office. It was him who represented the government.'

'You mean when Reginald Appleton decided against the islanders?'

'Yes. In its simplest form, it was Tevland versus the Sagossians – with Appleton's vote tipping it in the government's favour.'

So that was driving Ranjit, Iona thought, mind returning for an instant to the chase through the dark tunnels.

'Will this plot have ruined their chances of getting their island back?' Fenella asked, hands cupped round her stomach.

Wasim gave a sad shake of his head. 'They were never going to get it back. The present government is declaring the area around it a Marine Reserve. The only people who'll be permitted on and off the island are the Americans – it's their main base for bombing targets throughout the Middle East. And, as we're learning, a very useful stopping point for extraordinary rendition flights—'

'Can we not change the subject?' Muriel snapped irritably. 'They were planning on killing thousands of innocent people, including you and your daughter.'

Just as the silence was getting painful, a knock sounded on the door. Iona looked up gratefully. It opened a crack. Jim's face appeared.

'Come in!' Muriel jumped to her feet. 'Come in, you gorgeous man, you!' She was around the bed in a flash and yanking the door fully open.

Jim stood there looking mortified, a bunch of flowers clutched before him. Iona couldn't help beaming in his direction.

'Er,' he said. 'I'll come back later.'

'You bloody well will not,' Muriel said, taking his arm and practically dragging him in. 'We can't thank you enough, Jim. Really.'

Fenella was grinning up at him as Wasim got stiffly to his feet. He extended a hand towards the other man. 'Thank you.' His voice quivered.

The atmosphere in the room tightened as all eyes turned to Jim. Blushing, he took a step closer to Wasim and shook his hand. Iona quickly wiped a tear from the corner of her eye.

'I . . .' Jim faltered, hand still being clasped tightly by an earnest-looking Wasim. 'This is really embarrassing.'

Muriel planted a huge kiss on the side of his face. 'Bless you,' she said, gesturing to Wasim and Fenella. 'Come on, let's give the pair of them some peace.'

Once they were alone, Jim turned round and let out a relieved sigh. 'That seemed to go OK.'

Iona smiled. 'I've never seen Dad so emotional.'

'Or as pleased to see me.' He looked over at the row of cards. 'Anything from Wallace?'

'Funnily enough, no.'

'I hear he's not in the office.'

'Gardening leave,' Iona stated. 'The Chief Super who was in here earlier said he'll be putting in for early retirement.'

'They should cut him off without a penny.'

'I hear Tristram Dell has retired from his own company.'

Jim shrugged. 'He's made plenty to keep himself comfortable.' He started to read the various inscriptions, stopping at one and looking across at Iona with a smile. 'Is this from the CTU?'

She nodded as he looked at the card again.

'To the Baby-Faced Assassin.' He chuckled. 'See? I'm happy with them calling you that now. They've earned the right. Not before, but they have now.'

Iona shifted her legs to one side, grimacing slightly as she did so. 'Sit down.'

'Still hurts?' Jim asked with a concerned look as he perched carefully on the edge of the bed.

'I did kick the crap out of that tunnel's walls,' she said. 'My ankles are one big bruise.'

His eyes went to her hands resting on the bedcover. All her nails were jagged and torn.

She could tell where his mind was: back in that freezing little room with its smoke-blackened walls. 'How did you find me down there?'

'I heard your scream.' He looked up. 'So I ran back up the tunnel to where it was sealed off by new bricks. Just before it, this massive puddle stretched from one side of the tunnel to the other. Halfway across was a little alcove in the side-wall. I couldn't figure out why their tracks just vanished at the water. Anyway, it led round to a flight of steps. You were in the room at the top.'

She was silent for a second. 'What happened to him?'

Jim frowned. 'Ranjit?'

She nodded.

'They didn't tell you earlier?'

'I didn't ask. I didn't want to hear it from them.'

'Belmarsh.' He shrugged. 'No one will see him for weeks.'

'Vassen too?'

'And the old man – the uncle. He might be released sooner; it seems he didn't have a clue what they were really up to in his house.'

'Harish has been in touch.'

'Really?' Jim looked pleased. 'He rang here?'

'He left a message for me at work. Euan brought it in along with the card and grapes.'

'What did he say?'

'Harish? He was apologizing, believe it or not. After all that digging around he did.'

'Why was he sorry?'

'Ranjit Bhujun's background,' she said with a pained expression. 'The Creole thing.'

'I thought that's what they are.'

'Not really: he missed the fact they were originally from Sagossia. They're like a sub-class on Mauritius. Fallen through the cracks. Some have become Mauritian nationals, some are holding on to their Sagossian nationality in the hope they'll be allowed to return one day. They live in the worst parts of Port Louis. Harish had gone over Ranjit's police record in more detail. His mum was found floating in the harbour when he was four. In an area used by prostitutes. No other immediate family. He grew up on the streets—'

'Iona, do not – whatever you do – start sympathizing with the bloke.'

She let out a sigh. 'I know, I know. But when you start to hear what they all went—'

'Yeah, what they all went through. But only he decided to start killing people in return. He was trying to flood an entire building with ricin.'

'But who made him into a killer?'

Jim shrugged. 'Life isn't fair. We don't all try and murder people to get even. Listen, enough about him. What about you? Are you OK?'

She looked at her hands. 'I could do with a decent manicure.'

He slid his fingers across them. 'Are you sleeping OK? All that stuff?'

'I'm fine. Counselling has been duly offered, et cetera, et cetera.' She looked him in the eyes. 'What about you?'

'A short break while they look into the circumstances of how I came by that sidearm. I've had word things will work out fine.'

'The Chief Super said as much to me already. I mean, how are you? Sleeping and all that stuff?'

He blinked a couple of times. 'Yeah . . . yeah, I'm good. Sweet dreams and all that.'

Iona held eye contact. 'And the other stuff?'

His smile faltered. 'You mean the drinking?'

She lifted her eyebrows in confirmation.

'I'm going to get help about it.' He nodded, looking away. 'I am.'

She turned her hands palm-up and curled her fingers round his. 'I'll be there for you.'

He shook his head. 'You don't need to say that.'

She gripped his hands more tightly. 'You know, when you rang me that night? That rambling message when you tried to warn me about Wallace. I couldn't make out most of it – but I did hear you say that you'd always have my back.'

He looked at her. 'And I always will, Iona. I promised you.'

'I know.' She raised a finger and softly traced the scars running down his face. 'I know.'

AUTHOR'S NOTE

As a people, the Sagossians do not exist. However, the details of their story are based entirely on fact. In 1966 the Wilson government leased a small cluster of islands about 1,200 miles north of Mauritius to the United States – so enabling them to build a military airbase on one of the larger ones called Diego Garcia. There has since followed a truly shameful policy – pursued by successive British administrations to this day: firstly, to deny the island was ever inhabited and then, when this lie became impossible to maintain, to refuse the islanders' requests to return. This involved Tony Blair invoking the royal prerogative (the divine right of kings!) in 2004 to deny the islanders the right to go back and culminated in 2008 when the (then) Law Lords made a final ruling in favour of the government.

Since becoming an American airbase, Diego Garcia has been used as a launch pad by the U.S. for bombing operations throughout the Middle East and as a stopping-off point for extraordinary rendition flights.

Unlike the fictional Sagossians, the original inhabitants of Diego Garcia have only fought for their right to return home by peaceful means.

For more information I recommend you read:

Curtis, M. (2003), *Web of Deceit*, London: Vintage.
Plight of the Unpeople by John Pilger. http://www.newstatesman.com/human-rights/2008/11/pilger-british-chagos-law. Retrieved 15 July, 2012
The Chagos Islands: A Sordid Tale.
http://news.bbc.co.uk/1/hi/uk_politics/1005064.stm. Retrieved 15 July, 2012

The secret world of Manchester's uncharted tunnel system is a fascinating one.

For an overview (or should that be underview?) obtained by legal means, I recommend Keith Warrender's book, *Below Manchester: Going Deeper Under the City*. To read about explorations undertaken without permission of the authorities, www.28dayslater.co.uk (Retrieved 17 July, 2012) is a good place to start.

Finally, if you ever find yourself in Manchester city centre with time to spare, a visit to the John Rylands library on Deansgate is well worth your while. It is exactly as described in the book, including the Victorian gentleman's toilet!

ACKNOWLEDGEMENTS

My thanks to:

Ayoola Onatade – for such an invaluable insight into how the Justices of the Supreme Court (formerly Law Lords) operate.

Ian Simpson – for kindly taking the time to explain the architectural details of his magnificent tower.

Colin Wright – for demonstrating to me the formidable reach of Manchester's CCTV system.

Jeanette Zaman-Browne for sharing her experiences of growing up as a mixed-race child in Britain.

Those members of www.28dayslater.co.uk, who let me in on a few realities of urban tunnel exploration.

And lastly, to Chops, for continuing to put up with the man who lives at the bottom of the garden.